MW01106833

Available Titles By Joyce and Alexandra Swann

Non Fiction:

No Regrets: How Homeschooling Earned me a Master's Degree at Age Sixteen

Writing for Success: A Comprehensive Guide to Creative Writing Skills

Adult Fiction:

The Fourth Kingdom

The Twelfth Juror

THE TWELFTH JUROR

Alexandra and Joyce Swann

Frontier 2000 Media Group, Inc.

Media Group Inc.

Cover Design: Stefan Swann
Cover Artwork: Israel Swann
All rights reserved including the right of reproduction in whole
or in part in any form without written permission from
the publisher.
Copyright © 2010 by Alexandra Swann and Joyce Swann
Published in the USA by Frontier 2000 Media Group Inc., El Paso, Texas.

ISBN   1453615733
EAN-13 9781453615737

ONE

"What was the verdict?" called a voice to Jack Forbes as he slowly opened the glass doors of the once majestic residence that now housed the law offices of Pratt, Forbes and Magoff. Forbes was in no hurry to respond to that question. In fact, he had been hoping that his colleagues would not ask. Of course, jury trials are unpredictable at best, Jack reminded himself, and it is impossible to second guess the legal system. In spite of the outcome, he would get his check. His client's fate was not a source of great concern to him; Jack had begged Sam Dyer to plead guilty to manslaughter, and he had stubbornly refused. As far as Jack was concerned, it was Dyer's own fault that he was headed for prison.

"What was the verdict?" repeated the voice, and Megan Cleary walked out of her office to find out why there was no response to her question.

"Guilty," Jack replied a little disgusted.

"Guilty!" Megan's tone reflected her surprise. "How could you possibly have lost?"

"It wasn't hard," Jack muttered as he poured himself a cup of coffee. "The jury came back and announced, 'We find Sam Dyer guilty of murder in the first degree.'"

"But he didn't really do anything," Megan took the coffee pot when Jack had finished.

"He killed a man; I call that doing something," Jack retorted.

"He killed a thief who was breaking into his home. It was self-defense," Megan countered.

"People are not supposed to go around shooting other people. They're supposed to leave that to the police; that's why our tax dollars furnish this city with a police department. I told him to plead guilty to manslaughter. He didn't have a prior record. With parole he would probably have been out in a few months. But he wouldn't listen to me. He thought he knew more than his lawyer. So tonight he's sitting in jail waiting to be sentenced. You should have seen him as they led him away. He was screaming something about 'a man's right to protect his home and family.'"

"How long a sentence do you think he'll get?" Megan turned to go back to her office.

"It's hard to say," Jack thought for a moment. "My guess is he'll draw fifteen years."

Megan shut the door of her office and surveyed the desk covered with papers—last week's work still to be done on this Monday afternoon. It seemed that she was always running—and always running a little behind. She looked at the clock; the hour hand was nearing six, and she still had stacks of work to finish. No, those briefs could not wait; she would just have to stay late and finish them.

The last rays of sun had faded in the window behind her, and she adjusted the thermostat to take the December chill out of the office before she returned to her desk.

Images of Sam Dyer occupied Megan's thoughts as she began sorting through the papers. "Fifteen years is a long time to spend in prison for shooting a burglar," she thought. Megan had been certain that Jack would be able to get Dyer acquitted. Still, what Jack had said was true; people are not supposed to walk around armed to the teeth, shooting anyone who threatens them. The cornerstone of the legal system is "innocent until proven guilty," and Sam Dyer had not allowed a judge and jury to make that determination. Instead, he had been judge, jury and executioner, shooting an unarmed eighteen year old kid who would probably have stolen his television set and a few personal articles but had not posed any real physical threat to Dyer and his family. Sam Dyer might get a fifteen year sentence, but the thief had drawn the death penalty. If things had been different, the firm might have been defending the thief instead of Dyer. If only people would allow the courts to do their job and not take the law into their own hands. Perhaps she, too, would have voted for the guilty verdict if she had been on the jury.

In her four years with Pratt, Forbes and Magoff Megan Cleary had never been emotionally involved in any case. For some people the law is an obstacle, for others it is a symbol of justice, but for Megan it merely represented a livelihood. At twenty-eight she was a junior partner in a prestigious law firm in New York City. True, her father's connections had landed her the job after she graduated from law school, but she had worked hard and had proven herself to be a good attorney.

Megan's courtroom experience was not extensive, but she handled a judge and jury very well. She was bright, personable and ambitious. Everyone who knew Megan Cleary knew that she had a promising future. In a few years, when she had acquired more legal experience, her father would give her the boost that she needed to launch a political career. That was Megan's long-term goal. She might become mayor of New York City, or governor of the state, or the first female president of the United States. The one thing that Megan knew for certain was that whatever she decided to do she would succeed.

Megan's personal life was not as well mapped out as her professional one, but here, too, she had no reason for dissatisfaction. She owned a fashionable apartment in New York City, and she drove an expensive car. With her salary and the gifts that her parents sent her, she was able to afford a trendy wardrobe and still have a comfortable savings.

Megan was never lonely. Her parents lived in Buffalo, but she visited them frequently and spent every major holiday with them. With her long flaxen hair and eyes the color of emeralds, she attracted plenty of suitors. By almost anyone's standards Megan would be considered beautiful. She was tall, slim and shapely with small even features and a flawless complexion. Yes, many young men were interested in Megan, but she had not met any one special man she really cared for. There was Jeff, of course; he was a good friend and a pleasant dinner companion. They had been seeing each other off and on for a little over a year, but Megan did not think that she would want to marry Jeff.

"I'm leaving now," Jack was standing at the door of her office. "I'll turn out the lights in the front if you like."

"Thanks," Megan replied, looking up from her work. "See you tomorrow."

Darkness descended over the building as Jack turned out the main lights, and then Megan heard the door close behind him. Outside the sun had completely set and, except for the lights from Megan's office, the old house was engulfed in shadows.

The law offices of Pratt, Forbes and Magoff were in a part of the city which in the 1920s had housed some of New York's wealthiest residents. As time passed, the owners had died, and most of the houses along the street had fallen into disrepair until commercial enterprises bought and restored them. The brownstone housing the law offices was one of the most beautiful of these. The floors were solid oak, and a staircase with a heavily carved banister dominated the entry. The wood gave the offices a warm, comfortable feeling. Megan loved the wood, and she appreciated the fact that the building had been restored as well as renovated. It was pleasant to work in such luxurious surroundings.

In front and behind the building was bordered by streets, and on the right stood a wall designed to keep trespassers out. On the left an alley separated the brownstone from its neighbor, and a door leading from the hall to the alley gave employees convenient access.

Megan looked at her watch; it was a little past seven. These evenings spent working late were, in some ways, Megan's favorite part of her workday, for when the offices were quiet, Megan had a chance to think and plan as well as to work. Only the sounds of the heat coming on and the shuffling of papers on her desk disturbed the meditative atmosphere.

The silence was broken by the sound of someone fumbling with the handle to the alley door. It must be Jack, Megan thought. He had been gone exactly twenty minutes—just enough time to get about half way home, realize that he had forgotten something, and come back for it. From the way he was fumbling with the lock, he must have misplaced his keys. Megan rose from her chair just as she heard the door open.

"Come on in," she called. "I'm still here."

A man's shadow passed in the light of the open doorway. "Jack?" she called, but there was no answer. That was not like Jack Forbes, who always acknowledged her when he was in the office. Slowly Megan walked to the door of her office as a sense of panic began to grip her. The building was still dark; whoever had opened the door was obviously an intruder, and Megan was alone in the building with him. Peering out into the darkness she wondered where he might be. The light switch that illuminated the main part of the building was further down the hall. Quietly she stepped out of the doorway and made her way towards it. As she moved further and further into the hallway, the shadows deepened. This part of the hall was in complete darkness, and she groped along the wall for the switch.

Just as her hand reached it, Megan felt someone grab her from behind. His left arm caught her just under the breast bone, and his left hand sank into her ribs. At her throat she felt a knife blade. Terror engulfed her.

"Please," Megan begged in a broken voice, "my purse is on the desk in my office. Please…" Megan gasped as her captor released his grip and hurled her toward the wall. She was now facing him, but she could see only a vague dark form. He caught her long blonde hair in his left hand and pulled it while his free fist came down hard and smashed her cheekbone.

Megan cried out from pain and fear, "Please, please," she begged. "Don't hurt me. What do you want?" Her assailant did not answer; he continued to batter her with his fist. As she struggled he pulled her hair still more tightly and rained down harder blows. She could feel blood running from her nose and mouth.

He was going to kill her, but she didn't have the strength to stop him. Shielding her face with one hand, Megan tried to catch his fist as it came down, but he caught her wrist and twisted it until it snapped. Then he slammed her into the wall.

His hands began to tear at her sweater and skirt. "No!" she sobbed, "Please don't. Please let me go!" Megan could hear the fabric tearing, and she could feel his hands against her skin. She struggled and pushed him away from her. Completely disoriented, she ran madly down the hall in an effort to get to the door. In a second he was upon her again, and he pushed her down on her back. She could smell the staleness of his breath as he pressed his knee into her ribs while she sobbed and struggled. Through her tears Megan caught sight of something in his hand. There was just enough light from the doorway to reflect from the blade of the knife, and she screamed as it came down into her side. The screams continued as blows from the knife rained down and he tore away the rest of her clothing.

TWO

"Megan, Megan," from a long way off she could hear her mother's voice. It was the gentle coaxing tone Megan had heard as a child when her mother called her out of bed each morning. Now the voice sounded very distant and small, and it seemed to be calling Megan from the midst of a deep fog. She tried to answer, but she couldn't, and the veil of mist kept her from seeing her mother's face.

"Meg, can you hear me darling? Are you awake?" The voice sounded louder now and stronger. Slowly the mist was clearing, and Megan became aware that she was lying on a bed, though she still could not fully open her eyes. She was conscious only of being in pain. Every muscle, every nerve in her body felt as if it were on fire. Her side throbbed; every time she drew breath tiny knives seemed to slice her ribs. Her wrist and arm ached, but when she tried to move them, she discovered that they were tied down.

"Lie still," her mother told her. "You must not try to move your arm." Megan's head pounded, and every bone in her face felt raw and exposed. Slowly she forced her badly swollen eyes into little slits so that she could see her mother gazing down at her. Her lips felt loose and rubbery when she tried to speak, and her tongue was so swollen that she could hardly form words.

"How long have you been here?" she asked her mother.

"About an hour," her mother replied.

"We drove down as soon as Jack Forbes called," Megan's father interrupted. Megan turned her head slightly and saw him standing on the other side of the bed, gripping the rail. As ill as she was, Megan noticed that he was pale and shaken.

"Jack?" Megan wondered aloud. She was still disoriented from the medication and the trauma she had undergone. "Oh, the police must have called him," she finally said.

"No, you called him after you called the police," Megan's mother looked concerned. "Don't you remember?"

"I remember calling 911, and I remember the ambulance bringing me here, but I don't remember talking to Jack." Megan tried to move again and felt that her side was splitting open. "Am I going to be all right?" she asked her mother.

"Your wrist is broken. You have a number of stab wounds, but, fortunately, all of them are superficial. Your nose is also broken, but the doctors say they can fix it with no problem. Your face will look just like new." Her mother stroked Megan's hair softly. "You're going to be just fine, honey. You should be able to leave here in a few days, and then Daddy and I are going to take you home with us for a while. We'll take such good care of you." Tears welled up in her mother's eyes and her voice cracked as she said the last words. She had always tried so hard to protect her daughter. How could such a horrible thing have happened to her sweet little girl?

"Meggie," her father asked softly, "What happened?"

"I don't know, Dad," Megan began slowly. "Somebody broke into the office. I never saw him; I wasn't even able to give a description to the police." She stopped, unable to continue. She couldn't talk about all of the horrible things that had happened that night, and certainly not to her parents—to her father.

The nurse opened the door, "Mr. Forbes would like to see you."

Megan nodded, and her parents moved away to make room for Jack. Exhausted and distraught after having spent the night pacing up and down the hospital corridor waiting for Megan to awaken from the sedative, Jack was an unpleasant sight with his rumpled suit and uncombed salt and pepper hair, but his small, lash less, watery blue eyes bore an expression of genuine concern.

"Megan, I'm so sorry this happened," he began. "In all the years that the firm has been in existence, nothing like this has ever happened. I just can't imagine…" He stopped, and stared at her. Jack had never had any romantic interest in Megan, but he had always been aware of her beauty. Now her large green eyes were a grotesque swollen purple mass with broken red blood vessels. Her mouth was crimson and swollen to twice its normal size, and her entire face was so distorted that it had taken on a ghoulish quality.

"I talked to the other partners at the firm," Jack continued. "We all agree that you should take a paid leave of absence. Don't worry about your job; we'll make do until you get back. We want you to go to Buffalo with your parents to rest and recuperate. All we ask is that you call us once a week and let us know how you're doing. Okay?"

"Thank you," Megan replied quietly.

Jack turned to look at her parents standing close by. "I have to go to the office now," he said. "I'm due in court this afternoon. I just wanted you to know that all of us are behind you one hundred percent, and we want you to take care of yourself and get well as soon as possible." He smiled at her, said good-bye to her parents, and hastily exited the room.

"We've been up all night, honey," Megan's father told her. "Your mother and I need to go to a hotel and get some sleep."

"You go ahead," her mother told him. "I'm going to stay here for a while."

Mr. Cleary kissed his daughter on the forehead and left.

Mother and daughter passed a quiet morning. Neither of them discussed the attack, for Jennifer thought it was best to wait until her daughter was ready to discuss what had happened. Thus, Jennifer spent much of their time together talking about home, about the new outdoor kitchen that had been installed, and about the Christmas decorations. Megan responded, although inside she did not feel like talking.

In the afternoon Jennifer went to the hotel to get some sleep. Megan wanted to sleep too, but she couldn't without a sedative. Her body was still in too much pain, and her mind was in shock. She could hardly believe that she was lying in a hospital bed; that she of all people could have been raped and stabbed right in her own office building. As long as her mother had stayed with her she had been able to avoid thinking about what had happened. Now she was overwhelmed with a flood of feelings she did not understand. On the one hand, she was confused, hurt, enraged, embarrassed. She felt guilty, and, yet, she remembered how strong her attacker had been. There was nothing she could have done—every nerve and muscle reminded her of that whenever she tried to move. Still, there should have been some action she could have taken. Even Jack had said that nothing like this had ever happened before. Why had it happened to her?

Feeling dirty and helpless, and totally out of control, Megan could not keep her mind focused long enough to sort out her own feelings or to carry on a conversation with her mother. Without hearing much of what her mother had said, she had talked a little while inside a thousand emotions wrestled for attention. At moments an intense feeling of sadness washed over her, as though someone she had loved very much had just died. A lump formed in her throat and her head pounded, but she did not cry. It was not that she was trying to be brave; somehow no tears would come.

At other moments Megan was so angry that she felt that she could kill—not just her attacker but the first person she saw. None of the nurses who spent all day running in and out of her room checking on her seemed even the slightest bit interested in what had happened to her. It was easy to be angry with them, with the doctor, with the voices she heard from her bed. She could understand why terrorists go into buildings and shoot all the occupants at random. She could do that now if she had the opportunity.

Megan thought of the faceless figure in the shadows who had terrorized her the night before. If only she had been stronger than he. She would have taken that knife away from him and cut his throat with it. She wished that she had been waiting at the door with an axe when he opened it; she wished that she had blown his head off with a gun when his shadow passed her office. Nothing she could do to him would ever be too cruel; no anger was too strong, no penalty too severe, no action worth regretting.

Still, Megan was afraid, and no matter what else she happened to be feeling at any one time, fear was her most dominant emotion. Not fear of her attacker; logically, she knew that he could not hurt her in the hospital, although every time a figure passed her door she panicked. No, Megan told herself, he could not hurt her now. He would not come after her; he probably did not even know her name.

Another kind of fear dominated Megan's waking hours—fear of what people would think. Though she had never defended a rape case herself, during the time that Megan had been employed by Pratt, Forbes and Magoff, the firm had defended a number of accused rapists. She was well aware of the prevailing attitudes regarding rape and rape victims. At times, she had mentally accused rape victims of the same behavior of which others would now accuse her. She imagined that in the eyes of everyone she encountered she would recognize her own thoughts, attitudes and perceptions about rape coming back to haunt her. What would her parents think? Did they even know yet? They had raised her to be a decent young woman with good morals. They had given her a strict, even sheltered upbringing. They would be so disappointed.

What would Jeff think? Or Jack, or the other partners in the firm? What about the people living in her building—would they find out? A horrifying thought came to her—what if the story appeared on the news? She thought of all the crimes she had seen reported on the local news. Was some reporter sitting in an office somewhere typing her story for this evening's broadcast? Would they use her name? They might even photograph the outside of the law offices. Then everyone in New York City would know.

Megan quickly forced those thoughts from her mind. Probably the story would not appear on the news. New York City is so enormous; one rape case would probably not be considered newsworthy. Maybe no one would find out; the police knew, of course, and the doctors and nurses at the hospital, but it was possible that no one else knew. That meant that she did not have to explain anything to anyone.

She thought of her mother saying that they could talk when she was ready. She would never be ready—there would never come a time when she would be able to discuss everything that had happened to her. Megan was not that sort of person. She had always marveled at people who could appear on talk shows to discuss the most intimate aspects of their lives in front of millions of people. Not understanding them, she was disdainful of them. She believed that there are personal aspects of one's life that should be kept strictly private. Whatever problems she was experiencing she could work through herself, but she could not talk about them.

Megan had already made her decision when the counselor came to her room. The tall, middle-aged, bleached blonde woman entered uninvited and seated herself on the chair next to Megan's bed. "I'm the rape crisis counselor," she announced rather firmly. "I'm here to help you work through some of the problems you may be experiencing." She had a copy of Megan's medical chart. "I understand that you were attacked last night," she looked at Megan for confirmation.

"I can't talk to anyone right now," Megan began shaking her head. "I'm much too ill. I'm in terrible pain, and I really…"

"You need counseling," the woman interrupted her. "You've been through a terrible trauma, and you're going to go through a very difficult period of readjustment. It's important to begin working with a counselor immediately so that you can sort through your emotions."

"I understand," Megan replied. "But I simply am not well enough right now. When I leave the hospital, I'm going to Buffalo to stay with my family; I'll get counseling there."

"There's no reason why you can't start here at the hospital and then continue with a counselor in Buffalo." The woman leafed through some materials that she had brought with her. "The earlier you begin the easier it will be."

"There's a very good reason," Megan's tone was filled with irritation. "As I have already told you several times, I am very ill, and I cannot talk to anyone right now. When I get to Buffalo, I'll find a counselor."

"Fine," the woman replied. She took her materials and walked quickly from the room.

Megan watched her go. Her presence had reminded Megan that she could not hope to keep this attack a complete secret. She was indignant, though, that the hospital was handing out her personal information to total strangers. How dare they recommend her for counseling to some woman she had never seen or heard of? That had to be one of the most unprofessional acts she had ever witnessed. Surely she was capable of contacting a counselor on her own if she needed one, and if she didn't, she should not have one forced on her as though she were some deranged lunatic from the psychiatric ward. Megan was still angry when the nurse came in to give her another sedative.

Megan's remaining week in the hospital passed very slowly. Her parents came to see her every day, and sometimes one of them stayed alone with her for a while. It was hard for her to talk to them; it was hard for her to talk to anyone. Still, she felt better when they were nearby. Twice her mother brought Chinese Checkers, the only board game Megan had ever liked, and the three of them played in silence. She liked those times best. As long as they could play board games she did not have to talk, and her parents could not demand information about what had happened.

On Thursday another counselor came to see her, and Megan told her the same story. She was not in nearly as much pain now. The stab wounds had been superficial, and they were healing quickly. Intense pain had been replaced by a general feeling of overall soreness. Even her wrist no longer throbbed. The swelling in her eyes had gone down, and her mouth had nearly returned to its normal size. Still, the bruises were sufficiently discolored to convince her interrogator that she was in no condition to talk. Of course, she

The Twelfth Juror

promised, she would be getting into counseling the moment she arrived in Buffalo.

Finally, the day came for Megan's release, and she felt as though she were being let out of prison. Her mother brought her clothes and helped her get ready to leave. Her parents had packed some of her personal belongings from her apartment so that they would be ready to drive straight to Buffalo when they left the hospital. At last they were ready to leave, and the nurse arrived at the door of her room with a wheelchair. Megan protested strongly.

"It's hospital policy," the nurse insisted, and her mother nodded. The nurse wheeled her to the elevator and then to the door. Megan's parents helped her into the car, and she breathed a sigh of relief as they drove away.

Megan settled back in the car to enjoy the trip. Her mother was saying something, but she wasn't really listening. This was the first time that she had felt secure since the attack had taken place. She was glad to be getting out of New York City, glad to be going home for a while. Maybe that was exactly what she needed. She knew that *he* wasn't in Buffalo; the doctors and nurses and police officers weren't in Buffalo. She was getting an opportunity to hide out for a while.

The streets were congested, but her father drove as quickly as the heavy traffic would permit. The day was grim; it looked as though a snow storm were approaching. The pollution had turned everything in the city a dull brown. Megan was drinking in the sights, although she did not understand why. She had passed these buildings a thousand times since she had moved to New York. They had become part of the background of her life; like the furniture in her living room, they were always there but seldom noticed. Today these sights had captured her attention, and she found herself noticing the graffiti on the buildings and the cracks in the sidewalks. She noted how dirty the city was. Little patches of brown snow dotted the sidewalks and streets. She had heard on the radio that it had snowed while she was in the hospital, but, of course, she had not seen it. She did not like the snow in New York anyway; it was always dirty.

Eventually, they left the city behind and made their way into the country. It looked as though the entire state of New York must be frozen. Outside the city the snow was a little cleaner. The trees were covered with discolored frozen netting, and on the ground the snow was piled up to the middle of the tree trunks. Megan thought of the times when her father had insisted on coming to pick her up and take her home for the holidays because it was snowing. He did not like for her to drive when the roads were covered in ice, but he did not seem to mind driving four hundred miles one way to pick her up and then making the return trip. When she was in school, he had always driven down to get her for vacations, but she had assumed that when she graduated, he would discontinue the practice. He didn't; he still insisted that she fly or that he drive her, but he would not even discuss her driving home alone. She was old enough to live alone in New York and to work in a top law firm but not to provide her own transportation to visit her parents. Ian had always taken care of her.

Megan looked at her father as he drove along in silence. It had been sort of a promise when she was growing up; she would always be his little girl and he would always take care of her. Ian Cleary had always tried to provide the best for his daughter. When she was little he had taken her everywhere with him; he had introduced her to everyone. He had paid for her education and had arranged for her to go to Columbia Law School. When she graduated, he used his connections to secure her position with Pratt, Forbes and Magoff. He seemed to enjoy giving her things, but he never asked for anything in return. Megan now realized that he had not gotten much more from her than he had expected—presents at his birthday and Christmas, a telephone call every week, her love, of course; these were his rewards for all that he had done for her. Megan wondered whether it was enough.

Megan studied the handsome face that had always been so full of hope and expectation. Now it was masked with worry, and his warm brown eyes reflected dismay. Ian had said very little about her attack; since that first day at the hospital, he had not mentioned it. In some ways his silence was welcome; in others it was disturbing. They had always been so close. Now her attack was coming between them, putting them in a position where it was difficult to talk to each other. Perhaps it would be better if he said something—even if he said the wrong thing. At least she would know what he was thinking. His silence protected her secret, but it also seemed to shut her out.

Jennifer was saying something about the scenery. "Yes, Mother," Megan answered, half listening, "I love the snow, too." Megan turned toward her mother. Jennifer had been making light conversation since the first day at the hospital, but Megan suspected that even she was not really paying attention to what she was saying. Her tone was gentle—that of a mother talking to a seriously ill child who is too young to be told that it may not survive. She talked of home, of their plans for Christmas, of the future, and she smiled as though there were no problems. Sometimes, though, she fell silent for long periods of time, and Megan knew that her mind was far away. Then she came back to herself and once again began trying to lift Megan's spirits.

Megan thought of all the secrets she had tried to keep from her mother as a child. She thought of the time she had dyed her brand new shoes an awful shade of brown because they were scuffed. She had worked as quietly as possible on that project, but eventually Jennifer had discovered her and the shoes. She did not say much except to scold her daughter for not being more careful with the shoes in the first place and for not being more honest when she knew that the shoes were a hopeless mess. Megan smiled now as she thought of the incident. She had never successfully kept any secret from her mother, and she feared that her mother would guess what had really taken place in the office. If she figured it out, Megan would have to admit the truth, and that would bring on another series of questions.

The eight hour drive to Buffalo was fairly uneventful. At noon they stopped to have chicken for lunch and then they went on. As they moved further and further northwest, the temperature dropped considerably. It had been cold when they left New York City, but the chill of Buffalo winters was different even from that in New York. Ian turned up the heat in the car and Megan pulled her coat around her more tightly. As they reached the last leg of their trip, she felt her spirits lifting. She was glad that they had insisted on taking her home straight from the hospital.

It was seven o'clock when the car pulled up in front of the beautiful old two-story home that had served as the Cleary residence for thirty years. Ian took care of the luggage while Megan and her mother hurried to the door.

"Hello, Maria," Megan acknowledged the maid who let them in.

"Hello, Mija," Maria replied. "You came home for Christmas early this year."

"Yes," replied Megan as she gave Maria a quick hug and turned to go upstairs.

"Your room is ready for you," Jennifer called behind her. "Just take off your coat and wash your hands. Maria has sandwiches and potato soup waiting for us in the kitchen."

Megan nodded and walked slowly up the long winding staircase. She was tired from the trip but very glad to be home. She loved the house; she loved Maria's potato soup; she loved being near her parents. She reached the top of the stairs and felt for the light switch. As she groped in the shadows to find it, she felt panic rise up from somewhere deep inside her. She was terrified that someone was just behind her, about to grab hold of her. Quickly she flicked on the switch and turned around. The hall was empty. Downstairs she could hear her parents' voices.

Megan's heart was pounding as she opened her bedroom door and turned on the lights. It was exactly as it had always been. Her huge four poster bed with its fresh white comforter and mountains of snowy pillows stood against the wall to her left. To the right was her antique cherry dressing table with its large mirror. On the wall next to the door was a large walk-in closet where some of her clothes were kept at all times so that she did not have to take so many things when she came for visits. On the wall next to the dresser was a door connecting the bedroom to the adjoining bath with its jetted tub and separate shower. It was a very comfortable room—the room where she had spent many of the happiest years of her life.

Megan hung her coat in the closet, washed her hands, and brushed her hair. When she got downstairs, her parents were already seated and the soup and sandwiches had been served. They joined hands to pray over the food and began to eat.

"I'm doing some Christmas shopping tomorrow," Jennifer told Megan. "Why don't you come along and help me pick out gifts for Grandmother and Uncle Ted."

"That would be nice," Megan replied.

"There's a performance of Handel's *Messiah* Saturday night," Ian commented. "I have tickets for the three of us."

"Oh," Megan smiled enthusiastically, "I love the *Messiah*."

"Also," Jennifer added, "The American Ballet Company is presenting *The Nutcracker*. I know that you've seen it a hundred times, but it's nice for Christmas; it gets us into the holiday spirit. That's going to be the Tuesday after next?" She looked at Megan's father for confirmation.

"I think so," Ian replied. "I'll have to look at the tickets to see."

"We also have to pick out our tree," Jennifer continued. "On Monday we are having our tree decorating party. We always have to wait until later in the month so that you will be here when we put it up, but since you're already here, we thought we would go ahead just as we used to when you were a little girl."

Megan smiled again. Tree decorating parties were always tremendous fun. Her mother would make her special fudge recipe and Maria would prepare the rest of the food. The tree decorating party had begun as an occasion to provide a special Christmas tradition for Megan and her cousins when they were children. However, each year Jennifer still rounded up all of the cousins that happened to be in town for the holidays and got them there for the party. Cookies, fruit punch, popcorn, cupcakes and all sorts of candies did not seem like a particularly appropriate menu for a bunch of twenty somethings, but Jennifer still clung to the original menu that she had begun serving when Megan was five years old. To tell the truth, everyone would have been disappointed if she had changed anything.

This year, though, Megan and her parents would have the tree decorating party with just the three of them. She had told her parents that she wanted to wait until the family Christmas party to see all of the extended family members at one time.

"On the twentieth we'll drive out to see Niagara Falls," Ian stated.

"And the twenty-third is the Christmas party for all of our friends," Jennifer rejoined. "We want you to wear something absolutely gorgeous. Maybe you would like to call Jeff and ask him to come up for the party."

"No," Megan replied quickly. "Not this year." Out of the corner of her eye she caught a glimpse of her mother's startled expression, and she realized that her tone had been too hasty. She smiled a little and added, "He came last year. If I ask him up here again, everyone will think that we're planning to get married or something."

Megan swallowed the last bite of her sandwich. "I'm very tired. I'll see you in the morning." Rising from her chair, she kissed her parents good night and went upstairs.

The light in the upstairs hall was still on when she reached the landing. She went into her room and began changing for bed. Megan examined the bruises and wounds on her side as she undressed. It seemed to her that they were taking a long time to heal. She would be glad when they were gone; the sight of them and the soreness that accompanied them served as constant reminders of her attack. Quickly she put on her nightgown and turned out the bathroom light.

Megan walked back to her bedroom where she clicked off the light switch. The moonlight streamed through the window, casting eerie shadows. She lay in the darkness with the silver light lending a wicked glow to the objects in her room. Her heart began to race again, and her breath came faster as the feeling came over her that *he* was there, in the shadows, making his way slowly towards her in the darkness. Megan jumped from her bed, ran to the bathroom, and turned on the light. Opening the door as widely as she could, she looked carefully around the room. Then in the semi-darkness, she returned to her bed and went to sleep.

The next morning Megan woke to the sound of her mother gently knocking at her bedroom door. Jennifer let herself in and asked whether Megan would like to come downstairs to have some bacon and eggs. "Your father had some work to do. He's already gone. Why don't you come down and we can have breakfast together?"

Megan rose and dressed and then joined her mother downstairs. The crisp bacon and scrambled eggs with cheese were already on her plate, and after she was seated, her mother poured them each a steaming cup of coffee. Megan began to eat, and her mother watched her for a minute.

"Megan, we need to talk."

Megan swallowed a mouthful of eggs in one gulp. This was the moment she had been dreading since she had awakened in the hospital. She looked at her mother and pretended to be attentive without being concerned. "About what, Mother?"

"About what happened to you," Jennifer answered. "I know that you must be going through a lot of trauma right now. You need to know that what happened isn't your fault. Your father and I love you so much, and we want to help you in any way we can. Whatever problems you have as a result of this, we can work through together."

"I'm fine, Mother. I'm not having any problems," Megan looked at her mother, and then she looked away.

"Megan, you were raped," Jennifer looked at her daughter very seriously. "That's not something that you can just forget."

Megan was dumbfounded. "Who told you that!" she asked accusingly.

"The police told us," Jennifer remained calm. "The doctors talked to us very frankly when you were under the sedative, and they gave us a description of all your injuries. They also talked to us about some of the possible problems associated with what happened to you."

"They talked to you and who else?" Megan was still reeling from the shock of discovering that the hospital had given this information to her parents.

"I don't know. Jack Forbes, maybe, I don't think anyone else was there." Jennifer took Megan's hand. "That's not the point. You need to begin dealing with this and sorting through your feelings about it. You need to think about how this has affected you and how it's going to continue to affect you. You need counseling."

"I talked to a counselor at the hospital," Megan lied.

"Did it help?" Jennifer asked.

"No," Megan replied. "It was just depressing."

"I think you need long-term counseling," Jennifer resumed. "I have talked to a counselor here in Buffalo. You can have your first session with her tomorrow afternoon. She thinks it would be very good for you…"

"No!" Megan interrupted. "I've already seen a counselor, and I don't need to see anyone else. And I want you to promise me that you won't tell anybody else what happened."

"Megan…" Jennifer protested.

"No, Mother," Megan cut her off, "I have to deal with this in my own way. I don't want anyone to know."

"It might be easier for you to be open about it than to try to keep it a secret," Jennifer responded. "There are certain consequences that you may have to deal with," she paused, "You could be pregnant."

"I'm not," Megan looked both embarrassed and depressed. "The hospital…treated…me."

"What if you are anyway?" Jennifer studied her daughter soberly. Megan was disturbed and upset by the conversation, and that, to her mother, was another sign that she could not deal with the trauma by herself. "I know it's horrible to think about, but these are things that you need to start dealing with now."

"I can't deal with it now," Megan got up from the table and walked over to the sink. She pushed her hair back with her hands. "I can't talk about it now; I can't even think about it now."

Megan turned back to face her mother. "Look, if anything like that should happen, I will deal with it then. But I can't make myself crazy right now fantasizing about horrible hypotheticals." She sat down again and took her mother's hand. "I know you are trying to help me," her voice cracked with strain and emotion, "and you know that I love you. But I have to cope my way, and it's very important to me that no one knows what happened. Please, just tell your friends that someone broke in to rob the office, and I was beaten up because I surprised them." Megan looked at her mother pleadingly, "If you love me, promise me that you'll keep this quiet."

Jennifer was silent for a moment. "All right," she sighed, "I promise, but only if you promise me that if anything else happens you will tell me immediately."

Megan nodded, and Jennifer pulled her close and pressed her lips against her daughter's silky flaxen hair.

THREE

After she and her mother talked, it was easier for Megan to relax at home. They did not really discuss the attack again, but just knowing that her parents knew took away the burden of trying to keep them from finding out. Although Jennifer would have preferred for Megan to go into counseling, in a few days she decided that, perhaps, Megan was right—she was dealing with the attack in her own way, and her way seemed to be working.

Megan and her parents had a wonderful time shopping together for gifts and attending the various holiday performances. Megan had always loved going out with her parents, and she found that these times together were just what she needed. As the days passed, the tension that she had felt in the household seemed to be disappearing. Even Ian was convinced that his daughter was handling the experience well. She was laughing and talking, and she did not seem as nervous as she had been; she appeared to be adjusting.

Megan, herself, was surprised that she had not been more affected. At times she wondered why she was such an incredibly strong person. It was not that she was making an effort—rather, as the days passed, she felt more and more detached from her attack. It was almost as though it had happened to someone else. In Buffalo she was separated from all of the people and places associated with her attack, and she could almost convince herself that it had never really happened, that the whole incident had been part of some terrible nightmare.

The Christmas festivities played an important role in taking Megan's mind off her problems. Megan had loved Christmas since she was old enough to remember. She loved every aspect of the holiday, from the visits to the church for the Christmas services, to the social events, to the way the house looked and smelled during the holiday season. She loved the Christmas tree and its sweet fragrance of pine that scented the room where it stood. She loved the ornaments and decorations; sometimes she stole into the living room and sat watching the tree with its tiny lights and glass balls that reflected the dancing light of the fire in the fireplace. She enjoyed being in the kitchen with her mother, helping make Christmas candies and sweet breads. She even enjoyed addressing invitations for the Christmas party that the Clearys held every year for their friends. When she was involved in these activities, she could go for hours without thinking of her attack.

No matter how many distractions Megan had, though, she could not forget it completely. As the days passed, she began to experience times when feelings of great sadness or loss overcame her, and tears began to roll down her face without warning. At other times, rage rose up in her, and she wanted to lash out at whoever happened to be near. At still other moments, she found herself in a state of panic for no reason. She stayed close to one or both of her parents at all times; she never left the house without them, and she tried to be with them in the house as much as possible. Whenever these emotions overtook her, she found comfort and calm in having them near.

It was at night that Megan had the most difficulty. She had left the light on in her bathroom from the first night. Even with the light on, however, she often felt afraid. Sometimes she awakened in the middle of the night and lay awake for hours. Lying in the stillness, she replayed the attack over and over again in her head, and all of the emotions connected with it came flooding back. Sometimes she would get out of bed and walk the floor, desperately seeking some relief from the visions that haunted her. "How could I have been so stupid?" she asked herself. "Why did I call to him when I heard him open the door?"

Megan wondered what had motivated her attacker. Had he known she was working late? Had he been stalking her for days, waiting to find her alone and vulnerable? The thought gave her chills. Had he planned to just rob the offices? It was possible that he had not known she was there until she called out to him. Night after night the same questions filled her mind, as she grieved and feared and raged alone in the darkness.

On the twentieth Megan and her parents drove to Niagara Falls as they had every year since she was a small child. She had seen the Falls at various seasons—in the spring when the ice broke and they flowed free again, in the summer when the tourists came to stare at the rushing water, and in the early autumn just before the snows came. None of these sights fascinated her as much as that of the Falls at Christmas.

She and her parents now stood in the subzero weather to see hundreds of millions of gallons of water encased in ice, their force rendered impotent by the enormous power that bound them. Great sheets of churning water had been captured in motion to form a thick ice bridge. It was like looking at a freeze frame in a film. It seemed to Megan that the tremendous force of the water should be able to break those icy chains and flow freely once again in spite of the bitter cold. Yet, the Falls were subject to the season, and like an obedient slave they stood prisoner, suspended in time, until released by the spring thaws.

Megan felt that she, too, had been imprisoned by a force too great to control. Like those falls she had so much energy, so much creative power. She had so many ambitions and goals and so much drive. Now that energy seemed frozen inside her, and her heart felt numb. She could not find any of the drive to fulfill her ambitions; she no longer awakened eager to meet the challenges of each new day. It was as though someone had stopped time inside of her; her heart and mind were cloaked in a thick veil of ice. She was unable to gain control over her feelings, just as she had been unable to gain control over her attacker. Sometimes she felt as though he were still controlling her. He continued to force his way into her life. She was still his prisoner, and all of her will could not break the chains that bound her spirit.

Megan thought again of the Falls. In a few months they would be free. Spring would come to loosen the ice, and the water would burst through with its vast power, sweeping away the last remnants of its frozen dungeon. Would spring free her too? There must be someone, something to set her at liberty if she were ever to escape this nightmare. She could not break through this force on her own, of that she was now fairly certain. Yet, she could not imagine that anyone could help her. That was why even at her lowest moments she felt that going to a counselor was pointless. She would merely be rehashing grotesque details for a stranger who could not offer her any answers. How could someone else help her wage an emotional battle against a demon that now lived in her imagination? There was nothing she could do to the man who had attacked her—she could not even identify him for the police. All she could do was defeat the image he had left behind—the figure that haunted her fantasies. In order to do that, she would have to find something stronger than he— a power that could free her from the force that now controlled her.

Megan hoped that the happy spirit of Christmas would free her and that the time spent with her parents would help her forget. She threw herself into every activity, and she found that every project in which she took part helped her push the fear and anxiety out of her mind. She was determined to attend the party that her parents were giving on the twenty-third, although, secretly, she believed that she would be better off not going. However, she had already talked Jennifer into not inviting her cousins to the tree decorating party, using the excuse that by the time she saw them on the twenty-third her bruises would have cleared up. It would be her first social event since the attack, and she feared that she was not ready. Still, she knew that if she were ever going to fully recover, she would have to force herself to participate in these kinds of activities. Besides, since she had worked so hard to convince them that she did not need counseling, her parents would accept no explanation that she might give for boycotting the party.

On the night of the twenty-third Megan dressed carefully and gave extra attention to her hair and makeup. The bruises and swelling were gone, and she wanted to make certain that she looked her best. When she had finished her preparations, she studied herself in the mirror. Her hair was woven into a neat chignon, and her simple black dress was complimented by a double strand of pearls with an emerald clasp that matched the green of her eyes. When she was satisfied with her appearance, she went downstairs to help her mother receive their guests.

Many of the guests had been friends of the family for years, although a few were new acquaintances whom she had not previously met. Megan greeted everyone with a smile and exchanged pleasantries with them. Across the room she caught sight of her cousin Joanna. As children they had been almost like sisters. Smiling, she walked toward Joanna.

"Megan!" Joanna returned the smile as she gave her cousin a hug. "How have you been? I want you to meet Doug, my fiancé."

Megan shook hands with Doug, "Congratulations, you're getting a wonderful girl."

Looking at Joanna, she continued, "I'm so happy for you."

"Thank you," Joanna beamed. "We're going to be married in June. I'm counting on you to be my maid of honor."

"I'd love to," Megan responded warmly.

Joanna's mother, Megan's Aunt Martha, rushed toward them. "Megan," she put her arms around her niece. "I'm so sorry about what happened to you. It must have been so awful; I'm just glad to see that you're well now."

"What?" a startled Megan kept her voice low.

"Oh, your mother told me all about it when I talked to her a couple of weeks ago. She mentioned that you were home, and I asked why. She said that a burglar broke into your office and nearly killed you. I was so shocked. I've been meaning to call you, but I just haven't had the time."

"Why Megan," Joanna interrupted, "that's so awful."

"It wasn't serious," Megan responded, looking around the room.

"Not serious?" Martha interjected, "She was in the hospital for a week!"

"Will you excuse me? I need to check on things in the kitchen." Megan walked quickly away.

"That's just like Martha," she thought. "Rushing up to me and expressing sympathy was just her way of telling everybody. She is such an old busybody."

Megan fumed silently as she looked at the appetizers. Before the evening was over Martha would probably tell everyone at the party, and Megan would be dealing with condolences from all of them. It was a good thing she had gotten Jennifer to promise not to tell anyone about the rape. Otherwise, Martha would be spreading that story all over the room as well.

As Megan leaned over to reach for a shrimp she realized that someone was standing close behind her. Before she could turn around, she felt a man's arms encircle her. Suddenly she was back in the office, her hand outstretched to reach the light switch, and a man's arms were closing around her. She felt a chill go up her spine, and she spun around to face the man behind her.

"What's wrong, Megan?" asked her startled Uncle Ted, who was as alarmed by her actions as she was by his.

"Don't ever sneak up on me like that again," stormed a furious Megan. "You ought to know better than to come up behind somebody like that. You nearly scared me to death…"

"I'm sorry, Meg. Martha told me that you were in here, and I just wanted to give you a little squeeze. I haven't seen you since last Christmas."

"That doesn't make it okay for you to sneak up on me and scare me half to death. You should have spoken to me like a normal person." Megan was so angry that she could have slapped him.

"I'm sorry," Ted apologized again. "Don't you think you're overreacting just a little?"

"No!" her voice was choked with anger. "I don't think I'm overreacting at all."

Furious, Megan ran up the kitchen stairs to her bedroom and shut the door behind her. She sat on the edge of her bed and put her head in her hands. She was still enraged, and she told herself that she had been right to make a scene; after all, Ted should have more respect for her feelings. At the same time, a voice inside her told her that she had overreacted.

"What's wrong with me?" Megan wondered. She had begun the evening in high spirits, but the moment that Ted had put his arms around her she had felt anger burst out of her like some great uncontrollable beast.

Megan heard a short but firm knock at her bedroom door. Before she could respond, Jennifer walked into the room closing the door behind her. She sat down next to her daughter on the edge of the bed and asked, "What was that scene in the kitchen all about?"

Megan tried to defend herself, "Ted came sneaking up behind me and grabbed hold of me. Naturally I was startled, and I turned around and told him not to do it again."

"Ted came back into the living room and told me that he walked up behind you to give you a hug and you went wild. He asked me to come upstairs to make sure that you're okay," Jennifer studied her daughter.

"I suppose he's told everybody downstairs," Megan rose from the bed and walked over to the dressing table to gaze at her image in the mirror.

"No, he hasn't told 'everybody,'" Jennifer responded. "He called me aside and told me. He's worried about you; you need to go downstairs and apologize to him for exploding like that. Then you need to rejoin the party; the guests are asking about you."

"You certainly should not expect me to apologize to Ted," Megan looked aghast, ignoring the remainder of her mother's statement. "I'm the one who deserves an apology. He nearly scared me to death…"

"You're being ridiculous," Jennifer said. "Ted didn't do anything; you're the one who threw a fit."

Megan faced her mother angrily. "You don't care about my feelings; the only thing you care about is whether I spoil the party or offend your guests. You don't care anything about me."

"Stop that right now," Jennifer's tone was firm. "I love you with my whole heart, and you know it. That's not the point. I didn't tell anyone that you were raped because you begged me not to, and I haven't insisted that you go into counseling because you seemed to be getting along fine without it. But you're not going to go around attacking everyone else. This experience is something that you're going to have to live with for the rest of your life, and you might as well start getting used to it right now. Your father and I have been very patient with you since you came home because we know that you've been through a terrible ordeal. Other people are not going to be as patient or as understanding. Ted doesn't even know what happened; he thinks you're just spoiled, although that's not really the point either. What is important is that even if everyone on the face of the earth knew that you were raped, ultimately it wouldn't make any difference. You can't make excuses for your behavior forever. You're going to have to get a grip on yourself and rejoin the real world, at least in terms of your behavior in public. And, if you're not able to do that alone, you'll have to go into counseling."

Megan wanted to protest, but she knew it was a waste of time. She was much angrier with her mother than she had been with Ted. Her mother knew what she had been through, but she did not have an ounce of sympathy for her. Megan had been living on her own since she had begun college—nearly ten years. She was old enough and intelligent enough to make her own decisions, and she deeply resented Jennifer's authoritarian tone. Without looking at her mother, she pushed the door open and walked downstairs. She apologized to Ted and spent the rest of the evening with the guests, making a concentrated effort to look as though she were enjoying herself. Never-the-less, all evening her mother's words bothered her, and she remained very angry.

When the guests had left, Megan went to her room and dressed for bed. She was still seething from the events of the evening, and she did not say good night to her parents. As she turned out the light and lay in the semi-darkness she felt totally confused. Every nerve in her body seemed to be on fire. She could still hear Martha's nasal tone, "I am *so* sorry about what happened to you." Mock sympathy if she had ever heard it; Martha had probably gossiped to everyone in the room.

She remembered the terror she had felt when Ted put his arms around her; whatever else her mother might say, that fear was very real. She remembered her mother's firm tone, "You're going to have to rejoin the real world; if you can't do that you'll have to go into counseling." It was as if everyone were made of stone. She felt as though she were in some terrible nightmare where she was unable to communicate with the people around her. She lay awake, tossing and turning as a mass of confused thoughts tumbled through her mind until, finally, she found relief in sleep.

In her dreams Megan found herself running down a dark passageway. A man was chasing her; when she turned, she could not see him but she could hear him. She knew that he was large and fat;

he panted and wheezed as he drew nearer and nearer. Terrified she ran as fast as she could to stay ahead of him, knowing that when he caught her, he would kill her. Yet, no matter how hard she ran she could not escape. She could feel his breath, and she knew that he was just behind her. She could not see in front of her to find a means of escape; walls enclosed her on either side. "Please don't kill me," she sobbed. "Please don't kill me." There was no answer, only the sound of his congested breathing. At last he reached out to grab her, and she knew that she could not get away. She screamed as he caught hold of her.

At that moment Megan awakened. Her heart was racing, and she was covered in perspiration. She sprang from her bed and turned on the light. It was more than an hour before she was able to go back to sleep, and she slept the rest of the night with all the lights on.

FOUR

By the first of January Megan was feeling much better. She often remembered what her mother had said to her on the night of the party, and she worked hard to control her emotions when other people were present. In fact, after a couple of weeks of practice she was becoming skillful at the masquerade she had forced herself to play. It was not just a charade, though. With the coming of the New Year, Megan felt a desire to put all of the sad events of the past behind her and start fresh. Only one dark occurrence clouded Megan's thoughts. Since the night of the party, she had slept with the bedroom light on every night, and she had been afraid to go to sleep because she feared that her nightmare would return. She had dreamed about the man chasing her in the dark twice since that night, and each time she had awakened in a cold sweat, unable to fall asleep again. The dream was so frighteningly real that when she awakened she believed that *he* was in her room with her.

Ten days had passed since Megan had experienced the nightmare, and she believed that now that her life was returning to normal she would not be bothered by it again. Perhaps, it had simply been a result of her own anger and confusion, compounded by the people she had seen since she had been at home. She knew that it was time for her to return to her own apartment and her own life, and she believed that she would feel more in control when she did so. Some of her drive and energy were returning, and she was anxious to get back to work. Her life had been put on hold for a brief time; she now wanted to make certain that no more time was wasted.

Megan had kept her promise and called Jack Forbes once a week to let him know about her progress. She was relieved to find that his tone was always upbeat and positive. Jack was delighted to learn that she was ready to come back to work, and they agreed that she would be back at the office on Monday, January 24. Megan spent her remaining time at home enjoying her family and friends who dropped by, as she looked forward to her return to New York with a mixture of anticipation and apprehension.

The time passed quickly, and on the morning of January 23, Megan packed the last of her clothing into her suitcase. Her plane was leaving in a few hours; she would be back in New York City in plenty of time to unpack and prepare to return to work the following morning.

She looked out her bedroom window. The snow was piled in great heaps. She thought of other Sunday mornings when she was a child and the family had gone to church on cold winter mornings. After the service they had lunch at a restaurant close by. Sunday had been Megan's favorite day of the week. She remembered a few times when her father was running late, and they left the house so long after the service started that he suggested that they skip church and just have lunch out instead. Those were her favorite days; she got to eat out without squirming through a sermon.

Now that she was grown, Sunday was still her favorite day. The other six days of the week she spent working and going out with friends, but she reserved Sundays for herself. She no longer went to church; she now slept late, went out for lunch and spent a restful evening in her apartment reading or watching movies.

This Sunday morning she was filled with nervous excitement about returning to work. She wondered whether she would be all right when she was alone again in New York. She was doing so well at home; she hoped that she would be able to do equally well at work and in her apartment. She remembered what her mother had said to her about other people's lack of sympathy—she must not appear frightened or vulnerable.

Megan surveyed the room to see whether she had left anything behind. She would miss this room and this house, just as she had missed them when she went off to college. She turned off the bathroom light that had kept her company every night of her stay. Taking one final look around the room, she picked up her bags and walked downstairs.

Ian was still upstairs getting ready to take her to the airport. Jennifer was waiting for Megan in the kitchen, dressed in a black and violet sweater and black wool slacks. She had gotten up early and prepared strawberry waffles with whipped cream and a pot of coffee. Megan had long since apologized for her remarks to her mother on the night of the party, and any tension between them had passed. As they sat eating their breakfast, Megan looked into Jennifer's large dark eyes cloaked in thick black lashes. Mother and daughter were very similar in appearance—tall and slim with fine even features. The only marked difference was their coloring. Jennifer's hair and eyes were dark brown while Megan owed her flaxen locks and green eyes to her Grandma Cleary. Mother and daughter were also similar in other ways. They shared hobbies and interests and a zany sense of humor.

"Are you looking forward to going back to work tomorrow?" Jennifer asked as she poured them each a cup of coffee.

"Yes, I am," replied Megan, reaching for the sugar. "It's time that I got back to work. I'm sure that they will have plenty for me to do."

"I'm going to miss you so much," Jennifer put her hand on Megan's. "In spite of everything, it has been wonderful to have you home these last few weeks."

"I've loved being here," Megan replied as she looked at her mother affectionately. "In some ways I hate to leave; I wish that I could live here and work in New York," she paused. "I wish you and Dad were coming with me."

"I could come and stay with you for a while if it would make you feel better," Jennifer offered.

"No," Megan smiled. "Dad needs you here with him, and it's not fair to you for me to drag you away to babysit me. Anyway, I need to get back into my old routine as soon as possible. It's the only way I will ever be able to work past this. I'm taking your advice, you know."

"I know," Jennifer squeezed her hand. "But you also know that you don't ever have to put on a front for me. If you need to talk, no matter what time of the day or night, call me and I'll be here for you. If you decide that you do want me to come to New York and stay with you, I will get on the first plane. Remember, you promised to let me know about anything that happens."

"I will," Megan assured her.

Ian entered the kitchen wearing gray slacks and a matching sweater. "Are we going to be ready to leave soon?" he asked his daughter.

"Yes, Dad. Everything's packed and I'm almost through with breakfast."

"Good," he said as he poured himself some juice.

"Would you like a waffle?" Jennifer asked.

"No," he replied, "just some toast, I think."

Jennifer began to clear Megan's dishes from the table while Megan left to repair her lipstick.

"Do you think she will be okay in New York?" Ian whispered to Jennifer when Megan had left the room.

"I think she's having more problems than she'll admit," Jennifer looked worried. "A couple of nights ago I got up at two in the morning to get a drink of water, and when I passed Megan's room, I noticed that the light was on. I opened the door to ask why she was still up, and she was sound asleep in her bed. After that I checked on her nightly; she has been sleeping with the lights on every night."

"Did you ask her about it?" Ian looked surprised.

"No," Jennifer answered. "Every time I bring up the subject of her behavior she says that she is doing fine and that she is coping in her own way. Since she refuses to go into counseling, there isn't much that I can do. She seems to think that going back to New York will help her; I certainly hope it does. Frankly, I'm afraid of what may happen to her if she isn't able to start dealing with the attack."

Megan reappeared in the kitchen, and her parents rose from the table. Jennifer and Ian put on their coats and helped Megan take the last of her bags to the car. Then she settled into the backseat as they left for the airport. "Now, you already have your ticket," Ian reminded her as he drove. "You should be all set."

"Yes, Dad. All I have to do is get on the plane."

"Did Forbes have those extra locks installed in your apartment?" Ian asked.

"He said that he did when I talked to him on Tuesday. I asked for a couple of additional deadbolts and a security system. He said that everything would be ready for me when I get back today." Megan was relieved to have the extra locks. Even though her attacker had not been in her apartment, she felt that she was not really safe anywhere.

"Good," Ian was also more comfortable with the idea of extra security at his daughter's apartment, "You're going to be fine. Just be very careful."

Megan remembered all the times that he had warned her to be "very careful." She had always dismissed that phrase as the words of an overly protective father who could not accept that his daughter was an adult. For the first time she understood why he had always been so protective. In the recesses of her mind she had always believed that

New York was a dangerous city and that there were violent, unstable people who took pleasure in harming others. Still, she had never been afraid to live alone, or to stroll down the street as she window shopped on a Saturday afternoon, or to go to the park by herself, or to work late. She now realized that she had been incredibly naïve. Perhaps, if she had listened to her father, if she had been more careful, none of this would ever have happened.

Megan glanced at her window. Frost coated the glass, making it impossible for her to see the snow-covered countryside. For the last week she had been anxious to return to New York and get back to work and her normal routine. Even when she had awakened this morning she had been enthusiastic about the trip. Part of her was still enthusiastic, but another part wanted very badly to stay in Buffalo. She felt safer and more secure with her mother and father nearby, and she had enjoyed the time at home so much. She almost wished that she could ask her father to turn the car around so that she could remain with them for at least a little while longer.

Her father pulled into the airport parking lot, and Megan knew that it was too late to turn back. Ian took her bags from the car, and her parents walked with her into the terminal where she checked her luggage. They stayed with her until they reached the security check point.

"Call us tonight after you get to your apartment and let us know that you arrived safely," Jennifer said as she embraced her.

"I will," Megan promised.

"I love you, Baby," Ian said as he hugged her. "Let us know how everything goes."

"I love you, too," Megan replied.

She smiled at both her parents as she blinked away the tears that welled up in her eyes. Then she turned and walked into the secured area. Her parents watched as she placed her shoes and purse in a gray plastic container, set it on the conveyor belt, and walked through the metal detector. When Megan looked back for one last glimpse of her parents, they were gone.

Megan was filled with melancholy as she walked to her gate. A few minutes later when she boarded the jet that would take her back to New York, however, she felt much more optimistic. Soon the jet began to ascend, and she felt her spirits rise with it.

It was late afternoon when Megan arrived in New York, and from the airport she went straight to her apartment building. As she paid the cab driver and stepped out onto the crowded street, she felt a sense of relief to be home. She walked up the three flights of stairs leading to her apartment and let herself in. Shutting and locking the door behind her, she set her luggage down and turned to survey the new locks. In addition to the deadbolt that she already had on the door, there were two new deadbolts and a heavy bar that had been installed across the door. She looked at the security system. Jack had described it to her over the telephone, and he had left the instruction booklet and the keys to her new locks on her coffee table. She thumbed through the booklet. Jack had offered to pick her up at the airport, and she now thought that she should have taken him up on his offer so that he could have shown her how to use the system. After a few moments of studying the instructions, however, she had successfully activated the system and set all of the locks.

Megan turned and surveyed her apartment. It looked different somehow. The spacious living room with its gleaming hardwood floors and floor to ceiling windows seemed to have changed while she had been away. She straightened a picture on the wall and rearranged a couple of books on the bookshelves. She turned on the gas log in the fireplace and stretched out her hands to feel its warmth. She then walked into the adjacent open kitchen and studied the beautiful cherry wood cabinets and spotless stainless steel appliances.

When Megan opened the refrigerator to see what she could find for dinner, she recoiled at the smells that greeted her. The scents of decaying vegetables, sour milk and rotten meat filled her nostrils. She quickly dumped the spoiled food into the garbage disposal and wiped out the refrigerator with a mixture of water and lemon extract. When she opened the freezer, Megan found several frozen Italian dinners that were still edible. In the pantry she found a can of deviled ham, an unopened jar of mayonnaise, and a box of crackers. She put a packet of frozen ravioli in her microwave and set the deviled ham and the mayonnaise on the counter. Tonight she would use them to make a spread for the crackers; tomorrow she would go grocery shopping.

Megan walked into her bedroom to put away her coat and unpack her bags. When she opened her closet, she was amazed to find that it was so empty. She had not taken many items to Buffalo; she could not imagine what had happened to her clothes. Then she caught sight of a tag from the drycleaners with the words, "ready for pickup on Dec. 16" written on it. She had never given the dry cleaning a thought. She would have to pick it up tomorrow. The bathroom hamper was filled with towels and a pair of her stockings. She had been planning to wash them when she came home that Monday night in December. The laundry was still waiting for her.

The beeping of the microwave interrupted Megan's thoughts. In the kitchen she mixed the deviled ham with a little mayonnaise and spread it on a few crackers. She put the ravioli on a plate, poured herself a Coke and walked into the living room to sit by the fire with her food. Although she had been ravenous on the plane, now that she had her dinner ready she was not very hungry. Seeing the spoiled food in the refrigerator, the drycleaner's ticket on her nightstand and the unwashed clothes in the hamper had reminded her that she had not been in her apartment since the day she was attacked.

Everything was exactly as she had left it that morning when she had rushed off to work; it was as if time had stopped in those rooms. That realization brought back the memory of her rape with a clarity that she would not have thought possible. She vividly recalled every detail of that day—of her drive to the office, of her day at work, of her conversation with Jack Forbes when he returned to the office after his client's verdict was returned, and of being attacked. She could not have had more perfect recall if she had been watching a film of the entire day.

A loud thud made Megan jump from her seat so quickly that she knocked her fork onto the floor. She listened for a moment and heard it again. She rushed into the bedroom and forced open the closet doors. She checked the bathroom, and she looked out her bedroom window. She ran back into the living room and opened the coat closet and the closet that housed the water heater. She opened the pantry and pushed back the louvered doors that hid her washer and dryer. Having exhausted all of her possibilities for finding the source of the sound, she stood for a moment and listened. She heard it again, and then again, and then the banging became more regular. Finally, she realized that it was coming from the apartment above hers. Someone was hammering something into the wall. With her hands still trembling, she took a clean fork from the kitchen and sat down again with her food, staring at her bolted door as she ate.

When Megan had finished her meal, she returned to the bedroom to finish unpacking. She started the laundry and made out a shopping list for the following week. Then she walked into the living room and turned on the television. She looked at the schedule but could not find anything that interested her. She watched an old movie for a few minutes but found that she could not concentrate. After a while she turned off the television and took a book from the shelves. She could not remember where she had been in the story, so she started at the beginning of a chapter. She began to read only to find herself staring unintelligibly at the words. She tried to force herself to read aloud, but her voice drifted off and she caught herself again staring at the pages. She put the book back on the shelf and paced up and down for a while. Finally, she gave up and got ready for bed.

Megan left the light on in her bedroom when she lay down to go to sleep. She did not feel at all tired, and she lay there for a long time before she finally drifted off. In her dreams she found herself back in the tunnel, running wildly to escape the man who was chasing her. She could not veer to the right or left; she could not turn to look behind her. No matter how hard she ran he was always close behind, and she could feel his breath against her neck as he panted and wheezed. "Please don't kill me," she sobbed, but he did not answer. Finally, she felt him reach out to grab her, and she knew that he was going to kill her.

Megan awakened screaming hysterically. Terrified, she realized that she was alone; her parents were not just a few doors away as they had been in Buffalo. She sat up in bed, shaking and crying. Suddenly she sensed that *he* was in the room with her, lurking in the dark hall close to her bedroom. Springing out of bed, she ran to turn on the light in the hall, and then she went through the apartment, turning on the lights in every room. In the living room she checked to make certain that the door was still bolted and the security system was still activated. She did not want to return to her bedroom, and she was afraid to go back to sleep. With all the lights on, she sat down in the living room and turned on the television. She did not even attempt to pay attention to the program; she just sat staring at the screen.

Megan thought of her dream and of her actual attack. She had not seen her rapist, and she never saw the man who was chasing her in her nightmare, but she knew that she could easily pick him out of a crowd. She knew just how he looked. His skin was swarthy and leathery, and his eyes were hooded slits. His hair was black and greasy. His round thick head sat atop a short, fat neck connected to a short, fat body. She could visualize the way he would dress and walk and talk. He thought that he had been very clever, refusing to come into the light where she could see him, but one day she would get even with him. One day he would be walking on the street, and she would recognize him and kill him. He would feel perfectly safe because he would believe that there was no way she could identify him, and she would, therefore, have the element of surprise in her favor. He would not suspect anything until it was too late.

These fantasies haunted Megan for the remainder of the night. She stared at the television and plotted her revenge until the sun came up. Megan was exhausted, but she was grateful for the daylight. She rose stiffly from the sofa, turned off all the lights and went into the kitchen to make coffee. She had already decided on the suit she would wear on her first day back. Very soon she had applied her makeup, styled her hair and dressed. She looked at herself in the mirror but was not pleased with the result. Her head ached, and she thought that she looked terrible. Picking up her briefcase, Megan locked her apartment and walked downstairs to the garage. Mechanically, she drove to the lot where she parked when she was at work and walked the block to the law offices.

The faces on the crowded sidewalk reminded Megan that she would recognize her attacker if she saw him. Maybe he was here, one of the many people passing by. Perhaps he worked near Pratt, Forbes and Magoff and she had passed him every morning on her commute. Silently, she searched the crowd, scrutinizing every man who passed. A short overweight man lumbered past on his way to a construction site. Megan studied him critically. No, his eyes were too round, his hair too pale. He noticed her watching him, and when he passed her, he smiled. Her eyes left him and traveled back through the crowd, searching for the distinct individual who would fit her description.

The hunt ended when she reached her building. The sunlight reflected from the concrete of the familiar steps, and an almost cheerful atmosphere enveloped the old building, as if to hide the dark secret of what had taken place there only two months before. Resolutely Megan climbed the steps and pushed open the glass doors leading to the hall. Though she had worked in these offices for several years, when she entered, she was a little startled by the building's appearance. Artificial and natural light flooded the reception area and the hall which her imagination had painted dark and foreboding. The offices hummed with activity as the sounds of printers, copiers and telephones greeted her. There in the bright light with all the noise and motion, it was difficult to believe that the events of that night had ever taken place.

"Megan, welcome back," Jack had just stepped through the doorway of one of the offices.

"Thank you," Megan smiled. "It's certainly good to be here."

"Well, it's good to have you here," Jack continued smiling as the hall filled with Megan's colleagues gathering to welcome her back. She exchanged greetings with each of her co-workers, expressing her thanks for each chorus of, "It's nice to have you back." To her great relief, no one mentioned the attack, and she tried to act as though nothing had happened.

Bob Pratt, a short slightly overweight man in his sixties with thinning gray hair and piercing blue eyes, patted Megan's arm with his chubby hand. "We're sure glad to see that you're okay, Meg."

"And even more glad to see you back at work," smiled Henry Magoff, a tall thin man in his mid-forties with a bony face and beakish nose. Megan had often thought that between Pratt and Magoff the employees pretty well got to hear the long and the short of things.

"Are you ready to get down to business?" Jack asked, rescuing her from the crowd of employees who surrounded her.

"Yes," Megan answered emphatically, and they walked into her office.

Work had been piling up for two months. The morning sped past as she sorted through paperwork and returned telephone calls. She hardly had time to look up from her desk, and the work kept her too busy to think about anything else.

At lunch time Megan went to the office lunch room. The firm often ordered carryout so that the employees would not have to leave the offices for lunch. Today the aroma of pizza wafted through the rooms, informing Megan that the food had arrived. She went to the lunch room and took her place in line in front of the coffeemaker. As she stepped up to pour herself a cup, she became aware that a man was standing behind her, standing so close that she could feel his breath against her shoulder. Her nightmare came rushing back to her, bringing with it the confused torrent of emotions that she had been struggling with for weeks. A strong impulse to scream nearly overtook her, but her mother's words came back to her: "You can't make excuses for your behavior forever. You have to get a grip on yourself." Jennifer was right; Megan's co-workers would not have any sympathy for her. She had to prove that she was all right. She finished pouring her coffee and turned around to see Howard Breck, a junior partner. Howard took a step backward, and Megan sat down at the table with her coffee.

"It's a pretty stiff sentence, if you ask me," Anne Sutherland commented to Jack between bites of pizza. Megan took a piece for herself and tried to follow the conversation.

"Well, I think he deserved it," Howard interjected as he sat down at their table. "Anybody who buys a gun and sets out to enforce the law on his own ought to be locked up. It's lunatics like him that the legal system is supposed to protect us from."

"Who are we talking about?" Megan interrupted.

"Sam Dyer—the fellow who killed the burglar who was breaking into his house," Jack replied, and Megan nodded as she tried to recall the details of the case.

"Yes, I remember that you told me that the jury found him guilty," she said.

"Well," Jack continued, "on Friday the judge sentenced him. Fifteen years with no possibility of parole."

"Fifteen years!" Megan was incredulous. "That's a long time."

"The man's a murderer," Howard reminded her.

"He's not a murderer. He killed a man in self-defense. That's not the same thing at all!" Megan was shocked by their insensitivity.

"He had an illegal gun in his home, and he used it to kill a man," Jack looked at Megan carefully, surprised by her outburst. "The law doesn't permit that sort of behavior. Frankly, I think the court had an obligation to give him the maximum. If they'd been easy on him, it would have looked as though they were endorsing what he did. There can't be any excuse for the taking of a human life."

"What if the burglar had killed Dyer?" Megan asked. "Then he'd be on his way to prison and Dyer would be under the church yard. The police would close the case, there would be one more statistic on the books, and everyone would be happy. Instead, the burglar is the victim and Dyer's the criminal for protecting himself, his family and his property."

Everyone looked embarrassed, and for a few moments all were silent. Then Anne added quietly, "He was only a kid."

Megan did not respond. It was easy for them to sanctimoniously condemn Dyer for his actions, just as it had been easy for the judge and jury to condemn him. They had never been attacked or threatened; they had never been at the mercy of a heartless demon who took pleasure in torturing them. They had never known what it was to be truly afraid, but she had experienced all of these things, and she knew how Dyer had felt when he pulled the trigger. No court should have the power to punish a man or woman for killing someone who threatens them.

Soon the conversation picked up again on a different subject, but Megan stayed out of it—she was left out of it. People talked around her but not to her. When she had finished eating, she excused herself and returned to her office. The embarrassment that she had sensed at the table was not just the result of her position on the Dyer case; she had felt it all morning. Everyone had been friendly, yet they seemed uncomfortable with her. She began to ask herself why no one had mentioned the attack. She had elicited a promise from Jack that he would not tell anyone that she had been raped. She wondered whether the word had spread anyway—there was enormous office gossip, and if anyone had discovered the truth, they would have told the others in a matter of hours. The thought bothered her so much that she had to force it from her mind. Still, all of her co-workers were behaving strangely. Even Jack seemed ill at ease. When she had begun to defend Dyer, they had pulled back from the subject almost as though she were the one charged with a crime. They appeared to be embarrassed for her, ashamed of some horrible event in which she had played a part.

Megan had an impulse to stand on the top step of the staircase and shout, "I haven't done anything wrong." She had not committed any shameful act; she was a victim, just as Dyer had been a victim. Yet, she suspected that they had no more compassion for her situation than they did for his.

Megan returned to work, but as the afternoon wore on, her thoughts began to turn to her apartment and another terror-filled evening. She wished that she had a friend with whom she could spend the evening. She tried to think of someone; no names came to mind. She had to do something; if she locked herself up in that apartment again tonight, she was bound to go mad.

Suddenly, she remembered Jeff. They had not seen each other since before she had been attacked, although she had talked to him on the telephone a few times while she was in Buffalo. She took her cell phone out of her purse and called Jeff's cell phone.

"Hi, Jeff," Megan tried to sound cheerful. "How's everything?"

"Great! The market's up. How's everything with you?"

"Everything's fine. I got back in town yesterday. Today's my first day back at the office."

"Good," Jeff sounded pleased. "You're not having any problems then?"

"No, but there's lots of work to catch up on. Sorting through this stack of paper promises to be quite a feat," she laughed. "Listen, I was wondering whether you'd like to come over and have dinner with me at my apartment this evening."

"I'd love to," he responded. "What time would you like for me to be there?"

"Well," she thought aloud, "I'll leave here at six-thirty. I have to pick up some groceries on the way home. Be there about eight-thirty. I'll cook Chinese."

"That sounds good. I'll see you then."

Megan hung up her phone feeling much better.

At six-thirty Megan had her desk straightened and her briefcase in hand. She had promised herself that she would never again work alone after hours at the office. If she had any late-night work to do, she would take it home. However, there were no specific items that demanded her attention before morning, and she planned to spend a pleasant evening with Jeff. Turning out the light in her office, she walked down the hall to let Jack know that she was leaving for the day.

"Wait just a minute," Jack called through the door. "I'm on the phone, but I'll be right with you."

Megan stood obediently in the hall wondering why Jack wanted her to wait. It was dark outside, but the light was on in the hall. She caught sight of the light switch, and her mind returned to the last evening she had spent there. She forced the thoughts from her mind. Those memories were not going to dominate the rest of her life.

Jack appeared at the door, "Let me get my coat, and I'll walk you to your car."

"Thank you," Megan said appreciatively, for she had been nervous about walking to the parking lot alone. When he had his coat on, Jack held the front door for her and locked it behind him.

"Are you through for the evening?" Megan asked.

"No, I'll probably be there for another hour or so."

"Be careful," Megan warned.

"Oh, I will," Jack replied as if, under the circumstances, he had nothing to fear.

Megan remained quiet. A rapist was no threat to him; that was what he was thinking. They walked in silence to her car, and he stayed at her side while she unlocked the door and got in. He watched her pull out of the lot before he returned to the office.

Driving to the supermarket, Megan found herself once again searching the faces of the people on the sidewalk and of her fellow motorists. Once or twice she thought she saw him, but the man in question always turned out to be too tall or too short, too heavy or too thin. In the supermarket her eyes hunted the aisles for him, and she scrutinized the store employees. When she returned to her apartment building, the caretaker was sweeping the snow from the steps. She had never really looked at him. Now, he, too, was a suspect in her ongoing investigation. No, she studied him carefully, he was not the man. Balancing her bags of groceries in her arms, she started up the stairs of the refurbished brownstone that had been her home for several years.

She could hear a man's steps following quickly on the stairs behind her. The sound startled her; no noise was more disturbing than that of a man's step behind her.

"Excuse me," a young voice said. Megan moved to the side as the young man who lived in the apartment above hers ran past her up the stairs. Megan reached the landing and set down a bag of groceries in front of her door while she fumbled in her purse for the key. In a few moments the door was open, and the groceries were sitting on the kitchen table.

In half an hour her long hair had been brushed to fall in a mass of flaxen curls against her shoulders. Dressed in gray wool slacks and a gray wool sweater, Megan felt comfortable with her appearance for the first time since her attack. Going into the kitchen, she clicked on the television while she began preparing dinner.

The jingle of a tire commercial blared as she sliced celery and onions. Megan was half listening as she put the thin strips of beef into a wok to stir fry. Above the sound of the knife cutting the vegetables and the hissing of the beef in the wok, she heard a news report. "Following the sentencing of Sam Dyer on Friday, the District Attorney is taking a stronger stand against vigilantes. In a press conference this afternoon, District Attorney Jim Masters reaffirmed that law enforcement officials will not tolerate citizens taking the law into their own hands."

Megan rushed into the living room to see the D. A. at his press conference. "No person in this city is going to carry or own a gun without a license," he announced in his nasal tone. "We are going to enforce the law; anyone caught with an illegal firearm will be prosecuted to the fullest extent of the law. We are not going to be terrorized by vigilantes. Sam Dyer is the first of a number of people who are going to be prosecuted for murder because they took the law into their own hands. If a person is a victim of crime, that person has an obligation to report the violator to the authorities and let them handle it. The police force is trained to take care of these situations. New Yorkers don't want individuals assuming that responsibility, and we are going to make certain that it does not happen. The only way that we can have a safe city is for all of us to obey the law."

"You're not going to be terrorized by anybody," Megan argued at the screen. "You're the District Attorney. No one bothers you. You don't care what happens to the rest of us."

The aroma of the beef strips sent her back to the kitchen. She gave them a quick stir and resumed cutting up vegetables, but her mind was still on the news report.

"Police!" she thought, "What a joke." All day she had heard that the police are supposed to take care of apprehending criminals. She had lain bleeding on the floor for what seemed like an eternity while she waited for the police to arrive. The woman who answered the 911 call told her that the police were on the way, but as the minutes dragged by, Megan wondered what could possibly be taking so long. There must have been a patrol car reasonably close to her offices, but it took them forty-five minutes to arrive. Even if she had known that someone was breaking into the offices, and she had called 911 the first moment that she had heard him at the door, he would still have had time to do everything to her that he had done and make his escape!

The situation was ridiculous. The police had no leads as to the identity of her attacker; they would probably never locate him. Yet, if she bought a gun to carry on her person, or even just to keep in her apartment, she could be arrested. Thoughts of purchasing a handgun had been with her since the day she had left the hospital. She had not discussed the subject with her parents because she knew their feelings about guns. She was surprised, herself, to find that she was tempted to buy one. She had never even touched a gun; the thought of owning one frightened her a little. In her calmer moments she wondered whether she was losing her own humanity. As long as she had remained in her parents' home in Buffalo she knew that she would never have actually purchased a gun; it went against everything that she believed. Since she had returned to New York, though, she had thought more and more about buying one. When she felt safe, she convinced herself that it was wrong on principle, but then overwhelming fear would wash over her, and once again she would feel desperate to have some means of protecting herself.

The food was nearly ready when she recognized Jeff's knock. She opened the door to see a tall, slim, young man with neatly combed dark brown hair and a broad smile accentuated by deep dimples. He handed her a bouquet of red and white roses and kissed her lightly.

"Jeff, these are beautiful," Megan smiled. "Come on inside; dinner's almost ready."

He stepped inside and closed the door behind him. Megan took his coat and hung it in the closet.

"It's great to have you back," Jeff told her. He put his arm around her and pulled her close to him. Normally that would have pleased her; tonight it made her uncomfortable, and she pulled away abruptly.

"I'll put these in some water," Megan said as she retreated into the kitchen.

Jeff was a little puzzled by her response, but he did not comment. "Did you have a good visit with your folks?" he called as he sat down on the sofa and put his feet up on the coffee table.

"It was nice. I hadn't seen them for a while. I got to see all of the relatives…" she paused, remembering the night of the party. "What about you? How did you spend the holidays?"

"I went skiing with a couple of the guys from my health club, but I flew down to Boston to spend Christmas Day with Mom."

"That sounds like fun," Megan wondered whether Jeff had always been so dull or if he were just having a bad evening.

Megan was setting the food on the table as the evening news ended and the reporters recapped the major stories. Once again she heard them summarizing the District Attorney's comments.

"Did you hear that story?" Jeff called to her. "The D. A. is really stepping up prosecutions of those people."

"I heard it," she answered stiffly.

"I think it's great," Jeff continued. "These vigilantes have to be stopped."

Megan did not answer. She should have known that he would agree with the D. A. Jeff thought that the government had all the answers.

"Dinner's ready," Megan's tone was unenthusiastic. She was already regretting having invited Jeff to spend the evening. For a moment she entertained the hope that his cell phone would ring and he would be called away on an emergency.

They sat down together at the table, and Jeff filled his plate with food. As they ate he talked of the market and the rise and fall of various stocks. Megan was so bored that she could hardly concentrate enough to respond. He chattered incessantly, totally oblivious to her problems. It was true that he did not know that she had been raped, but he did know that she had been brutally attacked. He should have guessed that she had not yet fully recovered, but he did not seem to care. Every once in a while he fell silent and looked at her oddly. Then he immediately began rambling about another trivial subject.

Megan said very little; an occasional "yes," or "that's interesting," were her only responses as she struggled to control her growing irritation. She had always thought of Jeff as strong and intelligent. For the first time she realized how immature he actually was. For a man in his early thirties he was shallow and irresponsible. He lived in a city where people were raped, stabbed, murdered and kidnapped daily, but Jeff's only interest was in sitting at her table and gorging on Chinese food while he offered his opinions as if they were Gospel. His comment in support of the District Attorney had made her especially angry. It didn't matter whether the entire city agreed with him, the D. A. was wrong, and if Jeff were half the man she had believed him to be, he would have known that he was wrong.

In spite of her irritation, Megan waited politely for Jeff to finish eating. When the last grain of rice had reached his lips, she rose from the table and placed the dishes in the dishwasher while he sat at the table telling ridiculous jokes and laughing at his own wit.

Inviting Jeff into the living room, Megan sat down in the chair opposite him and looked at her watch. Exactly thirty minutes later she rose and announced that she had a splitting headache.

"I'm sorry," she tried to sound polite, but her annoyance was apparent. "Today was my first day back at the office, and I'm still recuperating. Would you mind cutting the evening short?"

Jeff's surprise was obvious. He had noticed that she had behaved oddly all evening, but he did not understand why she would ask him to go. "Fine," his tone was a little miffed. "I'll call you."

"Great," Megan smiled as she brought him his coat.

"Well, good night," he hesitated.

"Good night," she held the door open for him. Closing it gently behind him, Megan set all of the locks and activated the alarm. Then she returned to the sofa and put her feet up. Having Jeff gone was such a relief; she did not know how she would have endured an entire evening of his nonsense. After missing a night's sleep and working all day she was exhausted, and she felt that she could sleep for days. She closed her eyes and fell asleep on the sofa.

Half an hour later Megan awakened. She was startled and disoriented to find herself fully clothed on the sofa, and for a moment she did not know whether it was day or night. She looked at her watch. It was ten-thirty. She listened; total silence prevailed. The dishwasher had finished its cycle; even the kitchen appliances did not hum as usual. She rose to check her locks and the alarm. The silence reminded her that she was alone; she had no one to comfort or protect her. She quickly went through the apartment turning on all the lights. She returned to the living room, but she was not satisfied. No amount of light could ward off the fear that invaded her mind. The lamps cast dark shadows in every corner; even the furniture seemed unfriendly.

Why had she acted so stupidly toward Jeff? Why had she insisted that he leave early? She had invited him over expressly so that she would not have to be alone, but after he arrived she had practically thrown him out of her apartment. It was true that he had irritated her, but surely she could have tolerated that. She and Jeff had known each other for years and were good friends. Tonight was different, she told herself. Jeff had changed; he was not the man who had made her laugh uproariously on so many occasions; he was not the friend with whom she had spent so many happy times. He had become too self-involved; his only interest was in his own narrow world.

When had Jeff changed? Megan had seen him only a few days before her attack, and they had spent a wonderful evening together. She did not find him silly or shallow then. Was it Jeff who had changed so dramatically, or was it she? The thought of having her perspective altered so completely frightened her. She wished desperately that she had exercised more self-control and allowed him to stay. She thought about calling him, just to hear the sound of his voice so that she would not feel so alone, but she knew that she couldn't. She had seen the expression on his face when he left, and she knew that he was offended. It was her own fault that she was alone and terrified, and now she was going to have to find a way to get some sleep.

Megan did not even attempt to sleep in her bed. Instead, she put on her pajamas and brought her blanket and pillow into the living room. She lay down on the sofa and curled up under the blanket. She lay awake for a long time, but she forced herself to keep her eyes closed until, finally, she drifted off to sleep. Soon she found herself in the tunnel being pursued by her faceless attacker, and she was awakened by the sound of her own screams. Sobbing hysterically, Megan sat up on the sofa and put her head in her hands. As she cried and trembled something in her head spoke to her, and she slowly got control of her emotions. The solution to her problem lay within her reach, and her heart and mind supported the new resolve. As she contemplated her decision, she felt calmer than she had for weeks.

"No," Megan vowed. "I am not going to be afraid in my own home. I am going to be safe here, and I am going to feel safe here. No one will ever rape me again—no matter what I have to do." The rest of her thought she could not bring herself to say aloud, but for the first time she knew exactly what she was going to do.

The following day Megan told Jack that she had an appointment on her lunch break and that she would be back a little late. Shortly afterward she parked her car in front of Harry's Pawn Shop and walked quickly through the icy air into the small shabby building. She stood nervously by the door as the other customers were helped. An older woman stepped away from the counter; Megan started forward but then stepped back again. Her business would have to wait until the other customers had left. Behind her the bell on the door clanged as another customer entered. She allowed him to cut ahead of her, though she soon regretted having done so. The minutes dragged by as he argued with the owner of the shop over the price of a piece of silver. Megan looked at her watch; she would have to return to work soon. Why wouldn't he take the money and leave? At last they agreed on a price, and the customer left. The building was empty and Megan rushed to the counter.

"I'd like to buy a gun," she told the owner in a low voice. He studied her for a moment; then he walked into the back and returned carrying a small chrome-plated weapon with a pearl handle.

"What about this?" he asked.

"No," Megan shook her head. "I want a real gun."

"What kind of a real gun do you want?" the owner asked sarcastically. "What caliber?"

Megan stared at him blankly.

"What make?"

"I don't know," she finally answered. "What kind do you have?"

He began to reel off a list of names and calibers of various handguns. "...Colt .45, .357 Magnum."

"Yes," she stopped him at the only name she recognized. "A .357 Magnum."

"Oh," he grinned sardonically. "Well, you know that you have to have a license to carry a .357 Magnum, or any other gun for that matter. Do you have a license?"

"I...I didn't bring it with me," Megan swallowed nervously. "I was hoping that I could buy it anyway."

He looked at her for a minute. "It costs extra if you don't bring your license with you."

"That's fine."

"One thousand dollars, in cash."

Megan opened her purse and counted out the cash that she had gotten from her bank that morning. "Can you sell me some bullets, too?"

"Sure, if you've got another hundred bucks."

Megan gave him the money and picked up the gun and cartridges. "Show me how to load it."

The owner loaded the gun while she watched, and then she placed it in her purse. She walked quickly out of the pawn shop and drove straight back to work.

For the rest of the afternoon the gun's presence in her purse made her a little nervous. She was relieved to know that she would be armed as she walked from the parking lot to the office, but she worried that she would be discovered carrying an unauthorized weapon. Once or twice she thought of the owner of the pawn shop. What if he had called the police as soon as she had left. No, she reasoned, he would also be reporting himself. She worried that one of her co-workers might find it; they would report her. She could imagine the look on Anne's face if she were found with a firearm. It was important that no one should suspect that she had a gun.

In the evening when Jack walked her to her car, she put her right hand inside her purse and felt the butt of the pistol. It gave her a strange sense of power to know that in the palm of her hand she held a force capable of instantly killing a man. For the first time since her attack she did not feel so vulnerable; she was now a match for anyone who might try to harm her.

When she had reached her building and parked her car, Megan put her hand in her purse as she walked up the stairs to her apartment. Behind her she heard the click of a man's footsteps, and her grip automatically tightened around her gun. As she was about to unlock her door, she took her hand out of her purse for a moment, opened the door, and rushed inside. She placed the pistol on the counter while she cooked dinner and on the table beside her while she ate. When she went into the living room to watch television, her gun rested in her lap. She studied it carefully, experimenting with the safety and practicing holding it. The metal felt strangely heavy against her palm, and it seemed to resist her when she lifted it. Yet, she wanted to be familiar with it. That pistol would be her best friend, she determined, and her best kept secret. It would protect her, comfort her, and allow her to live in peace in her own home.

That night when she dressed for bed, the .357 Magnum found a place under Megan's pillow. She turned on all the lights, and after double checking the locks and the alarm, she went to sleep in her bed. Almost as soon as she closed her eyes, her nightmare began, and she soon woke screaming. Remembering that she now had her gun, Megan forced herself to settle back onto her pillow. Though her dream had badly frightened her, she was able to sleep for the first time since her return to New York City.

The following morning Jeff called her at work. Stacks of papers from the case she was working on covered her desk, and she was so engrossed in the project that when her line rang, she did not immediately recognize his voice.

"Hi," Jeff's tone was friendly, "I haven't heard from you, and I just wanted to know if everything is okay."

"Everything's fine," Megan replied stiffly. Although she had told herself that she had been unfair to Jeff on Monday evening, she now found the sound of his voice so irritating that she could hardly force herself to be civil.

"Great, how about having dinner with me tonight?" he asked.

"Not tonight. I'm very busy with a new case, and I'm sure that I'll have to take work home with me."

"Okay, what about tomorrow?"

"No, I'm going to work tomorrow, too."

"Over the weekend?"

"Jeff," she was now very irritated, "I'm busy. I don't have time to see you. I don't want to see you."

"Not ever?" was his startled, hurt reply.

"No, not ever," she snapped, and she hung up the phone.

She returned to her duties relieved to finally be rid of Jeff. At lunch her co-workers hardly spoke to her, or, perhaps, she hardly spoke to them—Megan wasn't really certain who had initiated the silence. She had to be careful when she talked to them now; she could not betray her secret, and she was afraid that she might say too much. When Jack told her that she was looking better, she thanked him, but she was careful not to say anything that might indicate that she felt safer.

Returning to her apartment that evening, Megan wondered whether she had not been too hasty with Jeff. They had been friends for a long time, and they had shared many pleasant experiences.

Surely things had not changed so much that they could no longer be friends. Then she reminded herself of their last evening together; she assured herself that she would be happier spending all of her evenings alone than with Jeff.

Still, Megan needed someone; she felt so isolated. Since her return to New York, she had not had anyone in whom she could confide. At times she longed to be back in Buffalo with her parents. There were so many things that she would tell them now. During her stay with them, she had been foolish to reject their offers to talk. She had naively believed that she did not need anyone's help—that she could work through this nightmare alone. Now she realized that she had been wrong. Occasionally she remembered her mother's insistence that she get counseling, and there were moments when the idea seemed like a good one. Yet, the thought of giving the details of her attack to a stranger was still abhorrent to her. Talking to an impersonal counselor in a clinical environment was not what she needed. She needed a friend.

When Megan reached her apartment, a newspaper idly tossed in front of her door caught her eye. Taking it inside with her, she unrolled it to read the usual headlines—collapsing bridges, faulty waterlines, the homeless and the criminals, all simultaneously tearing away at New York City. Megan wondered why "news" always had to be synonymous with disaster. She had sufficient problems in her own life without constantly being bombarded with everyone else's.

Leafing through the pages, she searched for something light—a human interest story, a book review, anything that might take her mind off herself. As she turned the pages, she caught sight of an ad in the Classifieds.

"Afraid in your own home?" the advertisement asked.

"Am I ever," she replied as she read on.

"Our dogs are trained to provide you with the comfort and security you deserve," the advertisers promised. "Call or come by Security Kennels." Megan tore out the ad and determined that she would visit the kennels on Saturday.

The ringing of her cell phone interrupted Megan's thoughts.

"Hello, Mother," Megan said as she answered the call.

"How's everything," Jennifer asked. "Are you getting along all right your first week back?"

"Everything's fine," Megan lied.

"Are you enjoying being back in your apartment and getting back to work? I know that you were anxious to go back by the time you left us."

"Oh, yes," Megan replied. "It's nice to be working again. I've been very busy. There's been so much to catch up on. I miss you and Dad, though. I wish I were still there in Buffalo."

Jennifer laughed, "I don't think so; otherwise, you'd have stayed longer. You have your own life, and Daddy and I understand that. Have you seen Jeff since you've been back?"

"Yes, he came over for dinner on Monday night."

"How nice. Did you two have a good time?"

"Yes, we had a very good time," Megan lied again.

"Jeff is such a nice boy," Jennifer said. "I feel better knowing that you have someone there whom you can count on. I would hate to think of you being all alone."

"Well, yes," Megan was embarrassed by the lies that she was telling.

"Your father is here. He wants to talk to you, too, so I'll let him have the phone. I love you, sweetheart."

"I love you too, Mother," Megan waited on the line until she heard her father's voice.

"Hello, honey," Ian spoke to her just as he had when she was a child.

"Hello, Dad," she responded warmly. "How are you doing?"

"I'm busy," he laughed. "What about you?"

"I'm busy, too, but it's not bad."

"Have you been a little nervous your first week on your own?"

"No," she responded. "The first night I was a little uneasy, but since then I've been all right."

"That's good. Is everything all right at work? Is everyone treating you okay?"

"Oh, yes. Of course, they know only that someone broke in and I was assaulted; they don't know the rest," her voice trailed off and then picked up again. "But everyone's been very friendly and supportive."

"So, you're not having any problems?"

"No, I'm not having any problems at all."

"Well, that good. I have to go, but we wanted to call and make sure that you're okay. Keep in touch and let us know what's happening. I love you."

"I love you too. Talk to you soon." After she ended the call Megan stared at her phone for a moment, surprised and disgusted with herself.

There were so many things that she had wanted to tell them—needed to tell them—but when the time came, she had lied about nearly everything they had asked her. Why hadn't she been honest with them? It was true that she could not have told them about her gun, but she could have been honest about Jeff. She could have told them about her dreams, her fear, her insomnia. She could have spent hours telling them how lonely and estranged she felt. The most disturbing part was that she wanted to be honest with them. They had called because they loved her and were concerned about her. Megan wanted to reach out and respond, but she couldn't. Something stopped her and caused her to tell neat little lies instead. Was it fear of worrying them or fear of their criticism? She did not know, but she felt that if she could not trust her parents with the truth, she would never be able to trust anyone. She sat down on the sofa and put her head in her hands wondering whether her life would ever return to normal.

FIVE

On Saturday Megan visited Security Kennels. Ed, the tall, gangly owner, escorted her through the facility extolling the virtues of a guard dog.

"An attack-trained dog is the greatest single force for your protection these days," he told her. "Guns get stolen, locks can be tampered with, alarm systems can be disconnected, but a dog is impossible to fool. He's always on the lookout; whether it's the middle of the day or the middle of the night, he'll always be alert. A good dog will give his life to protect his master."

Ed showed her a demonstration film of a dog attacking a criminal about to mug his master. The film depicted an enormous German Shepherd ripping into the arm of the attacker while his master watched.

"That's a first-rate dog," Ed announced with pride. "He could rip the throat right out of an attacker."

"If he's so dangerous, how do I know that I'll be safe with him?" Megan asked.

"Oh, your dog will bond to you," Ed replied. "We require that you go through training sessions so that you and your dog get to know each other. By the time you leave here with him, you'll be the best of friends."

"Will a dog be hard for me to take care of? I work long hours."

"Take him out once before you go to work and after you get home at night. Our dogs are completely housebroken, of course. A little walk every day is good for him so that he can exercise. Other than that, he doesn't require much. The most important thing is to keep him close to you whenever you're at home; that way he'll become very attached to you. Do you live in a house?"

"An apartment," Megan replied, "but I've already talked to the homeowners' association, and they say it's okay for me to get a dog."

"Good. Don't ever let anybody else pet or play with your dog. If someone else gets to know him, he may not sense danger right away. The more you keep him to yourself, the likelier he will be to respond quickly to an emergency."

Ed took Megan out to the kennels and showed her a large black and tan German Shepherd with yellow eyes. She studied him carefully, and, to her surprise, realized that he was studying her as well.

"This dog," Ed told her, "is one of our very best. He's eighteen months old, and he's expertly trained. Notice the muscles in his body and the strength of that jaw. He's strong and quick—an attacker wouldn't stand a chance against him. That's another advantage. Not many people are going to come in on a dog as big as this one."

"Yes," Megan remarked, "he looks very formidable." Megan admired the dog's size and strength, but his personality fascinated her. When Ed spoke, the dog watched him intently, and when she spoke, he turned his attention to her. Though she knew it was impossible, she could have sworn that he changed expressions; he seemed to understand every word they were saying.

Megan had never liked dogs, but there was something about this one that immediately captured her interest. He appeared to have great dignity; she could not imagine him running to catch a stick or performing silly tricks. He definitely was an animal who would prefer life indoors; she could easily see that he would be content in her kitchen and living room. He was more than just a dog; he was an animal who could also be a companion and a comforter.

"What's his name?" Megan asked.

"Kaiser."

"I don't like it," she responded. "I think I'll call him Holmes after the great detective."

"It's not a good idea to change a dog's name," Ed told her. "It will be very confusing to him. If this is the dog you want, we'll sign the paperwork and set up a time for your first class together."

"Yes," Megan answered, "I'll be right with you." She stood staring at the dog for a moment. Cautiously she extended her hand and touched the tip of his muzzle. "I still think Holmes is the best name for you; with any luck you'll be catching criminals too. What do you think?" Somehow, Megan felt certain that he agreed.

Megan and Holmes began their first training session together the following day, and they continued every day afterward for the next two weeks. She looked forward to those evening sessions after work, partially because she did not have to go home until later, and partially because she enjoyed the companionship. She was always happy to see Holmes, and she felt that he was glad to see her. She was impatient for the day when she would be able to take him home with her, and she would no longer return to an empty apartment every evening.

At last that day arrived, and Megan put Holmes in the backseat of her car. "Good luck, Ma'am," Ed called as Megan got into the car and pulled out of the kennel parking lot. Holmes sat up in the backseat and stared intently at everything around him. Megan wondered whether he was curious about where he was going. Holmes had spent nearly all of his life at the kennels; she wondered whether he understood that he was now starting a new life.

"That is where I work," Megan pointed to the law offices as they drove past, and Holmes turned his head in that direction. "That's the supermarket where I shop," she pointed out the location as they passed it. Through the rear view mirror she could see that Holmes appeared to be very interested in everything. She continued to talk to him and to point out places of interest. Then she suddenly felt self-conscious. Had she gone insane to be talking to her dog as if he were a person? She thought of their neighbor Minnie in Buffalo who talked to her houseplants. Everyone agreed that Minnie was eccentric at best, but she did have the largest peace lily in the neighborhood. Certainly, Megan reasoned, a dog is more aware of its surroundings than a plant. Besides, Holmes was no ordinary dog.

"We're home," Megan said as she parked her car in her parking space behind the building. She fastened the leash onto Holmes' collar and led him to the entrance of the building and then up the stairs. Behind her she could hear Mark Perkins, the young man from the apartment upstairs, running as usual. She could not count the number of times he had pushed past her or accidentally run into her during his perpetual marathon up and down the stairs. Now the footsteps slowed when he caught sight of Holmes, and he kept a considerable distance between Holmes and him.

"That's quite a dog you have there," Mark called from behind them. "Where did you get him?"

"I bought him," Megan turned around to face Mark. Since the night of her attack, she had made herself a promise that she would give out as little information about her life as possible. If Mark wanted additional information, he would have to ask direct questions.

"He's awfully big. Will he bite?"

"Under the right circumstances," Megan stroked the fur around Holmes' collar.

"I don't think we're supposed to have dogs in this building. I don't think the homeowners' association will allow this." Mark was intimidated and angered by the prospect of sharing the building with a large German Shepherd.

"I already spoke with Mr. Cukor," Megan replied calmly. "He called a special meeting of the HOA board, and they gave their permission before I bought my dog. There's nothing in the HOA covenants that prohibits dog ownership."

"There's a difference between owning a pet and owning a dangerous animal. I'm sure that Cukor didn't know that you were buying a police dog or the association would never have agreed to it."

"He's not dangerous," Megan countered. "He's trained, and that makes him safer for the other tenants than most pets. He'll attack if I'm in danger, but under ordinary circumstances he's not a threat to anyone."

"We'll see," Mark turned and headed back down the stairs.

Megan led Holmes to the door of her apartment. She let him inside and then set the locks and the alarm. After hanging up her coat, she knelt to take the lead off his collar. "That's just like Mark," she told Holmes. "He's going to try to make trouble because he doesn't want you here. I'm getting used to it, though; everyone tries to make trouble for me all the time."

Megan rose and walked into the kitchen, and Holmes followed. She washed her hands and went to the refrigerator. When she turned around, she was surprised to see Holmes sitting behind her. She saw in his eyes the same understanding, curious gaze that she had noticed when she first saw him at the kennels. Megan felt that she could talk to Holmes in a way that she could not talk to anyone else.

"There was a time," she began, "when I thought I had the world at my doorstep. People listened to me; they respected my ideas, they took my advice. I was up and coming, and everyone knew it. Just a short time ago people were assuring me that I was on the threshold of success, and I knew it too. I could almost taste everything that I had always wanted. It wasn't just the money; I wanted recognition and prestige. I had visions of being a young Gloria Allred and eventually of going into politics. It seems so long ago now, but really it has only been three months." Megan grew silent as she thought about the changes that had taken place in her life in such a short time.

"Then everything changed. You see, I was raped." It was the first time that Megan had been able to say that word aloud since the night of her attack. She pushed her hair back with both hands and turned to face her silent audience. "Since then my whole life has changed. At first, as horrified and humiliated as I was, part of me kept saying, 'You'll get over this.' I was in Buffalo with my parents for almost two months, and by the end of that time I thought that I was fine. I couldn't wait to come back here and get to work. Somehow I thought that the depression and sadness I still felt were the result of being up there with Mother and Dad constantly watching over me and reminding me of what had happened. So I came home, and I went back to work. I've been here for a month now, and since the first day, my life has been hell!

"I'm always afraid; twenty-four hours a day I live in terror. I'm afraid at work because I remember everything that happened to me in that building. When I come home, I'm even more afraid because I'm alone. Even in my sleep I don't get any relief. I have terrible nightmares that he's chasing me, trying to kill me. I run but I can't get away, and just as I feel his hands on my shoulders, I wake up screaming. As soon as I close my eyes that dream starts, and it repeats itself several times each night. No matter how tired I am, I can't ever rest. I feel like I'm serving some sort of sentence.

"The first week when I was back here in New York, I looked constantly for the man who had attacked me. Whenever I was on the street, I searched for him. I still do, and there are times when I hope that I will find him so that I can kill him. But there are other times when I feel that he is right next to me and I panic. I may be in a crowd, or a line in the supermarket when suddenly I know that if I turn around I will see him standing close by. Sometimes I hear a man's step behind me, and I'm sure that it is he, or the phone rings at work, and I wonder if he's on the line. I know that someday I will see him again, and I have to be ready for him."

Megan put a frozen dinner in the microwave and sat down at the table to wait for it to heat. Holmes sat motionless as she continued. "When I was in Buffalo, my mother wanted me to go into counseling, but I wouldn't. I was too angry and embarrassed to tell anyone that I had been raped. I still don't think that I could confide in a stranger, but there are so many times lately when I need someone to talk to. Everyone acts oddly around me now. At work the other attorneys avoid me, and if I try to talk to them, they act like they are afraid of what I might say. Everyone shuts me out. People who used to be my friends are embarrassed to talk to me.

"Jeff is the same way. When I was in Buffalo and we talked on the phone, he talked as fast and as long as he could to keep me from getting a word in edgewise. When I cooked dinner for him here at the apartment, he acted the same way. The subject didn't seem to make any difference as long as he kept talking. I don't know what he was so afraid of; I certainly wasn't going to tell him any deep, dark secrets. But his attitude hurt, and it was infuriating. No one else could be hurt by hearing about what I've gone through. I'm the one who's suffered, and now I'm the one who's living her life under a microscope. That's the way these things always work—I'm the victim so I'm the one who has to constantly defend her position. I've put on a very good act at work; no one even suspects what I'm feeling or thinking, and I'm sure that Jack's convinced that I'm almost back to normal.

"The thing that really makes me mad is that even though I have suffered so much, I'm sure that the man who raped me is fine. No one's looking over his shoulder to make sure that he can handle his job. His parents don't worry about whether he should be living alone in New York. His life hasn't changed at all.

"I could talk to my parents, I suppose, except that I've already told them one lie after another. In order to confide in them now, I would have to confess to all the lies. How would it make them feel to know that I didn't even trust them enough to be honest with them? They still don't know that I broke up with Jeff. Every week I tell myself that when they call, I'm going to tell them the whole story, no matter how long it takes or how hard it is for me to do it. Then, when the time comes, I can't. I catch myself lying to them instead. I don't even know why."

The microwave beeped, and Megan took her dinner out and set it on the table. She took a large bag of dry dog food from the pantry and poured some into a dish for Holmes and gave him some water in a separate dish. She placed his food on the floor near the table and sat down to her own dinner. Holmes looked displeased. Sitting up on his haunches, he placed his front paws on the table. Megan laughed.

"Oh no," she said. "You can't eat at the table. Get back down on the floor." Holmes sighed disgustedly and got down to eat his food.

The doorbell rang and Megan rose to answer it. She looked through the peephole to see Elliot Cukor standing outside. Turning off the alarm, she opened the door to admit the president of the homeowners' association.

"Hello, Mr. Cukor," Megan smiled. She already knew the reason for his visit.

"Good evening, Megan," he responded. "I'd like to talk to you about your dog."

"Please sit down," Megan motioned toward the sofa, but Mr. Cukor shook his head.

"No thank you; this won't take long. This evening I received a complaint from one of our homeowners who said that you had brought a vicious animal into the building. When the homeowners' association agreed to allow you to keep a dog in your apartment, we did so on the condition that you keep him confined so that he would not be a nuisance to the other tenants and that you pay for any damage he might do to the common areas. We respect your need for protection, but we also have an obligation to the other people in this building."

"I remember our agreement clearly, and I assure you that I will comply with it in full. Holmes is not a threat to the other tenants, and he did not exhibit any aggressive behavior toward Mark Perkins. "

"Megan, Mark said that you told him that the dog was dangerous when he met you on the stairs this evening."

"I did not say that Holmes was dangerous," Megan countered. "Mark asked if Holmes would bite, and I replied that he would if it were necessary to protect me. As I told you when I first approached you about buying him, Holmes is completely trained. He is not a threat to anyone who does not threaten him first."

Mr. Cukor turned to look at Holmes, who had followed Megan into the room when she answered the door and was now sitting next to her. "He certainly is big," Cukor commented. "He could do a great deal of damage. Does he obey you?"

"Perfectly," Megan answered, "I have a certificate from the kennel showing that Holmes and I completed a training course together before I brought him home."

Mr. Cukor looked at Holmes and then at Megan. "Very well," he finally said, "all is in keeping with our agreement. Keep him close to you at all times, and he may stay as long as you wish."

"Thank you," Megan smiled, holding the door for Mr. Cukor as he left. She could tell that he had been a little intimidated by Holmes, and this gave her a further sense of security. Both of the men who had seen Holmes had been cautious of him—she was certain that neither of them would try to come too close to her with Holmes at her side. Perhaps, everyone would have the same reaction. Megan felt that as long as Holmes was near her, she would be safe.

When the dinner dishes were cleared away Megan sat down in the living room to watch television, and Holmes curled up at her feet. When she got up to turn on all the lights in the apartment, Holmes followed.

When she was ready for bed, she placed her gun under her pillow, and Holmes lay down on the floor next to her bed. Megan soon fell asleep, and, as usual, shortly after she dozed off, her nightmare began and she awakened screaming hysterically. To her amazement, by the time that she was fully awake the room was a den of noise as Holmes matched her screams with piercing howls of his own. Jumping up on the bed, he licked her face until she was finally forced to laugh through her tears.

"Stop! You'll wake up everybody in the building." Megan pushed Holmes off her bed, but he immediately jumped up and looked at her with a puzzled expression. "I'll tell you what," Megan promised. "I'll stop crying if you'll get down and go back to sleep." Holmes seemed to understand and returned to the floor.

Throughout the night her nightmare repeated itself, but every time Holmes did his best to comfort her, and because she feared that he would disturb the other tenants, she made an effort to avoid screaming.

She rose early the next morning and took Holmes for a short walk before work. She realized that she had not gone for a walk in the early morning for years, and she enjoyed the relative quiet. She also noticed the attention that Holmes received and the way that people made an effort to keep a safe distance from them.

They cut their walk short so that Megan could have breakfast and get ready for work. When she put her gun in her purse and prepared to leave, Holmes followed her to the door.

"No," she said, "I know you want to go with me, but you can't. I'll see you this evening when I come home from work." Holmes sighed, and walking away from the door, sat with his face against the living room wall. Megan laughed at this display of temper and left for work.

During the next few weeks, Megan found that Holmes' presence had changed her life. He was her constant companion, and when she was at work she missed him more than she would have imagined possible. He made her feel free to go out again. Holmes required short walks daily, and she was, thus, forced to stop hiding in her apartment. His companionship took away the feeling of total estrangement that had plagued her for months. As she became less afraid, she found herself turning out some of the lights in her apartment before going to bed. Holmes afforded her excellent protection, but just the knowledge that a living, friendly being was in her apartment with her drove away many of her fears. Her nightmares began to subside because even as she slept, she was aware that Holmes was near.

When they spoke on the phone, her mother mentioned that Megan seemed calmer than she had been for a long time. "You sound so much more relaxed," Jennifer commented. "All of the tension has disappeared from your voice. You seem to be almost back to your old self."

"I'm feeling much better," Megan responded. "Having Holmes here has helped. I've started running again now that I can take him with me, and the exercise has been good for me."

"Be very careful," Jennifer cautioned. "New York is a dangerous city. Regardless of what kind of dog you have, you shouldn't take chances."

"I'm always careful now," Megan admitted. "I'm always looking over my shoulder. But for a while caution was turning into paranoia, and I was so paralyzed with fear that I couldn't even breathe. I was smothering myself because I was trying so hard to shut myself off from anything or anyone who might possibly hurt me. Holmes has changed that. I'm still aware of danger, but I now have a companion who is stronger than almost anyone who might threaten me. Last Saturday Holmes and I drove to the harbor and spent a little time on the waterfront. It was cold, and I was bundled up in my coat, but we enjoyed just being outdoors. You can't imagine what a sense of freedom he has given me. Between my dog and my," she started to say "my gun," and then remembered that her mother was not supposed to know about the gun, so she changed the last word, "me— between my dog and me I feel that I have life under control again."

"I'm glad that you're doing so well," Jennifer said, "but I can hardly believe that something so simple as buying a dog has been a cure-all for your trauma."

"It hasn't," Megan had made a concentrated effort to become franker and more open with her parents, and she was determined to answer her mother's questions with as much candor as possible. "I still have times when I think about what happened and an inexpressible sadness comes over me. I start crying without even knowing why. At other times I still become violently angry. Someone will say something or I will see something that triggers my emotions. I have finally come to the conclusion that there is no quick fix that straightens out your life after something like this happens, but I think that I will be okay, and that's what I concentrate on."

Jennifer remained skeptical, but even she had to admit that her daughter was improving, and Ian and she did their best to be supportive and encouraging.

On Saturday Megan and Holmes went to pick up her dry-cleaning. Parking her car in front of the shop, she left Holmes in the backseat with the window rolled down while she went inside. As she left the drycleaners with a bag of clothes draped over her arm, Megan felt a hand come up and grab hold of her purse. She turned and saw a boy of about sixteen tugging at her purse, but the shoulder strap did not allow him to snatch it from her grasp. Megan screamed, and the boy pulled out a knife to cut the strap.

From the corner of her eye, Megan saw Holmes leap through the open window, and in a couple of bounds he reached her and her attacker. The terrified mugger dropped his knife at the sight of the animal and began running, but Holmes knocked him to the ground and held him until the police arrived.

Megan was extremely proud of Holmes, and she felt much safer just knowing that he had actually saved her from an attack. Yet, her own behavior disturbed her as she recalled the incident. She had a gun in her purse, yet she had not reached for it. Since Holmes was there to protect her, it would have been both unnecessary and unwise to threaten the mugger with a gun. However, she had not known for certain that Holmes would jump through the car window to protect her. The moment that the mugger had grabbed hold of her arm she had forgotten about Holmes, about her gun, and about her resolution to never again become a screaming, struggling victim. Because of Holmes' presence she had not suffered any harm, but what if Holmes had not been there to protect her?

That night at her apartment Megan put her gun out where she could see it, and she began to practice holding it and working with it again. She had not depended on it for protection since Holmes had come to live with her. Now, though she knew that Holmes would take care of her whenever he could, she realized that she must be prepared at all times.

One night after work as she was walking to her car Megan had the feeling that the man who had raped her was close by. She had not sensed his presence for several weeks—now she felt that he was watching and following her. She turned around, but she could not see him. The streets were filled with people, but none of them fit his description. She could sense his presence so strongly, though, that she was certain that he must be only a few feet away. She glanced about her again, hoping for a glimpse of him. Jack asked her if she were looking for someone, but she shook her head and said that she thought she had seen an old acquaintance. Though Jack was near her, she felt threatened, and she began to walk rapidly. Jack saw her safely to her car, and she drove home as quickly as possible. Still, she felt that she was never out of his sight. She reached her building, and still she could feel him close by. She walked up the stairs, and his gaze seemed to accompany her. Only when she had finally shut herself up in her apartment did she feel that he was no longer with her.

Hatred gripped her. She knew that *he* had been nearby; she wished that he would come out in the open to face her. She would give Holmes an attack command and watch him rip the rapist apart, but he would not have the courage to face her with her dog at her side and her gun in her purse. He would try to sneak up behind her at night so that she would not have a chance to defend herself. One day he would come out of the shadows; one day she would see him face to face.

"And when that day comes," Megan said aloud to Holmes, "I will make him very sorry that he ever laid eyes on me."

SIX

In March Megan no longer had time for much outdoor activity with Holmes. She rushed to take him for a short walk each evening and then returned to her apartment. She ate a hasty dinner and denied herself any television. All of her energies were now consumed by the case she was preparing. It had been a long time since she had encountered a truly fascinating case, and the Dobson case had captured her interest.

Janet Dobson, a diagnosed schizophrenic, was accused of murdering four pre-schoolers who attended the kindergarten where she worked. The prosecuting attorney had an enormous amount of evidence against Janet, including the fact that each of the four children had disappeared after being taken to her house. Megan had in her favor the fact that Janet had never exhibited any violent behavior, and her psychiatrist would testify that she was not capable of committing the crimes.

It would be a difficult case, but that was what made it so fascinating. Secretly, Megan was certain that Janet was guilty, but she strongly believed that the guilty are just as entitled to a fair trial as the innocent. Megan never allowed the guilt or innocence of any client to cloud her judgment as legal defense.

As she became immersed in the case, Megan felt herself reawakening both personally and professionally. She and her colleagues discussed the case as she prepared the defense, and she felt that the ostracism that she had sensed for a while was gone. She was finally "back," and everyone was ready to forget about her attack.

Megan enjoyed every aspect of preparing the case, from the most mundane research to her long talks with her client. Mental illness had always intrigued her, and the research that she was doing gave her a new appreciation for the problems of the schizophrenic as well as for Janet's problems in particular. One thing became increasingly clear to her as she worked on the case—Janet was definitely guilty. Janet's guilt was obvious to anyone who heard her side of the story, and Megan knew that if she appeared on the witness stand, she would be transparent to a jury.

The only plausible defense was that Janet plead not guilty by reason of insanity. Megan could prove that Janet was insane, but the evidence was too overwhelming to convince a jury that she had not committed the murders. If Megan were successful, Janet would be committed to a mental institution without drawing a prison term. The strategy was a good one; the only difficulty would be in persuading Janet and her psychiatrist, Dr. Jameson, to agree to it. After a number of meetings Megan was still trying to convince them that the insanity plea was a good idea, and she spent an entire Wednesday afternoon with them discussing the matter.

"I don't think that Janet should use an insanity plea," Dr. Jameson protested. "I can testify that she is not capable of committing a violent act. Since I am her psychiatrist, my testimony will be credible. The police don't really have any evidence linking Janet to these murders."

"That's not true, Doctor," Megan countered. "As I have told you before, the prosecuting attorney has the gun that was used to kill the children; it is the same caliber as the one Janet was known to possess. If nothing else, she could go to prison for owning an illegal weapon."

"Janet's ex-husband was a policeman," the doctor interrupted.

"Janet's ex-husband could legally own and carry a weapon, but Janet couldn't. She can still be arrested for illegal possession. In addition, the police have statements from other children from the pre-school who say that Janet invited Billy, Henry, Rachel and Sally to go home with her and that she put them into her car in full view of the other children. Three hours later all four children were found shot to death near the harbor. The court is going to conclude that Janet put those children in her car, drove to the harbor, and killed them mercilessly."

"I didn't do it," a defiant Janet stuck to her original plea. "I took the children home and let them watch a DVD. Then I drove them back to the school. I don't know what happened to them after that."

"Frankly, Janet, I don't believe you," Megan told her candidly, "and neither will the jury. They are going to believe that you are a cold-blooded murderer of innocent little children. You've been in mental hospitals, and you're currently under the care of a psychiatrist.

You were seen with the children just hours before their bodies were discovered. Their parents will testify that you did not bring them home, and the other employees of the pre-school will testify that you never returned them to the school. After you took them from the school that morning, no one ever saw the children alive again.

"The jury is not going to accept your testimony over the testimony of a dozen respected individuals. One of the children's fathers is a doctor and another is an attorney. They are educated professionals, and they will make a good impression when they take the witness stand. Before the jury even goes out to deliberate they will have made up their minds, and when they come back, they will bring in a guilty verdict."

Megan sipped her coffee and stared at the little woman in front of her. Janet's mousy brown hair was pulled back and covered by a headscarf, but strands escaped to hang limply around her face. Her small round eyes, which did not bear even a trace of makeup, darted nervously around the room. Her face was pale and round with small pinched features. She wore a tattered dress covered with a red shawl and black oxfords with white cotton anklets. The nervous movement of her hands and tapping of her feet never ceased. Megan might be able to make the jury feel sorry for Janet, but only if she did not take the stand. She certainly would have no problem convincing them that Janet was insane.

Megan took another sip of her coffee and continued. "If you follow my advice and plead not guilty by reason of insanity, we will be disarming the prosecution from the very start. Instead of claiming that you did not commit the crime, we are simply saying that you are not responsible for your actions, and the prosecuting attorney will have a very difficult time disproving that. You will be sent to a mental hospital rather than to prison, and you will probably be out in a few years. If you are sentenced to prison, you could be there for the rest of your life."

"You're only doing this to protect yourself," Dr. Jameson turned to Megan. "If you persuade Janet to plead guilty, you don't have that much work to do. You can go in, present your case, and walk out a winner. If you don't want to give Janet a proper defense, maybe we should find someone who does."

"For your information," Megan retorted angrily, "I've already put a great deal of effort into this case, and I'll be putting a great deal more time in before I'm through. I have just as much work to do regardless of how Janet pleads. Your only problem is that you're afraid of losing part of your paycheck when they send her to a mental hospital. Well, I've got news for you; you're going to lose her as your patient anyway because if she doesn't agree to this, she's going to prison for the rest of her life."

"Stop!" Janet cried. She looked at Megan with tears in her eyes. "Do you really think that saying I didn't know what I was doing will save me?"

"I think it's the only thing that will save you," Megan replied.

"All right then, do whatever you have to, but, please, don't let them put me in prison." Taking a handkerchief from her pocket, Janet wiped away the tears that had begun to stream down her face. Megan wondered whether she should feel sorry for her. Then she thought of the four little victims; they had probably cried too before Janet shot them.

Megan was celebrating a personal victory as she left her office that evening. In spite of Jameson's protests, she had finally persuaded Janet to use the insanity plea. She discussed the case with Jack as they walked to her car, and he agreed that Megan had chosen the best possible defense for Janet.

"I must tell you, Megan," Jack commented, "that over the last few weeks I have seen you really perk up. You have come back to life again."

"Thank you," Megan laughed, "I feel like a different person. Working on this case has been a tonic for me."

"I'm glad. It's good to have you back again." They exchanged smiles as Megan closed her car door and drove out of the parking lot.

It was true, she thought. Jack's attitude about her had changed. He was once again the good friend she had known before her attack. Her own attitude had also changed. She had rediscovered the challenges and excitement in her work that she thought she had lost forever. It was wonderful to be rediscovering the joys of life.

Megan was so preoccupied that she had driven a third of the way home before she realized that she had left some important briefs at the office. She hated to go back for them; she wondered whether they could not wait until morning. No, she finally decided, she had to work tonight in order to be ready for Janet's trial. She looked at her watch; it was six-forty. If she hurried, she could be back at the office by seven. Nearly every evening someone was there until at least six-thirty. With luck, she could get back and pick up her briefs before everyone left.

Megan turned her car around as soon as she could and drove back to the office as quickly as the traffic would permit. Parking her car on the street about a block from the law offices, she held her keys in her left hand and slipped her right hand into her purse where she nervously gripped her gun. Before Megan reached the building she could see that the lights had been turned off. Megan began to run and turned when she reached the alley so that she could slip in the back entrance unobserved by anyone on the street. This was her first night to be at the office alone since her attack, and her heart was racing as she ran up the steps to the back entrance and reached out to insert her key into the lock. The alley entrance was well lighted by a security light Jack Forbes had placed there after her attack to discourage anyone from attempting another break-in. She was glad for it now. She didn't think she could have forced herself to use that entrance if it had not been so well lighted.

Just as her key touched the door handle, a man's left arm came up around her, and his hand sank into her ribs as a knife blade came up beneath her throat. Her heart seemed to stop beating as horror gripped her. Megan was too frightened to scream. She had known that one day *he* would come back, and now that day had arrived. She could feel his breath against her neck as he pushed his face close to her hair.

"I've been waiting for you to come back, baby," his voice was breathless and excited. "You been on a trip or somethin'?" Megan did not answer.

"Huh?" he grunted. "We're gonna have another party, only this time you won't be comin' back."

He was going to kill her, just as in her dream. She had sworn that no one would ever rape her again, but he was actually planning to kill her this time. Megan's hand was on the gun, she tried to move her arm, but he tightened his grip around her.

"Stop moving," he ordered, and he cursed at her. "You make any noise and I'll cut your throat right now."

He dragged her down the steps and shoved her onto the ground. Her hand was free for just a moment; and she pulled the pistol from her purse. She was in an awkward position, but she knew that if she did not fire immediately, he would take the gun away from her and kill her with it.

"What's that in your hand?" he moved toward her. She pulled the trigger. She was not sure that she had hit him; he just stood over her for a moment. Then blood spewed from his chest, and he fell on top of her.

Megan struggled wildly to get to her feet, and as she did, she rolled his body off of her. In the bright stream of light she could see his face. He looked nothing like she had thought he would; her "description" had been all wrong. He was young and handsome and very well groomed. Blond curls fell against a pale brow; dark lashes accentuated large, wide-set eyes. He lay gasping as his life slipped quickly away. Megan stared in horror at the dying face with the eerie glow cast by the harsh security light and the silvery moonlight. At last, he let out a heavy sigh, and his body went limp. He was dead; she had killed him. For the first time she became aware of the evening chill, and it spread through every fiber in her body. Her hands were shaking; she realized that she was still holding the gun. She had been pointing it at him to see whether she would have to shoot him again; now she shoved it into her purse. She was alone in an alley next to the building where she worked, standing beside a man whom she had just killed with an illegal gun.

What should she do? She could not even form a coherent thought. Her palms were cold and wet, and she could almost hear the sound of her heart beating. Should she call the police? She looked around; she could see no one else. Why would they believe her? She had no witnesses. Even if she could prove that he was her rapist, she had no proof that she had killed him in self-defense. They would say that she had conspired to kill him in revenge. After all, hadn't she? She had bought the gun; she had carried it with her. No one would ever believe the truth. She caught a glimpse of her hands in the moonlight; they were covered with blood. She must have gotten it on them when she pushed him off her. Megan looked down and saw that she was standing in a pool of his blood; blood stained her coat and dress.

Megan stood up straight at the sound of a siren screeching down a nearby street. It must be the police, she thought. Someone had heard the shots and called them. She listened as the sound became louder. They would be there in a few moments. Once again she looked at the face of the man she had killed and at her own blood-stained hands. Suddenly she turned and began to run as though demons were chasing her. She tore out of the alley and down the street without slowing until she reached her car. Breathless, she fumbled with the keys until she opened the lock. Getting in, she locked the door and sped away. She nearly did not see the car in front of her brake for a turn or the young woman in the crosswalk. Her hands were shaking too hard, and her mind was racing too fast for her to concentrate.

When, at last, she reached her building, Megan ran up the dark stairs to her apartment and opened the door. Without first setting the locks, she rushed to the kitchen and scrubbed the blood off her hands. Holmes followed her. Turning off the water, she stood looking at him as she dried her hands. Without warning, all of the nervous energy that had sustained her disappeared, and her legs became weak. Collapsing to her knees, she threw her arms around Holmes' neck and began to sob.

More than an hour passed before Megan regained her self-control. Her body felt stiff as she rose from the floor and sat down wearily in a chair. She looked at her watch. It was only 9:00 P.M. It seemed much later—she felt as though days had passed. It was strange to think that in a matter of minutes she could kill a man much larger and stronger than she. She thought of his face in the moonlight; only two hours earlier he had been alive. Was someone waiting for him to return home tonight? Would they wait all night for him wondering where he was and what he was doing? She did not know why she allowed herself to think these thoughts. She had hated him with every fiber of her being. She had wanted to kill him; she had spent hours fantasizing about the moment when she would extract revenge. Yet, now that he was dead, she found no pleasure in having killed him. It all seemed totally unreal to her.

A police siren howled past her building, and the sound of it startled her out of her chair. Someone would find him in the alley, if they hadn't already. The police car she had heard not far from the alley had probably discovered him. They had taken him to the hospital or, perhaps, to the morgue—whatever they did with corpses they discovered in the street. They would identify him and begin a search for his killer. For an instant Megan imagined that the police were on their way to arrest her—the car that she had just heard going past the building would turn around, and the officers would come up to her apartment, handcuff her, and take her away. The thought brought on a new wave of panic. No, she reasoned desperately, grasping for control of her frayed emotions. They did not have anything to connect her to the shooting; she must make certain that they never would. She had to protect herself.

Megan looked at her clothes. She was still wearing her coat, but she now took it off. She was surprised to see how much blood she actually had on her dress and shoes. The drying blood had already stained the gray fabric brown in several places. Taking off her dress, she saw that the blood had soaked through onto her underclothes. Everything would have to be disposed of. She left the clothes on the kitchen floor and put on a bathrobe while she tried to decide how to get rid of the garments. She could throw them into a dumpster far from her apartment, but she was afraid that they would be discovered and traced back to her. She could throw them into the river, but what if she should be seen getting rid of them? There must be a way to get rid of this crucial evidence without further endangering herself.

She caught sight of the fireplace. "Why didn't I think of that sooner?" she said aloud to Holmes. Picking the clothes up off the floor she laid them carefully in the fireplace and turned on the gas jet. Soon the clothing began to disintegrate under the blue torch. Megan watched her bloody clothes burn, stirring the mass from time to time with the fireplace poker to make certain that everything was reduced to ashes.

While her clothes burned, Megan moved around the apartment making certain that there were no signs of blood anywhere. She mopped the kitchen floor with disinfectant to remove any fibers that her clothes might have left behind. She bathed thoroughly and washed her hair; then she sterilized the sink and bathtub with bleach. She checked the walls to make certain that they did not bear her bloody fingerprints. She opened the door and cleaned the outside handle to remove any traces of blood that her hands might have left behind.

When Megan was satisfied that the apartment was clean, she sat down on the sofa to watch the fire. Thus, she passed the night staring into the fire and listening to the sounds of the city. Every siren from every police car and emergency vehicle that passed added to the fear and horror that she was already experiencing. It seemed that every few minutes she heard the shrill sound as another vehicle raced by, and she half expected each one to stop at her building. Once she heard the sirens grow louder and then die right outside her building.

"This must be it," she told herself as her palms began to sweat. Walking slowly toward the window, Megan carefully pulled back the curtain just far enough so that she could see outside. An ambulance was parked outside the building across the street, and the lights flashed in the darkness as paramedics carried a stretcher inside the building. With a sigh of relief, she returned to the sofa.

When dawn came, she dressed in running clothes and went down to the parking area to inspect her car. She saw no traces of blood, but she carefully wiped the seats and dash with a leather cleaner. She found nothing that might link her to a shooting, but she knew that even a hair or fiber that could be traced back to her rapist would be very incriminating. With a hand vacuum, she cleaned the carpet, going over every inch of material until she was satisfied that nothing was left behind. When she had finished, she drove to a car wash and thoroughly cleaned the outside.

When Megan returned to her apartment, Holmes was anxious for his walk. He had been her faithful companion the night before, sitting beside her on the floor for most of the night and following her around the apartment as she worked to remove any evidence of her guilt. Now she had no choice but to stop ignoring him for a little while.

They stepped out onto the street in the cool morning air, and Holmes tugged excitedly on his lead. Megan had learned to enjoy these morning walks with Holmes. This morning, however, she felt as though everyone they passed was staring at her. She imagined that they knew what she had done and that they were waiting for her to be exposed. She felt as though her guilt had been announced on the morning news.

It was ironic, she thought, that after her attack she had searched the crowds of New York to find her attacker. Now the faces in the crowd seemed to be searching for her, and she turned her eyes from those around her. She did not need to search the crowds to find the face of a criminal—she had only to look in the mirror.

Megan cut their walk short and returned to the apartment to get ready for work. For the first time since she had purchased it, she would not have her gun with her that morning when she left for work. She had carried it with her religiously; she had relied on it to protect her. Now, that same gun that had given her so much comfort could result in her spending the best years of her life behind prison bars. She knew that she could not have it in her purse when the police came to question her.

Megan wondered whether she should get rid of it, just in case they should search her apartment. Then she remembered the terror that she had felt the night before. Without that gun she would now be dead—of that she was certain. The thought of disposing of it frightened her even more. She never wanted to be without protection again. On the other hand, perhaps she would have been better off if he had killed her. At least she would not have to face the police, her friends, and her parents. She thought of Jennifer and Ian; she could not imagine their reaction if they discovered that she had killed someone. The horror and disappointment they would feel; the shock and humiliation of seeing their only child go to prison would devastate them. It would have been better if she had not been armed. The police would have found her in the alley, and they would have called her parents and her colleagues at the firm to tell them that she had been murdered. She would have become a heroine of sorts, a helpless victim who was stalked and murdered by a savage rapist.

"Stop it!" Megan told herself, as she caught a glimpse of her reflection in the mirror. "If I hadn't done what I did," she could not even say to herself that she had killed him, "I would be dead now, and he would be walking the streets terrorizing other women the way that he terrorized me. Who knows how many other women he brutalized and how many more he would have brutalized if I hadn't stopped him?"

Megan turned to Holmes. "I was right," she stated with conviction. "I did exactly what I should have done. The police weren't able to protect me. I not only protected myself, I protected the rest of society as well. I was the victim."

Those arguments would not help her with the police, however, for the law said that she was wrong. For the first time, Megan realized that even if she had one hundred eye witnesses who would swear that he had attacked her, she could still be charged with murder. The circumstances made no difference; she had deliberately broken the law. She had shot a man willfully and purposefully with intent to kill. She could not prove that he was going to kill her, though she knew that he would have. In any case, she had no defense because the law said that only the legal system had the right to punish criminals.

Megan thought of Sam Dyer screaming as they dragged him out of the courtroom, "It's a man's right to protect his home and his family." Her argument was very similar, "It's a woman's right to protect her body," and it would be just about as effective. She was going to end up like Sam Dyer, serving a fifteen year prison sentence for murder. When she did, all of her "friends" would say that she deserved it because people aren't supposed to go around shooting other people. No one would understand—not her family, not her co-workers, and certainly not the police.

Megan stared again at the gun. It was time for her to leave for work; she could not decide what to do about it right now. She looked around for a hiding place. Going to her closet, she pulled down a hat box. Wrapping the gun in tissue paper, she hid it under the hat and returned the box to the closet.

When Megan reached the offices of Pratt, Forbes and Magoff, she stayed as far away from the alley as possible. Walking straight to the front door, she let herself in and responded to the few "good mornings" that greeted her as she walked directly to her office. On the desk in front of her were the briefs she had needed the night before for Janet Dobson's case. She had completely forgotten about them. She looked at the clock; she had so much to do. With all of her problems, Janet's case hardly seemed important, but she knew that she had to have everything completed before the upcoming trial date.

Sitting at her desk, Megan began to sort through the material. Though she tried, she could not concentrate on the papers in front of her. Her mind kept returning to her own problems as she anticipated what she would do when the police arrived.

Since the body had been found in the alley next to the building, she guessed that they would be arriving soon to question everyone working there. What would she say? She had to be careful; she had to act as though she had nothing to hide. Yet, she also had to respond to their questions in such a way that she did not betray herself. The key was to stay calm and to behave as if nothing out of the ordinary had taken place. She had the perfect alibi; Jack had walked her to her car and watched her drive away. He knew that she could not have been there when the shooting occurred. Yes, Jack would be her alibi; he would have no reason to believe that she had returned to the offices. The police would not doubt his word; he was the respected partner in a large legal firm, and he had been a friend of the police commissioner for many years. Megan's spirits lifted as she realized that all she had to do was remain cool. If she appeared nervous, they would suspect that she had something to hide. If she remained calm, they would suspect nothing.

Megan jumped when she heard the front door open. "That must be the police," she thought. She listened carefully, but she could hear only the usual office sounds. Finally, she cautiously approached the door of her office. She peeked out into the hall and saw no one. She waited, but she still did not see any sign of the police. Not wishing to attract attention, Megan returned to her desk and waited. Fifteen minutes passed, and still no police appeared. It must have been someone else.

The ringing of the telephone gave her another start. Megan wondered whether the police were calling for information before coming over. When she saw that the line was clear, she was tempted to run to the reception desk and demand to know who had been on the phone. "Get a grip on yourself," Megan tried to calm her nerves. "If you start running all over the building like some sort of lunatic, everyone will know that something's wrong." Never-the-less, whenever the door opened or the telephone rang, she had the same reaction, and it was only with the utmost effort that she was able to control herself.

Megan looked at the clock. It was nearly noon and she had not accomplished anything. While she had been busy mentally arguing her own defense, she had left Janet's future in a jumble on her desk.

Megan's line rang, and she answered it.

"This is Dr. Jameson," the voice announced imperiously on the other end. "Janet and I need to talk to you."

"I can't meet with you today," Megan replied.

"Janet's trial is coming up right away," Jameson argued. "There are still some issues that we have to resolve. For instance, is Janet going to testify on her own behalf? What witnesses will you be calling? What are you going to ask the court to do for her?"

"I'm going to ask the court not to put her in prison," Megan snapped. "Look, I'm working overtime to get this case ready. I do need to meet with you, but I can't do it today. What if we get together Monday afternoon at two? In the meantime, have Janet compile a list of people she thinks might testify for her. Keep in mind that we're using the insanity plea, so people who will testify that she was not responsible for her actions are the kinds of witnesses we need. Is that all right?"

Jameson agreed, and Megan hung up the phone. "That man has a lot of nerve harassing me about his client at a time like this," she thought disgustedly. "We wouldn't be going through this to begin with if she weren't a murderer." Megan had completed the thought before she realized that the same thing might be said of her when her turn came, if it ever did. Megan shook her head. Janet was going to trial because she had gotten caught; Megan was not going to get caught.

Megan ate lunch at her desk trying to focus on Janet's defense. The books she had read about schizophrenia in preparation for the case were stacked on the corner of her desk. She picked one up and thumbed through it absentmindedly. For the first time she wondered what had gone through Janet's mind as she pulled the trigger. Until now she had assumed that Janet had killed the children for some sort of sadistic pleasure or that she was so far removed from reality that she was not truly conscious of hurting anyone. Megan's perspective had now changed. Sane or not, Janet must have felt something. Had she been frightened, believing herself to be threatened by them? Had she acted out of anger? What had induced her to murder four pre-schoolers? The more Megan thought about it, the more she had to ask herself those same questions in connection with the act she had committed. Was there any difference between shooting a group of children and shooting a man in an alley? Everything had happened so quickly; she could not remember what she was thinking when she had shot her attacker. Had she shot him out of fear, or anger, or both?

Megan had always believed that she would meet her attacker again, and she had planned to kill him when she did. Was there some force that had driven her back to the office that evening knowing that *he* would be waiting for her in the alley? If she had taken those briefs with her when she had left the office, none of the events of last night would have taken place, or if she had been a few minutes earlier or a few minutes later she would not have met him. Janet claimed to hear voices that told her what to do; Megan had read that this is a symptom of schizophrenia. Perhaps, Megan had heard voices too, and though they were not audible, perhaps, they had persuaded her to do something that she had not wanted to do.

Megan waited all afternoon for the police, but they never arrived. At the end of the day, she was angry with them for not having come. She was ready with her alibi; she was prepared to answer their questions. They should have done their duty and taken everyone's statement so that she could stop anticipating their arrival. Every phone call had made her jump; every sound at the door had made her heart race. Megan wanted this ordeal to end. Now, thanks to the inefficiency of the NYPD, she would have to wait for them all the next day. "It's like waiting to be shot," she murmured as she put on her coat at six-thirty.

Looking around the office, Megan made certain that everything she needed for her work that evening was in her briefcase. Then she walked out into the hall where Jack was waiting for her. They went outside and walked down the steps of the building together.

"Just a minute," Jack called turning the corner into the alley. "I need to check this door."

Nervously, Megan stood at the alley entrance. Enough daylight remained for her to see everything clearly. The scene looked totally different than it had the previous night. She took a few timid steps towards the spot where his body had lain. She could see the blood stains on the pavement. She wondered whether Jack had noticed them.

Jack climbed the steps leading to the door and checked to make certain that it was secure.

"Is there a problem?" Megan asked, trying to hide her apprehension.

"Somebody tampered with the door last night," Jack said. "They apparently were using some kind of gadget to pick the lock. They didn't get it open though; an officer on patrol spotted them and ran them off before they had a chance to finish their work."

Jack smiled as he stepped down. Megan shuddered. Jack had made up the last part for her benefit. It was her own arrival into the alley that had kept her attacker from opening the door and entering the building. In a few more moments he would have been inside waiting for her. He would have heard her enter. In the darkness, without the benefit of moonlight, she would not have been able to see well enough to shoot him. He would have overpowered her and killed her in the same spot where he had raped her. Even if she had been able to shoot him, she would not have been able to conceal the shooting from others.

"What's wrong?" Jack asked with concern in his voice. "You're shaking."

"It's just the evening air," Megan lied. "I'm a little cold."

SEVEN

Three months passed, and the police never came. After waiting a week for them to arrive, Megan determined that they were not going to interrogate her or her colleagues.

"I guess," she said to Holmes in the privacy of her kitchen, "there are so many murders here that the police don't even try to solve them. They just pick up the body and question whoever happens to be in the area at the time. After all, the offices were locked, and if they had checked the building, they would have known immediately that no one was inside. There would really be no point in them questioning the people who work there in the daytime."

Megan was relieved that the police had never arrived, and she had been able to relax enough so that she was certain that Jack and her colleagues would not suspect that anything was wrong. After the first week had passed she bought a kit to clean her gun so that no one could tell that it had been fired recently, and then she returned it to its place in her purse. She was now more careful than ever. She knew that it was not just important, but imperative, that no one suspect she was armed.

Megan never let her purse out of her sight because she was afraid that someone would discover her weapon. She avoided having her co-workers in her office, for she feared that one of them might pick up her purse to move it and notice that it was unusually heavy. One night when she was putting on her coat, Jack had reached out to pick it up and hand it to her. To his surprise, she snatched it up before he could touch it. Immediately, she realized that her reaction had been too abrupt. She worried that at some point she would be caught, and she feared that if she were caught, it would be as a result of being overly cautious.

Megan's attitude about her gun had also changed. She had never appreciated the power contained in that small metal object. She now knew first hand the damage it could do, and she felt that she could never use it again without being certain that her life was in danger. It was an old promise; she had never intended to use the gun for any reason other than her own protection, but now her resolve took on new meaning. The gun made her feel safe, but it also served as a constant reminder of the shooting, and that event now overshadowed her concerns for her personal safety.

During the first week after the shooting, her nightmare of the man chasing her through the dark tunnel occurred for the last time. Shortly after the dream began she had awakened calmly and told herself, "He's dead. I don't ever have to be afraid again." After that she had been able to sleep in peace for several weeks.

After a few weeks, however, the first nightmare was replaced by a second one. Now when Megan closed her eyes at night, she could see herself standing over *his* body. She stood looking into the young face illuminated by the silver glow of moonlight, and then she looked at her own blood-stained hands. She awakened from this dream with a new kind of horror accompanied by guilt instead of tears. Then she would begin rethinking her actions on the night of her second attack.

Megan's first reaction was to wonder how she could have killed him. He was so young and handsome, and he looked like such a wholesome clean-cut boy. If someone had been chasing her in a crowd, she was certain that she would have run to him for help. He was well dressed, obviously affluent, and probably well educated. She guessed that he was no more than twenty-three; he was probably a university student. How was it possible that he could have been the sadistic monster that she remembered?

Surely, she must have been confused. She must have killed the wrong man because the face she had seen in the alley could not have been capable of inflicting the pain and terror she had experienced at the hands of her attacker. Megan was a murderer; she had killed a respectable young man in cold blood.

"No," she told herself aloud, "I am not a murderer, and he was not a nice young man. He was evil and insane, and if I had not killed him, he would have killed me. No matter what he appeared to be, I know the truth, and I know that I did only what I had to do." Sometimes she argued the matter with herself for hours, but she still was not satisfied.

Other times she became angry with herself. Why did she feel so guilty? Why couldn't she have just shot him and walked away as she had always imagined she would? There was no doubt that the man she had shot was the rapist. He had even identified himself so that she would know that it was he. Megan had never planned to feel guilty, and now she was surprised to find that she was so weak. She had always believed that she was strong and determined; she had never suspected that underneath she was completely lacking in courage.

Megan believed that she would have lost her mind had it not been for Holmes and her job. Holmes sat patiently listening to her debates, and she imagined that he was sympathetic. Although he could not add to the arguments, the varied expressions on his face led her to believe that he understood.

At work she was busy preparing Janet's case, which went to court in July. In spite of her many personal problems, she gave Janet an excellent defense. She called five witnesses, all of whom testified to Janet's deranged state of mind. Just before the trial began, Dr. Jameson became angry and refused to testify, a move that Megan had been expecting. She believed that the case was probably stronger without him since he was opposed to Janet's plea. Janet wanted to testify in her own defense, but Megan refused to allow her to take the stand, and the ensuing argument nearly resulted in her being fired. In the end, however, she won and kept Janet off the stand.

She knew that even with the best defense Janet's case would be a difficult one, and when the prosecutor gave his opening arguments, her fears were confirmed. The prosecutor presented his case with a precision that Megan had seldom encountered in the courtroom. In the first few days of the trial he recounted every ghastly detail of the crime to the jury, and Megan noted that they began to avoid looking at Janet. Describing in detail the wounds that were inflicted on the children, he quickly made his case that Janet was an inhumane monster. He presented ample evidence that the crime was premeditated and that Janet had, in fact, been planning it from the first day she went to work at the pre-school. By the time he had finished presenting the state's case, the prosecutor had even succeeded in convincing Megan that Janet deserved life in prison.

When it was time for Megan to present the defense, she did not attempt to minimize the facts about the crime itself. Instead, she tried to gain some sympathy for Janet by arguing that she was not competent enough to be aware of her actions. The insanity plea was convincing, and she was certain that she had won the case even before the jury returned with a verdict.

Never-the-less, leaving the courtroom that day, Megan did not feel victorious. She knew positively that Janet was not only guilty but that she was fully aware of all of her actions. There was no question that she was mentally disturbed, but Megan wondered whether the same could not be said of anyone who would commit such a heinous crime. She saw the parents of the children standing in the corridor as she left the building. She did not look at them then, but she had looked at them during the trial and seen in their faces the pain and grief that they would have to live with for the rest of their lives. Nothing would bring their children back; their only comfort had been that they would see the person responsible punished. Now, thanks to her, even that had been denied them.

She had experienced very similar emotions only a few months earlier. She could not tell herself that revenge would not bring their children back and that punishing Janet would not serve any purpose. Only people who had never experienced a great loss and known that the person responsible had escaped punishment could justify those neat little clichés. Not so long ago she would have proclaimed those sentiments, and she would have returned to her perfect ordered little world without a second thought for the people she had left behind. That was no longer true; she now knew what it was to be hurt and angry and forgotten.

As she drove back to the office, Megan passed a large church with a sign that questioned the passerby, "What have you done for mankind lately?" She forced herself to think about the question. "I killed a man and freed a murderer," she thought. "I'm sure that both of these acts will benefit the human race tremendously."

What had she ever done for mankind? She had become an attorney as a professional stepping stone, and she had helped a great many Janets gain their freedom. Not once had she ever questioned the methods she used—her clients' guilt or innocence had never been important. She had been in courtrooms where she had heard details of cases more brutal than this one, and she had never once asked herself whether she had done the right thing in working to give her clients the best possible defense. It was not so much that she supported the great American legal system, although she knew the rhetoric by heart and could recite it if anyone questioned her ethics. Rather, she had simply never given her actions any thought. Being an attorney was a job like any other job. Some women typed letters for a living; others took people's temperatures; she defended criminals. There was nothing immoral about it. Her clients might be malicious, but their guilt did not taint her in any way, any more than the executive assistant who puts the calls through to her employer's mistress is guilty of adultery.

Yet, Janet Dobson's case had changed everything. For the first time in her career Megan had felt some of the anger of the victims' families, and she had imagined the children's terror before they died. It was as though, against her own will, she had put herself in their place as Janet's victims. She knew something of the terrible sense of grief and helplessness that the parents had experienced. Their lives had been torn apart by an insane stranger who had no sympathy for them or their children. By the time the trial ended Megan hated Janet because she saw in her traces of her own attacker. Perhaps he, too, had been on trial at some time and an ambitious attorney had persuaded a jury to set him free. They might have saved him from prison so that he would be free to rape her.

In a bizarre way, however, she could also identify with Janet. Janet was on trial for shooting four little children; Megan had shot one young man. She could not forget the distinct feeling that she should be in Janet's place. What right did she have to judge and condemn her client when she was guilty of murder herself? The day might come when she would be consulting an attorney about her own defense. At some point she might have the choice between a mental institution and prison, except that she would not have any evidence to substantiate her insanity plea. She and Janet were not so very different, but only Megan knew it.

Depressed, Megan returned to her office and shut the door. She saw the day's mail on her desk and walked over to pick it up. The usual assortment of junk mail awaited her along with a few notices from the Bar Association and some business correspondence. She sorted the envelopes into piles based on their priority. She was left with one plain white envelope with no return address.

Taking out her letter opener, she slit the envelope and produced a sheet of lined note paper. Written across the paper in large block letters was the word, "MURDERER." Megan gasped and dropped the note.

Someone knew what she had done, but who? Megan had seen no one in the alley. Besides, why would they wait three months to write to expose her? If they had seen the shooting, why wouldn't they have reported it to the police at the time?

She drew a deep breath and sat down behind her desk. The alley was empty; she was certain of that. No one could possibly know what had happened. The note must be a reference to the trial; someone in the courtroom had seen her defense of Janet and had sent the note to upset her. Perhaps it had come from one of the parents; Megan knew that they were very angry with her. That was the only logical explanation.

There was one problem, however. The note had been mailed, and the trial had concluded today. Surely it was not that obvious to the spectators that Janet would be freed. Megan looked at the postmark. The letter had been mailed two days earlier. Was it intended to be a threat during the trial?

She tore the note into tiny pieces and tossed it into the wastebasket. It didn't matter who had sent it; they could not harm her. She reminded herself that in every sensational murder trial at least one disturbed spectator tries to find a way to get some publicity. They call the press or post comments on websites or contact the participants in the trial. In most cases it is a harmless ploy for attention. She tried to calm her nerves.

"Congratulations!" Jack was standing in the doorway. "I was over at the courthouse this afternoon."

"Yes," Megan smiled. "It went really well."

Jack laughed, "I know the D. A. is steamed. They thought they had a sure winner with Janet. This afternoon his assistant was bragging about how they were going to send her to prison for life, and there wasn't anything you could do about it. I didn't say much to him because, just in case he turned out to be right, I didn't want to end up looking like a fool. I guess they're singing a different tune this evening. Remind me to call him tomorrow."

"Adam did look upset when he left," Megan laughed for the first time all day. "He keeps hoping for a break to advance his career, and so far he hasn't found one. He thought that if he won this case the media would make him into a hero."

"There was a little more furor over the trial than I had anticipated," Jack commented. "It started out so quietly, but after that parents' group got involved with their protests outside of the courthouse the media started coming around. One of that bunch of troublemakers called here this afternoon and said that we should not be defending 'that Dobson woman' after what she did. She said that we were co-conspirators with Dobson for helping her to escape justice. I wouldn't be surprised if they hassle you a little, too."

"I'm sure. All this week they yelled at me every time I entered the courthouse. I think they were mostly parents of other children at the pre-school and a few attention hogs who showed up hoping to get on the evening news. I didn't think that they would go so far as to call us, though." Inwardly, Megan breathed a sigh of relief as she realized that the note must have come from one of them.

"Well, it's over now, and you won the case. That's what's important. I've been wanting to talk to you about something, but I was waiting until the trial ended so that you would have time to consider the offer."

Megan smiled; she thought she knew what Jack was going to say, and she also knew that he had been waiting to see whether she won the case before he asked. She looked at him attentively as he took a chair on the other side of her desk.

"As you know," Jack began, "Bob Pratt is retiring in six months, and that leaves an opening for a full partner in the firm. Now, you're very young, and ordinarily we would want an older, more experienced attorney in the position. But we feel that you are also exceptionally talented. For the past six months I have been reviewing every case you have defended since you first came to us. You have maintained an almost perfect track record. You are precise and efficient, and you communicate extremely well. You possess the maturity of someone five or ten years your senior. We believe that you are right for the position."

Jack leaned forward and continued, "Now consider very carefully before you answer one way or the other. This is a great opportunity, but it also carries with it heavy responsibilities. You would have to be willing to devote long hours and to take on a lot of extra duties, but an opportunity like this won't come around again for a long time."

"I am delighted to accept," Megan responded.

"Wonderful!" Jack slapped his knee in his enthusiastic way. "I thought you would. As I said, it'll be six months before the position is open, but we are delighted to know that you will be on board when Bob leaves."

Megan drove home that night turning the name over in her mind, "Forbes, Magoff and Cleary." It had a nice ring to it. She had been sure that they were going to offer her the position, and she had already decided that she wanted it. Becoming a full partner was one of her many ambitions, and she had now reached that plateau. She was one step closer to achieving her career goals. Someday she would be wealthy and famous. She would not just have claim to her father's money and connections; she would have money and connections of her own. Whether she chose politics or law as her ultimate profession, everyone would know her name. When she arrived in a city, her presence would be noted on the local news. She would be one of those few lucky individuals to whom other people look as role models. Little girls would want to grow up to be exactly like her.

Since Megan was a little girl she had dreamed of being rich and famous; she had never doubted that everything she wanted would someday be hers. Never-the-less, the last few months had changed her, and although the ambition and drive were still there, she no longer felt the satisfaction that she would have a year earlier.

She was excited about the new opportunity, but in her heart, she wondered whether she was emotionally ready for more responsibility. A year earlier she would have had no doubts, but much had changed. She was now struggling to deal with emotions that she could neither control nor understand. Megan could feel herself changing in ways that frightened her. The more she tried to fight those changes and return to the person she had been, the more she realized that this, too, was beyond her control. When she tried to analyze her own feelings, she found that she could not make sense of them.

She had lived in fear for eight months, and at times that fear paralyzed her. At first she had lived in fear of her attacker; now she lived in fear of being exposed. Fear was like a demon that reached out to torment her every hour of the day and night. She was never free; even now she was sometimes gripped by unreasoning terror, and she had the impulse to run from her office or apartment and to keep running until she reached some far off destination where no one could find her. Feelings of guilt about the shooting and about having hidden the crime constantly gnawed at her. Frequently, she wished that she had called the police at the time of the shooting; it would have made everything easier.

Megan dreaded her parents' phone calls. With every word she feared that she would give something away. Every sentence seemed to be a lie. She had specifically promised her mother that she would tell her if anything else happened. That promise had been broken, and there was no way that she could tell the truth now. Even if she wanted to confess everything, she would not know what to say. Her conscience reminded her that she lied whenever she said "everything's fine." Her parents had wanted her to come to Buffalo for her birthday, but she could not face them. She knew that she might break down and tell them the truth, and that would be disastrous.

Finally, she was faced with a growing sense of disgust—disgust with herself and disgust with her life. The Dobson case had raised questions in her mind that she had never thought she would ask and for which she had no answers. Whether she was developing a conscience or a complex she did not know, but in either case it was professional suicide.

A full partnership presented a new challenge for her, both professionally and emotionally. She had to conquer her own phobias and fears if she were to be successful in her new position. The opportunity gave her another goal to work towards; she must find a way to regain control of her own mind.

She was reviewing all of this for Holmes while she fixed dinner that evening when the ringing telephone interrupted her. She answered to hear a familiar voice on the other end.

"Hi, Megan. This is Mike," the caller informed her. "How have you been?"

Her face lit up with an enthusiastic smile, "Hello, Mike. I haven't heard from you in ages. What have you been up to? "

"Well," he replied. "I'm here in New York City now, and I've got a restaurant."

"That's great! I know you always wanted one. What kind of food do you serve?"

"Mostly Italiano," he responded in his bad attempt at an Italian accent, "although we also have grilled steaks and salmon."

"I'm very happy for you. I missed seeing you at the Christmas party last year. Were you here then?"

"No, I just couldn't find anything to wear. What about you; you didn't go to Joanna's wedding in June. She was really upset; she said that she had asked you to be her maid of honor and that you had agreed, but at the last minute you bailed. Aunt Martha was flitting all over the place complaining to everyone who knows you."

"I didn't exactly stand her up," Megan responded. "She did ask me at Christmas, and I agreed, but when she called me back in the spring to talk about the wedding arrangements, I told her that I couldn't come. She had two months to find someone else, for Heaven's sake, and I had told Mother that I couldn't make it before then. I'm sure that she had already told Martha."

"Why didn't you come? You and Joanna were always close."

"I was working on a case that was going to trial in July. I just didn't have the time. Anyway, you've heard the saying, 'Always a bride's maid, never a bride.'"

"Whatever. I know that Jennifer and Ian were disappointed that you weren't there."

"I'm sure," Megan responded. "Mother practically begged me to come, but I really couldn't." She abruptly changed the subject, "How long has your restaurant been open?"

"As of midnight tomorrow, about seven hours. That's why I called. I want you to attend the grand opening."

Megan thought for a minute, "I'd love to. What time?"

"We officially open at five, but, of course, I have to be there all day. Why don't you come around four-thirty and beat the huge crowds we're going to have all evening." She could hear Mike knocking on wood in the background, and she laughed.

"I'll probably just have to beat my way through; I can't leave work that early, but I think I can make it by six-thirty. What's the name of your place?"

"Little Sicily."

After writing down the address, Megan said, "All right, I'll see you tomorrow about six-thirty." She hung up the phone smiling.

Her cousin Mike had been Megan's closest friend when she was a little girl. They were constantly together, and everyone said that he was more like her brother than her cousin. She was just six months older than he, and they enjoyed many of the same things. Mike had never been as driven as she; he had always enjoyed the lighter side of life. There was no question that he was the family eccentric. He was wonderfully witty and kept everyone laughing, but his unpredictable behavior caused most of the family members to shake their heads in dismay if they spent too much time with him. She was almost sorry that she had not gone to Joanna's wedding just to see Mike. She could imagine the comments he would have made about the groom, the bride and the wedding party. She would have laughed until tears ran down her face.

Megan was glad that Mike was in New York; he was exactly what she needed to take her mind off her problems. Mike would not inspire her to confess any deep dark secrets. He would simply entertain her and be her friend.

As she ate dinner, Megan anticipated the following evening with enthusiasm. "I haven't been out socially since the night of the Christmas Party," she told Holmes. "I've been bottled up in this apartment for so many months that I had nearly forgotten that anything else existed. The opening night at Mike's restaurant should be fun: no court cases to worry about, no co-workers complaining, no crazy people sending me threatening letters. I'll enjoy good food and good company. I'm sorry that Mike didn't call me when he first came to town."

The next day passed quickly, and at six o'clock she drove straight from the office to the restaurant. She was disappointed to see that the parking lot was practically empty. She knew that no restaurant is an overnight sensation, but she had hoped that Mike would have a good crowd on his opening night. He greeted her as she came in the door.

"You look great, Meg," Mike called to her. "This brown air does wonders for you."

"Thank you. I can see that you haven't changed a bit; you're still exactly like you were when we were in kindergarten." Megan looked around the restaurant. A glazed brick floor, plastered walls and a huge stone fireplace at one end made the room inviting and cozy. Snowy white table linens and gleaming crystal goblets adorned the tables. The establishment was informal but upscale, just the kind of place where successful young professionals love to spend their evenings.

"Very nice!" Megan said as she caught the spicy scent of Italian dishes wafting from the kitchen. "How did you manage all of this?"

"Dad provided the financing—made me a loan actually. His only condition was that I open the restaurant any place other than Buffalo. If it doesn't take off, I owe him a small fortune, so I was careful to invest wisely. I found this little location with a pretty good lease for New York. By doing a lot of the renovations myself, I was able to get it looking good without going over budget. I bought the equipment from an expensive restaurant that went out of business after four months. Apparently the owner had invested his life savings, and he was desperate to sell everything as quickly as possible. I was able to get virtually new top-of-the-line kitchen equipment at bargain basement prices. My pride and joy, however, is our chef, Alfredo. He costs plenty, but the food is amazing, and that's what counts. Come back, and I'll introduce you."

Mike led her to the kitchen where Alfredo was hard at work. "Al, meet my cousin Megan."

"Good evening, Beautiful Lady," Alfredo said, making a slight bow in her direction.

"It's a pleasure to meet you," Megan replied trying to hide her amusement at Alfredo's attempt to play the part of the macho Italian male. She surveyed the kitchen and was impressed by the numerous dishes in their various stages of completion.

"Everything looks and smells wonderful," she said, acknowledging both Mike and Alfredo. "If you can get people in here once, I know they'll come back."

"I'm pretty sure that we can get them in," Mike responded. "Here, taste this." He speared a small savory morsel on a fork and held it to Megan's lips.

"Delicious," Megan responded as she swallowed. "Friday night is probably the best night for your grand opening; I'm sure that will work in your favor."

"Wait until seven," Mike predicted. "Then you'll see business really start to pick up."

She felt doubtful as she surveyed the nearly empty dining room, but she smiled brightly, as if she were certain that Mike was correct. For the next fifteen minutes Megan told Mike about the Dobson case and her promotion.

"I'm really happy for you, Meg," Mike said when she paused. "You shouldn't work too hard, though. Staying in all the time, working late every night, that's not good for a girl. Life is passing you by. What about Jeff? Doesn't he mind the long hours?"

"Jeff and I broke up," Megan replied.

"Do you have a new guy?"

"No."

"Megan Cleary, the most popular girl at Jefferson High, doesn't have a boyfriend? I don't believe it! That's what I'm talking about; your work is eating you up. You're losing sight of the important things. How are you going to enjoy all that fame and fortune without someone you love by your side?"

"Everything's changed, Mike. I haven't looked for a knight in shining armor since I was sixteen. Now I'm not even looking for a knight. I don't know; I can't seem to find anyone I like. They're all too shallow or too opinionated or too immature."

"Hang out here with me, Kid. You'll meet all types. Eventually you're sure to find someone."

"I'm not sure that I want to find someone—maybe my career is enough."

"A job is no substitute for people," Mike responded. Although she remained quiet, Megan thought that if the people she had been involved with for the past few months were any example of humanity, she would prefer to be alone.

"That's the difference between you and me. You're a people person, and I'm not. You want everybody and his brother around all the time."

"It's true that I enjoy the company of my fellow human beings. I like to believe that I'm part of their existence, and they're part of mine. I listen to their problems, and I'm drawn into the great web of humanity," Mike responded magnanimously.

"And if you find that the web has spiders in it, just remember that your cousin is a successful attorney who can help you beat back the masses," Megan replied jokingly.

Mike turned, "It's seven; I have to get ready for the crowd."

Megan looked at him fondly, but she was unconvinced. Only five people had entered the restaurant during the previous thirty minutes. To her surprise, exactly at seven a steady stream of customers began to appear. By seven-thirty people were waiting to be seated. She went into the kitchen to ask Mike how he had known that a crowd would arrive at precisely seven o'clock.

"Elementary, my dear. I advertised free drinks with dinner between seven and ten this evening."

"Free drinks!" Megan was aghast. "Mike, you'll be bankrupt before you even get started."

Mike shook his head, "I'll lose money tonight, but once they taste the food, they're mine."

The evening was a great success for Little Sicily in terms of a huge crowd, though Megan feared that it would take Mike quite a while to make up the money he had lost on the free drinks. Still, it was apparent that the customers had enjoyed themselves, and Mike was elated when he closed the restaurant at midnight.

"Didn't I tell you?" he beamed. "We're off and running. What an introduction to New York!"

"I think it's terrific," Megan smiled. "I just hope it keeps up."

"It has to keep up," Mike looked a little startled, and then he laughed. "I have to start making payments to Dad next month. If I fall behind, he'll have people knocking at my door threatening to break my kneecaps."

At this, they both laughed. Mike's relationship with his father had always been a little strained. In fact, Megan was surprised that Dick had financed this venture for his son.

Megan looked at her watch, "I have to go. I'm not used to being out this late anymore. Usually if I'm still awake at midnight, I'm sitting on my couch going through papers from the office."

"Remember what I said about all work and no play," Mike said as her walked her to the door. "Take a little time to smell the roses. We only have a few years in this world, and it's a shame for a girl like you to waste hers in an office."

Megan stepped out into the parking lot and stood for a moment drinking in the sights. The tall silhouettes of the buildings were lighted like Christmas trees, and the traffic formed a constant stream of red and white lights. She was aware of the pulse of the city and the excitement and sense of adventure that it offered. This was New York as she remembered it from happier days.

Tonight reminded her of her college days and the carefree times she had enjoyed before her world was turned upside down. This evening marked the first time in months that she had been able to spend hours without thinking of her problems. She had not once felt frightened, or guilty, or depressed. She was glad that Mike had come to New York; he would be a tonic for her to help her overcome her pain.

EIGHT

Megan slept until eleven o'clock the following morning. After a leisurely brunch she took Holmes for his walk. As they returned to the apartment, she stopped to pick up her mail. She mentally counted off the contents: the electric bill, the gas bill, two credit card bills, a card from her mother. She was left with one plain white envelope addressed to "Miss Megan Cleary." She turned the envelope over; there was no return address. It was identical to the envelope that had contained the note calling her a murderess, and she felt a growing sensation that it had been sent by the same person.

"This is ridiculous," she told Holmes. "I am certainly not going to be harassed by some irate courtroom spectator or emotional parent. Whatever those people think of me, I was only doing my job."

By the time she reached her apartment, Megan had almost decided to throw the letter away unopened. She was a little uneasy, though, and sitting down at the table, she used her car keys as a letter opener and drew from the envelope a sheet of note paper. Unfolding it, she saw the same block letters that were used in the first note. "DID YOU TELL HIM TO BEWARE THE IDES OF MARCH?"

A chill went through her body. March 15—the night of the shooting. The notes had nothing to do with the trial; whoever sent this note and the first one did know. Who could know? Who could have seen it? She thought of the buildings bordering the alley. Perhaps someone had looked out the window and seen the shooting. Perhaps a vagrant in a doorway had heard the shot and seen everything. She had thought that she was safe; she had naively walked around for four months believing that safety lay in silence. Now she knew that she would never be safe. While she had been out last night thinking that she had outsmarted everyone, a stranger had been waiting for her to receive this note. The first note had been delivered to her office, but this one had been mailed to her home. Whoever it was had been following her. He knew where she worked and where she lived. He probably knew every other detail of her life as well.

She picked up the note and carried it through the apartment wondering what she should do. What did the writer want? Would he go to the police? More than four months had passed; his testimony would seem suspect now. What if he had some sort of proof? Surely he could not provide evidence that would actually link her to the shooting. Yet, even an accusation could hurt her. He might contact the authorities who would begin an investigation, and that investigation might provide the evidence they needed.

Suddenly, Megan realized that she had no reason to believe that the author of the notes was a man. Perhaps they had been written by a woman. A number of women who worked for the firm might be jealous of her position there. Could one of them have been waiting to discover something that could derail her career? Were these notes meant to frighten her enough so that she would quit her job? Were they meant to send her into hiding? Did the author believe that she could be manipulated into confessing to her crime? For a moment she entertained a mental image of Anne Sutherland sitting at her desk with a smirk on her face as Megan was handcuffed and taken away by two of New York's finest. As she considered this possibility, she was overcome with such loathing for Anne that she would gladly have smashed her face in.

Megan still had the gun; that gun could be linked to the shooting and to her. Whoever had witnessed the events of that night knew about the gun. The "smoking gun" might actually be her gun. She had stupidly allowed herself to bask in false security. She had never considered that anything or anyone could implicate her after four months.

"I am such a fool!" She said to Holmes. "Why did I run?" She thought of the sirens screeching toward the alley. She had assumed that they were from a police car, but they might have been from any type of emergency vehicle. If only she hadn't panicked. If only she had called 911. She shook her head, "No, I couldn't have told anyone when it happened. They would have sent me to prison."

Now Megan was again faced with the possibility of prison, and she had no recourse. It was too late to report the incident to the police. Any hope she had of a self-defense plea had been thrown away when she ran from the alley and disposed of the evidence. If she were caught now, she would be charged with murder, and her attempts to hide the crime would be used as evidence to convince the jury that she had intended to kill her attacker.

She was once again at the mercy of a stranger, and she knew how cruel strangers can be. She spent most of the afternoon pacing up and down the apartment with the note in her hands.

"Why is this happening to me?" she angrily asked Holmes. "I never did anything to hurt anyone. I've always just gone about my life minding my own business. In less than a year I've been attacked twice, raped once, and forced to kill a man to save my own life. Now I'm being terrorized again. Is this ever going to end?"

Finally, Megan sank into a chair. "I'm sick and tired of this. I'm sick of being chased and hounded and persecuted. Real criminals don't have to suffer like this. New York is full of people who ought to be in prison. Is anyone making their lives miserable? Of course not! I'm the one who has her life crashing down around her. I'm the one who never has any peace. I was the victim, and I'm the one who's suffering. That maniac who raped me probably never suffered a day in his life until I shot him, and even then he didn't suffer very long. I've been suffering for eight lousy months!"

She tore up the letter and crumpled the pieces before tossing them into the wastebasket. Holmes licked her hand as if to say that he understood. She patted his muzzle. Even Holmes could not comfort her now, though. She was frightened, but she had been through so much trauma that fear was losing its potency in her life. She could absorb only so much fear, shock and anger, and these emotions were beginning to give way to a growing sense of frustration. It was as if the entire planet were conspiring to destroy her. She had tried not to let any of the things that she had experienced ruin her life. She had worked to put on a good front. She had forced herself to go back to work, and she had thrown herself into her job. Yet, every time she struggled up for air someone was always waiting to push her back under. It was as though she were the victim of a secret pact like those she had read about in novels when she was a child. She could easily imagine that somewhere a group of individuals had bound themselves with an oath to make certain that Megan Cleary would never again have any peace.

Megan wished desperately that she had someone with whom she could talk. "I should have gone into counseling the way Mother wanted me to when this first happened," she sighed. "But, would I listen? No, I knew what was best for me. I was stubborn and rude, and I wouldn't even discuss it. There was no way that I could tell a stranger about what had happened to me. Now I need to talk to someone; I would gladly pay anyone just to sit and listen. But I can't. I can't tell anyone about anything that's happened because if I get started, I might never stop. So here I am—all alone because I thought I was so smart. I ought to be taken out and shot for being so stupid."

She was so upset that she did not eat any dinner, and when she took Holmes for his walk that evening she did not notice the touches of autumn in the air. She wondered whether the author of the notes was watching her. After she was raped she had a very clear picture of her attacker, but this time she could not formulate any image of her tormentor. Was it a man or a woman? Was the person young or old, what race was he or she, was he or she tall or short, overweight or under thin? She felt like a creature being stalked by a hunter, knowing that her unseen predator could be anywhere waiting to strike.

The note ruined Megan's weekend, and on Monday she was unable to concentrate on her work. She had to make an effort even to hear what was said to her, and Jack mentioned that she seemed preoccupied. She tried to shrug it off, to remind herself that she must conceal her emotions. Somehow, though, that no longer seemed important. She was tired of putting on a good front, of pretending that she was carefree when her life was falling apart. The act was over— she would no longer bury her feelings. She remembered her mother's warning at the Christmas party that other people would not understand or excuse her behavior, but she no longer cared.

On Tuesday she recognized another plain white envelope on her desk at work. Rising, she shut the door to her office and, with shaking hands, opened the letter and read the enclosed note. "I SAW WHAT YOU DID TO THAT MAN IN THE ALLEY. GET FIFTY THOUSAND DOLLARS TOGETHER AND WAIT FOR MY INSTRUCTIONS."

Megan's palms were sweating as she sat down behind her desk. "Fifty thousand dollars!" she whispered. She had no idea that the blackmailer would ask for so much. Where was she to get fifty thousand dollars? Her parents might loan it to her, but they would want some explanation, and that was out of the question. She thought of her stocks; her parents had been making investments for her since she was born, and she now had a sizable sum tucked safely away. She could cash in some of her stocks.

She picked up the envelope and examined it for any clue as to the identity of the author. The postmark read "New York City." There was nothing to indicate where it had come from or who had written it.

What should she do? If she paid the blackmail, she would be putting herself in a position from which she would never be able to escape. The blackmailer was asking for fifty thousand this time; how much would he demand the next time? "Of course," she thought to herself, "Maybe this is all he will ever demand. If I pay this, maybe I will never hear from him again." She smiled weakly, unable to convince herself that this would be the end of her blackmailer's demands. She had heard stories of people who had been blackmailed for years until every penny had been taken from them. Was she destined to meet a similar end?

Megan considered her alternatives. If she refused to pay, the blackmailer would go to the police. He might not have any evidence to convict her, but he might. She would not know the truth until it was too late. In any case, she would most likely go to prison if an investigation were launched. Even if she were not charged, her reputation would be tainted so that she could not launch the political career that she and her father had envisioned for her since she was a child.

She was caught in an impossible situation. Trembling, she picked up the phone and called Jeff about selling the stocks. They had not spoken since his phone call shortly after they had dinner at her apartment and she had told him that she never wanted to see him again.

"Jeff, this is Megan," her tone was almost sharp when Jeff answered his cell phone. "I want you to sell fifty thousand dollars worth of my stock and get me the check today."

Jeff was shocked. "But, Megan, that's a terrible idea. The market's down and…"

"I don't care what the market's doing. Get me the money, and get it today."

"Okay, I'll sell the stock, but I can't get you the money today. It will be at least Thursday."

"Thursday's too late," Megan snapped. "I need it now. It's urgent."

"I'm sorry, Meg, but you know how this works. You've cashed in stock before, and you know that the money doesn't come in immediately. Look, I'll have it ready for you Thursday at noon, and you can come by and pick it up."

Megan was silent for a moment, and then her tone softened. "I'm sorry, Jeff. This is very important. Can you possibly have it for me tomorrow?"

"Well, I don't know. Maybe. If I can get it for you tomorrow around four o'clock, is that okay? That's absolutely the very soonest that I can do this."

"Okay, I'll pick it up tomorrow at four."

"Good," Jeff was encouraged by Megan's friendlier attitude. "What's so urgent?"

"It's a personal matter," she responded.

"I hope everything's okay. I haven't seen you around at the club for months. I was wondering what had happened to you."

"I don't go to the club anymore. I'm very busy with my job now."

"That's what I've heard. Barbara and Lisa told me they tried to call you—left a bunch of messages on your phone. No one's been able to get in touch with you for months. Mike said that you're up for a big promotion and you've kind of been buried in work."

"When did you see Mike?" she asked without interest.

"He called me and told me about his restaurant, and I went over there Monday night. It's a great place. Have you been there?"

"I was there Friday for the opening."

"I'll bet that was fun. When I was there on Monday, he had a lot of business. I think the place is going to be a success. Anyway, Mike hasn't changed; he's still the same crazy guy he's always been. I went over with a couple of friends, and we had a great time."

"That's good," Megan responded dully, looking at her watch. "I hope he does well. He always wanted a restaurant."

"Yeah. Well, anyway, I thought maybe you and I could have dinner there sometime. You know? What do you think?"

"Sure."

"This weekend, maybe?" Jeff asked.

"Not this weekend. Sometime. I'll let you know."

"Okay," Megan knew that he was shrugging just by the tone of his voice. "Well, I'll see you tomorrow."

"I'll be there at four. Thanks, Jeff." She hung up the phone.

She would pick up the check from the brokerage house tomorrow. Then, she would take it to the bank and cash it. The note said that she would be contacted with instructions. She would have to let the blackmailer know that she was getting the money, but there would be a slight delay. She wondered what would happen if he demanded the cash immediately.

Megan was so nervous that she was unable to work. Leaving the door to her office closed, she paced the floor staring blankly at the work on her desk until six o'clock. At six she took the papers with her, hoping that she would be able to concentrate enough to complete her work that evening. She had to remember her promotion, she told herself. But what did a promotion mean now—more money to give to a blackmailer? She took the documents with her anyway so that she could not be accused of neglecting her work.

That evening even Holmes was affected by her nervousness, and he paced the apartment with her. She thought of the blackmailer; perhaps she could discover his identity. That would give her some advantage. She was guilty of the shooting, but extortion is also a crime. Perhaps she could force him to leave her alone; she might even be able to find something in his past that would give her an edge. The key lay in discovering who was doing this and exactly how much he knew. It might be nothing more than someone who had heard the shot and seen her run from the site. In that case, he had no real proof and was simply playing games with her.

"I must find out who it is," she told Holmes. "That's my only hope of stopping this."

Megan was startled by the ringing of her cell phone. The caller ID showed "unknown name unknown number." She did not answer. In less than a minute another call came in from "unknown name unknown number," and this time she answered it quickly. "MEGAN

CLEARY," an electronically distorted voice addressed her. "IF YOU EVER IGNORE MY CALLS AGAIN, YOU'LL BE SORRY. DO YOU HAVE THE MONEY?"

Megan could not tell whether the caller was male or female, young or old. "Not yet," she replied nervously. "I'll have it tomorrow."

"I WANT IT NOW!" the robotic sound unnerved her.

"I can't get it today. I'll have it tomorrow after four o'clock."

"THAT'S TOO LATE! GET THE CASH, AND I'LL CALL YOU TOMORROW WITH INSTRUCTIONS. YOU DON'T WANT TO GO TO PRISON, DO YOU?" As Megan tried to think of something she might say to reason with her caller, he ended the call.

"What should I do?" she asked Holmes. "How am I going to get out of this mess?" The electronic voice had made the message seem even more horrible. Her blackmailer did not even seem human; he had taken on a machine-like quality. Whoever he was, he knew everything about her. He knew where she lived, where she worked, and what she had done to protect herself. She, on the other hand, knew nothing about him. She had not learned one thing about the person's identity from the phone call; she was completely on the defensive.

"It's probably a transient who was in a doorway or out on the street when it happened," Megan thought aloud. "It might even be one of the people from the other office buildings who happened to be working late and had looked out the window when he heard me scream." Megan shuddered as a new thought occurred to her. The blackmailer might be someone from her own offices. Although she had briefly entertained the possibility that Anne Sutherland might be the blackmailer, she had not seriously considered the notion that the blackmailer might be someone from her own offices. Now, she thought about this possibility in a new light. She had assumed that the building was empty, but she was not sure of that. Nearly every evening someone worked until at least six-thirty. Perhaps one of them was still there and saw what had happened. That would explain how the blackmailer knew so much about her. It might even be Jack Forbes.

She leapt to her feet and shook her head. "Am I crazy, or paranoid, or both?" she asked. "No one there could hate me enough to do this. Certainly not Jack!" Still, the uncertainty gave her chills; she had to find out once and for all who was responsible. Depressed, she curled up on the couch with Holmes close by and tried to think of a plan to discover the blackmailer's identity.

The following day Megan left work at three-thirty to drive to the brokerage firm where Jeff had her check waiting for her. He wanted her to stay and talk, but she told him that she had another appointment and headed straight for the bank. She had already phoned her account manager and had informed her that she would be bringing the check in. The transaction was completed quickly enough so that she arrived at her office at five-thirty

As Megan walked down the hall, her cell phone rang. The call came in as the now familiar "unknown name unknown number." Entering her office, Megan shut the door and answered her cell.

"DO YOU HAVE THE MONEY?"

"Yes," she replied, "it's all here."

"GOOD. PLACE THE MONEY IN A PACKAGE. TOMORROW MORNING LEAVE IT WITH THE RECEPTIONIST AT THE FRONT DESK, AND TELL HER TO GIVE IT TO THE COURIER WHO WILL COME FOR IT. DO YOU UNDERSTAND?"

"Yes, the receptionist at the front desk. It will be waiting there."

"DO NOT TELL ANYONE WHAT YOU ARE DOING. DO NOT TRY TO FIND OUT WHERE THE MONEY IS GOING, OR I WILL CALL THE POLICE AND TELL THEM WHAT I KNOW. IF YOU WANT TO STAY OUT OF PRISON, DO EXACTLY AS I SAY."

The call ended abruptly. Megan had never felt more alone as she sat staring at the satchel containing the money. So, she was to give the money to a courier. The couriers were a common sight—young men and women on bicycles weaving in and out of traffic for their deliveries. Each day several came to the law offices for pickups and deliveries.

She spent the next hour thinking about what she should do. The blackmailer thought he was very clever, but, perhaps, he had outsmarted himself. The courier who came for her package would wear some sort of badge or jacket identifying the company for which he worked. Further, he would have to sign for the package. Megan would wait for him to arrive and then follow him. The courier would lead her either to the company that the blackmailer had hired to pick up the package or to the blackmailer himself. This newly formulated plan gave her quite a lot more confidence. She might have to pay one fifty thousand dollar sum, but she would be able to quash future blackmail attempts.

Megan looked at her watch. It was six-forty-five. She jumped from her chair; this was the first night in ten months that she had not been out of her office at the stroke of six-thirty. She grabbed her handbag and the papers on her desk and started for the door. Suddenly, she wondered why she was hurrying. Was it even possible for her to get into more trouble than she was in already? After all, the purpose of going home early had been to protect herself against future attacks. She had to smile at the irony; at one time she would have believed that if the day ever came when she was no longer afraid to be at work after closing, it would be a sign that she had completely recovered emotionally. Instead, she could now take more chances because it was inconceivable to her that her situation could get worse.

Howard was waiting for her in the hall. "You want me to walk you to your car?" he asked in the half-hearted tone he always used when Jack was away, and it was his responsibility to escort her to her car.

Megan looked at Howard and remembered her theory about her co-workers. "No, thanks," she replied. Slipping her hand into her purse so that it touched the butt of her gun, she walked out the door alone.

The following morning she left the package with the receptionist. "A courier will pick this up," she said.

"Fine," Marge answered. "I'll give it to him."

She returned to her office and waited. She tried to work, but every time she heard the front door open she rose and went to the doorway of her office to see who was there. The first time it was a client; the next five times various colleagues were coming and going. At last, she saw a young courier walk into the office. Her heart beat faster; this was it. Megan watched carefully.

"I've got a package for Bob Pratt," the courier announced. Disappointed, Megan returned to her desk. To have been so anxious to get his money, the blackmailer was certainly taking his time about collecting it.

All morning she waited for the courier as she tried to finish her work. At two o'clock she had to leave the offices to be in court for an arraignment. As she passed the reception desk, she saw that her package was still waiting to be picked up. She wondered whether anyone would come for it after all.

An hour and a half later Megan returned and saw that the package was gone. She had feared that the courier would come for it after she left; now she felt that the blackmailer had arranged it on purpose. He had been watching the offices to see when she would leave and had called the courier as soon as she was gone. Once again Megan was left defenseless. She had believed that the courier would lead her to her blackmailer, but he had seen through her plan. He was deliberately playing games with her.

"Marge," Megan said to the receptionist, "who picked up my package?"

"The courier, of course," Marge replied without looking up.

"I know," Megan responded, "but which courier? Which company was he from?"

"I don't know; I wasn't paying that much attention."

"Well, can you tell me anything about the person?"

"It was just a kid. They rode up on a bike and came in and got the package."

"Was it a boy or a girl?"

"I don't know."

"Were they black or white, tall or short? Come on, Marge. You must remember something."

For the first time during the conversation Marge looked up at Megan. "We have couriers coming and going all day long. You can't expect me to remember yours out of all those faces. They asked for the package from Megan Cleary, and I handed it to them. I didn't look up. What difference does it make anyway?"

Megan tried to appear unconcerned. "It doesn't make any difference. I just wanted to make certain that the right party came for it, in case there were any questions later on." She started to walk back to her office when she thought of something else. "Marge, the couriers have to sign a log when they pick up packages, don't they?"

"Sure."

"Let me see the log."

Marge handed Megan the log, and she scanned the list of couriers and dates. Just as Marge had said, there had been a number of pickups and deliveries that day. Each courier signed next to the name of the person in the firm for whom the pick up or delivery was made. Megan found the entry she had made in the book that morning, "Package by Megan Cleary for pick up," but no one had signed next to the entry.

"Marge, no one signed for my package."

Marge took the book and looked at the empty signature space. "You're right. How about that? Well, I gave 'em the book and told 'em to sign. I was on the phone, and there was another call coming in. When they handed it back to me, I just assumed it was signed."

"So there's no way that I can find out anything about who picked up the package?" Megan knew the answer already.

"Look, give me the number of whoever was supposed to receive it, and I'll call them to make sure that it got there. What was in it that's so important?"

"That's okay; I'll take care of it," Megan responded. "It was just some legal documents for a client."

Marge laughed, "I'm glad. I was beginning to think that it was a box full of money."

Megan smiled weakly and returned to her office. She couldn't continue to ask questions. She was already calling too much attention to the package and its contents. Shutting her door and picking up her telephone directory, she called all the courier services in the vicinity. She asked each of them if they had picked up any packages from the offices of Pratt, Forbes and Magoff between two o'clock and three-thirty that afternoon. Several confirmed that they had made pick-ups and deliveries to those offices that day but not during that specific period of time. When she had finished making her calls, she knew little more than she had when she started.

The one thing that she did know was that the courier did not work for a courier service. Either the blackmailer had hired someone to pick up the package, or he had picked it up himself. In either case, no one had seen him who could identify him.

Megan had lost again. Everyone seemed to cheat her, to outmaneuver her, to outsmart her. She had thought that when she gained control over her rapist, she would also gain control over her life, but that was not true. The control that the rapist had exerted on her life had been replaced by the merciless grip of another stranger. She was still a victim struggling to be free with no one to help her. Had the entire world gone completely crazy? What kind of person would ignore the screams of a young woman fighting for her life and then blackmail her for shooting her attacker in self-defense?

It made no difference now. She had protected herself and bought this person's silence. Fifty thousand dollars ought to induce him to remain quiet and allow her to go on with her life. Her debt was paid, at least for now.

NINE

Four months passed, and Thanksgiving was approaching. Jennifer wanted Megan to come home early for the holiday. Ian was thrilled about her upcoming promotion, and he wanted to help her make new contacts in the state. The chairman of their political party, who was an old friend of his, was going to be in Buffalo the week before Thanksgiving, and Ian wanted her to take a long holiday in order to meet him. "This is a great stepping stone to a political career," he told her during their weekly phone call. "I can see it now, 'Megan Cleary, Governor of New York.' In a few years you could be President of the United States if we introduce you to the right people and get you started. That's why I want you to meet Fred. With your background and experience you'll impress him as a young woman with a future. It's time you started working for the party so that you can get your name up there."

Megan smiled a little sadly when she heard the enthusiasm in Ian's voice. How was she going to tell her father the truth? "Megan Cleary is never going to have a political career," she told herself bitterly. Even if she were emotionally ready for the challenges of political life, she would never be able to withstand the microscope of public scrutiny. The goals she had set for herself, her dreams and ambitions, all were gone. She had been stripped of everything: her self worth, her dignity, her future. At twenty-nine she had nothing left to look forward to. Since that Monday in December, she had been fighting to keep her head above water; now she realized that she was drowning.

At night she lay awake for hours staring into the darkness. After she had been attacked, the darkness was frightening to her, but now it seemed to be a comforting veil that hid her from the world. Tossing and turning, she pondered a thousand useless questions as she tried to think of what she might have done to spare herself the pain and grief she had endured. "If only I hadn't forgotten those briefs that night," she told herself. "If only I had called the police instead of trying to keep from being caught." Ultimately she heard herself saying, "If only I hadn't worked late that night in December." She had never found the solution; it was as if she were destined to live this nightmare.

When Megan paid the first blackmail demand, she had been certain that others would follow. When she did not hear from the blackmailer again for a few weeks, she hoped that he had forgotten about her. Then, at the end of thirty days she received another phone call demanding an additional fifty thousand dollars. She called Jeff and told him to sell more stock, and in a few days she had the money ready. The instructions were the same as before. She was to leave the money at the reception desk to be given to the courier who would come for it.

This time Megan did not have a court date in the afternoon, and she waited all day for the courier. No one came that day or the following day. The day after that she had to leave the office for a few hours, and while she was gone, the courier came. Again, no one remembered anything about the person who had picked up the package and there was no clue that would allow her to trace the blackmailer.

She and her blackmailer had followed this pattern every thirty days for the past four months. The courier always came when she was away from the office, even if it meant waiting several days for her to leave. She had given up hope of ever discovering her blackmailer's identity. He was, obviously, watching her, but she had no way of finding him. She was always aware that when she stepped out on the street during the days of the pickups, one of the faces belonged to her tormentor. Sometimes she scanned the crowd of passersby hoping to see someone watching her or to recognize a face. Everyone was a suspect—the people in her office, the people in her apartment building, the strangers that passed her on the street. Yet, Megan never saw anyone whom she felt was the right person.

Megan knew only that at the end of November she would receive another phone call, but this time she had nothing left to pay. To compound her other problems, the stock market had been constantly down, and every time she sold stock she took an enormous loss. She had nothing left; she had sold the last of her stocks and her car in order to raise the money to make the October payment. She had talked to a realtor about selling her apartment in the brownstone, but with the housing market depressed it would probably take her at least until the New Year to sell it, and her combined checking and savings accounts totaled less than ten thousand dollars. There was no way that she could make another fifty thousand dollar payment.

"What am I supposed to do?" she asked herself. "I could ask my parents for the money, but they would want to know why I needed it. At any rate, they can't make a fifty thousand dollar payment every month. So that's the end; I've given everything I have, and it still isn't enough. If I had known how this was going to turn out, I would have let him kill me. It would have been so much easier."

The music playing on the radio was interrupted by an advertisement for a Methodist Church. "A man who never appreciated anything was given one million dollars," the pastor began in hushed tones, "and on the same day another man was given ten dollars. The first man stormed that his million would not even begin to cover his needs. 'While you're giving money away, why didn't you make it two million,' he snapped at the giver. But the man who had been given the ten dollars said, 'Oh, thank you, Sir. This will allow me to buy food for my family tonight.' I think too many of us take the first man's approach and forget to be truly thankful for the good gifts that Life gives us. This Thanksgiving remember to count your blessings and be thankful for what you have been given, however insignificant it may seem to others."

"Thankful?" Megan snapped, turning off the radio. "What could I possibly have to be grateful for? A year ago I had everything I wanted: I had two hundred thousand dollars in stocks and a job that I looked forward to every day. Now I'm broke, I'm probably headed for jail, and I can't even work anymore. Every day is a nightmare—I can't concentrate at the office, I don't care what happens to my clients, I don't even care what happens to me. There's no way I can replace Bob Pratt. I can't even stay on top of the job they hired me to do.

"Life has kicked me in the teeth," she continued railing as Holmes stared at her. "I was allowed to be successful just so that I could lose it all to some maniac. I always thought that I was going to get through this, but now I know I'm not. Things are never going to get any better. I'm going to have to tell my father that I can't meet his friend. I can't take the promotion at work, and I can't pay the next blackmail demand. I'm sick of fighting; there isn't even anything left to fight for. I just want to get this over with; I want out of this mess!"

Megan saw her pistol lying on the sofa where she had laid it after arriving home from work that evening. "Maybe there is a way out," she told herself. In a few seconds she could end all of the trouble of the past year. It would be quick and painless—no more wrestling with blackmailers or her parents' ambitions for her. The neighbors would hear the shot and call the police, and the police would find her dead. She picked up the gun and held it in her right hand. It was ironic—the same gun that had brought her all this trouble would also bring her peace.

Holmes licked her hand as if he sensed what she was planning. She stroked the fur around his neck. He had been a good friend, and his company had probably kept her from losing her sanity. If she committed suicide who would take care of him? She ought to leave him with someone, she thought. No, Holmes would be all right. He was obviously expensive and well trained. The police would take him to a shelter where he would be adopted—he might even be sent to live with her parents.

Her parents—she hadn't thought about them. They were the only two people in the entire world whom she truly loved. How could she do this to them? Megan gripped the gun with shaking hands and thought of all they had done for her. They had never denied her anything. If she pulled the trigger, she would be ending their lives as well as her own. They would never recover from her suicide. For the rest of their lives they would blame themselves for not having been able to prevent it.

Suicide was the only thing she could ever remember her parents telling her was a sin. She supposed that it was a product of the Episcopalian-Roman Catholic heritage. Her father once told her that people who commit suicide go to hell. She didn't know whether she believed that; she wasn't sure that she wanted to find out. Perhaps what mattered was that they believed it, and for the rest of their lives they would mourn her soul as well as her death.

Megan wiped away a stray tear rolling down her cheek and put the gun away. "No, I've always been selfish, but this is more selfish than all of the other things I have ever done combined. I've managed to destroy my own life; I won't destroy theirs too."

She called a taxi and then waited downstairs until her cab came to take her to Little Sicily.

Even the festive atmosphere of the busy restaurant did not lift her spirits. She asked the hostess for a table and told her that she wanted to see Mike. In a few moments he appeared.

"What's the matter, Meg?" Mike asked as he sat down next to her. "You look depressed. Over the past four months, you've wilted."

"I am depressed. I don't know; I've had a lot of problems lately. I just feel like I'm losing control of everything."

"What problems?" Mike laughed. "You've got a gorgeous apartment and a great job. In January you're going to be a senior partner. And, if all that weren't enough, you live in the world's greatest city. Oh, Megan, I love it here. New York is everything I always wanted—there's so much to see and buy and do. It's like living in a magical world where the fulfillment of all your desires is right outside your door. I love the hustle and bustle; the crowds, the nightlife—even the traffic."

"I don't," Megan looked at him very seriously. "I can't stand it here anymore. This is all new and exciting to you—just like it was to me when I first came here. Now I'm sick of it. I hate the crowds; I hate the people; I hate the nightlife; I hate my job. New York is killing me—it's strangling the life out of me. I've got to get out of here, Mike."

"Get out of here? What are you talking about? Your whole life is here."

"Not anymore. I don't have a life. All I have is work. I work and pay bills; that's not living. I'm ready to go crazy here; I've got to have a change."

"You need to get out more, see your friends, make some new friends. You don't have to leave New York to do that. The city has millions of people—all you have to do is get out and meet them. The richest, most handsome, most desirable men in the world are living right here. Why don't you go out and find one?

"Get back into your club and start going out with some of your female friends. Join a spa, work out, have a facial, have your hair done, buy some new clothes. Pamper yourself a little, and you'll be amazed how much better the world will look."

"You don't understand," Megan responded. "A new dress or hairdo won't fix what's wrong. The only way anyone could straighten out the mess I've made of my life would be to replace me with a girl who would handle everything differently. Going shopping, having a facial—that's how women cope when some jerk they've been dating dumps them. I've got real problems. My life has been turned upside down; I'm not even sure that I can start over somewhere else. But I know this—as long as I stay here things can only get worse."

Mike looked concerned. "I knew you were upset, but I didn't realize it was this serious. You want to tell me what's bothering you?"

Megan shook her head. "I can't. All I can say is that I have to get away."

"Think about what you're saying. If you pass on this offer to become a senior partner, the opportunity won't come around again for a very long time, and it won't ever come around again with Pratt, Forbes and Magoff. You're twenty-nine years old, and you've already gained a reputation as a young, hotshot attorney. If you drop back into some menial position, you will lose all of the ground you've gained.

In ten years or so when you try to reappear, it won't be the same. People won't remember you, and they won't have any interest in you. Other ambitious young women will be fighting for the best positions, and you'll be crowded out. I just want you to consider this very carefully before you do anything foolish."

"I've already considered it. I'm handing in my resignation tomorrow afternoon."

Mike searched her face for any clue as to what might be driving his cousin's announcement. Finding none, he said, "I guess you've made up your mind. What are your plans?"

"I don't have any."

He paused. "There's a job that you might be right for, but I'm not sure that you'd want it. It's in Buffalo..."

Megan shook her head, "I don't want to move back to Buffalo. I'm going to have a hard enough time explaining this to Mother and Dad as it is. I don't think I want to live in the same town with them; it will just be embarrassing for all of us."

"Look, your problem is that you've shut yourself away from people. I told you that months ago. I know how much you love your family, and I think right now you need to be with them. You're going home for the holidays anyway—right?" She nodded. "Okay, go back to Buffalo, spend the holidays with your parents, and try the job out. If you don't like it, you can always quit."

"I guess that's good advice. Tell me about it."

"It's legal counsel for a non-profit daycare center. The pay's not very good, and you couldn't afford a condo or a great car, but you would be working with good people. The lady who's in charge of the place is an old friend of mine, and they desperately need an attorney to represent them. The people in the neighborhood are broke; it seems like somebody is always trying to make some money by suing the center. They would keep you busy, and the work would take your mind off your problems until you can decide what you want to do with your life."

"A non-profit daycare—for the poor and underprivileged?"

"Exactly! It's located in a very poor neighborhood. A lot of the people from the tenements leave their children there while they work. The state subsidizes part of it and also pays all or part of the cost of leaving the children there. Each family is charged according to their income, but no one is charged more than twenty dollars per week, no matter how many children they have there. The rest comes from private donations.

"It's one of those projects where everybody is encouraged to participate and help themselves and each other. To tell the truth, Megan, I can't really see you there. It's not glamorous, and it won't make you rich or famous. But a lot of the kids are really cute, and their stories are touching. If you really want to get away and experience something new, I think this is the place for you."

Megan thought for a moment. Tenements, slum children, the underprivileged—it did not fit her image of what she wanted for her career. She didn't like children, and she hated the thought of social work. However, it was out of town, and she had to leave. Trying to disguise the contempt she felt, Megan smiled and asked, "When do you think that you could talk to your friend about me?"

"I'll call her first thing tomorrow morning if you'd like. I'm sure she'll be interested. Their last attorney quit six months ago, and they haven't been able to replace him. If she wants to meet you for an interview, when can I tell her you can be there?"

"Right away. Call me tomorrow morning, and tell me what she says. I can leave immediately."

"Fine, I'll let you know as soon as I find something out."

"There's one other thing, Mike. I need for you to do another favor for me."

"What is it?"

"After I'm gone, will you put my apartment up for sale for me? I also need you to ship the furniture and my personal belongings to my parents' address in Buffalo. I'll pay you a commission after the place is sold. Fair enough?"

"Sure, I think I know someone who'd be interested."

"Great. And Mike, if anyone asks about me, please tell them that I went to Florida."

"Florida?" Mike looked at her suspiciously. "Why not the truth?"

Megan smiled at him, "I just want to make a clean break."

The following morning Mike called and confirmed that Linda Pearson was interested and wanted to interview her about the position. From Megan's office she called her parents and told them that she would be arriving in Buffalo in a day or two.

"Wonderful," Jennifer said, "Give us your flight schedule and we'll pick you up at the airport."

"I don't have my schedule yet, but I'll call you and let you know as soon as I do."

After talking with her mother, Megan told Jack's secretary that she needed to see him that afternoon. She then went to the bank and closed her checking and savings accounts, taking the balances in cash. Returning to her office, she cleaned out her desk and straightened up the office. Her files were in order to be taken over by another attorney.

At two o'clock she met with Jack and explained that she was taking her vacation early. Handing him the files she had compiled, she informed him that she would not be returning to work.

"I've been offered a job in a law firm in Florida," Megan told him. "They want me to start immediately."

Jack was stunned. "You're supposed to take over for Bob in January. How could you just walk out on us like this? You're moving to Florida, and you haven't even given us any notice?"

"I'm sorry," Megan said. "The position opened up suddenly, and I have to accept immediately if I'm going to take it. Today is my last day here."

"This is the most unprofessional thing I have ever heard of!" Jack exclaimed. "After all we have done for you, you could have at least had the courtesy to let us know that you were leaving. I believed that you were better than this; I thought that you had the maturity and the professionalism that we needed. I can see now that I was wrong— you weren't at all the right person for a full partnership. Good-bye, Megan." He looked down at the work on his desk and did not speak to her again.

Megan left the office carrying a box containing her personal belongings that she had carefully taped shut so that if she were being watched her blackmailer would not suspect that she had cleared out her desk. She took a taxi to her apartment and spent the remainder of the afternoon packing. Mike would take care of sending the furnishings and the rest of her clothing; she had only to pack clothes for the next few weeks. An hour later two suitcases and an overnight case were packed and waiting by the door of her apartment.

Picking up his brush, she brushed Holmes' fur and then took him for his walk. They then returned to the apartment and waited for nightfall.

At nine o'clock Megan again called a taxi. While they waited, she tucked the cash carefully into the overnight case where she would have easy access. She made certain that the lights were out in her apartment, and she locked the door. She locked the door key in her mailbox, where she had told Mike it would be, and gave the mail key to the lady across the hall, telling her that a friend would come to pick it up. She and Holmes then went downstairs to wait for the taxi.

When they reached the airport, Megan took Holmes and the suitcases and went to the counter of the first airline. "I would like to buy a ticket on the first flight leaving New York City," she told the ticket agent.

"What destination, ma'am?" the agent asked.

"Any destination."

The ticket agent eyed her suspiciously. "The next flight out is going to Boston. It leaves in forty-five minutes."

"That's fine," Megan told her.

She paid cash for her ticket and put Holmes on his flight. By the time everything was ready, she heard the boarding call. "Is this the solution?" she asked herself as she stood in line to board the plane. It might be the man in the gray pinstripe suit holding his briefcase and looking at his watch. It might be the young woman in tight blue jeans and a leather jacket. She had tried to be careful. She had not told anyone where she was going, and she had waited until dark to leave to decrease the chances of being seen. Still, no plan was infallible.

Even if the blackmailer did not know where she had gone, once he determined that she had left, he might call the police. On the other hand, now that she had paid blackmail money, he too could be charged with a crime. Megan did not believe that he would be willing to take that chance. She believed that once she was gone she would be safe. Whatever else she had to face—tenements, dirty children, low wages, her parents' disapproval—it would all be worthwhile just to never again have to hear the electronic voice on the telephone.

The forty-five minute flight to Buffalo took three hours because she had gone first to Boston and then purchased another ticket to take her and Holmes to Buffalo. Tired as she was, Megan thought that the additional travel time was time well spent if it meant that the blackmailer would not be able to trace her steps. When she finally arrived in Buffalo after two A.M. and caught a taxi to her parents' house, she was feeling good about her decision and safer than she had for months.

She had second thoughts the following morning when she told her father that she had quit her job. The next two hours were taken up by his eloquent and impassioned plea for her to return to her job in New York. He was so convincing that, at moments, she wondered what had ever possessed her to leave, and it was only with the utmost effort that she recalled the circumstances of her resignation. Of course, she could not tell her parents any part of what had happened, and since they didn't seem to accept her argument that as an adult she was free to live her life as she chose, she had to listen to their ominous warnings.

"You have to realize, Megan, you won't be young forever," Ian told her in a speech reminiscent of the one Mike had given her. "You're almost thirty years old. In another ten years you'll be an old woman. No one is going to want you. Right now you have an opportunity to move into the best circles. In five years that opportunity will be gone. If you give up your career now to go into social work, you're finished. The years you spent in law school and the years you spent at Pratt, Forbes and Magoff will have been wasted. I think you should reconsider before you throw your life away."

"Dad, I know you want this, and it's important to you…"

"It's not important to me; I won't benefit in any way if you have a great career, and I won't suffer if you don't. All I want is what is best for you. Your mother and I have given up a lot to get you where you are, and I don't want you to throw it away."

"Megan," Jennifer brushed her daughter's hair away from her face, "we want you to be successful because we think that's what will make you happy. Since you were a little girl all you've talked about has been being an attorney and someday being Governor of New

York. You've laid the groundwork to make that happen, but suddenly you act as if none of it matters."

"Maybe in a few years I can go back," Megan said in a conciliatory tone. "Right now I just have to take a break."

"It doesn't work that way," Jennifer argued. "If you drop out now, you won't be able to go back later, even if you want to."

Ian interrupted, "Everything changes when you get old. Nobody's interested in you. They'll promote a young ambitious attorney but not some old woman who dropped out of sight years ago and has nothing to show for it. If you do this, you need to understand that there's no going back."

Ian's warnings were still ringing in Megan's ears as she drove his car to her meeting with the administrator of Safe Haven Daycare Center. "Safe Haven," she thought contemptuously, "What a name! No place in this neighborhood could possibly be either safe or a haven." She surveyed her surroundings; the center was exactly one block from city housing and one block from a large tenement. Though she had grown up in Buffalo, she had never seen the "slums." Crumbling buildings with rags hanging in the windows to afford the occupants some privacy lined the street. Drunks slept in the doorways, and groups of young people with nowhere to go gathered on the street corners. The sidewalks were cluttered and filthy; graffiti covered every wall and trash was piled up in every corner. This wasn't a place she wanted to drive through, much less work in every day. Mike must have a vicious sense of humor to have sent her here.

She reached the parking lot of Safe Haven and stepped out of her car. Someone had smashed a beer bottle against the black top and left the jagged glass. She made a mental note to have someone clean up the parking lot if she took the job. Having broken glass in an area where children would be exposed to it was tantamount to begging for a lawsuit.

Megan studied the building carefully from the outside. The roof had been repaired in so many places that it looked like a patchwork quilt. The red brick was covered with graffiti and the mortar had crumbled and fallen out in many places. The concrete steps were worn and the edges were broken. The building suited its neighborhood—old, untidy and undesirable.

Megan pushed open the front door. Inside, children ranging in age from newborn to ten years filled the room. A few women were looking after them; at one table a woman was teaching pre-schoolers the alphabet, and at another a group of even younger children were being shown how to draw rabbits. The infants were in cribs in another room; Megan could hear their cries. The toddlers played on the floor with an assortment of blocks, dolls, and stuffed animals.

Although the interior was clean, it was not any better cared for than the exterior. Where the walls were not covered with the children's artwork and crayon scribbles, peeling green paint created the illusion that they were ready to splinter into a million pieces and come crashing down on the occupants. A pungent but familiar odor that instantly repelled her permeated the air; she tried to remember where she had smelled it before. "A hospital," she suddenly realized. "This room smells like a hospital. It must be the disinfectant."

"You need some help?" one of the attendants asked cheerfully.

"Yes, I'm Megan Cleary. Linda Pearson is expecting me." The attendant smiled, but as she turned toward Pearson's office, she rolled her eyes and looked toward heaven as if to say, "Hey, God, I think this is the wrong lawyer for us."

A tiny hand tugged at the hem of Megan's coat, and she looked down. A small child stood with her arms extended upward. Megan studied the little girl. She had the most beautiful face Megan had ever seen. She guessed that the child was Puerto Rican; her skin was the color of pale honey, and her hair, eyebrows and lashes were blue-black. She peered expectantly at Megan through liquid black eyes and shaped her rosy little mouth into a perfect "o".

Megan stood staring at the child. "Hello," she finally said. Still the little girl stood silently looking at her and reaching upward.

"Maria wants you to pick her up," one of the women said.

Megan looked uncomfortable—she had never held a baby before. Bending down, she put her arms around Maria and lifted her up. The little girl smiled and with her tiny hands patted Megan's blonde curls. In a few moments she began to squirm and pull away, and Megan set her back on the floor.

"I see that you're getting acquainted with some of our children," a voice said behind her. Megan turned to see a woman about her age with short unkempt brown hair wearing blue jeans and a sweat shirt. "I'm Linda Pearson," she smiled and stuck out her hand in a friendly fashion.

"How do you do, I'm Megan Cleary."

"I'm glad to see that you're punctual. Come into my office where we can talk."

Megan followed Linda into a very small office and sat down opposite her in a dusty vinyl chair. "That's a beautiful little girl," she commented.

"From the shoulders up," Linda answered. Megan looked surprised, and Linda continued. "When she was six months old, her father dipped her in boiling water, and it left her entire body badly scarred. Only her face was untouched—it's incredible that she's still alive."

"That's horrible! I hope he's in prison."

"He is. Maria's mother works to support herself and the baby, and Maria stays here with us. I'm surprised that she would let you pick her up; in the three months she's been with us she hasn't wanted anyone to touch her. You're the first person she's responded to.

"Now," Linda continued, "let's get down to business. You're applying for the position of legal counsel?" Megan nodded. "Your cousin Mike told me a lot about you. He said that you were a junior partner in a big law firm in New York City, but you decided to leave. May I ask why?"

"Personal reasons," Megan answered carefully. "I needed a change."

"Well, this is about as far as you can get from a high powered law practice in New York. Why do you want to work here, specifically?"

"I became an attorney in order to help people," Megan lied. "I didn't feel that my former position allowed me to do that as completely as I wanted to. Here I will be able to put my talents to work for the community, and I think that will be very rewarding."

"I'm afraid that the only rewards you'll find here are emotional, and even those are negligible." Linda looked critically at the pampered young woman in her cashmere coat and Manolo Blahnik boots. Megan's long, manicured fingernails tapped lightly against the arms of her chair.

"Megan, I want to be honest with you. Social work is very demanding, both physically and emotionally. Basically, you'll be just a social worker who happens to have a law degree. Most of the cases you will handle will be neither challenging nor rewarding. They will involve some parent suing us because after they come home from a three day drunk, they decide that we haven't given their child good enough care in their absence. In addition, you'll have to research grants and help us petition the state for funding. You'll also have to go into the business community with your hand out to get donations from them.

"At first, you'll feel sorry for most of the people you encounter here—until you hear their stories and find out that nearly all of them caused their own problems. Much of the time you'll feel tired and overwhelmed. Eventually, you'll become cynical and decide that these people can't really be helped. The only thing that will keep you going is the hope that you can help one or two of these kids break free and make something of their lives. Do you think you're ready to handle that?"

"I think so, and I do believe that I can be an asset to you."

"Good. Mike had only good things to say about you, and that gives me some confidence. When he was here, he was very instrumental in helping us get the funding to add new workers. I must confess, though, you're nothing like I expected. I can't understand why you would choose to leave a promising career for this."

"We all have to do whatever fulfills our personal needs. Why did you choose social work?"

Linda laughed. "I wanted to become a psychiatrist, but I couldn't afford to. I became a psychologist instead. When I finished school, setting up a private practice was too expensive. They offered me this job, and I took it. It's only temporary, though. I'm getting out of here just as soon as I can."

Megan smiled faintly. She wanted to add, "Me too," but that didn't seem appropriate so she kept quiet.

"You can start right now," Linda told her. "Your office is just down the hall, to your right. Your predecessor left files he hadn't even started working on, and during the past six months we've added to them. No one knows what's what. I imagine it'll take you quite a while to sort through it all."

She followed Linda down the hall to a room approximately the size of a large closet. The desk and the floor held boxes of papers. Megan stood silently in the doorway staring at the smallest, ugliest, darkest office she had ever seen—it didn't even have a window. Taking off her coat, she searched for a place to hang it. Not finding one, she laid it across the back of a chair and began to drag the boxes off the desk. When it had been cleared, the desk proved to be a scratched, scuffed piece of dusty furniture that must have been purchased second hand. She needed to wash it and swab it with lemon oil, but she had neither soap nor oil. Anyway, she would ruin her suit if she attempted to clean up this little hovel. Wiping some of the dust off the orange vinyl chair with a paper towel she found in the bathroom, she sat down in her new office and wondered whether she ought to laugh or cry.

That night when she returned to her parents' house, she was not eager to respond to their questions of, "How was your day?" She wanted to tell them that her day was horrible. She had been in the worst place, with the worst people she had ever encountered, but if she admitted the truth, they would respond with, "I told you so," and she could not face that. Her only understanding listener was Holmes, and since Jennifer was adamant about not allowing him in the house, Megan went out to the garage to chat with him.

"This is worse than I imagined," she told him. "I could just wring Mike's neck for getting me into this mess. I can't even hear myself think in that place. How am I supposed to concentrate on figuring out this mess of paperwork the last attorney left behind when children are crying and fighting all around me? This afternoon one of the little brats threw a temper tantrum and screamed for an hour."

"Linda introduced me to the other women in the center. One of them is a social worker from the neighborhood who says she came back to help the people of the community. I don't understand her; I don't understand any of them. I have to do this because I'm a victim of circumstances, but I don't know why anyone would choose to work here when they can do something else. All this talk about helping people is nonsense. The only person I want to help is me, and if they were honest, they would admit that's true for all of the rest of them too.

"The other women aren't social workers; they're mothers from the neighborhood who work there so that they can watch their children. They seem nice enough, I guess. I don't have anything in common with them, though. They're from the barrio; they have no education; they've never known success. They're used to filth and squalor and poverty and crying children. I'm not; I'm educated, and I've had money. I know what it is to enjoy art and music and the theatre. People talk all the time about how hard it is for the poor, but I think it's much harder for people who have had everything and then seen it all taken away. People who have never had anything don't know what they've missed." She hugged Holmes and then rose from the floor and went inside to say good night to her parents.

The following morning she went to work more suitably dressed in slacks and a sweater. She took with her a small bottle of Murphy's Oil to clean her desk and the worn paneling on her walls. On her way she stopped and bought new folders and the few office supplies she would need to get her filing done. Her father dropped her off at Safe Haven.

"If this is going to be a permanent arrangement, you'll have to get your own car," he told her.

"I know. I'll take care of it this weekend. I'm also going to have to get my own place."

"Why? Your mother and I love having you with us. Anyway, Buffalo is expensive, and you're not making the kind of money you used to. You would be much better off living at home for a while."

"I have to try to get myself re-established, Dad. I adore you and Mother, but as long as I stay with you, I will always feel like a child living under your roof again. I have to get control of my life, and part of that is having my own place."

"Whatever," he replied. "You've always done exactly what you wanted to anyway. I know it won't be any different this time."

Megan sensed the frustration in Ian's tone, and it hurt her to know that she had been such a disappointment to her parents. She knew that they would view her leaving as a sign of personal rejection. Certainly they did not intend for her to live with them forever, but they had expected that she would want to stay in their home at least through the New Year. Yet, she feared that if she stayed longer she would begin to tell them everything that had happened to her. At times she felt so close to them and so lonely for someone with whom she could talk. She wanted to tell them why she had left New York so suddenly; she hated not being able to share with them the most important events of her life. Yet, she knew that she could not. If she confided in them, she would be making them a party to all that she had done during the last year. They probably believed that she was still suffering from the trauma of having been raped, and that she had resigned from Pratt, Forbes and Magoff for that reason. She must never give them cause to believe otherwise, and it was only through distance that she could keep her secret.

Her father left her in the parking lot of Safe Haven, and she walked through the door carrying the bags containing the supplies she had purchased. As she entered, the other women greeted her pleasantly.

"Good morning," she responded. She set the bags down and took off her coat. Out of the corner of her eye she saw Maria rise from her play and toddle over to her.

"Good morning, Maria," she smiled at the little girl. The child lifted her arms and waited expectantly. Picking her up, Megan wrapped her arms around the child's small body and held her close. Again, Maria reached out to pat Megan's hair, and then she touched her face. Megan brushed away the wave of black hair that had fallen against Maria's forehead, and the two smiled at each other. Soon Maria became restless and began to squirm. Megan returned her to the floor, picked up her bags and walked into her office.

By afternoon her office was relatively neat. After hours of sorting through boxes, she had identified and filed most of the information. When the filing was finished, the real work would begin—reviewing all of the files and putting everything into good legal order.

Megan leaned back in her chair and stretched. It was early afternoon, but she thought that she had never been so tired. Always before clerks and assistants and interns had done most of the unpleasant work for her. Never in her life had she encountered such a mess. Any attorney who would leave unmarked documents stacked in boxes ought to be disbarred, she thought.

A baby was crying in the next room. She suspected that afternoon tantrums were a ritual at Safe Haven. The older children appeared to be playing tag indoors—she could hear running and laughing in the main room. Two little boys had gotten into an argument in the hall outside her door and were yelling at each other. How would she ever be able to work amid all of this bedlam?

The shouts from the little boys grew louder. "You pushed me!"

"Did not!"

"Liar."

"Stupid."

Megan opened her door just as the first little boy gave the second one a shove that sent him flying back into her office. Megan grabbed his arm and pulled him to his feet. "Both of you stop it right now," she scolded. "This is a daycare, not juvenile hall. Decent people are trying to work, and I'm not going to have you shouting and pushing each other. Now get back in the other room where you belong; I don't want to hear from you again this afternoon." The two culprits looked shocked and silently slinked back to their play area.

She had no sooner sat down behind her desk than she heard a knock on her door. She opened the door for Carmen, the social worker from the neighborhood who had returned to give something back to the community.

"I see that you made an impression on Carlos and Gilbert," she smiled. "They came back to the play area quieter than I've seen them for a long time."

"I only told them to stop fighting," Megan replied. "Surely they've heard that before."

"It wasn't what you said; it was the way you said it."

"You heard me?"

"Of course, we all did. You were right to break up the fight— they're at a difficult age, and they argue nearly every day. But, it takes patience to work with children, and especially these children. You mustn't be too cross with them, Megan. More than anything else they need love."

"Tough love, maybe," Megan retorted jokingly.

"All love is tough. Few things take the strength and energy that it requires, and to love the unloved requires the greatest strength of all. These children have been exposed to such terrible things. Poverty, crime, divorce all take their greatest toll on children. They live in a neighborhood most people are afraid to walk through. They grow up around drugs and violence. They go to schools where the older children carry weapons. Most of the time they come home to empty houses. Many of them are being raised by single moms who are alcoholics or addicts. Their fathers are dead or in jail or disappeared years ago. Like Maria, many of them have been the victims of child abuse. They are largely forgotten—welfare provides some of their material needs, and social workers compile statistics about them, but no one really cares what happens to them. That's why the center is important. We keep the children safe and fed while their parents are working, but we also let them know that someone loves them. That's the most important thing we give them. Only three things last—faith, hope and love, and the greatest of these is love."

Megan smiled but said nothing. Though naïve, it was a nice philosophy that Carmen preached. Unfortunately, she knew that life just didn't work that way. No amount of love could conquer real suffering. No matter how loved the children felt at the center, they still went home to their same wretched lives.

Carmen seemed to sense her skepticism because she changed the subject. "I wanted to invite you to a meeting on Wednesday night at Mother Harriet's."

"Who?"

"Mother Harriet. I think her real name is Harriet Porter, but ever since I can remember, everyone's called her Mother Harriet. She's been a widow for thirty years, and she's spent most of that time helping others. She lives on social security and widow's benefits from her husband's pension, but she gives most of that money to people in this neighborhood and to Safe Haven. She provides a sort of free counseling service for the people around here. The kids go to her when they get into trouble, and they tell her things they don't feel comfortable telling their parents. She listens to their problems and offers her advice. They know that she won't tell their secrets, so everyone trusts her. She's a wonderful person, Megan; I know you'd like her."

"I'm sure I would. Maybe I'll see her around here sometime."

"No, she's very old, and she's blind. She almost never leaves her house. But on Wednesdays she has a little meeting for anyone who wants to come. We each bring a few refreshments, and we talk. There's a prayer service and Bible study, too. It's nice. You should come."

"Thank you for inviting me," Megan tried to sound pleased, "but I'm afraid that I already have plans for Wednesday evening."

Carmen nodded. "It's okay. If you change your mind, let me know. Right now I have to get back to work." She rose and left Megan's office.

"A prayer meeting at a blind woman's house," Megan thought. "What could be more depressing?"

Megan was delighted when the clock finally struck six. Picking up her coat, she walked out of her office and into the nursery to wait for her father. As she waited, she saw that two children still had not been picked up by their parents. Carmen was putting their coats on them.

"It's late," Megan said, "I thought all the children would be gone by now. Do you think their mother forgot about them?"

"No," Carmen responded, "she gets off work at five o'clock. Her job is fifteen minutes from here; when she's going to come for them, she's here by five-thirty at the latest. She's either high, or she's brought home a man, or both."

"Where will they go if no one comes to get them?" Megan asked.

"I take them home with me," Carmen told her. "They'll spend the night at my house until their mother finally comes for them."

Megan was surprised. "That's very generous of you. Do parents often fail to pick up their children?"

"Fairly often," Carmen answered. "It depends on the parent. This woman disappears for a few days about once a month. I think she gets enough money for drugs and takes about three days to enjoy them. Sometimes the mothers don't come because they've been arrested for drugs or prostitution, but most of the people here love their children and take good care of them."

Carmen led the children to the door. "Do you need us to drop you somewhere?" she asked Megan as she took the keys from her purse.

"No thank you. My father's coming for me."

Carmen said good night and walked the children to her car. It was old and dented, and Megan heard the engine sputter when she turned on the ignition. Just then Ian drove up in his new Mercedes, and Megan rushed to get in.

On Saturday Megan bought a car using part of her savings for a down payment. It was a new Honda Accord, a practical car with a good engine, but she could not help making comparisons between it and the Jaguar she had previously owned. Every comparison only served to heighten her sense of loss—not just of the vehicle, but of an entire lifestyle that had been ripped from her.

She also began looking for an apartment, and it proved to be difficult to find one. She finally settled for a clean but modest one bedroom with a parking space. After signing the lease she had special locks and a security system installed. Mike had sent her personal belongings and furniture, and they were packed safely in a storage facility in Buffalo. Everything was ready for her to move right after Thanksgiving. She would again have her own place, and Holmes would no longer be banished to her parents' garage.

The following week was a short one as it included Thanksgiving. Megan looked forward to the holiday as a break from her job—she had always loved the holidays, and she hoped that they would lift her spirits. At work she felt that she was beginning to learn her way around, and in spite of her inherent prejudice against the underprivileged, she was making a new friend. Every morning Maria greeted her by insisting that she pick her up. Megan was growing attached to the child, and soon she began taking a few toys from the nursery into her office and allowing Maria to play on the floor while she worked.

She also discovered that Maria was one of the main culprits in the afternoon crying jags—she did not want anyone except Megan to touch her. When the other women tried to care for her, she cried and pulled away from them, and she refused to play with the other children. With Megan, however, she was content at all times, and Megan discovered that by keeping Maria nearby she not only pleased the little girl, but she achieved some of the peace and quiet she sought.

Busily sorting documents and organizing material, Megan hardly had time to notice the little girl who played on the floor. As she moved from her desk to the file cabinet one afternoon she noticed Maria frowning as her tiny hands slapped her sides. Setting the files on top of the cabinet, Megan knelt to look at the child.

"What's the matter, Maria? You look so unhappy." Maria continued to frown and fuss. Megan looked at her carefully and noticed that her diaper was drooping badly. "You must need changing," Megan observed.

"Marla," she walked to the play area and called one of the mothers who worked there. "Maria needs to have her diaper changed."

"Just a minute," came the reply.

A short time later the door to Megan's office opened and Marla entered carrying a stack of diapers, a packet of disposable wipes, and a tube of diaper rash ointment. "There you go," she smiled as she turned and left the room.

"Wait!" Megan called. "What am I supposed to do with these? I want you to change her."

"Can't. I'm busy taking care of other kids. Anyway, Maria don't want nobody but you touchin' her."

"But, Marla, I don't know how to change a baby. I've never done it before."

"It's time you learned if you're gonna work here. There's not much to know. You take the old diaper off; you put a new one on. You're a smart girl; you'll figure it out." Marla left smiling sweetly.

Megan rose from her desk. Was it just her imagination or did she sense a trace of sarcasm in Marla's voice? Taking a diaper from the stack, she got down on her knees and undressed Maria.

Repulsion mingled with horror swept over her when she saw the little girl's body. The beautiful honey-colored complexion that Megan so admired was marred by purple scars. From her toes to her armpits the little girl was covered with thick, reptilian-looking skin. Megan remembered Linda having said that Maria's father had dipped her in boiling water when she was a baby, but she was not prepared for the massive damage that he had done to his child. Fury rose in her; prison was not punishment enough for someone who would commit such an act.

She put the clean diaper on Maria and dressed her. Pulling the child close to her, Megan thought of the scars on her own body—

knife wounds that would forever remind her of the crime that had been committed against her. The two of them had something in common. Yet, Megan knew that she was much more fortunate than Maria. Megan's father had been kind to her and had given her as much as any parent could. Regardless of what she might have suffered at her attacker's hands, she would always have his love—no stranger could hurt her as much as Ian had helped her. Maria had no one—she had been attacked by her own father. No one else could ever help her as much as he had hurt her. Only a few months ago Megan might have been this man's legal defense; she might have advised him to plead temporary insanity and persuaded the court to let him go with minimal psychiatric care.

Megan had mourned the loss of her career as most people mourn the loss of a loved one. For the first time, she wondered whether that career had even been worthwhile. She missed the prestige that came with her job; she missed her income and her friends; and she certainly missed her lifestyle. Still, as she knelt on the floor of that tiny, dark office holding Maria in her arms, she experienced a warmth and tenderness that she had never felt at Pratt, Forbes and Magoff.

Later that day Marla again came into her office. "I guess you're looking forward to tomorrow," she said to Megan.

"Oh, yes! I just love the holidays. How about you—do you have something special planned?"

"Sure. It's one of the few days that I get to spend with all my kids. We're gonna have dinner and see the parade. It'll be nice. I just wish everybody had a family to be with tomorrow."

"I think that most families get together for Thanksgiving and Christmas," Megan commented. She wondered whether all of the mothers would come for their children this evening or if Carmen would have unintended company for Thanksgiving dinner.

"We're getting together a Thanksgiving basket to take over to Mother Harriet this evening," Marla began. "She never has nothin' of her own because she gives it all away, so every year we all put in some money and buy her a turkey and dressing and cranberries—the usual meal. Would you like to chip in?"

The honest answer to her question was, "no," but Megan was embarrassed to refuse. Since her first day there she had heard everyone sing Mother Harriet's praises. According to urban legend, Mother Harriet was the sweetest, kindest, gentlest, most generous saint ever to lend a hand to the poor. She could not very well say, "I'm sure she's wonderful, but I don't care whether she has dinner tomorrow or not." Everyone at the center knew that Megan's family was prosperous. They had seen her father's car when he picked her up from work, and even the "casual" slacks and sweaters she wore to work were designer labels. If these women who had nothing were contributing, she could not justify refusing to help.

"I'd be delighted to," Megan answered as she forced a smile. "I'll give an equal part along with everybody else."

"Good. We're gonna leave here at six and go shopping for her, and then we'll make it over to her house about seven. We always have a little prayer meeting on Wednesday nights—it's a good time for fellowship."

"I don't think I can stay for the prayer meeting, but I'll certainly enjoy meeting her."

Marla looked at Megan understandingly, "That's okay. We're glad you're coming."

When Marla left her office, Megan called Jennifer to tell her that she would be late. She knew that her mother was a little disappointed, and she promised to come home as soon as she could.

Participating in the cost of the Thanksgiving meal for Mother Harriet would help the other women accept her, Megan reasoned. Carmen, Marla, Patricia, Veronica, and Rachel would see that she did not think of herself as "too good" for the community. Mother Harriet might even be impressed enough with her generosity to say a few kind things about her. After all, she had never met the woman, yet, she was giving her money and time to help her. More important, by going Megan would be relieving herself of the pressure the women had put on her to meet Mother Harriet. In the future when they mentioned Mother Harriet—as they did every Wednesday when they tried to convince Megan to accompany them to the prayer group—she could say that she had met her and that she thought the old woman was "wonderful." She could then politely excuse herself from any further involvement in the prayer group. To be free of their harassment was certainly worth a few dollars and a couple of hours of her time.

The women arrived at Mother Harriet's house a little after seven o'clock. Megan had been sure that they were buying too much food for one old woman, but when she expressed her concerns, she was told that Mother Harriet would most certainly invite other lonely people from the neighborhood to have dinner with her, and there must be plenty of food for all. Though annoyed at the thought that the food she had purchased would be given away to a group of undeserving strangers, she smiled resolutely and determined to be as gracious as possible.

Mother Harriet's home was a small detached residence at the end of a block of tenements. Like the other buildings in the area, it was old and dilapidated. The roof bore the same patchwork of repairs as the other buildings, and the tiny yard was strewn with litter that passersby had carelessly tossed onto her property.

"Whose turn is it to sweep Mother Harriet's yard?" Marla asked.

Veronica replied, "It's Marco's, I think. I'll tell him to get out here Friday morning and get it done."

Carmen turned to Megan. "Once a week one of the neighborhood boys cleans up the yard for her. They also look in on her to see if she needs anything."

"They don't mind doing her yard work free?" Megan looked surprised. She would not trust the boys in the neighborhood to do something she paid them to do, and she would know better than to expect a service to be performed without charge.

"It's not free, really," Carmen replied. "Mother Harriet has done a lot for them. At one time or another, she has helped every kid in the neighborhood. In a way, they are just paying her back a little bit of what she's given them."

The door opened to Marla's knock and revealed a tiny, frail black woman holding a cane.

"Hello, Mother Harriet," Carmen said.

"Hi, Carmen!" the old woman responded joyfully. "Who's with ya?"

"Veronica, Marla, Patricia, Rachel, and Megan Cleary, the new girl at the center I told you about."

"I remember," Mother Harriet groped for Megan's hand, and when it was finally given, she squeezed it in her own. "Come on in children," she said. "It's cold outside. The other folks is already here."

They stepped through the doorway and into Mother Harriet's living room. Megan guessed that someone in the neighborhood also donated housekeeping services, for the place was relatively clean and certainly too neat to have been kept by a blind woman.

"We brought you Thanksgiving dinner," Patricia said. "There's turkey and dressing, and a pie for dessert."

"Thank ya, Jesus!" the old woman clapped her hands. "The Lord always provides! I done invited six people to eat with me tomorra, and here I was wondering what I was gonna feed 'em with."

"We figured as much," said Veronica. "There's plenty here for everyone."

"Well, that's good," Mother Harriet smiled as she took her seat.

Megan was shocked. "The Lord always provides," she repeated the old woman's comment in her head. Was that all she had to say? She and the other women at the daycare had provided this meal; it seemed to Megan that Mother Harriet ought to be thanking them.

Megan studied the woman about whom she had heard so much. Less than five feet tall with withered black skin stretched over frail bones, Mother Harriet was one of the most unappealing people Megan had ever seen. Her large sightless eyes darted aimlessly around the room, and though Megan pitied her for her blindness, she thought that the lack of expression in the old woman's eyes made her look insane. Her white hair was cut short and formed a fuzzy white cap on her head. Her youth spent in the Deep South was apparent in her speech, and when she became excited, she clapped her hands. She reminded Megan of a grotesque voodoo doll. The fact that the people in this community followed after her as though she were the Virgin Mary showed how desperate they were.

Even though her senses were offended, Megan had to admit that there was something sweet and guileless about Mother Harriet. In spite of having lived most of her life in a neighborhood filled with crime and vice, the old woman seemed uncorrupted by her surroundings. Lacking the education and sophistication that are the products of affluence, she also lacked the pretensions that accompany social status. Though she lived alone in poverty and darkness, Mother Harriet beamed with the joy of living. Her unabashed happiness caused Megan to wonder whether she had the intellect to know that she ought to be resentful about the lot life had dealt her. Yet, simple or bright, good or bad, Mother Harriet was totally genuine and sincere. It would never occur to her to try to hide her problems or to put on a show for others. Her openness and enthusiasm reminded Megan of the pathetic children at Safe Haven. Mother Harriet behaved as though she were one of these children grown old, having had nothing in her youth and expecting nothing in her twilight years.

"I's so grateful that we can all be together like this tonight," Mother Harriet was saying to the group that had assembled in a semi-circle of chairs around her. "Nobody's been real sick or hurt; we've all got a place to stay. How many of ya know the Lord's been good to ya this year?" Everyone except Megan said, "Amen." Mother Harriet clapped her hands again. "Hallelujah! How many of ya believe the Lord will take care of ya next year?" Another chorus of "Amen!" was heard. "Tomorra's Thanksgivin' and we think on all the good things God's done for each of us. Let's go 'round the room now and hear from each of you 'bout the good things God's done this past year that you's grateful for. Marla, you start."

"This won't take long," Megan thought as she looked around the room at the ragged, wretched group congregated in the miserable little house. Nothing very good had ever happened to any of them, or they wouldn't be there. To her surprise, everyone found not just one thing for which to be thankful, but several. One woman was thankful that her son had come home and that he was off drugs and had not been in jail for six months. A man was thankful that he had found work and he and his wife were back together. Several were thankful for their jobs, their children and the company of their friends. A newly married couple was thankful for each other and for the baby she was expecting. But the most touching was a young mother whose three children sat at her feet. "I'm just so thankful that we got a place to live this year, and I'm not out on the street with my kids no more."

When Megan's turn came, there was a long silence. It was not that she wanted to create a scene; she simply could not think of anything for which she was thankful. The past year had been the worst of her life, and to pretend that she had anything good to remember was a travesty. Finally, seeing that she had to say something, she blurted out, "I'm grateful that I've been able to come back to Buffalo to visit with my mother and dad."

The statements of gratitude continued around the room until, at last, Mother Harriet's turn came. "I'm grateful for this house and for each of these people here in it tonight. I'm grateful to be a part of this community and to know the people here—they's been such a blessing to me. Mostly, I'm grateful for Jesus and the life He gives to all of us. Ain't no better life than the one we got in Him."

"Ya know children, we's so blessed," she continued. "There's people that don't know 'bout the Lord, and we need to remember them tonight and tomorra. We need to remember them that don't got no place to live, and the ones that can't get no work. Let's make special mention of 'em in our prayers tonight. There's refreshments in the kitchen; why don't everybody get somethin' and talk to each other for a minute, and then we'll have our prayer and Bible service."

Seizing the opportunity, Megan rose from her chair. "I really must go," she told Mother Harriet. "I'm already late."

The sightless eyes darted about even more rapidly. Mother Harriet reached out her withered hand and took Megan's. "All right, Child. Go if ya must, but 'fore ya do, I'm gonna pray for ya."

A startled Megan did not know how to respond. She wanted to refuse, but Mother Harriet was already rising from her chair and pushing Megan down into it. Putting her hands on Megan's head, Mother Harriet began to pray, but Megan did not hear the words. She was aware only of her own annoyance. This ignorant old woman tried to take control over every situation. She acted as though she had authority over Megan. Obviously, she did not understand that it was very rude to insist on praying for a total stranger, particularly in a room filled with other strangers. Megan had nothing in common with any of these people, and she realized that she had made a serious mistake by coming. Talking with Carmen and the other women at Safe Haven, she had been aware of the vast differences, but in the presumptuous old matriarch she saw the reasons that she would never be able to really be a part of Safe Haven or these people's lives. They were unwilling to leave her alone; they insisted on dragging everyone down to their level.

When she finally heard the old woman say, "Amen," and felt the hand lift from her head, Megan jumped from the chair and hastily said good-bye to Mother Harriet and the other women. Picking up her coat, she fled from the tiny house as though pursued by devils, determined that she would never return.

The following day should have been a happy one for Megan, but she was not at peace. She sensed tension in the Cleary household, but she was not certain whether she was the cause or merely feeling its effects. Waking in her childhood room on Thanksgiving morning gave her a strange feeling, though she always came home for Thanksgiving and had already been living with her parents for two weeks. Gazing out the window to see the snow piled up beside the house, she remembered that cold morning last January when she had looked out this window before catching her plane back to New York. For the first time, she did not feel a sense of sorrow that New York was no longer her home; she was haunted, instead, by a feeling of estrangement from her surroundings. It was as though the holiday, her parents' home, her job at Safe Haven, and the events of the night before were all part of some bizarre illusion.

Megan helped her mother with the pumpkin pies and then sat down to watch part of a Thanksgiving Day parade on television. Later she and her parents went for a walk and then returned home for dinner. Jennifer's mood was especially cheerful, and even Ian behaved as though he were in high spirits.

When they sat down together at the polished mahogany table, carefully set with crystal and fine china, Megan looked critically at the exquisite room. It was warm and comfortable, and the aroma of holiday cooking filled the air. A fire crackled in the fireplace. It was a scene straight from a Norman Rockwell painting. Father, mother, daughter—a perfect family enjoying the holidays together. Yet, Megan did not feel like celebrating.

Her thoughts unwillingly returned to the previous evening. Twenty or more people had crowded into a hovel recalling their blessings. They had nothing in their lives except misery and hardship. Mother Harriet's statement forced itself back into her mind, "Ain't no better life than the one we got in Him," and she remembered the little woman clapping her hands eagerly.

"What life?" she asked herself. Those people had no life; they merely survived. They had no future, no possibility of ever having anything better. Megan was a thousand times better off than they. Whatever her personal problems, she still had a beautiful home and two wonderful parents. Even now, at the worst time in her life, she had more than those people could ever hope for, but she was miserable. How could they be happy with nothing?

When Maria was older, what would she celebrate on Thanksgiving, Megan wondered. If she belonged to Mother Harriet's group she might sit in the circle of chairs and give thanks for her mother or the tenement apartment where she lived. She would never mention the scars or the grief that her father had caused her. She would go through her life counting small blessings but overlooking major difficulties. Such an approach was not wise; it probably was not even mentally healthy. Surely it would be better for Maria to be honest—to stand and say that her father had ruined her life and that she had nothing for which to be thankful. Megan, herself, had been forced to lie by saying that she was grateful to be back in Buffalo when that was the last place she wanted to be. No matter what those people might believe, nothing good could come from a meeting where people were forced to hide behind a mask of false hope and joy.

TEN

The Saturday after Thanksgiving Megan moved into her apartment. The disappointment was apparent on her parents' faces the day she left, but she was relieved to be moving to a home of her own. Holmes was also happy to move out of the Clearys' garage.

Never-the-less, leasing the apartment gave a certain finality to her move to Buffalo. She had run away from New York to escape her blackmailer; now she was running away from her parents to escape feelings she did not understand. She wondered whether she would ever stop running.

The heavy locks on her door and the security system made her feel safer, but they also seemed to shut her away from the rest of the world. Living with her parents had made her realize that she missed human companionship. She had become accustomed to the aroma of breakfast cooking when she awoke each morning and to having her mother there when she came home at night. Although she had lived alone for years, the time spent with her parents had made her aware that she was lonely.

She wondered whether she had made the right decision in moving out of their house.

She consoled herself that Christmas was quickly approaching and she and her parents would be repeating their usual rituals. She noted all of the December engagements on her calendar, but one date overshadowed them all.

On the morning of December 5 Megan woke depressed. She still vividly recalled every detail of that evening exactly one year ago. December 5 would always live in her mind as one of the most heinous dates in history. On the one-year anniversary of her attack she remembered the lamentations of Job that she had been required to memorize as a child in Sunday school. "Let that day perish…let not God regard it from above, neither let the light shine upon it…let it not be joined unto the days of the year, let it not come into the number of the months." Yes, Megan thought, if she had the power to do so she would have December 5 stricken from every calendar and written record so that it could never be remembered.

She soon realized, however, that she could not even strike the date from her own memory. The other women at Safe Haven had no idea what she was dealing with that day. Even her parents did not seem to associate the date with the event.

Driving to work, she had fantasies of coming across the mythical time warp and traveling back through it to that morning a year before. If only she had a way to go back, to change that one day, her life would be permanently altered. At times the inexpressible grief that she had felt after her first attack washed over her, and at other times she felt oddly detached and logical. How strange to think that the simple act of working late one evening could change the course of a person's life.

Absorbed in her own thoughts, Megan did not notice one of the older youths from the neighborhood leaving a baby at the center. She would not have seen him at all if the other women had not appeared so surprised by his presence. "Linda had an early class today," he told Carmen. "I told her I'd drop Beto off for her. I'll be back this evening to pick him up so she can study."

"Good," Carmen responded. "I'm glad to see that you're taking more interest."

The youth shrugged, "I've been talking to Mother Harriet, and I've decided that maybe I should take more responsibility for him. He's my kid too."

When the boy left, Carmen turned to Megan. "It's good to see him here like this. A year ago when Linda found out she was pregnant he wouldn't even discuss the baby."

"Mother Harriet changed his mind?" Megan asked skeptically.

"She had a lot of talks with both of them. Mother Harriet persuaded Linda to keep the baby. She's been talking to Manny about it ever since, and it looks like he's starting to come around."

"What did she say to them?"

"Nobody knows. Mother Harriet wouldn't even have told anyone that she was talking to them if they hadn't told everyone first. It's sorta like going to a priest; anything you say to her is held in confidence. By the way, we missed you at our last meeting."

Megan took a couple of steps towards her office. "I've been moving, and I was tied up."

"I hope you'll come again soon," Carmen urged.

"Sometime," Megan called over her shoulder as she entered her office and shut the door.

She sat at her desk without any desire to begin work. From the day she had started her job she had forced herself to work diligently, but today it seemed as though some invisible force was pulling her away from her desk and forcing her down a path of painful memories. Even the sight of Maria playing quietly at her feet did not distract her. Though she forced herself to begin some of her duties, she passed the day without accomplishing much.

Like the young people in the neighborhood, Megan needed someone with whom she could discuss her problems. When counseling was available and the counselors were eager to see her, she had refused their help; now circumstances had closed those doors. It was ironic that she worked with two psychologists, but she dared not talk to either of them. Her parents already knew about the rape, of course, and she could talk to them, but that was no longer sufficient. She must tell someone the entire story from December 5 of the preceding year through December 5 of this one. She immediately discounted her parents. She was certain that they would not want to know all that had happened.

Even the thought of telling her whole story was frightening. At six o'clock, however, she had made her decision and left Safe Haven for the home of someone who would listen patiently and quietly to everything she had to say.

"Mother Harriet, I need to talk to you," Megan said to the old woman when she opened her door.

"Come in, Child," she stepped back from the door and allowed Megan to enter. "What's your name?"

"I'd rather not tell you," she replied. "When you hear what I have to say, you'll understand why."

"Fine, Child," Mother Harriet nodded as she took a seat. "Tell me what your trouble is."

Slowly, methodically, Megan told her story, beginning with her attack one year before and recounting all of the events that had taken her to Buffalo. At times her voice was filled with sadness and bitterness; at other times she nearly shouted from agitation. Omitting nothing except the name of the center where she worked, she recounted her tale with sufficient pathos and passion to stir the heart of even the most indifferent listener.

Mother Harriet was tacit, though her eyes darted about more actively at times. Never interrupting or asking questions, she maintained such silence that at the end Megan wondered whether she had even been listening. Was that quiet old mind incapable of absorbing her sordid tale?

When the story concluded, Megan sat quietly for a moment waiting for her listener to speak and wondering whether she had made a mistake in coming.

"That's all," she said at last as she rose from her chair. "I guess I'll be going now. I just had to tell someone."

"Sit down, Child," Mother Harriet called her back to her seat. "Ain't nobody that's never been attacked by the devil."

"I was attacked by a lunatic and some vicious person who saw me defending myself," retorted Megan, stunned and annoyed by Mother Harriet's remark. "I don't believe in the devil."

"Ya should. He believes in you." Mother Harriet smiled, and her tone softened. "Ya been through a bad time—ain't no doubt. You say ya can't never go back to New York City?"

"No, my life there is over; my career has ended. Everything I ever wanted has been taken from me. I'll be here in Buffalo trying to make ends meet for the rest of my life. And the terrible part is that no one can help me. I came here tonight hoping somehow that you could, but now I see that you can't do anything for me either."

"No, Child; I can't help ya. But there's Somebody that can. Ya need to talk to Him 'bout your problems and let Him solve them for ya."

"I can't tell this story to anyone else. I could hardly come here and tell you. Don't you understand that there are repercussions? I have to think about the consequences of everything I say. If I talk to the wrong person, and they tell the police…"

"Ya don't got to tell Him nothin', 'cause He already knows it all. He saw it when it was happenin.' Ya just gotta talk to Him and ask for His help."

Megan looked up with a puzzled expression. "Who are you talking about?"

"I'm talking 'bout Jesus. If ya ever wanna get your life straight, ya got to turn it over to Jesus."

"I believe in God," Megan said thoughtfully. "But I don't think He can help me."

"It ain't enough just to believe in God. Ya gotta know Jesus. Ya gotta have a personal relationship with Him and believe that He's your friend."

"But God should help me anyway, if He can."

"And He might, but ya won't ask if ya don't know Him. It's like if I wrote to the President of the United States. He don't know me from no one else, so I don't got no reason to believe that he'll do what I ask him to. But if I know him and I write to him, then I know he'll answer me 'cause he's my friend. When ya know Jesus, and ya ask Him for somethin' ya expect Him to answer ya 'cause He's your friend. And even if the answer don't come right away or it ain't what ya was expectin', ya know that you can trust Him because He cares about ya."

"I don't think you understand. I broke the law; I killed a man. I'm guilty of a crime. How am I supposed to reconcile that with God?"

"We've all broke God's law, Child. Ya killed a man, and the law says you're guilty. The law don't know no mercy toward ya even though you can justify what ya done. Ya just wait to get caught, knowin' that one day somebody's gonna find out. What ya gotta understand is that everybody on this planet lives the same way. Everybody's guilty. We live out our lives hopin' that nobody knows 'bout all the things we done. Sometimes we think we've got away 'cause during our lifetimes nothin' happens. But in the end, the law always comes for us—it comes in death. That's what death is; it's the price we pay for the evil we done, and it's also the moment of accountability. We die, and we go before the Judge of all the earth, and we're sentenced for eternity."

Mother Harriet continued. "But if we got someone to plead our case, then we're counted not guilty of breakin' the law. It's like we never done nothin' wrong; we're washed clean. Then we becomes part of God's family; He adopts us as His very own children. That's why Jesus came—to take the burden of all our sins on Hisself so that we can be counted not guilty now while we're alive and not guilty when we die and stand before God. 'For the law came by Moses, but Grace and Truth by Jesus Christ.'"

Megan shook her head, "You're talking about God's law; I'm talking about civil law."

"There's only one law," Mother Harriet corrected her. "Every just law of man is based on the commands of God. Ya broke those commands—not just once when ya shot that fella, but many times. Every time ya told a lie, or swore, or got angry with someone, you was just as guilty then as ya is now. The only way to get free is to confess what ya done."

"You mean I should turn myself over to the police?" Megan asked.

"Not unless you wanna go to jail. Ain't no real point in tellin' the police no how; they can't forgive ya. I meant that you need to confess to Jesus and ask Him to forgive ya. Then He'll help ya start all over again with a new life."

"If God already knows, what's the point of confessing?"

"Because ya gotta ask forgiveness. Then ya gotta commit your life to Him; ya gotta promise to change. Ya gotta be willin' to be what He wants ya to be and do what He wants ya to do. Your heart's gotta become like a little child's. Ya gotta be born again."

"Born again—I've heard of that—born again Christians. My parents had me baptized in the Episcopalian church when I was a baby. I went to Sunday school. That ought to be good enough."

"Jesus says, unless a man gets born of water and the spirit he cannot enter the kingdom of God. That's what I was sayin' 'bout committin' yourself. When you gives your life over to Jesus, and ya start a friendship with Him then you's born again. You gets to fix your mistakes and start again, just like you was startin' out for the first time."

Megan shook her head, "I can't even make a commitment to people right now, much less to God. I came here to tell you my story, and I have. You've given me your advice, and I thank you for it. I trust that you won't repeat anything I told you to anyone."

"Course not, Child. 'Fore you go, though, there's somethin' I want to give ya."

"Not another prayer, please," Megan moaned silently. To her surprise, Mother Harriet rose and walked to the bookshelves. Groping, her hands searched until she found the right book. Then she walked to Megan's chair.

"Read this book," she thrust it into Megan's hand. "Read every word, front to back. This book is gonna tell ya things that's wrong with your life—things ya don't even know 'bout. And it's gonna tell ya how to start over and fix all the mistakes ya made. When you finish readin', ya read it again. I started readin' that book forty years ago, and I ain't finished with it yet. Told me more about myself than I ever knew. I done read it every day till I lost my eyes, and every day I learnt something new from it. That book contains the secret of livin'—real livin'. It's an instruction manual for life."

"Thank you," Megan said stiffly as she rose from her seat. "You've been very kind to listen all this time. I have to be going now."

Walking toward the door, Megan heard the gentle voice behind her. "Good night, Child. If ya want to talk again, feel free to come back anytime." Megan hurried from the premises, certain that her shadow would never again fall across Mother Harriet's doorstep.

Yet, that evening in her apartment and the following day at work, Mother Harriet's words haunted her. What was it that she had said to make such an impression? Megan did not agree with her—she did not share the simple faith that this old woman treasured. The Bible that Mother Harriet gave her sat on her bookshelves untouched. Perhaps, she would read it someday when her life was more under control and she had more time.

Still, something about Mother Harriet drew Megan to her. Without understanding the attraction, Megan felt its effects. She did not even like Mother Harriet very well; in her presence she felt troubled. In Megan's opinion, Mother Harriet did not make a very good comforter. She had hoped that the old woman would extend great sympathy to her; instead, she had tried to give her a recipe for correcting her problems through religion. It was as though Mother Harriet had laid the guilt for all that had happened at Megan's feet. She talked to Megan of repenting, confessing, changing—that was not what she wanted to hear. If it had not been for Mother Harriet's complete openness and sincerity, Megan would have been angry with her. Yet, she knew that whatever Mother Harriet said came from her heart and that made it difficult for Megan to feel angry.

Three days passed and Megan could not forget Mother Harriet's statement that she must make a commitment. Perhaps God would help her; it couldn't hurt to ask. But what would she pray? When she was a little girl, she had learned some selections from the *Book of Common Prayer*. Many years had passed, however, and she had forgotten them. "Talk to Jesus," Mother Harriet had told her, making it sound as simple as talking to a friend. Still, Megan was fairly certain that prayers are supposed to be handled in a certain way. Praying alone might not be sufficient; she wondered whether she should have a priest pray for her. That, however, would entail involving other people, and she could not take that chance. No, it had to be as Mother Harriet had suggested or not at all. If God existed as Mother Harriet believed that He did—an all-knowing, all seeing, all powerful God—then a simple prayer would suffice. If the old woman were wrong, an entire army of priests could not communicate with Him.

Kneeling on the floor of her apartment, with her elbows pressed into the cushions of her armchair, she tried to think of what to say. Holmes came up beside her and nudged her as if to get her on her feet and away from this foolishness. She tried to ignore him, but he persisted until she rose and shut him in the bedroom. Returning to her kneeling position, she felt the same awkwardness. The ticking of the clock and the sound of her own thoughts interrupted her efforts. Praying silently did not seem sufficient, yet when she opened her mouth to speak, she was self-conscious. Mother Harriet's words came back to her over and over again. "Just talk to Jesus and ask for His help."

"God," she finally said aloud, and then remembering Mother Harriet's instructions, she changed it, "Jesus, I don't know if you can help me or not. But if you will come into my life and forgive me for everything that I've done and help me get out of this mess, then I'll try hard to do what you want me to. Amen."

Continuing to kneel, she waited for something to happen. She did not know what to expect, but from the way Mother Harriet had talked, she was certain that something must happen. She had never given much thought to angels or the supernatural, but now she half expected a visitation or a bright light or an audible voice—some sign that someone was listening. Nothing happened that indicated anything had changed, and she felt nothing at all.

When Megan finally rose, she was thoroughly irritated with Mother Harriet and herself. She could understand how an old woman such as Mother Harriet might believe that prayer made a difference, but she was an educated woman. She should have known better than to be taken in by this superstitious nonsense. Living in a dark, lonely world where her only joy came from barrio children who told her their problems and poor women who brought her food, Mother Harriet had to believe that God could see and hear her. The blindness from which the old woman suffered was more than physical; she lived behind a veil of ignorance that prevented her from understanding the world. Megan's world was illuminated by knowledge and reason, and both told her that her little "conversation" with God could not possibly benefit her. Though she was annoyed with Mother Harriet for having convinced her to make a fool of herself, she took some satisfaction in determining that she had been right from the beginning and Mother Harriet's faith was misguided.

On Monday Linda Pearson called Megan into her office. "I want you to know that we are very pleased with the job that you're doing," Linda told her. "We were not certain that you would adjust to the work here at Safe Haven, but I must say that you have surprised us very pleasantly."

"Thank you," Megan answered. "I am certainly enjoying the work."

"That's good. I wanted to ask you, Megan, have you ever done any teaching?"

"Not in a classroom setting. However, when I was in New York our firm allowed various law students to intern with us. I trained many of the interns."

"The reason I asked is that the community college here is putting together a course on the legal aspects of correctional science. I know the director of the program and he has been looking for someone to teach the course. Frankly, with your experience, I think you're a good candidate for the position, and I wondered whether you would be interested in applying."

Megan thought for a few moments, "Yes, I would be very interested."

"Good. Gerald Humphrey is the chair for the Correctional Science division. Contact him for an interview today. He has to hire the instructor before Christmas vacation begins."

After thanking Linda, Megan returned to her office to call Gerald Humphrey. She scheduled an appointment with him for that afternoon. Arriving promptly at two o'clock, she was seated in a large room where the clerks' desks were separated by partitions. She glanced at the dirty green carpet and dusty file cabinets with papers stacked on top. How different from her alma mater with its spotless buildings and professional personnel. The fact that she was there at all was one more indication that her life was no longer what it used to be. Reminding herself that she needed the money, however, she forced a friendly smile and brushed a white thread from her black wool slacks.

Gerald Humphrey finally appeared at the door. His brown shoulder-length hair and bushy beard were unkempt, and his clothing was rumpled. At least fifty pounds overweight, he wore a white dress shirt without a tie, and his large stomach hung loosely over the waistband of his brown corduroy trousers. Megan again thought of her own law school days when she had worked with numerous Gerald Humphreys. It gave her some encouragement to see that he was so like the other members of the academic community she had known.

"Good afternoon, Dr. Humphrey," Megan rose to shake hands.

"Come on into my office," he said as he turned and led the way to a small, cluttered cubicle and moved a few books from the chair so that she could be seated.

"So, you're interested in the instructor's position we have open for the spring semester? What qualifies you to teach the legal aspects of correctional science?"

"I have a degree in criminal law, and I've been a criminal attorney for almost five years. Prior to moving to Buffalo, I was a junior partner at Pratt, Forbes and Magoff in New York City."

"And what are you doing in Buffalo?"

"I'm legal counsel for the Safe Haven Daycare Center," she replied trying not to hesitate.

"That's kind of a step down; why did you come to Buffalo?"

"I wanted to spend more time with my family, and I wanted to give something back to the community."

"Giving something back to the community is part of the mission of the community college system. We are dedicated to enriching the lives of the people of Buffalo by providing training and opportunities that might otherwise be unattainable to them because of financial or personal reasons. Here in the Correctional Science Department most of the people we train are looking for some sort of career in law enforcement.

Basically, you will be giving the students an overview of the history and philosophy of modern criminal and correctional laws with an emphasis on the rights of the convicted. You will be discussing the application of certain statutes and leading case law, and you will be reviewing the elements of crime and punishment. You will also teach the general provisions of the New York Code of Criminal Procedures as they apply to correctional settings. Since you have experience as a practicing criminal attorney, you should be able to relay this information to your students so that they can readily understand it. Does this sound like something that interests you?"

"Yes, I think it would be just right for me. What is the class schedule?"

"It's a three credit course. Beginning on January twelfth, the class will meet at seven o'clock Tuesday and Thursday evenings for an hour and a half. It's a fifteen week semester. Will that work for you?"

"Yes, that would fit in well with my schedule."

"Very well. Have your official grade transcripts sent directly to us from your law school. We also need two letters of recommendation. The sooner you can get these to us, the better. When everything is in order, I will call you to come in and pick up your materials so that you can prepare during the Christmas break."

Thanking him, Megan left his office and returned to work. That afternoon she called the records division of her alma mater and made arrangements to have her transcripts mailed to Dr. Humphrey's attention.

After returning to her apartment that evening, she pulled a scrap book from the shelf and searched for suitable letters of recommendation. Considering how angry Jack was when she resigned Pratt, Forbes and

Magoff, she felt certain that he would not write one for her, and she was equally skeptical about the other partners at the firm. However, she had carefully saved the letters that had been written about her when she had been employed at the firm, and she was able to produce two that she thought would be acceptable. Moreover, each was dated just prior to the time of her resignation, and they praised her excellent work there.

Within a week Humphrey had received her transcripts and the letters of recommendation and notified Megan that the job was hers. At her apartment that evening she looked through the books and materials with enthusiasm. She had always loved school, and the idea of teaching really appealed to her. Knowing that she had very little time in which to go through the course and familiarize herself with the material, she threw herself into the project and worked late every night that she was home.

With Christmas approaching, Jennifer wanted Megan to spend more time with her family, and she attended all of the Christmas performances with them. Yet, when she was with her parents, her mind was on the course and the adjustments she ought to be making. At night she thought of Maria and Safe Haven. She and the little girl had become such good friends that she hated to be separated from her in the evenings, but during the day as Maria played at her feet, Megan was so busy with her other duties that she hardly had time to notice her. At work and in her apartment she felt guilty because she knew that she ought to be spending more time with her family, but when she was with them, she did not enjoy them.

Suddenly, everything had become mundane to her, though she could not explain the reason. A few days before Christmas she and her parents made their annual trek to Niagara Falls, and Megan found herself making comparisons between this trip and the last. A year before she had been disturbed by her own comparisons between her emotional state and the Falls; now she saw nothing except frozen water. She wondered why they even bothered to make the trip. Every year for as long as she could remember the three of them had gone to see the Falls at Christmas, and every year she had been awed by them. Now she asked herself what there was to see. The same sight always greeted them; the ice formations might vary slightly, but to the casual observer the sight was identical from year to year.

This attitude invaded her other Christmas activities as well. When they attended a performance of Handel's *Messiah*, she found herself asking the same questions that she had of Niagara Falls. They had attended this performance for years, and every year in the past it had delighted her. Now she felt like a silly child who had unexpectedly stumbled upon adulthood and suddenly saw life through the eyes of a cynic.

On Friday evening the three of them attended the annual production of "The Stingiest Man in Town," based on Dickens' *A Christmas Carol*, and she noted that the lead actor was similar in makeup, costume, and talent to the actors who had played the role every year previously. She even thought that she recognized some members of the cast who played the same parts year after year with the same enthusiasm as the year before.

Megan did not intend to be unpleasant, and she tried to disguise her boredom from her parents. She had not forgotten how much she had relied on them all those years when she was living in New York, and even now there were many evenings in her apartment when she felt lonely for them. She knew that they would have welcomed the idea of her living with them, but though she longed for their company, she did not want to be in their house. Whether it was her own refusal to be subject to their authority, or whether she resented their treating her like a child, she could not say. She just knew that there was some indefinable force that kept her away from them.

Christmas shopping with Jennifer, Megan noted with displeasure the gaudy ribbons and glass ornaments that decorated every store. As she sorted through piles of sweaters looking for gifts for various family members, she thought about this year's Christmas party. They would all be there reminiscing among themselves about how oddly she had behaved the previous year. A year earlier she had feared that they might think badly of her if they knew that she had been raped. Now, she no longer cared what they thought; their opinions did not matter in the least.

The night of the party everyone behaved pleasantly, though Joanna and her new husband were obviously a little miffed that Megan had not attended their wedding in June. Megan moved among the crowd laughing and talking without ever really hearing anything that was said. She felt as removed from her surroundings as Scrooge on his Christmas Eve journeys. It was as though the people around her were in a different dimension where she could not reach them to communicate. They were interested to hear that she was in Buffalo, and since Mike had told his mother that he had recommended the position at Safe Haven, most of the family members were aware that she was now employed by a daycare center for low income families. The looks on their faces told her much more about their reaction to this news than pages of eloquent discourse would have. The room was almost equally divided between those who were uncomfortable with the idea of a member of the family throwing away her talents on the underprivileged and those who derived a secret pleasure in knowing that Megan's promising career had obviously fallen through. Mike had always been eccentric; none of his projects surprised anyone, but for Megan to be following in his footsteps told them that something was amiss.

As for Megan, after two hours she settled with her back against the wall and stood staring at the Christmas tree. It occurred to her for the first time that the other people in the room were actually enjoying themselves. This dull, lifeless, little social event was pleasant to them, as were all of the other holiday activities. Not one of them had ever stopped to wonder whether it might all be meaningless. They stood sipping champagne and discussing topics that were of absolutely no importance. Their lives had always been the same—most of them had known no great tragedies, but neither had they experienced any deep joy. They had been born in comfort, and they had lived without ever having any meaningful contact with the rest of the world, or even among themselves. The questions that plagued her constantly had probably never even crossed their minds.

From the corner of her eye, Megan glimpsed the flashing lights of the Christmas tree, and she turned to look at it once again. She had always loved the tree for all that it symbolized—tonight it symbolized this gathering. Gaudy, green and gorgeous with its snow tipped branches and frosty white decorations, it was as beautiful a tree as could be seen in any home in Buffalo that night. Yet, for all its beauty, it was dead. Once alive, it had fallen victim to someone's axe, and now it stood in the living room in just enough water to keep the needles green until after the holidays ended. Then it would be stripped of its ornaments and taken to a recycling center where it would be reduced to mulch. Its usefulness had ended. It had been sacrificed to become a splendid centerpiece for the Cleary's living room.

The people at the party were very much like that tree. If they had ever truly been alive and capable of questioning their surroundings, they had long since cut away that part of themselves. They had sacrificed themselves in favor of a public image. Was she to age and become a part of this shallow self-serving little clique without ever finding out whether real life existed somewhere outside the sheltered walls of their neat little lives?

Perhaps Christmas itself was like the tree—all show and no substance. Christmas, which she had loved so much as a child, had disappointed her. It was nothing more than the ultimate commercial holiday. Gift giving and holiday parties were part of the trappings of an enterprise supported by merchants in order to keep the economy healthy. To add the finishing touches and make a hedonistic celebration seem like a humanitarian enterprise, small children sang, "Joy to the World" outside houses throughout the city. Those innocent little carolers and the shallow adults who heard their song had never stopped to reason that there might well be no joy in the world at that moment nor would there ever be. It was more a ritual than a celebration; people participated out of habit and social custom rather than true feeling. She wondered whether anyone over the age of five really enjoyed Christmas. Unwillingly her thoughts traveled back to the people in the barrio that surrounded Safe Haven. What must they think of this holiday when the stores were filled with expensive gifts they could not afford to give their children? They would not be deceived by sentiments of "peace on earth, good will toward men." They must dread the coming of the holiday and be grateful for its passage, for if the wealthy were unhappy at Christmas, the poor must certainly be despondent.

When the party ended, Megan walked up the stairs to her old bedroom. The room brought back memories of her childhood and of the year before. It seemed strange that only a year earlier she had been so totally defeated, and, yet, her ordeal was just beginning. A year later she had emerged on the other side of the tunnel and found that the road she had been traveling led nowhere. After months of believing that she would forever be a victim, she was free—with her move to Buffalo she had finally outmaneuvered her blackmailer and set herself at liberty from his demands. Though she had not been happy at Safe Haven, she had made a place for herself there, and she was again beginning to receive the praises of her colleagues. Now, with her pending position at the college, she saw an opportunity to have her life return to normal. She had taken a long detour, but she saw in her future a stable and successful existence. For the first time since the nightmare had begun, she had definite plans. She would find a position in a law firm in Buffalo, and she would move back into the arena she had left.

The thought should have given her pleasure, but it was an empty dream. What was missing from her life to make her feel its absence so? Not long ago all she had wanted was to be successful, but now she felt that no amount of success would ever be enough. She could not overcome the feeling that if she had not been working late that night in December—if no one had interrupted her peaceful life and stolen her security—she could have gone on forever as she had been. Yet, things had changed, and whether she chose to admit it or not, she had changed. She could never go back to that carefree, innocent girl she had once been.

Megan was almost glad to be back at Safe Haven the following day, for she was learning to enjoy the children. Mike had been correct in his assessment of them—they were cute and, for the most part, they behaved pretty well. Besides, there was something about the innocent honesty of children that Megan liked. Expressing their feelings without hesitation, they described the world as they saw it, without trying to hide its blemishes. Like her, those children were victims—if not victims of physical abuse, at least victims of a system that reduced them to poverty and gave them very little hope of bettering their situations. She had learned to empathize with them, and she welcomed their company.

Megan was, therefore, delighted to hear Carmen announce that on Christmas Eve a party would be held at Safe Haven for the children. Carmen asked that everyone bring food, and all volunteered to help. Within a few minutes the women had offered to bring various kinds of sandwiches and casseroles, cakes and candies. Megan volunteered to bring a variety of chips and dips.

"Okay," Carmen announced when she finally had completed the list of foods that everyone had agreed to furnish, "remember that the whole neighborhood is invited, so there will be a lot of people. Whatever you're bringing, make sure there's lots of it." The rest of the women laughed, but Megan did not even smile. To have a party for the children was one thing, but to invite the whole neighborhood was something else entirely, and it seemed an open invitation to every lazy degenerate and free loader looking for a free meal.

The day of the party Megan brought enough chips and dips to feed several dozen people, but she was still angry at the thought that adults from the neighborhood would attend. She forced herself to put on a happy face and smiled broadly for most of the morning, but a little of her testiness slipped through the facade every now and then. The party would begin at twelve noon, and just as she feared, by eleven-thirty the place was beginning to fill. Many of the mothers of the children who stayed at the center, followed by the young people she had seen on the street corners, were now crowding into the main room. The mother of the twins who had gone home to stay with Carmen on so many occasions was there, as were the fathers of some of the children. The gathering looked as though it had been gleaned from every miserable alley in the vicinity. It was exactly as she had expected—people who lived off others 365 days of the year were there for still another free meal.

"Who's gonna get Mother Harriet?" Marla was asking.

"Mother Harriet?" Megan asked with surprise. "I thought she didn't leave her house."

"She don't usually. Every year we send somebody to bring her to the party. Who's gonna get her this year? Carmen?" Marla inquired, looking at the subject of her question.

"I can't," Carmen replied. "This morning when I got up someone had slashed all my tires; I had to take the bus to work."

"I don't have no car," Marla said. "I ride the bus every day."

"Veronica," Carmen asked, "would you get Mother Harriet for us?"

"I would, but my car's in the shop."

Carmen turned to Megan. "I guess it'll have to be you. You remember where she lives, don't you?"

"Unfortunately," Megan thought, "I remember exactly where she lives." However, she did not want Carmen to suspect that she might have gone to see her, so she asked for the address and directions. Taking her keys, she left the center and got into her car.

This new twist was unexpected. Having chosen Mother Harriet as her confessor for the very reason that she was blind and homebound, Megan was now very uneasy. The person who was privy to her darkest secrets would be going to the place where she worked to talk with her colleagues. She was glad that she had not revealed her identity to Mother Harriet that night when she had gone to see her alone. She had been to her house only twice, and it was very unlikely that the old woman would recognize her; it was probable that she would not even remember that Megan had come.

She pulled up in front of Mother Harriet's house, locked her car, and walked quickly to the door. It opened, and Mother Harriet stood before her in a starched, neat dress holding her white cane firmly. "Hello, Mother Harriet," Megan greeted her warmly. "I'm Megan Cleary; I work at Safe Haven Daycare Center, and I've come to drive you over for the Christmas party."

"Good morning, Child; it's good to have ya here again." Mother Harriet put her hand on Megan's arm. "Has ya been thinkin' 'bout what I told you the other night?"

Megan was horrified; within five seconds Mother Harriet had recognized her voice. She had thought she was being very clever, but she had not fooled the old woman, and now she could identify her. "Are you ready to go?" Megan asked in a shaky voice.

"Yes, Child, I's ready," she said as she shut and locked the door of her house. Making her way to the car, she slipped into the seat without difficulty. "This sure is a nice car you got here," she commented as Megan started the engine. "Nice and quiet."

Inwardly Megan groaned. "She's already thinking about what a nice car I have. Next it'll be what a nice bank account. I've opened myself up to another blackmailer, and this old bat will try to take me for a fortune." Of course, now there was no fortune to be taken, and Megan began contemplating ways of escaping Mother Harriet's greed. She could begin looking for a job in another city, and the moment she found one…

The sweet sound of Mother Harriet's voice broke through her thoughts, "Ain't Christmas wonderful?" she was saying. "When I was a child we always looked forward to Christmas. My father didn't have no money and there wasn't presents much, but my folks tried to get us each a little somethin'. Then after we was through with dinner we would sit, and Mama would read from the Bible. It was the most beautiful time of the whole year.

"I remember the first Christmas after Mama died. She'd been sick a long while, and we kep hopin' she'd make it through the holiday, but she didn't. Christmas came, and I was grievin' so bad for her I didn't even feel like celebratin'. Papa got the Bible down off the shelf and said that I mustn' cry so on Christmas, 'cause it was because of Christmas that Mama was alive in Heaven where she was well again and happy. And he read to us 'bout Jesus and His birth, and even though I missed Mama, I felt better. I's lived eighty-nine years now, and I's seen Papa die, and my brothers and sisters, and my husban'. Every year at Christmas I remember 'em all and I wish they was here with me, but I ain't sad, 'cause I know what Papa said was true. They's all alive in Heaven because of Jesus, and one of these Christmases I'll be there too." She paused, "There's lots o' people that grieve at Christmas time and feels a loss. Instead of bein' happy, they's sad and grievin' 'cause they don't understand what Christmas is about. Jesus said that He come so we could have life and have it more abundantly, and Christmas is a celebration of that life. Not this miserable unhappy life we got down here, but the everlastin' life that He gives us."

Megan remained silent for a while, and then she spoke up, "If you ask me, there's a little too much celebrating at Christmas—all of the shops advertising goods and trees everywhere, stale parties in people's houses and too much food. Nobody seems to really enjoy it. Everyone talks about 'peace on earth, good will toward men' in a world filled with war and famine. Frankly, I don't see the point."

"Well, of course, Child," Mother Harriet responded. "And if ya think all there is to Christmas is parties and presents, ya ain't never gonna enjoy it. Most of those people at those parties ain't celebratin' Christmas at all. They's celebratin' havin' money and bein' with their friends and family, but they ain't thinkin' at all 'bout the reason behind it. They's hopin' to get somethin' in a box with a ribbon 'round it that'll make 'em happy, and happiness just don't come that way. Has ya ever thought 'bout why folks gives presents at Christmas?"

"I suppose because it's custom," Megan thought back to her childhood Sunday school lessons. "The wise men gave gifts to the Christ Child."

"Yes they did, but God gave this old world a gift, too, and that gift was His son. Two thousand years ago Jesus was born, and He taught people how to live and love and work and get along peaceable with each other. He gave us freedom from sin; He gave us an example to follow, and He showed us how to get right with God. And with His death, He gave us life that never ends. On the first Christmas even the angels in Heaven was so happy that they come down rejoicin' and singin' just to tell the world that the Lord had come. And if angels that live in the presence of the glories of God get that excited over His birth, we folks on earth ought to be happy just thinkin' 'bout it."

They pulled into the parking lot of Safe Haven and Megan helped Mother Harriet out of the car. To Megan's surprise, by using her cane, the old woman was able to find her way about without much assistance. Megan opened the door to the center, and Mother Harriet entered amid shouts of delight from the children and warm greetings from the older guests and employees.

The sight of Linda Pearson standing in the doorway of the children's play area caught Megan's eye, and she guessed that Linda was not one of Mother Harriet's converts. She had heard Linda mention Mother Harriet only once and that was to say that because Mother Harriet lived in the same desperate circumstances as the other people in the barrio they were less inhibited about telling her their problems, and the act of talking with someone proved to be therapeutic for most of them. Though she was inclined to agree, Megan also sensed that Linda was a little jealous because the old woman was such a valued part of the community.

When Mother Harriet took her seat, everyone in the room sat down, and Megan noted how much quieter it became. "I's brought some candy for ya kids," Mother Harriet announced, and from a small grocery bag she had been carrying, she produced several bags of miniature candy bars. "Ya can have these in a minnut, but first let's talk. What's tomorra?"

"Christmas," yelled the children in one voice.

"And why do we have Christmas?"

Various answers came back dealing with Santa Claus and presents and breaks from school, but one child cried, "It's Jesus' birthday!"

"That's right," Mother Harriet said. "It's Jesus' birthday. That's the greatest event ever in the history of the world. Carmen, are ya gonna read to these kids 'bout it from the Bible?"

"What I thought we'd do this year is let different children read the story. We've been practicing with the older children who come to the center after school, and I think we have a nice little program lined up."

Carmen picked up a book of Bible stories which contained a version of the annunciation and birth of Christ. Megan had heard the children practicing their reading each afternoon, but she had not known that it was in preparation for this event. Now, beginning with the youngest, five of the best readers read excerpts from the story as everyone quietly listened. Megan saw Linda slip back into the kitchen where the food was waiting to be set out, and she followed.

"You're not one of them, are you?" Linda asked.

"No," Megan replied. "Although they would like me to be."

"You never will be, though. They're not like us. They have no hope; all they have is religion and the belief that things will get better for them in the next life. Religion is the ignorant man's way of dealing with life."

"Obviously, you don't approve."

"No I don't. I don't approve of their group or of Mother Harriet. Unfortunately, there's very little that I can do. Mother Harriet has been a fixture in this community for longer than any of them can remember. Before she lost her sight, she had what she called a 'street ministry.' She spent her days working within a five-mile radius of this place going out on the streets and talking to the people she met. I think that occasionally she ventured out a little further, into the heart of Buffalo, but she said that God had called her to help the people in this community. She gave money to people who had nowhere to go, she invited them into her home, and she fed them and gave them a place to sleep. I think it's amazing that no one killed her. Later, when she lost her sight, she started the Wednesday night prayer meeting and invited strangers into her home to talk. Most of the people here today are her 'converts'—they just know that she's good for a handout. As far as she's concerned, I think she enjoys being the big cheese."

Linda sighed, "Like I told you, this job is not forever; it's only until something better comes along. In the meantime, I have to work with what I've got, and that means not rocking the community's boat too much. I put up with Mother Harriet's little Christmas visit because keeping her away would cause too many problems. By the same token, I let Carmen teach the kids to read the Christmas story as long as they understand that it's only a story and no different from any of the other fairy tales we read them. I tell myself that no matter where I had gone into social work I would have had to contend with local superstition, and

I try to be as tolerant as I can. I know that Mother Harriet can't help these people, but they don't, and I think it's the placebo effect—they believe what she says is true so they begin to change their lives."

Suddenly, Megan realized that the reading had ended. She remembered that Mother Harriet had recognized her and knew her story. She must keep an eye on her so that she would know if the old woman should start repeating her story to the others. The daycare workers were filing into the kitchen to serve lunch, and Megan excused herself to find Mother Harriet. Sitting in the same chair she had taken when she arrived, the old woman was talking to a little girl, and Megan rushed over to hear what was being said.

"My birthday's on Christmas, too," the child was saying.

"Well, ain't you lucky!" Mother Harriet exclaimed. "I think that deserves a big hug." She squeezed the little girl in her arms. The child returned the embrace and slipped down from Mother Harriet's lap and went into the kitchen.

Mother Harriet turned her head slightly, and her eyes darted around rapidly. "That you, Megan?" she asked, turning in her direction.

"Yes," Megan responded nervously.

"That's real nice perfume ya got on. I can smell it real easy. Somethin' ya need Child?"

"Ah, well, I just wondered what you would like for me to bring you from the kitchen."

"Oh, just a little of whateva' you got in there. Ain't no kinda food I don't like or can't eat, so just put somethin' together."

The children were starting to come back with their plates filled with treats. Megan hated to leave Mother Harriet alone for even a minute lest she tell the secrets with which she had been entrusted. Yet, now that she had said something, she had to get her a plate. Rushing into the kitchen she grabbed a plate and impatiently took her place at the end of the line. The seconds dragged on as hours, and in her mind Megan could hear Mother Harriet's soft voice and awful grammar as she told Megan's story to everyone there. They would be shocked; Megan would be the last person they would have suspected of harboring such a past. The line moved slowly as the guests took their time filling their plates, and Megan grew more and more nervous until she wanted to scream. By the time she got back with the food, it would be too late; the entire story would have been told without her being there to stop it.

At last the suspense was too much for her, and she could no longer wait to reach the food. Taking the paper plate with her, she flew back into the play area where Mother Harriet and the other women were sitting in a circle of chairs talking. With sweating palms and a racing heart she strained to hear their conversation as she drew near them.

"Back in Puerto Rico, my mother has a wonderful garden," Carmen was saying. "When I first came here I missed the fresh vegetables."

"I miss fresh peas," Mother Harriet laughed. "My cousins in Georgia bring me some when they come to visit, and they's just as sweet as sugar. And corn; ain't nothing like fresh corn right outta the garden..." Sensing Megan's presence she turned to her, "You brought the food, Child?"

Megan brushed the hair away from her face with the back of her hand, "Well, ah, actually I wanted to know—do you prefer chicken or ham on your sandwich?"

"Chicken's fine," Mother Harriet answered, and Megan returned to the kitchen.

All afternoon she dogged the old woman's steps, never letting her out of ear shot. Mother Harriet talked of Christmas, religion, gardening, and her childhood, but nothing in her conversation indicated that she was about to tell any stories about Megan. Still, Megan wanted to be certain, and for the remainder of the party she became Mother Harriet's shadow.

When at last the time came for her to drive Mother Harriet home, Megan knew that the best thing to do was to confront her directly. She could not endure days and nights of waiting for the first blackmail note; she had to know exactly what she was dealing with, and she had to hear it from the old woman's lips. As soon as they pulled out of the parking lot and were on their way, she seized the opportunity.

"All right, you know who I am. What are you going to do about it?"

Mother Harriet looked surprised. "Ain't nothing I can do 'bout it, Child. It's your life; only you and Jesus gonna be able to get it straightened out. But I's your friend, and I'll help ya in any way I can. If ya need anybody to talk to day or night, or if ya want somebody to pray with ya or talk to ya 'bout the Bible, I'm here for ya."

It was Megan's turn to be surprised—and embarrassed. Mother Harriet had no intention of blackmailing her; the thought had never even occurred to her. For the first time she realized that the old woman was sincere; the only thing she wanted was to be Megan's friend. She would never tell her story, and she would work without pay to help Megan in any way she could.

For the first time since her attack, Megan realized that there are a few decent, caring people in the world. For so long she had not trusted anyone. But after hearing her talk and seeing the way she conducted herself, Megan knew that Mother Harriet could be trusted. She could be counted on to exercise discretion and to provide a shoulder to lean on in a crisis. She felt a rush of warmth towards this blind, poverty-stricken old woman who, in spite of her own problems actually cared about what happened to her.

Pulling up outside the modest little house, Megan parked the car and helped Mother Harriet to the door. Then, as impulsively as a child, she threw her arms around Mother Harriet and kissed her cheek. The action surprised even Megan.

"God bless you, Child," Mother Harriet said, patting her gently. "You come back and visit with me soon."

"I will," she promised. Returning to her car, Megan watched as the tiny black figure disappeared into the house and the door closed behind her. Then she drove away, feeling more at peace than she had in months. Linda Pearson was wrong; Mother Harriet was a great help.

ELEVEN

On January 12 Megan's classes began, and she soon discovered that a few of her students did not attend class regularly or simply could not be induced to improve their grades, but for the most part, they were eager to learn. When the results of the first test were in, she was pleased to discover that the class average was high and many students had earned A's.

Her Tuesday and Thursday night teaching schedule fit in well with her job at Safe Haven. She had no social life since coming to Buffalo, and the classes kept her from sitting in her apartment and staring at Holmes. He was still her companion and a good sounding board for her ideas, but now she yearned for human companionship, and the camaraderie of the classroom made her feel less lonely.

Monday and Friday nights were taken up with research for the blog on the correctional system that she had started writing. Her own experiences as both a criminal attorney and a victim told her that much needed to change in the legal system's handling of criminals; therefore, she wanted to produce as comprehensive a work as possible, and this meant spending her free evenings at the law library researching cases and legal theory.

Saturdays were spent exercising Holmes and running errands, and Sundays were spent with her parents. Having decided that she missed their company, she was determined to include them in her life. The Sunday afternoon meal they ate together was pleasant, and the tension that had previously been present when she visited was gone.

Wednesday evenings were reserved for Mother Harriet's prayer group. Since Christmas Eve Megan had been more inclined to visit Mother Harriet's home, and she was beginning to enjoy the prayer meetings. Having never read the Bible, she found the Bible study portion especially interesting. She joined in the prayers with the rest of the group, and although she was not entirely certain that they would be answered, she could not help being a little inspired by the faith of the other members.

One evening when she arrived, she saw a stranger talking to Mother Harriet. Normally, this would not have interested her, but this man was obviously not from the neighborhood. He was tall and slender but well built, and he had the clearest, deepest blue eyes Megan had ever seen. His thick dark hair was graying slightly at the temples. His dress and manner suggested that he was affluent and certainly too sophisticated for this humble little group. Yet, he laughed and talked with Mother Harriet as affectionately as if she were a well-loved member of his own family.

Carmen insisted that Megan go over to meet him, and Mother Harriet introduced them. "Megan, this is Dr. Jonathan Andrews. Jonathan, meet Megan Cleary."

"How do you do," he greeted her in a deep cultured voice with a slight British accent.

"Hello," she responded.

"Ya'll sit down," Mother Harriet called to everyone. "It's time for the meetin' to begin. Jonathan's just got back from bein' in England, and he's gonna tell us 'bout his trip."

When everyone was seated, Jonathan began to speak. "Six months ago I had the opportunity to go back to my native England for the first time in three years. I went as part of a faculty exchange program, and, fortunately, most of my time there was spent in London. I was able to see many of my family members there and share with them my testimony of Jesus Christ. One day when I was on the street, I ran into an old acquaintance, and she asked about Jill. I told her what had happened and about the changes that had taken place in my life since. When I finished, she said, 'I'm so glad that you shared that story with me, because my husband is dying of cancer, and I have been so grief stricken. But I remember how much faith Jill had and how she always believed that God could do anything. After seeing you today and hearing you talk, I know that she was right, because her fondest wish was always that you would come to really know the Lord.' She asked me to pray for her, and when I did she asked me to visit her and her husband at their home that evening. When I arrived, I learned that Ann had become a Christian several years earlier but that Anthony had never made a commitment. After talking to both of them for several hours, I was able to pray for him, and he committed his life to Christ. The following week he died, and I saw his wife at the funeral; she was more serene than I have ever seen her."

"Praise the Lord!" Mother Harriet clapped her hands. "Death is swallowed up in victory! We always got victory in Jesus. Life can't defeat us, and death can't defeat us 'cause we is more than conquerors through Him that loves us."

Everyone said, "Amen" except Megan, who wasn't sure that she agreed. Jonathan's story wasn't beautiful; it didn't even end happily. If this poor fellow turned his life over to God, she didn't understand why God allowed him to die the next week. After all, if God weren't going to take care of people, what was the point of being a Christian? She wanted to have faith as strong as Mother Harriet's; she wanted to be able to accept life as easily and complacently, but she couldn't. There were too many unanswered questions.

As the song service began, she could hear Jonathan's strong voice lending power to the choruses, and when the time came for the Bible study, he participated without being aggressive or monopolizing the conversation. Again, she was surprised that he could be so comfortable in this place. She had never come to feel fully at home in the group, though she was learning to respect the other members. She could not help wondering what strange events in this man's life had brought him to this meeting.

At nine the service ended, and Megan, who had not been able to get into the spirit of the meeting as much as usual, prepared to leave. She walked over to say good night to Mother Harriet, but the old woman caught hold of her arm and held her fast. "Jonathan says his car is bein' fixed, and he done had to take a taxi. And I told him, ain't no use in his payin' out good money for a taxi when Megan Cleary's got her car here, and I know she won't mind givin' ya a ride.'"

Megan's brow wrinkled with irritation. Surely Mother Harriet was the pushiest old woman she had ever met. Without first discussing it with her, she had offered Megan's services to chauffeur a complete stranger. It is not true that blind eyes are without expression, for in Mother Harriet's eyes Megan could see the method behind her friend's actions, and that irritated her still more. Certainly, she found Jonathan attractive—he was the type of man nearly all women find handsome. She, however, was not looking for a man. Her life, such as it was, was at least once again orderly and planned, and in it there was no room for a suitor. Even if there were, she was capable of finding one without any help from Mother Harriet.

She was tempted to say that she was sorry, but she simply could not give him a ride home. Yet, she knew that she couldn't, for if she did, she would offend them both. Besides, she could not help being curious about him. This would give her an opportunity to talk to him alone.

Jonathan was standing quietly close by. "I don't want to put you out of your way," he said quickly. "If it is inconvenient for you to drive me home, I can easily call a taxi."

"No, that won't be necessary. Where do you live?" He gave her the address and she recognized it as being relatively close to her parents' home. "Actually, that's sort of on my way," she said.

"Good," he smiled. "whenever you're ready, then."

"I'm ready now. Good night, Mother Harriet. I'll see you next Wednesday."

"Good night, Child. God bless," and she smiled so sweetly that Megan had to smile, too.

Leaving the house, they stepped out onto the dark street and walked to Megan's car. The one thing she did not like about these Wednesday night prayer meetings was that they required her to walk alone on the poorly-lighted street of this dangerous neighborhood. It always sent chills down her spine, and more than once she had imagined that she heard footsteps behind her or caught a glimpse of someone crouching in the shadows, waiting to pounce on her. As a result, she walked quickly, and Jonathan commented on it after they got into the car and were safely buckled into their seats.

Megan laughed a little nervously, "I'm sorry. I wasn't aware that I was walking so quickly." Turning the key, she realized with some apprehension that this was the first time since she had been raped that she had been alone in a car with any man except her father. Her first inclination was to be uneasy, but she knew that Mother Harriet would not send her out alone with a man who might harm her.

"It's a beautiful evening, isn't it?" he began.

"Yes, although I think it's a little too cold. I prefer the spring and fall to winter or summer. I suppose it's very different from England."

"It get's cold in London, too. Are you originally from here?"

"Yes, but I lived in New York City for several years, and I just recently returned." She didn't know why she had added that last part; she had grown accustomed to telling people as little about herself as possible. After a brief silence she said, "Mother Harriet said that you are a doctor."

"A Ph.D. I'm a professor of literature at the University of Buffalo."

"How interesting. What field of literature, specifically?"

"I teach English literature, but my specialty is nineteenth century French literature. Do you read French?"

"Yes, I read it very well, but I don't speak it so well. Do you?"

He nodded, "Linguistics is one of my hobbies, although to be fair, I learned to speak French as a boy when I lived with my parents in Paris. That's where I developed an interest in French culture and, eventually, French literature."

Megan could contain her curiosity no longer. "If you don't mind my asking, how did you meet Mother Harriet?"

"I don't mind at all, but it's a long story and it will take me a while to tell it." Megan nodded, and he began. "I was born in London and educated at good schools; when I was old enough to attend the university, I went to Oxford. It was there that I began to develop my interest in literature, and by the time that I had earned my undergraduate degree, I was fairly certain that teaching was going to be my profession."

"At Oxford I met and married a beautiful girl named Jill Wheaton. Though I had always gone to church, I had never been very religious, but Jill was devout. She read the Bible constantly and prayed and told me that God has a special purpose for each person's life. She was kind and quick to help other people, and she had as generous a heart as anyone I have ever met. I did not agree with much of what she believed, but I was tolerant of her views because I was very much in love with her.

"While I was completing my graduate studies, Jill and I had the opportunity to come to the U.S. so that I could study in New York City as part of a transfer program. I fell in love with the city and all that it offered, and in spite of her homesickness, Jill supported my decision to remain in the United States. After our son was born, I took a teaching position with the university and began working on my Ph.D. while Jill stayed home with the baby.

"The next year Bethany was born, and I had everything a man could desire. When I completed my post graduate work, I was offered an excellent position with New York University. I was earning a good salary, and we were very comfortable. I thought my son and daughter were the two most beautiful children that had ever been born, and I tried to spend all of my free time with my family. Jill had taught them to be well behaved, and she took them to church every Sunday in the hopes that they would grow up to share her faith."

"Then one day," he paused and his voice faltered, "my entire life came to an end. Jill was taking the children shopping when a drunken driver ran a red light and collided head on with her car. The police came to the university and called me away from a class I was teaching to tell me that my wife and children were dead. At first I could not take it in; I thought that the faculty was playing some sort of cruel joke, for there was a lot of teasing among us. But when they took me to identify the bodies, I realized the truth—there were my beautiful wife and precious children smashed and bruised almost beyond recognition. I couldn't even stand to look at them; I fled from the room like a small child. For months, whenever I closed my eyes, I saw my family, cold and gray and mutilated."

"I'm very sorry," Megan apologized. "I didn't mean to bring up painful memories."

"No," Jonathan stopped her. "It's all right. All things work together for good for those who love the Lord and are called according to His purpose. I am confident that my wife and children are in Heaven and that one day I will see them again. In the meantime, all of this is crucial to the reason that I am here tonight. You asked how I came to know Mother Harriet, and if it had not been for that tragedy, I would never have met her.

"After my family was killed, I lost interest in everything. My professorship at the university that I had worked so hard for meant nothing. I could not bear to be in our house, because when I came home at night, I was so alone there. Every room was filled with memories. I even came to hate the city because of what had happened there. I could not help telling myself that if I had never come to New York they would still be alive; they would not have been at that particular intersection at that particular time. In one moment everything I loved had been taken from me. When my family died, my own will to live died with them. I sold the house and resigned from the university. A few months later I left New York City, and for a while I wandered like a nomad around the state until I, finally, settled in Buffalo."

He paused and looked at his young driver. "You are very young and beautiful, and it's obvious that you have led a well-ordered, peaceful life. I hope that you will never know the anguish of having your entire life snatched from you."

Megan stared at him for a moment but remained silent. Unfortunately, she knew all too well what it meant to lose everything—to be destitute and desperate and alone. However, she said nothing—perhaps someday when she knew him better she might tell him her story; in the meantime, she let him finish his.

He continued, "I had some money saved, and after I came to Buffalo I did not even attempt to work. I did not want to see anyone; I did not even stay in contact with my family. I began to drink as a way of escaping my grief. The more I drank the more bitter I became. At times I was angry with Jill for having taken the children out that day, and at times I hated myself for not having been with them. Most of all, I was angry with God for having allowed such a horrible thing to happen. Jill had always spoken of God as though she knew Him personally; she had been faithful to do everything that she thought was right. How could he have abandoned her, allowing her to die in the prime of her life with her children at her side? If Jill's virtuous life brought only misery and grief, I could see no point in trying to live a godly life. The angrier I became with God the guiltier and more burdened I felt, and I increasingly turned to alcohol until, finally, I was no longer aware of anything. I was beginning to fall into debt, my apartment was a hovel, and I looked and acted like a raving lunatic, but I no longer cared. On several occasions I contemplated suicide, and if I had not met Mother Harriet, I would undoubtedly be dead today.

"One day I was lying on a park bench in a stupor when I looked up to see a small, withered old black woman peering down at me. I stared at her blankly, and then I heard her say, 'Get up on your feet; ain't no call for nobody to go and get drunk like this.' I muttered to her to leave me alone, but she took her little hands and began dragging me to my feet. Though I was dirty and drunk, she was not at all afraid of me and led me back to her home. When I reached the tiny house, I collapsed on her sofa, but she pulled me into a sitting position."

"'Where do you live?' she demanded.

"England."

"'Well, you's a mighty long way from home. I think ya better be stayin' with me awhile.'"

At this point Megan laughed out loud. She remembered Linda Pearson saying that Mother Harriet had a street ministry before she lost her sight, and she could well imagine the frail little woman with her gentle touch and bold personality being a match for anyone.

"I can just hear the way she said it," she commented, and then added more seriously, "It's strange to think that she wasn't afraid to have strangers in her home."

Jonathan nodded, "From that first moment until this one I have never known Mother Harriet to be afraid of anything. Though completely non-violent herself, she has never backed away from situations that might lead to someone harming her. She was very old even then, but she was the toughest person I had ever known, and she taught me how to be tough too.

"I stayed with her for several weeks, and during that time she cleaned me up, and she sobered me up. The first day she said to me, 'If you's gonna stay in this house—and you is—you gotta be clean.' I was ill for days, but when I finally recovered to the point where I felt almost human, she began talking with me, and I told her my story. To my surprise, when I had finished, she told me about losing her husband. I learned right then that Mother Harriet could match almost any story I told her. She was always compassionate, but she refused to give me any more fuel to feed my self-pity. Then she told me that the only way I would ever find peace was through trusting Jesus.

"'My wife was as good a Christian as they come,' I told her, 'and you can see where it got her. If that's where serving God leads you, I don't want any part of it.'

"She looked surprised, and then she said, 'That's your whole problem right there. You ain't grievin' 'bout your family; you's mad at God. Well ya better get over it right quick, 'cause ya can't win a fight against God. You gonna destroy yourself, and He'll still be there. Best thing ya can do is just accept what happened and trust Him.'

"'How can I trust Him?' I asked. 'If God is just, how could He allow a wonderful young woman like my wife to die? How could He take my children away from me? That's not justice; it's not even fair.'

"'I don't know,' she answered honestly. 'And I ain't gonna tell ya that I got all the answers, 'cause I ain't. Nobody knows why some folks lives to be old and others dies real young, and it's usually the good ones dyin' and the bad ones livin'. I think mebee God gives some folks a longer time on this earth so they has a opportunity to change, and sometimes He wants somebody to come home to be with Him sooner than they planned. I do know this—everybody's got to die sometime, and when it's all said and done, nobody lives on this earth very long. I can't tell ya why your family went when they did, just like I can't tell ya why my husban' went when he did, but I can tell ya this—in Jesus they's alive forever. Death ain't permanent; it's just a separation, a move from this place to the next. On this earth eighty, mebee ninety, years is the most we can hope for, but when we die we's facin' eternity, and that's what's important. Every second counts; everything we says and does matters. It's like havin' five minutes to prove yourself for a career you's gonna have for the rest of your life.'"

Jonathan paused again. They had arrived at his house, but Megan wanted to hear the rest of his story. "To put it very simply, Mother Harriet continued to work with me. I went back to my apartment, but she continued to visit me. At her insistence, I began attending the Wednesday night prayer meetings. Eventually, I determined that she was right; until I committed my life to Christ, I could never hope to change anything. I turned my life over to Jesus and promised to serve Him if He would help me change. Almost immediately things began to improve. I went into a rehab program and stopped drinking completely. Without alcohol to blur my perspective, I began looking at my life realistically. I was in debt, and my career was non-existent. After praying about it, I applied at the University of Buffalo and landed a position in the literature department. I then began working to pay off my debts and get my life in order.

"That was over three years ago, and I now have a full professorship; I am financially solvent, and I no longer drink any alcohol. For the first time in my life I know what it means to be a 'born again Christian' because I have truly been born again. I have become a totally different person through my relationship with Jesus Christ. Although I don't want to give her undue credit, for it is only as a result of God's mercy that I am here at all, I owe a debt to Mother Harriet for working with me and sharing her faith. She is like a mother to me, and I love her as if she were my mother. I attend the prayer meetings every week when I am in town, and I support some of her projects in the hope that I can give back to others some of what has been given to me."

"That's very inspirational," Megan said quietly. "You should consider writing a book."

Jonathan laughed. "My past would certainly shock most of my colleagues and students." He then added more seriously, "I don't think most people would appreciate it. No one who has not suffered a great loss understands the pain and heartache and bitterness that follow."

"That's true," Megan replied. "But I think that there are enough suffering people out there to make it worth your while." She smiled at him, "I'll see you next Wednesday?"

"Yes, and I'll bring my car so as not to inconvenience you."

"It wasn't an inconvenience. I enjoyed talking with you."

"Same here. Thanks for the ride. Good night."

"Good night," she called and watched him as he went inside his house—a beautiful Victorian in an upscale neighborhood. Handsome, prosperous, educated, intelligent—no wonder he already seemed so wonderful. As she pulled away from the curb, Megan unconsciously hummed a hymn they had sung in their prayer meeting that evening. The night air was crisply cold, but Megan was wrapped in a warm glow. She looked at her watch and noted that it was still early. Only a few streets separated her from her parents' house; it seemed a shame not to stop and say hello. Yes, she thought, she would drop by for a while and tell them all about Jonathan Andrews.

Her parents were surprised to see her and smiled with delight at the unexpected visit. When Jennifer had made a pot of hot chocolate, they each took a mug and sat in the den next to the fireplace. "I was just thinking about you," Jennifer said. "We are going to the ballet Saturday evening, and we wondered whether you would like to join us."

"I'd love to," Megan replied.

"Good. It's all set then. We get to see so little of you now with all of your projects."

"What have you been up to?" Ian asked.

She told them briefly about her class and her work at Safe Haven. Her work was not her parents' favorite subject of conversation now, and she could see from their responses that they still had not completely gotten over her decision to leave Pratt, Forbes and Magoff. Realizing that she was only reminding them of a bitter disappointment, she turned to the real reason for her visit and began to tell them about her new acquaintance. She left out very little except the circumstances under which she had met him. Her parents strongly disapproved of her working in the barrio, and they would have been horrified to think that she was walking those dangerous streets alone at night.

They listened quietly as she talked about Jonathan, but when she had finished, her mother said, "He sounds nice enough, dear, but you probably shouldn't become too friendly. People like that stop drinking for a few months, but then they start again. They never really change. If you get too close, he'll only disappoint you."

"Drunks are dangerous," her father added. "The world is full of crazy people; you need to be careful."

Megan did not reply. Her father certainly did not have to remind her about danger—she knew firsthand what it meant to be at the mercy of a lunatic. Never-the-less, she could hardly believe that her parents would put Jonathan in that category or that they would refuse to accept that he might be capable of changing. It occurred to her that from their perspective, he could not change because they could not comprehend a spiritual change. The idea that he might really be "born again" was totally foreign to them.

In the back of her mind a voice reminded her that only a few months earlier she would have agreed with them and judged Jonathan as harshly as they did. Now she could only vaguely remember that naïve person who had thought herself to be an expert in human affairs. Her life had changed in many ways. She had known deep sorrow and seen the results of cruelty in her own life, but she had also experienced great compassion. Through Mother Harriet and Carmen, she had learned that for a person who truly commits his life to Jesus, external circumstances are not as potent a weapon as they are for those who live their lives without purpose.

For the first time, she realized that her parents had lived their lives entirely on the surface, without any real depth of emotion or experience. She had often envied them because their lives had been relatively problem free, but now she understood that they had also never experienced real joy. They loved one another as much as they were capable of love, and to her they gave everything associated with parenthood. Yet, they lived their lives to be accepted, and they had tried to keep from being tainted by other people's problems. They gave to charity less out of any real concern for the poor than because it was fashionable to do so. They calculated every word and action to conform to the rules that society had written for them, and they never questioned whether anything existed beyond that which they understood in their own sphere.

The realization caused Megan to understand how much she had changed. Only vague memories remained of the young girl who had lived in this house before going off to college. Equally blurred were the recollections of the ambitious young attorney who saw every case as no more than a means to advance her career. She had been raised by Jennifer and Ian; she owed them everything she had, and she loved them—nothing would ever change that. She thought that in this regard one's parents and one's children are very much alike—in both a person sees her own image, as though reflected in a mirror. Her parents were a part of her for as long as she lived, but she no longer belonged in the neat little niche they had carefully carved out for themselves. Circumstances beyond her control had sent her world spinning off in another direction, and she was now beginning to understand that she would never find her way back; that girl was dead. If she were dead, perhaps she needed to be born again.

She did not mention Jonathan again that evening, and she promised herself that she would not mention him again to her parents. She wondered whether she was something of an embarrassment to them now—they could no longer boast to their friends of her career or her political aspirations. She wanted to believe that she was judging them unfairly, but something told her that if she could hear their private conversations concerning her, she would have been deeply hurt.

Undaunted by their lack of enthusiasm, she determined that she would press on. Turning to Holmes, she told him all of the things she had wanted to say to her parents, and the never critical, ever patient Shepherd listened for hours with an interested expression. After that first evening he heard Jonathan Andrews' name mentioned frequently, for Megan thought of him often and never tired of talking about him. Every week she looked forward to Wednesday night, knowing that he would be there.

Though he brought his car after that first night, she found a little time to talk to him when each meeting ended. Holmes always heard the outcome of these discourses, and if he had been a person rather than a dog, he might have realized that she was very attracted to Jonathan.

One Wednesday night she announced to Holmes, "You're going to meet him." Holmes looked pleased that at last he would be able to satisfy his curiosity about the object of Megan's attentions. She proceeded to explain that after the prayer meeting that night Jonathan had called her aside and told her that he had two tickets for a play, and he wondered whether she would like to go with him. "It's probably nothing personal," she told Holmes, trying to contain her own excitement. "University professors get free tickets to all sorts of events, and he probably invited me because he had no one else to take. After all, most of the other people at Mother Harriet's would not be very interested in theatre. He's probably just being friendly, and I'm sure there's nothing to get excited about." Still, she was excited, and she hoped that there was at least a little interest on his part. She liked him so very much, and it pleased her to think that he would want her to go out with him socially, whatever his primary reason might be.

For the next few days she could not overcome her giddy enthusiasm. She bought a new dress for the occasion—a simple emerald satin that exactly matched her eyes and was very flattering to her figure. She made an appointment to have her hair done and get a manicure the day of her date. She also purchased new makeup and a bottle of expensive perfume.

"You're too old for this," she told herself on the morning of the date as she caught a glimpse of herself in the mirror. She hardly recognized the breathless girl gazing back at her, and she realized how little attention she had paid to her appearance from the day that she had been attacked. Now she could not help being annoyed with herself for spending so much money and time to please a man she hardly knew. "You're thirty years old," she scolded her image, "and you're acting like a silly teenager going on her first date."

"But I am," she countered back in her own defense. "This is my first date since I was attacked, and since then my whole world has changed. It was the old Megan Cleary who dated Jeff and put up with his nonsense. She died, and I would be bored to death by the things that she found amusing. I'm a new person now, and this is my first date."

Smiling at her own argument, she glanced around her apartment. Jonathan would be stopping here first and everything must be perfect. Certainly, it was not the beautiful residence she had enjoyed in New York City, but it was clean and presentable. She left Holmes to be groomed while she spent the morning cleaning the apartment and buying food for the hors d' oeuvres she planned to serve. Forgetting Jonathan's past, she nearly made the mistake of buying a bottle of wine. After a little thought, she purchased a bottle of sparkling cider instead.

By five o'clock the apartment was spotless, and the food was ready. The broiled shrimp wrapped in bacon filled the apartment with delicious smells. Holmes had returned from the groomer looking as neat and proper as possible, and he now lay on the living room carpet watching Megan survey herself in the elegant floor mirror propped against one wall of the living room.

With her long pale fingernails she nervously smoothed out a curl or two left rough by the hairdresser while she studied herself in the mirror. Her pearls with the emerald clasp were the perfect accent for her dress, and the gleaming blonde curls that brushed her shoulders made her look young and carefree. In the mirror she could see the opera length black mink coat lying against the arm of the sofa. She had not worn it in well over a year. She tried it on in front of the mirror to see the full effect and was pleased to see that the glamorous young woman looking back at her bore no traces of the trauma she had suffered. It was almost as if the clock had been turned back to a gentler time in her life. She thought that it was a shame that none of her old friends would see her looking so well. For a moment she thought of dropping by her parents' house. No, she told herself, even though the sight of her all dressed up would please them, they would want to know where she was going and with whom, and that would only spark another unpleasant series of warnings about Jonathan. Better to leave her parents out of this.

Taking off her coat, Megan returned it to its position on the sofa. "Well," she turned to Holmes. "What do you think?" His expression assured her that he approved and thought that Jonathan would too.

Megan jumped when she heard a knock at the door. Smoothing her dress one final time, she walked to the door and opened it to reveal a smiling Jonathan bearing a bouquet of pale pink roses. "Good evening," he said as he handed her the flowers.

"Good evening, and thank you," she said as she took the roses. "These are gorgeous! Have a seat, while I put them in some water." From the kitchen, she studied Jonathan as she filled the vase from the tap. Impeccably groomed, in his black wool suit and custom made shirt, he looked more handsome than she had ever seen him. His cologne filled the apartment with a warm masculine scent that made Megan's heart race. Judging from his appearance, he had also spent a long time in his preparations, and it pleased her to think that he wanted to look his best for her.

Returning with the cut crystal vase and placing it on the table, she found Jonathan and Holmes studying each other curiously. "This is Holmes, Jonathan," she introduced them patting the dog's head. "He's my watchdog and companion."

"It's a pleasure to meet you, Holmes," he smiled at the dog and then turned to Megan. "He's a beautiful specimen. Attack trained?"

She nodded. "I've had him for about a year, and you'd be surprised how much safer he's made me feel."

"I wouldn't be surprised at all. I have a female Shepherd at home, and she's quick to alert me if there's any sort of problem. In this day and age a dog is a good investment."

Megan brought the hors d' oeuvres from the kitchen along with the cider which she served in chilled silver goblets. Holmes did not try to interfere with the food, but he stayed close by Megan's side, as if to ward off any danger to her.

Jonathan complimented her on the food. "I must confess," he told her, "that I've been a little nervous about tonight. This is the first time since my wife died that I've been out alone with a woman, and frankly, I wouldn't be surprised if I've forgotten some of the finer points of escorting a lady."

Megan laughed, partially in relief because she realized that he was feeling some of the anxiety that had filled her waking hours for the past several days. In a way, this was his first date as well. "I know what you mean," she smiled. "I haven't been out for quite a while myself."

Jonathan smiled and looked at his watch, "We should be going. I made the dinner reservations for seven, and there is an eight-thirty curtain." Megan glanced at the clock and was surprised that an hour and a half had passed.

She took the empty plate and goblets to the kitchen and Jonathan helped her with her coat. Turning out the lights and setting the security system, she walked with Jonathan to his car waiting on the street below.

He drove a new Lexus, but for the first time in her life, Megan was not preoccupied with possessions, and she did not mentally compare it to the cars of her friends or family. She loved the car because it was his, because when she got into it, she could smell his cologne, and because it responded to his touch. As she sat beside him, she felt happier and more contented than she had for months.

"I'm afraid that you have something of an advantage because you know a great deal about me, and I know almost nothing about you. Tell me about yourself."

She laughed. "What would you like to know?"

"Where you were born, where you went to school, what kind of work you do, what your family is like. Whatever you'd like to share with me."

"All right. I was born and raised in Buffalo. I'm an only child, and my parents were relatively indulgent; they had great plans for my life and wanted to see to it that I attained their goals. When I was eighteen, I entered New York University, and I eventually earned my law degree from Columbia. For almost five years I was a junior partner with Pratt, Forbes and Magoff, but a few months ago I returned to Buffalo."

"That sounds like a bio from Who's Who," Jonathan laughed.

Megan did not like talking about her past, but she regretted that she could not have been a little more forthcoming. After all, he had been totally open with her.

"Well, it's really not much of a story," she said smiling.

"Are you glad to be back?" he asked.

"Yes, I am. New York City is too big and busy for me. When I was in college I loved it, but that wonderful excitement wore off after a while. When the shock and awe was gone, the only things left were bumper to bumper traffic, crime and pollution."

"The crime is unbelievable," he agreed. "When I lived there, my house was robbed twice; it was absolutely infuriating. Though it's never happened to me personally, I have friends who were mugged while they were walking on the sidewalk in broad daylight."

"That's New York City," she commented. She was afraid to say more on the subject. Fortunately, they had arrived at the restaurant, and they were seated at their table before he resumed the conversation.

"In New York I felt a coldness in the people. I know that Americans complain of the same thing when they visit England, but it wasn't only that they were aloof. I always sensed a general insensitivity and lack of concern. Anywhere where you have to step over homeless people on your way to work must have something fundamentally wrong. There is some of that in Buffalo too, but it's not nearly so prevalent."

"That's true. I think the problem is that there are so many people on the streets that you can't help them all. Even if you give money to one street person, there are ten or fifteen more waiting for you. You can't help everybody, so you learn to help no one. That doesn't make it right, but I think that people who live there adopt that attitude as a self-defense mechanism. Once you take on that mindset, it's easy to let it take over other aspects of your life."

"It is very difficult to find someone to talk to there. The more that you need people, the further they seem to pull away. When my wife and children died, I couldn't talk about it for weeks. Then later, when I wanted to talk, no one wanted to listen. They had their own lives and their own problems, and they didn't want to hear about mine. It was as if everyone was embarrassed. They treated me as if I had committed some social faux pas, and they wanted to keep me from further humiliating myself. It's a shame, because I really believe that if I had been able to find someone supportive to talk to, I might not have become a drunk."

Megan responded. "I know what you mean. About a year ago I started having some real problems." She paused at his inquisitive look, "Someone broke into the law offices where I was working late, and they beat me up pretty badly and stabbed me several times. I went through exactly the same thing. At first I didn't want to talk to anyone, and when I was ready, no one wanted to listen. As a result, I have become a very different person, and I don't seem to have anything in common with the people I knew before."

"How did you get through it?"

"You met my dog, Holmes. I bought him for protection shortly after the attack, and soon I found myself talking to him. I've gotten used to telling him all the things that no one else wants to hear. He's the only one that understands me."

Jonathan laughed. "If only dogs could talk back. Although, it's probably a blessing that they can't repeat the things we tell them. I told you about my Shepherd. Her name is Heidi, and she was both a protector and a pet for my children. After they died, she was my only living tie to them, so I kept her. But Heidi isn't a good conversation dog; she's about as hospitable as my neighbors in New York."

The meal concluded too quickly, and soon they were on their way to the theatre. The show was entertaining; the performances were good, and the music was delightful. Megan wished that she could have concentrated on it more, but she found herself thinking of the man sitting next to her. He was so comfortable; she felt as though she had known him all her life. She regretted all the time she had wasted on people like Jeff and all the evenings she had spent working late. Seated next to him in the semi-darkness of the theatre, she wished that the evening would never end, and they would never have to go home. She was disappointed when the final curtain fell and the house lights came up.

"Do you have plans for tomorrow?" Jonathan asked on their way back to her apartment.

"No," she replied, hoping that he would suggest they do something together.

"Would you like for us to exercise our dogs together? Jill and I used to show dogs, and I still have a camper with dog kennels in the back. If you're interested, we could take Heidi and Holmes out to the woods and let them run."

"I'd like that very much."

"Good, let's get an early start. What if I pick you and Holmes up about seven tomorrow, and we'll have breakfast at this little place I know outside town."

"That sounds wonderful."

As he walked her to the door of her apartment, she wondered whether he would ask to come in. Instead, he smiled and said, "I'll see you tomorrow at seven," and he turned and walked away.

"Good night," she called and waited for his reply before she stepped inside and closed the door.

She hardly slept that night, and in the morning she and Holmes were up early waiting for him to arrive. By seven she was dressed in a cream-colored wool sweater, blue jeans and boots. She was seated at the window when she saw the camper stop in front of her building. Grabbing her keys and her sheepskin coat in one hand and Holmes' leash in the other, she nearly ran to the door, opening it before he had a chance to knock.

"Good morning," she greeted him enthusiastically.

"Good morning," he returned pleasantly, "Are we ready?"

"Absolutely," she pulled Holmes out into the hall and locked the door of her apartment. The dog was suspicious and seemed to cooperate reluctantly.

"Better put that on," Jonathan told her noting the coat slung over her arm. "It's freezing out there."

He held it for her as she slipped into the soft warmth. She noticed that he also wore a sheepskin coat with a wool sweater, blue jeans and boots. She was relieved to see that he had not resorted to the rumpled corduroys and parka that was the usual attire of university professors.

Jonathan put Holmes into one of the kennels. Except for the flight from New York City to Buffalo, Holmes had not been caged since Megan had owned him. Now, he fairly scowled at her when she ordered him inside, and for a moment she felt a little guilty. He seemed to already know what she was only beginning to realize—he had been permanently displaced by the Englishman standing by her side.

She and Jonathan climbed into the front of the camper and started on their way. It was a beautiful morning—cold, crisp and dry. Megan was elated at the prospect of spending the day outdoors with her new friend, and she sat quietly enjoying the early morning air.

They had turned onto the country road that led out of town before she remembered her parents. She had not thought once to let them know that she was not going to their house for dinner today, and they would be expecting her. Megan felt a tiny twinge of guilt that she had not remembered to call, but she promised herself that when they arrived at the restaurant, she would call from her cell and let Jennifer know that she couldn't make it. With that, she turned her attention back to Jonathan and did not think of her parents again all day.

Before long they stopped at an old-fashioned country inn. "This place," Jonathan told her, "serves the best breakfast I have ever eaten. See if you agree."

Megan was instantly charmed by the informal atmosphere and cozy décor. Rich wood and natural stone gave the restaurant the charm and quiet simplicity of a century past.

A polite young woman showed them to a table next to the fireplace and handed them each a menu. Megan picked hers up, but Jonathan interrupted her. "Would you mind if I ordered for us?"

"Not at all," she smiled and returned the menu to its place on the table.

"Do you like eggs Benedict?"

"It's one of my favorites."

He ordered eggs Benedict for each of them, fresh fruit, crisply fried bacon and fried potatoes. While they waited for their food, the waitress brought each of them a steaming mug of coffee.

Megan sipped the rich brew and smiled at her companion. "This is lovely. I'm so glad we came."

"I rather like it myself. But it's the food that makes it special." He paused and looked a little embarrassed. "Actually, I've eaten here only once, with a colleague who brought me, and that was several months ago. I hope that after I've done all this boasting, the food will be good today. I've wanted to come back, but there's something inherently lonely about sitting by oneself in a restaurant full of happy people."

"Ah, now I see the method to your madness," Megan replied with a twinkle in her eyes. "I'm just an excuse to allow you to have the best breakfast you've ever eaten for the second time."

Jonathan looked startled for an instant, but when he saw her expression, he burst out laughing. "You can't help feeling self-conscious when you're the only person at a table for two," he said, "but even I would not go to this much trouble for an order of eggs Benedict."

"I understand," Megan replied more seriously. "I don't eat out very often for the same reason, although I'm almost too busy to eat out during the week."

"What are you doing now that you're here in Buffalo?"

"I'm the legal representative for Safe Haven Daycare Center," she paused. After what she had told him about her career in New York, this admission seemed to be an announcement of professional failure. Never-the-less, he had asked, and she had to answer honestly. Megan's experiences were teaching her that the truth had to be good enough. "And in the evenings I teach at the Community College."

"Safe Haven—that's the daycare near Mother Harriet's house, isn't it? That's certainly admirable work; I know the center has had a lot of problems in the past retaining competent counsel. I'm sure that they value your help."

Megan did not comment, but she was shocked. He assumed that she had gone to work for Safe Haven as a way of helping the underprivileged; he had no idea of the circumstances that had forced her there. Remembering the numerous negative comments she had made, both verbally and silently, about the daycare center and her work there, she now felt guilty. He was giving her far more credit than she deserved.

The food had arrived, and Megan immediately saw that they would not be disappointed. Every dish was expertly prepared, and at the conclusion of the meal, she determined that it was also the best breakfast she had ever eaten.

When the time came for Jonathan to pay the check, Megan rose reluctantly. They were having such a wonderful time; she did not believe that the rest of the day could possibly go as well as breakfast.

They were soon back on the road again with the heater blowing warm air into the cab and light classical music playing softly on the radio. As they entered the woods, Megan was grateful that no snow had fallen for four days, and the temperature had risen. Only small white patches remained under the trees and in the shaded areas by the roadside. The leafless gray boughs were kissed by patches of pale muted sunlight that peeked through steel gray clouds. Jonathan parked the camper and got out the food that he had brought for the animals. Letting Heidi out first, he secured her leash in his left hand and held her dish in his right hand. He then gave Megan instructions for freeing Holmes, and when she had picked up his dish, they led the dogs out into the morning air.

Megan kept a tight grip on Holmes. She suspected that Heidi's presence bothered him, but she knew that he would be obedient to her above everything else. "That is a beautiful dog," she said as she watched Heidi greedily devouring her food. "She's really big for a female."

"Thank you. When Jill and I showed dogs, Heidi was one of our best. She has excellent confirmation, and she loved the attention of the judges. Of course, when I got her, she was just a pup. I bought her in the hopes that she would someday be a good watchdog, so it was sheer Providence that I happened to end up with such a fine animal."

"She looks as though she might have come straight from Germany," commented Megan, who had spent some time studying German Shepherds' bloodlines since purchasing Holmes.

"Her parents were both imported from Germany. I named her Heidi because of that, and I thought that I was being very original. Then I started attending the shows, and I found out that about 60% of female German Shepherds are named Heidi."

At this they both laughed. "Well, I don't think that there are many German Shepherds named Holmes," Megan commented as she stroked her dog's fur.

"No, I wouldn't think so; although I have a friend who named his English Terrier 'Sherlock'."

When the dogs had finished eating, their owners allowed them to run while they followed close behind. Megan and Jonathan continued to talk, and although later she could not remember anything they said to one another, she always remembered that morning fondly.

Morning quickly became afternoon, and rain began to fall in spite of the continued presence of pale sunlight. "The devil is beating his wife!" Megan exclaimed when they had taken cover inside the camper.

"What?" Jonathan laughed.

"It's an old Irish expression to explain why it rains when the sun is shining."

"I've never heard that, although it's certainly cold enough for the devil to be working in some way."

"Yes it is," Megan nodded, noting that the rain was beginning to freeze on contact as it hit the wind shield. "This would be a good afternoon for a nice cup of tea."

"This would be a good time for Afternoon Tea," Jonathan corrected her.

"Isn't that what I said?" Megan asked.

"Not exactly. Afternoon Tea is different from a cup of tea in the afternoon. In the 1800s the Duchess of Bedford began having tea with bread and butter served to her every afternoon because she got too hungry between lunch, which was served at noon, and dinner, which was not served until eight or nine o'clock in the evening. During the afternoons when the other ladies of her social class visited her, they joined her for tea. They liked the idea so much that it became quite popular. Soon the bread and butter expanded into a light meal to include pastries, scones, small sandwiches, and other such refreshments."

"Really? I had no idea."

Jonathan studied her in surprise. He had thought that everyone was familiar with Afternoon Tea. "There's a restaurant just a few miles from here that serves a superb Afternoon Tea. It's owned by a British couple, and they have captured the essence of what Afternoon Tea represents. Would you like to go there?"

"I would love to."

"Well then, let's put the dogs back in the kennels and drive up. By the time we get there, tea will be underway."

They arrived at the inn just as tea was beginning, and Megan found that it was as delicious as Jonathan had promised. Every variety and flavor of tea was served along with delicate sandwiches and cream-filled pastries. She was very hungry, and her introduction to "Afternoon Tea" proved to be a delightful addition to her day.

When at last they drove back to Buffalo and stopped in front of her apartment, Megan hated to say good-bye. She invited Jonathan inside and served them each a glass of chilled sparkling cider. They sat in her living room and talked without a break as comfortably as if they had been members of the same family. She felt safer and more secure than she had since she was a small child, and she realized that in Jonathan she had discovered everything that she had been searching for. The cheerful fire crackling in the fireplace and his warm gentle voice made her forget that anything bad had ever happened to her.

At midnight he rose to go, though he seemed as reluctant to leave as she was to have him do so. At the door he took her delicate hand and pressed it between his as he said good-bye. Then he opened the door and was gone, leaving Megan alone with her thoughts.

It had been the most wonderful day of her life. A few years earlier she had dated a great deal, and she had always thought that she enjoyed herself on these outings, but she now realized that until last night she had never known what it meant to have a really good time on a date. Every aspect of her outings with Jonathan had been perfect; she only regretted the thought that subsequent dates could never measure up to the standard they had set today.

Her hand still felt his warm, strong grip, and her heart felt full to overflowing. She lifted her palm to her face and smelled his cologne. She would not take her shower tonight; she would wait until morning so that she could smell the masculine scent he had left behind as she slept. She locked the door and set the alarm without thinking about what she was doing, and after she had gone to bed, she lay awake reliving every moment of her day with him. When she finally drifted off to sleep, he remained near her in her dreams. For the first time in her life, Megan Cleary was falling in love.

TWELVE

The air was cold and crisp in the woods, and the night was still. He stopped for a second to listen. On the path behind him lay the twigs and leaves he had trampled; the trail would be clear for anyone wishing to follow. That was not his concern, however; by morning he would be far away. He had thought he heard someone chasing him; he now stood with his back against a tree to listen for his pursuers, but the silence of the night was broken only by his own breathless panting. When he was satisfied that no one was following, he raced off again through the dark maze of trees lit occasionally by patches of moonlight.

He was young, about twenty-two years of age, with thick black hair and deep dark eyes. His dark skin was scratched from his frequent falls and brushes with trees, and his light blue jeans and shirt were torn and dirty. Lean and strong, he was able to continue running at his fierce pace although his heart pounded wildly. At least, he thought, he was now free to run without bars and fences to restrict his movements. That they would come for him was not a source of great concern; he had never allowed himself to look very far into the future. They would not even notice that he was missing until morning, and by the time they began their search, he would be long gone.

Faint touches of color lit the horizon as the darkness began to lift. With daylight approaching, he would have to make his way more slowly so as not to attract attention. Continuing to wind his way through the woods, he worked like a meticulous mouse in a maze, stopping occasionally for a puff of his marijuana cigarette. At last the city lights loomed before him, and he knew that his journey had nearly ended. Sitting down with his back against a tree, he rubbed his blistered feet and cursed in Spanish because he was forced to travel on foot.

The sky grew fully light as he sat there. Extinguishing his cigarette and brushing back his hair with his hands, he rose and made his way toward the highway. The cars flew past him as he stood with his thumb up trying to attract their attention. At last a truck pulled up beside him and rolled down the window.

"Where are you headed?" asked the pretty young driver.

"Buffalo," he replied.

"Get in," she opened the door. "We're just outside of town."

The stranger grinned broadly as he slid into the seat. She returned his smile and pulled back onto the highway. Half an hour later he was at the wheel of the truck, and its young owner lay in a ditch alongside the road with her throat slit.

He drove the truck to the barrio where he had spent his whole life before going to prison. The tenements and narrow streets represented everything he hated. He blamed the barrio for his poverty, for the girl he had married and the child she had born. For the last two years he had told himself that everything had been her fault—if she had not gotten pregnant, if she had not refused to have an abortion, if he had not married her, if she had not nagged him to support her and the baby—none of this would have happened. He was the one who had been made to suffer, but it was she who deserved punishment because she had ruined his life, and then she had sent him to prison.

Nervously tapping his fingers against the steering wheel and puffing a cigarette, he now sat staring up at the window of the apartment they had shared together. What would she say when she saw him? Grinning at the thought of the expression on her face when she opened the door and saw him standing there, he imagined every word that she would say. He had envisioned this scene every day and night for two years. Now that the time had come, his heartbeat quickened and his palms felt cold and damp.

Pushing open the door of the truck, he stepped onto the sidewalk. Across the street he recognized the group of young men who stood aimlessly on the curb laughing and talking. Once he had been one of them, but now he hurried inside the building so that they would not recognize him. Climbing the stairs, he looked around and savored each moment. Familiar sights and smells lent an air of reality to his homecoming. He had returned to do as he had promised. He walked down the hall and knocked at number thirty-seven. When no answer came, he knocked again, and then cursing and threatening, he began to pound the door with his fist. Taking his pocket knife, he used one of the blades to trip the lock and let himself in.

He looked around the small, clean apartment. She was not there; he wondered when she would return. Looking at the clock, he realized that it was almost noon. He was hungry, and he looked in the refrigerator for something to eat.

Hours passed before he heard footsteps in the hall and the sound of a key in the lock. Stepping behind the door, he waited. Holding sacks of groceries in both arms, a young Puerto Rican woman, no more than twenty years of age, entered. As she pulled the door forward to close it, she saw him and cried out, but he grabbed her arm and slammed the door shut.

"Aren't you glad to see me, Yolie?" his smile was menacing.

"Hector, please," she dropped the groceries and tried to wrestle away from him, but he held her fast.

"Please what, huh?" He forced her closer to him. "I told you I would come back. You thought you were safe, didn't you, Bitch? You told all those lies about me in court, and you were so glad when I went to prison. You thought I'd never get out. But I'm out now, and you're going to be sorry."

"Please, Hector," she begged. "If you kill me, it'll be worse for you when they find you."

"Shut up!" he barked. "Where's Maria?"

The blood drained from the young woman's face. "No, Hector, please. Don't hurt Maria; she's just a baby."

"Where is she!" he screamed.

"She's not here," tears streamed down the young mother's face. "I don't know where she is."

"Liar! Whore! I'll kill you!" He slammed his fist into her face. "Never mind. I know where she is. Jose wrote me in prison and said you were leaving her at a daycare around here. I'm gonna find her and kill her too so she can't grow up to be a filthy whore like you."

"No," she screamed. "I won't let you hurt her again." She tore away from him and ran toward the door, but he caught her with his left hand and pulled out his knife with his right. Grabbing hold of her hair, he cut her throat and left her bleeding on the floor of the apartment. Slipping the bloody knife back into his pocket, he walked from the building and went to find Maria.

THIRTEEN

At four o'clock Megan still had a considerable amount of work piled on her desk, and she realized that she had a long evening ahead of her. Maria was playing quietly on the floor with her toys as Megan typed the final paragraphs of the letter she was writing. She hated to interrupt her work just at that moment, but she knew that Carmen had to leave at five o'clock to pick up her husband.

Maria began to fuss, and Megan pulled the little girl up onto her lap.

"Now, let's see what's the matter with you. You've been fed, you're warm, you're dry. I think you're just ready to go home." The little girl put her arms around Megan's neck and lay her small head against Megan's shoulder while the young attorney softly patted her. Rising with the child in her arms, she walked out of her office to speak with Carmen.

"Holmes is finished at the groomers, and I have to pick him up before five," she told Carmen. "I know you have to leave at five to pick up Mario, so I thought I would go over now and get Holmes. Then I'll come back and stay with whatever children are left until their mothers come so that you can leave when you need to."

"Good," Carmen agreed.

When Megan arrived at the groomers, Holmes was waiting for her and jumped eagerly into the backseat of her car. "We're not going home yet," Megan announced. "I have some work to do at the office, so you'll just have to wait there for me and play with the children until I finish." Megan had taken Holmes to Safe Haven on two other occasions when he had to come back early from the groomers, and she knew that he was a safe companion for the children. She admired the respect he showed for their inferior size and strength. He was never rough or aggressive with them; he had the even disposition of a family pet combined with the intelligence of a trained animal that discerns dangerous situations and handles them accordingly.

It was nearly five o'clock when Megan arrived back at Safe Haven. The main play area was empty, and as she entered with Holmes, she called out to Carmen, "Has everyone left already?"

"No," Carmen shook her head, "Maria's still here, and that's odd because Yolie's usually pretty punctual or else she calls if she knows she'll be late. I don't know where she could be." Carmen looked at her watch.

"You go ahead and leave," Megan smiled. "I have some work to finish up here anyway, so I'll stay until six, and if Yolie doesn't come, I'll take Maria home with me tonight."

Carmen looked relieved. "Thanks, Megan. That would be a big help." Grabbing her keys and coat, she hurried out the door. Megan immediately locked the entry door behind her. Maria had been playing near Carmen's desk, but Megan now carried her back into her office with Holmes following close behind, and then she settled the little girl on the floor with her toys and the dog while she resumed her work.

Twenty minutes later she heard a car stop in front of the building and someone press against the door in an attempt to enter. "That must be your mother," she looked down and saw that the little girl was sound asleep. Holmes had also heard the car, and he was on his feet staring intently in the direction of the door. He seemed very displeased when she closed the door to her office, shutting Maria and him in together while she went to open the door for Yolie.

Megan was surprised to see, instead, a young man dressed in blue jeans and a blue shirt standing outside. Megan had never seen him before and was immediately suspicious of him. "Open the door!" he called.

Megan shook her head. "We're closed!" she called back through the door.

The young man walked away for a minute and returned holding a piece of paper with the word, "MARIA" written on it in large letters. Megan opened the door reluctantly, for she thought that he might be bringing a message from Yolie. She did not let him in, however, but spoke to him through the partially-opened door.

"I'm here to get Maria," he said. "Her mother sent me."

"I'm sorry," Megan responded. "We can't release the children to anyone but their parents."

"Yolie can't come." His tone was agitated. "She sent me instead. Now give the kid to me."

"No," Megan replied firmly. "When Yolie gets here, I'll give Maria to her." With this she tried to push the door shut, but he threw his weight against it and forced it open.

"Where is she!" he yelled.

"Get out of here, now," Megan ordered, but as she spoke, he pulled the bloodstained knife out of his pocket.

"See this?" he waived the bloody knife in front of her. "I used this to cut her mother's throat, and I'm gonna use it on Maria, too. If you don't get out of my way, you'll be next."

The steel blade flashed in the glare of the fluorescent light. Megan was not afraid for herself; she thought only of the harm he would do to the slumbering child. Whatever happened to her, she would not let him harm Maria.

Bracing herself, Megan stood still and tried to remain calm. She looked around, but there was nothing with which she could defend herself. She knew that he could easily overpower her, and there was little hope of reasoning with the lunatic railing before her. If she did not think of something quickly, he would kill her, and then there was no hope of saving Maria. As Hector continued to threaten and rave, Megan's mind raced until she recalled a verse that she had often heard repeated at their prayer meetings, "In my distress I called upon the Lord and...he delivered me from my strong enemy."

Silently she prayed, "Jesus, please don't let him kill me and this child." Then she spoke, "You can't hurt me or Maria. We belong to Jesus, and He protects us. No weapon formed against us will prosper."

Hector stared at her wordlessly. He had already killed two women that day, and both had begged for their lives. No one had ever faced him with the steely determination of this woman. He was so taken aback by her statement that it took him a moment to regain himself. Then he thought again of prison and of the risk he had taken to get out and find his ex-wife and daughter.

"Shut up!" he yelled, cursing at her violently. Grabbing her arm, he swung the knife up under her throat and maneuvered her into the hall leading to her office. Silently she prayed all the way that something would intervene to stop him. He opened Linda's office first and pushed her into the room while he turned on the light. He overturned furniture and file cabinets until he had satisfied himself that no one was there. Always he held tightly to Megan's hair with one hand. After he had wrecked the room, he turned again and stared at her. For the first time since he had entered, Megan became really frightened for herself, for he spoke to her in Spanish, and though she could not understand what he said, she felt certain that he was talking about raping her. Nothing else, including the prospect of dying, frightened her as much. He moved toward her, and then something caught his attention. Forcing her in front of him again, he dragged her towards the room across the hall, and pulled open the door.

There in the doorway stood Holmes, teeth bared, tail raised, and fur standing high. Maria was behind him, and even she seemed to understand that she must keep her distance. Seeing Megan in front and Hector behind her, Holmes did not move to attack immediately, but he snarled and moved toward the intruder.

The knife touched Megan's throat. "Call him off!" he screamed.

"I can't. He's attack trained. He will kill you if you harm either Maria or me."

Holmes snarled and moved forward, forcing Hector to step back while he held Megan fast. Steadily, the growling dog continued to advance until he had again forced Hector and Megan back into the reception area. The terrified convict now realized that he couldn't get past the dog, and he couldn't kill his hostage. Dragging Megan to the door, he opened it and released her just before he stepped outside onto the dark sidewalk. Before Megan could call him off, Holmes bounded out the door barking ferociously. Hector panicked and dashed into the heavily trafficked street in front of a stream of oncoming cars. Holmes stopped at the curb and watched as Hector rushed half way across the four lane stretch before he was hit by a speeding truck and crushed beneath its wheels.

Megan slammed the door of the center and locked it before calling the police to report the incident. From them she learned of the prison break. It saddened her to think that both of Maria's parents were dead, for she knew that in spite of Yolie's many difficulties, her world centered around her daughter. That night when she took Maria home with her, she felt a special burden for the sweet little girl who had endured so much tragedy. Megan fixed special foods for her and allowed her to sleep with her in her bed. Once in the night, Maria awoke and called, "Mama," and Megan put her arms around her to comfort her. How could she tell a two-year-old that her mother was never coming back?

The next morning when they arrived at Safe Haven, the center was buzzing with the news of what had happened. Everyone praised Megan for her bravery and marveled that she and Maria had survived the incident. Linda Pearson gave credit to Holmes, although she disapproved of having the dog in the center. Though Megan loved her pet and usually credited him with everything positive, this time she knew that Linda was wrong.

It was Jesus who had saved them; she knew that for a fact. She had been the victim of two other attacks, and she could recognize the difference between those and this one. When she was raped, the fear of dying had eclipsed all other emotions. A few months later, when she had again been confronted by her rapist, she had reacted the same way. Her only thoughts were of self-preservation. Last night she had realized that for the first time in her life she was not afraid to die because she trusted in the eternal life that Jesus Christ had provided for her. More important, perhaps—for the first time since her attack she was not afraid to live.

She could have died the previous night—she had been alone with Hector for at least ten or fifteen minutes before he released Holmes, and at any point during that time he could have slit her throat. It was no accident that Holmes had been there—in all of the time that she had worked at Safe Haven he had been at the center only two other times.

Megan had been both a successful criminal attorney and a shattered victim, and she knew that there are no coincidences. Everything that had happened that night had been carefully calculated to save their lives. This morning she and Maria were alive by Providential decree, and that knowledge gave her hope for the future. She had finally found the Friend of whom Mother Harriet had so often spoken, and she realized that He could not only help her face death, He could give her the courage to face life—to reconcile her past with Him and to share her future with Him. He had already extended His help to her; all that remained was for her to make her commitment. She regretted only that she had waited so long.

That Wednesday night at the prayer meeting she asked that everyone pray with her to receive Jesus Christ into her heart. They gathered around her, Mother Harriet with the same strong hand on her head that had once forced her into a chair when she had insisted on praying for her at the first meeting; Jonathan with his light soft touch against her brow. "Lord Jesus," she asked, "Come into my heart. Forgive my sins and give me the life that you have for me." She thought of the journey that had brought her to this point and realized that everything had begun to change the night that she had gotten down on her knees and asked God to show her what He wanted her to do. She had not known it at the time, but that prayer had changed her life. She heard Mother Harriet quoting the words of Christ in prayer, "If anyone clings to his life he shall lose it, but anyone who gives up his life for my sake shall find it again." She had not given up her old life, it had been ripped from her, and she had bitterly grieved its loss. Now she renounced if freely, knowing that in Christ she had found a better life, one that promised a future and a hope.

FOURTEEN

Megan asked Linda to allow Maria to stay with her rather than placing the child in foster care, and Linda passed the request on to the Department of Human Services. "The child has always been withdrawn due to severe physical abuse by her father, and she has been further traumatized by the death of her mother," Linda informed the case worker from DHS. "Megan Cleary is one of the few people she trusts. Besides, Megan works at the center, and the child is assured of excellent care during the time that she is working." The DHS agreed, and Maria was placed in Megan's temporary foster care.

Megan had not spent much time with children prior to going to work at Safe Haven. Thus, she had never learned to enjoy their company, and she knew almost nothing about caring for a child. Never-the-less, she welcomed Maria into her home because she believed that she could help her adjust to losing her mother better than a stranger could. To Megan's surprise, she soon discovered that Maria was not the burden she had imagined she would be. Rather, she was a constant source of laughter and joy. From the first night, Holmes accepted Maria's presence; it was as if he understood that she needed their help, and her stay was only temporary. Placidly he watched as she played on the floor with her toys and followed Megan around the apartment. Occasionally, she approached him and stroked his fur. When he grew tired of feeling her small fingers tug at his coat, he rose and walked away, but he never snarled or snapped at her, and this pleased Megan immensely.

After Linda informed her of DHS's decision, Megan took Maria shopping for a crib, a high chair, and a few other necessities. When the crib was arranged close to her bed and the high chair had taken its place in the kitchen, Megan thought that her apartment seemed much cozier. Every night she bathed the little girl and put her to bed in the crib, sitting near her until she went to sleep. For the first few nights Maria slept fitfully, but by the end of the week she had adjusted to her new residence and woke only once in the night to call for her mother. At these times Megan's heart went out to her, and she got out of bed and picked Maria up to reassure her.

Although the police had given Megan Maria's belongings, Megan was concerned to see that most of her clothes were old and worn. Yolie had made barely enough money to keep her rent paid and purchase the bare necessities, and Megan guessed that many of the ragged items had been purchased at used clothing shops in the barrio. On their first Saturday together, Megan took Maria shopping and outfitted her in a colorful new wardrobe for the approaching spring and summer.

The two settled comfortably into their new routine. On weekends they took walks in the park with Holmes, and Maria, who had overcome her initial unwillingness to speak, chattered endlessly. Megan could not understand much of what she said, for she spoke a combination of

Spanish and English held together with infant gibberish, but she enjoyed hearing her talk anyway. When Maria bubbled over with laughter over something that Megan would normally not have found the slightest bit amusing, Megan would fall prey to the child's infectious gales, and she would find herself laughing along with her.

On Tuesday and Thursday nights Carmen baby-sat while Megan taught her class at the college, but on all other occasions she tried to keep her as near as possible. Jonathan liked Maria from the first minute he met her, and he often took Megan and her to family-style restaurants where children were welcome. "Bethany was just a little older than she when the accident happened," he mused quietly on one occasion, and Megan understood that in Maria he saw traces of the little girl he had lost. For her part, Maria kept her distance from Jonathan, although she did not object to his presence as long as he did not try to pick her up. Maria's wariness of men led Megan to wonder whether Maria had known any sort of father figure after Hector had gone to prison.

One evening as the three of them were having dinner in a neighborhood restaurant, the waitress remarked, "What a beautiful child! But then, how could she not be with you two for parents." She turned to Jonathan, "She looks like you." Jonathan smiled, and Megan said, "Thank you."

To Megan they were beginning to seem like a family. Although after their first date Megan feared that they would never be able to recapture the magic of that evening, she soon found that every time she saw Jonathan she found something new to love about him. Whether she caught a glimpse of him across the room at Mother Harriet's or she spent an evening with him at the most elegant restaurant in Buffalo, his presence warmed her heart and filled her with joy. They went out for coffee every Wednesday evening after the prayer meeting and spent almost every weekend together. Most other nights he phoned, even if they could talk for only a few minutes. In conversation and manner he was always a perfect gentleman, but when she looked into his blue eyes, Megan suspected that he felt all of the emotions that she did.

Megan did not realize that she was in love, for she had convinced herself that people do not really fall in love. She had grown up understanding that people meet other people of their social class to whom they are attracted and eventually, for mutually beneficial reasons, decide to make the arrangement permanent. She had dated a number of socially acceptable young professional men while she was living in New York City, but she had never had a relationship of any substance with any of them. Her relationship with Jonathan, however, had not followed any logical pattern. Almost from the first day she met him she had not been able to envision a future without him. She hoped that behind his genteel reserve he also planned for them to have a life together.

One evening Jonathan called to ask if they could have dinner alone at one of their favorite restaurants. Megan made arrangements for her parents to watch Maria, for, in spite of themselves, they had learned to love the little girl, and they enjoyed spending time with her. Megan dressed in a black silk suit and coiled her hair into a chignon that she pinned at the nape of her neck. She opened the door at the sound of his first knock to see him standing in a black suit holding a dozen red roses. Megan took the flowers to the kitchen and put them in a vase, but Jonathan refused to sit down. He seemed nervous and insisted on going straight to the restaurant. During the drive, they talked of various matters—Maria's progress, how glad they were that summer had finally arrived, his work at the university, and the different projects on which Megan was working. As they talked, Megan realized that the coming week would mark six months since they had met. To her it seemed as if it had been only a few days since she had driven him home after the prayer meeting.

At the restaurant the waiter seated them at a table by the window. As they talked and laughed and ate, the time passed so quickly that Megan was surprised when she noticed that only a few patrons remained.

After a brief silence Jonathan put his hand on hers. "Megan, will you marry me?"

She was stunned. The question had been preceded by none of the flowery declarations of love that she had imagined would accompany a marriage proposal, and she sat silently staring at him, trying to process what he had just said. Jonathan realized that he had caught her off guard and began to speak again. "During the past six months, I've begun to live again. I know this may seem sudden, but I love you. I've learned how unpredictable life can be, and I don't want to spend any more of my life without you."

Megan searched for the words that would express all of the love that she felt for him, but none seemed adequate, "Yes," she answered, "I will."

Lifting her hand to his lips, he kissed her palm and then leaned over and kissed her lightly on the lips. From his pocket he produced a box containing an engagement ring—an emerald surrounded by diamonds. "I had this made especially for you," he said almost shyly, "in the hope that you would say 'yes.'" He slipped it on her finger. Too large, it would have to be sized; for safety's sake she returned it to the box, but she was delighted with the way that it looked and felt on her hand. It was not the ring that made her heart race, though, but the idea of becoming Mrs. Jonathan Andrews.

"Megan Andrews," she thought to herself, "Megan Cleary-Andrews." Either way, it was the most beautiful name she had ever heard, and this evening was the most wonderful she had ever experienced. She smiled at Jonathan who was beaming at her.

"When do you think we can have it all arranged?" he asked.

"The wedding? I don't know; you've only met my parents a couple of times, and you have no idea how demanding they can be. I want us to be married as soon as possible. I've never wanted a big wedding. I'd like to have the ceremony in the rose garden of my parents' church with just a few friends and family attending. Is that okay with you?"

"That's perfect; I prefer small ceremonies too, but I do want traditional vows."

"Of course," Megan's mind began to race, and they spent the next hour making plans over coffee—where they would honeymoon, where they would live, how they could best arrange their vacation time. Finally, she looked at her watch and saw that it was after midnight. Her parents had been baby-sitting for hours.

"We have to go," she said. "I forgot that Maria is with my parents. If I leave her there too long, they'll stop taking care of her for me." Jonathan paid the check, and five minutes later they were in his car heading towards her parents' house.

Ian looked irritated when he opened the door. Megan guessed correctly that his annoyance stemmed only partially from her leaving Maria in their care for so many hours. On the two previous occasions when he had briefly met Jonathan, he had not been impressed. Even though he was very disapproving of Megan's continuing relationship with him, he forced himself to be polite.

Jennifer heard their voices and came downstairs to suggest that since Maria was sleeping soundly there was no reason to disturb her before morning. When she entered the room and saw Jonathan standing next to Megan, however, she forgot about Maria. With a mother's keen and unerring instinct, she surmised that Jonathan had proposed, and from Megan's flushed and glowing face, she guessed that she had accepted. She felt that, at the very least, she owed it to her daughter to tell her that she thought she was making a serious mistake.

"I'm sorry for leaving Maria with you for so long," Megan began. "We sort of lost track of the time..."

"That's not a problem, Dear," Jennifer interrupted. "Maria's sleeping soundly; there's no reason to wake her. Why don't the two of you sit down?" At Jennifer's insistence, they were seated on the sofa with Ian and Jennifer sitting across from them in large wingback chairs.

"Did you have a pleasant evening?" her mother asked, hoping to open the conversation to the subject of their engagement.

"It was very nice," Megan responded, wondering whether this was the right time to tell her parents about her decision to marry Jonathan. She looked at Jonathan and then at her parents; something told her that it was better to make the announcement now and get it over with.

"Jonathan and I are going to be married," she could not help smiling as she made the announcement, "and I wanted you to be the first to know."

Ian, who was not as perceptive as his wife, looked genuinely surprised, but Jennifer was careful not to change expressions.

"Congratulations," she said quietly, but it was clear to Megan that she was not pleased. "Have you set a date?"

"Not yet," Megan replied, "but we would like to be married as quickly as possible."

"Why the rush?" her father looked at her suspiciously. "You're our only child, and this is your first marriage. I would think that you would want to take the time to do it right."

"There's no special reason," Megan resented her father's implication. "We love each other, and we want to be man and wife. If we're going to get married anyway, I don't see the advantage in waiting."

"It certainly is to your advantage," Ian argued. "A few months can change everything. Marriage is a serious matter—you're going to spend the rest of your lives together. Surely you're not opposed to taking a little time to get to know each other better before you make a final commitment."

"You and mother always say that you don't know a person at all until after you marry them," she countered.

"Well, you could certainly know *him* better than you do; you only met a couple of months ago."

"We met in January," Megan replied. "We've known each other for six months, and we've seen each other often."

Jonathan looked uncomfortable. He now knew what had escaped him for the past six months—Megan's parents were opposed not only to the idea of their marriage; they were opposed to him personally. He did not know what Megan had told them concerning his past, but he suspected that she had told them about his behavior after he lost his family, and that played a part in their opposition to him.

"I know that, generally, what you are saying is true," he addressed Ian respectfully, "But Megan and I are not children. We are mature adults, and we know that this marriage is right for us."

"Nobody's arguing that you're not a kid," Ian retorted. "You're forty years old—certainly too old for Megan. You've been married before and had a family. You're an alcoholic. I think you've lived enough for all of us."

Jonathan remained silent for a moment, and then he spoke, "I am a recovering alcoholic," he finally said, "While it's true that I will never be cured, I have been sober for more than three years, and I will never go back to drinking. As for my family, they were my whole life. It's not my fault that they were killed by a drunk driver. Your daughter is the first person I've dated since I lost them, and I have grown to love her very deeply. I know that my past is checkered, but I have become a Christian and re-evaluated my priorities. I'll take good care of Megan and do my best to be a good husband to her."

Ian shook his head, "I'm not saying that any of this is your fault. Obviously, you've been through a hard time, and I'm not insensitive to that. I'm only saying that there are too many differences between the two of you. This is for your benefit as well as Megan's. The fact that she's the first person you've dated in three years indicates to me even more that you really aren't prepared for marriage. I don't want my daughter put in a position where she'll always be competing with your former wife, and I don't want her to spend the rest of her life trying to keep a drunk on the wagon. She deserves better than that."

"Dad!" Megan protested, but he cut her off.

"Look, I'm not opposed to your getting married. You're certainly old enough, and you've been on your own for a long time, but I want you to marry the right person. You need to find someone closer to your own age who shares a similar background. The world is full of nice young American men who are much more suitable. If you're interested in getting married, I can help you start looking. But this," he waived his hand at the two of them, "is not acceptable."

"I'm sorry that you feel that way," Jonathan said.

"Well, I do, and that's just the way it is. I don't want to hear any more about this, and I would prefer that you two not see each other again."

Jonathan stared at Megan disbelievingly, and she forced a smile filled with both disappointment and amusement. Gently she patted his arm, and he correctly interpreted the signal as his cue to leave. Rising, he said good night to her parents, and Megan, who had decided to stay the night, walked him to his car.

"Don't worry," she smiled. "They'll come around, but even if they don't, we have a wonderful future ahead of us."

"I know. I wish that they could be happy for us, though."

"Oh," she shrugged, "eventually they will be. My father is really a very nice person. You'll like each other once we get past this hurdle and you get to know each other better. It's just that he's very controlling, and he likes to have his own way. In a couple of days he'll have reconciled himself to the idea of our getting married, and everything will be fine."

Megan waved to Jonathan as he drove off and then stood for a while enjoying the starlight. Part of her wished that she could hold onto this moment forever and not have to face anymore confrontations. She hated to disagree with her parents; she had seldom won an argument. Still, she knew that what she had to say must be said, though it would result in still more arguing. Turning, she walked resolutely back into the house. Her parents were still sitting where she had left them.

Taking her seat opposite them, she began: "Mother, Dad. I'm very sorry that you are unhappy about my marrying Jonathan. When I gave you the news tonight, I hoped that you would be supportive. I understand your feelings, but you must also understand mine. I'm thirty years old, and for the first time in my life, I'm in love. Jonathan is a wonderful man. When you look at him, you see only his troubled past. You don't appreciate that he is bright, well-educated, successful, and prosperous. Whatever problems he may have had, he has overcome. He's kind, generous, caring, honest, forthright and honorable. He has put Christ at the center of his life, and he has dedicated himself to serving Him. I love him, but I also respect and admire him, and I'm going to marry him."

"So what you're saying is that you don't care what we think; you're going to do this whether we like it or not," replied her father.

"I do care what you think, but you're not going to change my mind about this."

"No, obviously you don't care, and that's about what I should have expected from you. All my life I worked hard to give you everything, and you never appreciated it one little bit. I had to struggle when I was young, but you never had to do anything. I handed you the very best so that you could have a good life, and what have you done with it? I worked to send you to school—you didn't have to take out student loans or work while you were in school like most people do. When you were fresh out of law school, I got you a job with Pratt, Forbes and Magoff. Believe me, they wouldn't have even spoken to you if I hadn't pulled a lot of strings to get you in. Now, you've thrown all of that away to work in a slum daycare and teach a bunch of dopes at a community college. I taught you all the social graces and introduced you to society when you were sixteen. I kept you right by my side and took you to the best clubs and parties so that someday you could marry someone with wealth and influence and a name that amounted to something. Now, you can't wait to throw that away too. Well, I've been a fool! I should have invested my time and money where I would have gotten a decent return on it."

"Dad," Megan regretted that she had so deeply disappointed her father, and she didn't know what to say. "Don't say that. None of that is true. You know that I love both of you."

"You may love us; in fact, I'm sure that in your own selfish way you do, but you don't care about our feelings. To you, we're just old, meddlesome baggage, and since that's the way you feel, I don't care what you do. I'm tired of doing things for you, and I'm through taking care of you. From now on, you're on your own." With that Ian rose from his chair and stormed upstairs to his bedroom, leaving Megan and her mother alone. Jennifer sat silently for a moment and then followed her husband upstairs. Megan went to her old bedroom.

She had been angry with her parents so few times in her life that she could almost count them on her fingers, but as she lay in her childhood bed staring into the darkness, she was angrier with them than she had ever been. Logically, she could tell herself that she understood their apprehensions, but she could not understand their reaction to her engagement. Jonathan's proposal was the first positive thing that had happened concerning her future in nearly two years, and she wished that they could have appreciated that and been considerate of her feelings. Telling herself that she didn't care what they thought and that she didn't need their permission or blessing to marry, she tried to sleep. Yet, whatever she might tell herself, she was hurt by the things that her father had said to her.

The following morning she got up early with Maria. Making an effort not to wake her father, she did not even have breakfast before having her mother drive them back to her apartment. Dreading another confrontation, she rode along silently waiting for her mother to reiterate what Ian had said the night before. Jennifer had not been surprised when Ian had taken the initiative in discouraging their daughter from marrying Jonathan, but she had been surprised at the vehemence with which he objected. She was sorry that the happiest event in Megan's life was being spoiled. She was torn between Megan's feelings for Jonathan and her own, but her conflict sprang from her desire for her daughter's happiness. Cautiously she approached the subject.

"You know," she said, "Dad loves you very much. He's always wanted what's best for you. I know that you're angry, but don't be too hard on him; he only wants you to be happy."

"Maybe he could want it a little less," Megan replied ruefully.

"No," Jennifer shook her head, "a parent's instinct is to protect his child from any sign of danger, and we've devoted thirty years to protecting you. I know that you're all grown up—you've reminded us of that every single day since you were eighteen—but no matter how old you get, you'll always be our baby. In your Dad's eyes you'll never grow up, and he'll always try to protect you."

"But I don't need to be protected from Jonathan," Megan protested.

Jennifer was silent for a moment. "Do you really think he's changed?" she finally asked.

"Of course," Megan replied. "You have to put this in perspective, Mother. It's not as though the man was always a derelict. He has a Ph.D.; he was a respected member of the academic community for years. He had never had any problems until his wife and children were killed. At that point he dropped out of the academic world and began drinking. He dropped out of sight for about a year, and then he returned to academia and has been sober ever since. It was never a matter of regaining professional respect because, as far as his colleagues know, he took some time off after he lost his family and then returned to teaching when he was emotionally ready. They never saw him drunk or witnessed his work suffering as a result of his drinking. He didn't have to work to regain other people's confidence; he had only to rebuild his own. Now he's written a series of papers that have been very well received, and he is becoming well known in academic circles. His career has come back stronger than it was before.

"You've never suffered a great loss," she looked at her mother lovingly. "You don't know what it means to have your entire life snatched away from you. When that happens, you don't just get up and go on as before. When people experience real tragedy, the person that they were ceases to exist. That's what happened to Jonathan; when his family died, he died too. His whole life disappeared in that car accident, and the man that was left mourned not only the loss of his family but the loss of the best part of himself as well. In spite of everything, Jonathan made it through, and the new man is much stronger than the old one."

"How can you know that for certain?" Jennifer asked. "You've never suffered a great loss either."

"Yes, I have," Megan replied. "When I was raped, I experienced a terrible loss. People who thought that I had only been beaten and stabbed said to me, 'You're so lucky that he didn't kill you,' but what they didn't realize was that he had. The old Megan Cleary, the naïve self-confident girl who knew what she wanted and how to get it and had always been in control of her life—that person never made it to the hospital. She was dead long before the ambulance arrived. I think that's what made it so hard for me; every day I grieved the death of the person I had been. Whenever I looked back at myself as I had been before the attack, I never wished for the day that I would be like that again, because I knew that I never would be. Death is the most final of all things upon this earth—anything else can be fixed or changed, but death is permanent. When the person inside you dies, that is also permanent—there's no resurrecting that person. The best you can hope for is to survive, and if you can make it past the experience, you find that you're very different, but much stronger and more resilient. Jonathan made it through, and so have I. Neither of us is ever going back to what we were. We have only the present and the future, and we plan to share that together. Maybe we'll draw strength from each other."

Jennifer stared silently at her, and it was impossible for Megan to tell whether her mother even understood what she had said. Kissing Jennifer good-bye, she got out of the car with Maria in her arms and climbed the stairs to her apartment. A note had been pushed under the door, and when she picked it up, she saw that it was from Jonathan. "Sorry about last night," it read. "See you at the jewelers at 12:30 to have your ring sized. We'll have lunch afterward. Love, Jonathan." Smiling, Megan pressed the note to her lips and then rushed to get Maria her breakfast before they left for Safe Haven.

At noon she met Jonathan, and before leaving the ring with the jeweler, she put it on her finger. She turned her hand under the bright lights and watched the stones produce a spectrum of colors. That ring seemed to reflect all the hope and beauty of their future, and the happiness and joy it represented were far more valuable than the emerald and diamonds of which it was created. Jonathan smiled at his bride-to-be's enthusiasm.

They stopped at a delicatessen for a sandwich before returning to work, and each was careful not to mention her parents. Instead, they led the conversation to more pleasant topics such as where they would live after they married.

"I own a beautiful piece of property just outside the city," Megan was telling him. "It was a graduation present when I finished law school. It's four acres of the most beautiful wooded land you've ever seen, and all I have to do is pay the taxes on it. If you want to, we can build a house there. We would have room for a pool and a place for horses, and Maria would have a big yard to play in..."

She stopped abruptly; she had made the last statement without meaning to. She had surprised herself by the inclusion of Maria in their lives, but Jonathan laughed.

"You know," he said. "I've been thinking that we might want to adopt her after we're married. We both love her, and she's certainly attached to us. She needs a real home, and we could provide that for her. She would have plenty of family—she's even won your parents over, and that does seem to be the acid test."

"Obviously, I've been thinking the same thing," Megan replied, "although not consciously."

Jonathan glanced at his watch and saw that he was late. "I've got to run," he said. "I'll call you tonight."

Two days later Megan was surprised by a call from her mother. "Since it looks as though Jonathan is going to be our son-in-law, we need to get to know each other. Why don't the two of you come over for dinner this evening?"

Megan was taken aback by the invitation. "What about Dad?" she asked.

"You know your dad," Jennifer replied. "He's always polite to guests in his home. He'll be all right."

"I hate to contradict you, but he wasn't very polite the last time we were there," Megan replied.

"Well, Sweetie, you took him by surprise. I'll handle Dad if you'll take care of Jonathan. You just get him over here, and we'll take it from there."

"Thanks, Mom. We'll be there."

"Good, I'll expect you at seven."

Megan hung up the telephone feeling that her mother was on her side, and she knew from experience that her mother had her own way of controlling her father.

Immediately, she called Jonathan who accepted the invitation politely. If he had any reservations about spending the evening with her parents, he kept them to himself, and for this Megan was thankful. She prayed that they would get through the evening without an argument and that her parents and Jonathan might learn to genuinely like one another.

They arrived promptly at seven, and Jennifer greeted them with unusual warmth. Ian was quieter, as though he had resigned himself to an unpleasant evening, and he greeted the two of them politely though coolly. Dinner was ready, and when they had taken off their coats, they went into the dining room to eat.

To Megan's great relief, after a few minutes the conversation between the two men began to pick up. Ian was an accomplished horseman who loved horseracing, and they soon discovered that Jonathan shared his love for the animals and the sport. Having found this common ground, the two men spent the remainder of the evening discussing horses.

After dinner, Megan and her mother left the men alone while they went upstairs to the master bedroom where Jennifer had spread out various bridal magazines. As she began to show her daughter the various designs in formal gowns and veils, Megan groaned inwardly. Knowing her mother as she did, she was certain that she would insist on a formal, showy, expensive wedding with many guests. Jennifer had already begun planning the details, and Megan saw her own dream of a small intimate ceremony dissolving. Yet, she also knew that there had already been enough dissension over the wedding. Smiling, she pretended to be enthusiastic as she looked at the gowns with her mother.

On the way home, Megan told Jonathan of the impending compromise. "My mother has always dreamed of my wedding, and she has already begun making plans for it. I think I need to concede this issue in order to restore peace. Can you live with that?"

He nodded understandingly, and she smiled at him, "The marriage is for me," she said. "The wedding is for my parents."

Her parents ordered her a custom bridal gown, and Jennifer occupied herself by making arrangements. Megan also allowed her mother to take the lead in preparing the guest list, which was soon filled with friends, business acquaintances, and numerous members of the Cleary and Donovan families. An announcement of the engagement resurrected relatives and friends whom Megan had not seen for years. At the numerous bridal showers, luncheons, and parties given in her honor, she smiled and chatted politely and breathed a sigh of relief when they were over.

She and Jonathan looked forward to their announcement to Mother Harriet's prayer group with much more enthusiasm, for it was this group that had brought them together. Megan, however, felt that Mother Harriet should be told before the other members of the group, and so on a breezy Saturday afternoon she took time off from her preparations to drive to the old woman's house to give her the news.

"Praise the Lord!" exclaimed Mother Harriet when she heard the news. "I knowed you two was right for each other the minnut ya met.

See, Child, I told you that God has a way of workin' out our lives for us. You's gonna be real happy together."

"We're happy already," Megan smiled. "We wanted to be married right away, but my parents insisted on giving us a big wedding, and that has delayed things a bit. We'll be getting married just before Thanksgiving, and that's my favorite time of year." She paused, wrestling with herself over what she had come to ask the old woman. "Do you think I should tell Jonathan about what happened?"

Mother Harriet sat up straight in her chair. "Why I thought you done that already!"

"No, I've been afraid to. In fact, I'd decided not to, but now that he's getting to know my parents, I keep wondering whether at some point they'll make some reference to what happened to me in New York. Then he'll want to know why I didn't tell him. I'm so afraid that something will slip out without them thinking about it."

"How much do they know?"

"Only that I was beaten and raped. I never told them the rest of the story."

"And they know that you ain't told Jonathan nothin'?"

"Yes. We haven't really discussed it, but I think they believe that if he knew, he wouldn't marry me. I don't think he would either."

"Well," said Mother Harriet firmly, "only one way to find out, and that's to tell him. You's plannin' to marry this man and spend the rest of your life with him. That's a relationship built entirely on trust. When ya gets married to a person, you's more vulnerable to them than ya ever gonna be to anybody else—they knows your secrets, they lives in your house, they supports ya and you supports them. Ya can't hide nothin' from each other. So ya don't wanna start with lies and secrets. Call him and tell him ya gotta talk to him, and then ya sit down and tell him the truth."

"About the rape?"

"'Bout everythin'. 'Bout bein' raped, and shootin' that boy and getting' all them notes for money. Tell him the whole thing."

"But what if he doesn't understand," Megan sounded desperate. "What if I tell him, and he stares at me and then he tells me that he can't marry me? What if he calls off the wedding? Oh, Mother Harriet, I love him so much; I can't stand the thought of losing him; that's what I'm most afraid of."

"I think he'll understand. I's knowed Jonathan Andrews when he was worse off than you's ever been. When I found him layin' on that bench he couldn't even tell me his own name. He knows 'bout grievin' and havin' bad things happen, and I think he'll understand. But if he don't, you'd be better off findin' somebody else. Any man that wouldn't understand that ain't worth marryin'."

"But you're forgetting that I committed a crime. I actually killed somebody. What if he reports me to the police?"

Mother Harriet looked shocked, "If ya can't trust him no better than that, ya ain't got no business marryin' him. Anybody off the street can keep a confidence; that's the least ya should expect." The old woman smiled and her tone grew softer, "But I knows him, and I knows he loves ya. I can hear it in his voice when he speaks out your name. I ain't never knowed him when he was so happy. He'll understand, Meggie; if I was a bettin' person, I'd put money on it."

Megan looked at the dry little face she had come to love and trust, and the confidence with which the old woman spoke gave her hope. She could not remember ever having known Mother Harriet to be wrong about anything, and she hoped that she was not wrong about Jonathan.

The old woman invited her to have a cup of coffee, and they spent about an hour chatting before Megan had to leave. From Mother Harriet's home she went to her own mother's house where they were to choose wedding colors and select the bridesmaids' dresses. Thoughts of Jonathan filled her mind, and she was so distracted that finally Jennifer became annoyed with her. She could think of nothing except what she would say to him and how he might react. Finally, Jennifer determined that they were not going to accomplish anything, and she sent her daughter home. On the way Megan tried to muster the courage to call Jonathan, but when she pulled up in front of her apartment, her cell phone rang, and she was fairly certain that he was on the other end. The decision to talk to him had been made for her. As she looked at the caller ID, she was tempted not to answer.

"I've been calling you all day," his voice was cheerful. "Finally, I called your mother's house, and she told me that you had just left."

"I'm sorry. I left my phone in the car. We were making the never-ending wedding arrangements. I'll have to show you the options so that you can give me your input."

"I'm sure that whatever you like will be fine. I called because I want you to come over to my house this evening. With all of the wedding preparations, I haven't gotten to see much of you. I'm afraid I'm not much of a cook, so I thought we could order a pizza and just enjoy the evening."

"That sounds nice," Megan answered, "but why don't you come over here instead? Maria does best if she goes to bed right on time, and I need to talk to you."

"Is everything okay?" he sounded a little concerned.

"Yes, everything's fine. When can you be here?"

"Half an hour. I'll stop and get the pizza on my way over."

"Fine, I'll see you then." Megan suspected that Jonathan thought she was about to break the engagement; in a way, she might be. She wondered whether she should have gone to his house as he had suggested, but there was something about the security of being in her apartment and having Holmes there when she told him—not for protection but as a friend who had heard the story many times and suffered through it with her. Anyway, she thought bitterly, if he should receive the news badly, she didn't want to drive home alone.

When Jonathan arrived, Megan smiled at him warmly. He seemed reassured by her smile, and though dinner was dominated by Maria's chatter, they enjoyed a pleasant meal. Yet, it was obvious that Megan was troubled about something, and when the pizza was gone and Maria had been put to bed, they sat on the couch together.

"You said that you have something to tell me."

"Yes," she nodded slowly, unsure of how to begin. "You mentioned after we first met that I knew a great deal about you, but you knew very little about me. You've trusted me with the story of your past and the events that brought you to where you are, and now it's time for me to trust you with my own past." She paused, but he said nothing.

With difficulty Megan tried to make sense of a series of events that she had never fully understood herself. "Soon after we met, I told you that when I was in New York City I was attacked in the offices where I worked by someone who broke in one night when I was working late. I told you that I was badly beaten and stabbed, but more than that happened—I was raped. He beat me, and stabbed me, and raped me, and left me on the floor for dead."

She had been looking down as she spoke, but now she lifted her gaze to meet his. His brow was wrinkled and his expression had changed, but whether he felt compassion or disgust she couldn't tell. Averting her gaze again, she continued, "What happened wasn't my fault. I was working late, all the doors were locked. When I heard someone come in the back entrance, I walked out into the dark hall, and he grabbed me from behind; I never even saw him. I tried to fight but he was much stronger…"

"I'm sorry," Jonathan said as he reached out to pull her into his arms.

Instantly, she stiffened and said, "There's more. Please let me finish." He moved back to his former position, and she continued. "Afterwards I was sad and depressed and enraged. I was terrified of everything. I spent Christmas with my parents, and when I returned to my apartment, I had several deadbolts and a security system installed. I bought Holmes for protection, and I also bought a gun. I didn't tell anyone, but I carried it in my purse with me everywhere I went. I swore that no matter what happened, I would never be raped again.

"One evening when I left the office I forgot to take some papers for an important case that I was working on. When I was about half way home, I realized what I had done. Because it was still early, I thought that there would be someone in the building when I got back. I parked in a lot not far from the office and then cut through the alley to enter through the alley door. I was on the steps unlocking the door when he came up behind me and grabbed hold of me. He told me that he was the one who had raped me before and that this time he was going to kill me afterwards. He dragged me off the steps, but I was able to reach into my purse and put my hand on the gun. Before he could rape me, I pulled out the gun and shot him. He fell across me, and in the lamplight I could see his face. He was so young—so unlike what I had expected—that I just stared at him in disbelief. For an instant I even imagined that I had shot the wrong man. I managed to get to my feet, and then I heard a siren, and I thought someone had called the police. I ran back to my car and drove to my apartment as fast as I could.

"All the next day at work I kept waiting for the police to come to our offices to question us about the body in the alley, but they never came. As time passed, I realized that no one was coming, and I thought I was safe. Every time I thought about the man I had killed, I felt horribly guilty, but at the same time, I was relieved that he could never come back to hurt me, and I was determined to move on with my life.

"A few months later I received a note written in large block letters. That first note referred to me as a murderer, and I thought that it was sent in connection with a case that I was defending, but a few days later I received another note in which the writer told me that he had seen me kill the man in the alley. He said that if I did not pay him fifty thousand dollars in cash he would go to the police. I had no choice but to pay it, and although I tried to find out who was blackmailing me, I never succeeded. Every month after that I received an additional demand. In only four months, he took two hundred thousand dollars from me—all of the money that my father had given me in investments. To pay the final demand I even had to sell my car. I was dead broke. It was impossible for me to make any further blackmail payments, so I resigned from my job and left New York City. My cousin Mike got me the interview at Safe Haven, and Linda Pearson hired me at our first meeting. Mike agreed to sell my apartment for me and have my belongings shipped to my parents' address.

"My parents know about the first attack, and they know that I was raped, but that's all they know. They have no idea that all the money they gave me is gone. Mother Harriet and you are the only ones who know the whole story. "

When she had finished, Megan lifted her eyes. Jonathan bore the troubled expression of someone who is hearing something so far outside the realm of reality that he is having a difficult time processing it. At last, he spoke, "You weren't going to tell me any of this, were you?"

"No."

"What made you change your mind?"

"I talked with Mother Harriet about it, and she convinced me that we should have no secrets between us."

"Mother Harriet was right." He reached out and took her hand, "I'm glad you told me. I can't change what happened to you, Megan, and I can't promise you that nothing bad will happen to you again. But I will promise you this: I will always do everything in my power to protect you and keep you safe." He pulled her close to him and wrapped his arms around her.

She was glad that she had told him; he had understood after all. He loved her in spite of everything, and he wanted her to be his wife. If she had ever had any doubts about whether he was the right husband for her, in that one moment he dispelled them all.

FIFTEEN

One evening Megan was looking through an on-line job site that specialized in listings for legal professionals when she came across a posting from a large law firm in Buffalo that was looking for a criminal attorney to fill a recent vacancy. She e-mailed them a copy of her resume and requested an interview. Shortly after she arrived at Safe Haven the following morning her cell phone rang, and John Kindale of Kindale, Howard and Schwartz identified himself. He told her that he had received her resume and asked her to meet with him at his office the following day. Megan arranged with Linda to take the time off from work, though she did not tell her the nature of her appointment, and at two o'clock the following afternoon she was sitting across the desk from John Kindale.

"We're looking for someone with at least three years' courtroom experience in criminal cases and an excellent track record," Kindale informed her as he glanced over her resume.

"I have almost five years of courtroom experience. I was a junior partner with Pratt, Forbes and Magoff in New York City, and during my years there I handled several jury trials. By the time I left, I had earned a reputation as a competent defense attorney." She wondered whether she should tell him that she had been offered a full partnership with the firm.

"Why did you leave?"

Megan was prepared for this question, and she answered carefully. "After almost ten years of living away, I felt that it was time to come home. My parents live here in Buffalo, and I have a lot of extended family here besides. New York City is intoxicating to a young person just starting out, but as I matured, I began to realize that Buffalo had more to offer in terms of a family-friendly environment. I had come to the point where I was beginning to think in terms of where I wanted to put down roots. I could see myself having a successful career here, but I could also see Buffalo as a place where I would want to raise my children. I have many friends and family here with whom I can share my life. I'm satisfied that I made the right choice."

"How long have you been back?"

"I've been here eight months."

"And I see that during that time you have served as legal counsel for the Safe Haven Daycare Center—a government-sponsored institution for the underprivileged. Why did you choose to go there?"

"A friend of mine told me about the center while I was in Buffalo," Megan replied. "He said that they were badly in need of legal counsel, and he thought that if I were moving back here, I might be willing to help them through a difficult period." Then, being careful to answer honestly but to also accentuate the positive aspects of her work, she answered, "When I arrived at Safe Haven, they had been without legal counsel for six months, and open files and documents were stacked haphazardly in cardboard boxes. I worked hard to bring everything up to date and to give them good legal representation for their pending cases, but now any competent attorney could step in and take over."

"So, now you feel it's time to move on?"

"Yes. My work there was never meant to be permanent. In many ways it has been rewarding, but I have finished everything I went there to do. It's time for me to get back to criminal law; I miss the challenge of arguing cases before a jury."

"That would certainly be a very real part of your work here," Kindale told her. "Your caseload would require that you spend a good deal of time in hearings and conferences and in court. The rest of the time you could work out of your home via computer and telephone hookup. Many of our attorneys are doing that now, and it is working out well for all of us. We require only that you be here for all consultations with your clients. Of course, if you prefer to work from here everyday, we can arrange that as well."

"Actually, right now I have a foster child, and I would prefer to work from home. My parents will look after her whenever I need to be in the office or in court."

"Good. I see that you have also taught classes at the community college."

Megan nodded, "I teach a correctional science course there."

"That's always good experience and good PR for the firm. Teaching heightens one's awareness of his subject, and it also heightens the public's awareness of the firm. Teaching is considered a noble profession, and we like to have our attorneys involved in that sort of thing. I occasionally conduct workshops, and I've taught a few classes in legal theory at the university, so I know the advantages."

Placing her resume on his desk, Kindale studied Megan. "I think that you would be a good fit for us. I'll need a list of references from your former employers, but pending some unforeseen problem, I don't see any reason why you couldn't have the job. How much time do you need before you could begin working?"

Megan was surprised; she had not imagined that he would make a decision so quickly, and she had to think for a moment before she answered. "I need to give Safe Haven two months' notice so that they can find a replacement. I could begin the first of October."

"Great. E-mail me a list of references, and I'll get back with you."

That evening as she talked with Jonathan and her parents over dinner, she said, "I think I have a really good shot at this. John Kindale seemed to think that I was well qualified, and he more or less said that I could have the job if I got good recommendations from Linda and Pratt, Forbes and Magoff."

"And you will," Jennifer assured her, "You've always performed well for them. You have an excellent record, and that's what they'll judge you by."

Megan was thoughtful. "I'm sure that Linda will give me a good recommendation—we've always had a good working relationship. I know that the college will have good things to say about me because I received a very high evaluation from them last semester. The only one who worries me is Jack Forbes; he was so angry when I left that I don't know what he will say."

Ian frowned, and she was sorry that she had brought up the subject of her former job. But in an instant, the frown disappeared, "Jack will say that you deserve the job. Did you tell this fellow that they had offered you a full partnership just before you left?"

"No, I didn't think it was wise. Anyway, I was afraid that Jack would deny it."

"Well, you should have," said her father emphatically, "and stop worrying about what Jack is going to say; he's not the only person there. They'll recommend you highly; I can almost guarantee it."

Megan looked at her father with loving suspicion, wondering whether he planned to use a little of his much touted influence to ensure her a good report. "If the Lord wants me to have it, I'll get it, and if He doesn't, I won't. Either way, it's up to Him, and I'll be happy with the outcome."

"Well, I think they'll hire you," Jonathan sounded optimistic. "If they do, you'll be getting a new job and a new husband all at the same time."

"Yes," Megan smiled, "I have a new life ahead of me, filled with good things."

That evening after Megan and Jonathan had gone, Jennifer commented to Ian, "Megan is so excited about the prospect of this job, even though she's reluctant to say so. I certainly hope she gets it."

"Yes," he responded, "it would be very nice for her. After she quit her job in New York and moved here to go to work for that place, I thought her life was over. I was so upset; I couldn't understand how she could just abandon everything. But now I do believe that she's making a comeback. She's almost back to the girl we used to know."

"I think that after she was raped she went through a lot more trauma than we realized," Jennifer mused. "She wouldn't discuss it, and she refused to go into counseling. I think that she fell apart inside, and she had so many bad memories of New York and what had happened to her there that she had to get away. She's finally beginning to heal, but I don't think that she's at all the same girl she used to be."

"Jonathan's been good for her, I think," Ian replied. Jennifer looked at him in surprise. He noted the look on her face and added, "I know that I was opposed to him initially, but he does seem to really love Megan, and that makes up for a lot. Besides, now that I've gotten to know him, he's actually a nice guy. He seems bright enough, and he's rather interesting to talk to. The only thing I don't like about him is that he's going to marry my daughter."

"I don't think that you would have liked anyone she had married."

"I'm sure I wouldn't have. My expectations were just too high. I think that she deserves someone perfect, but Jonathan's probably a good choice. He'll be good to her and take care of her, and that's important."

"I think they'll be happy. They're planning to adopt Maria after they're married."

"I know. Jon told me. There's no sense in my telling them it's not a good idea; they'll just do it anyway. I wish they wouldn't add the strain of parenthood to the first few months of their marriage, but I guess that's up to them."

"Oh, it'll work out," Jennifer sighed. "Megan is determined to have a good life, and people who are determined to have good lives usually do. She's gotten very religious, and she believes that God has something special for the three of them. Maybe she's right—things do seem to be falling into place for her."

"Maybe." Ian kissed his wife's cheek and turned out the living room lights before they went upstairs to bed.

Three days later John Kindale called to say that Megan had the job, and they wanted her to begin the first Monday in October. She was ecstatic when she called Jonathan and her parents to tell them the news. Though she never knew to what extent Ian had been involved, she could tell from Kindale's remarks that she had received very positive recommendations from all of her references, and for this she thanked God.

That afternoon Megan gave Linda her notice. As she entered her office, she remembered clearly the first time, eight months before, that she had walked into that office to apply for the position of legal counsel. Vividly she recalled how repugnant the sights and smells had been to her when she started working there. Now she realized that Safe Haven had lived up to its name. It had been a safe haven for both her and the children. The past eight months had given her an opportunity to recover spiritually and emotionally from the trauma she had undergone. Here she had found a new life and a new faith, and it was with some sense of loss that she tendered her resignation. She knew that the time had come for her to move on, but she also realized that for the first time in her life she was leaving genuine friends behind.

Linda was interested to hear about the job. Kindale had not contacted her, and this was the first she had heard about it. When Megan had finished, she said, "It sounds like a great opportunity. I'm very happy for you." Linda seemed sincere, but she looked around the office a little ruefully, as though she wished that she could tender her resignation as well.

"I don't want to leave the center in a lurch," Megan said. "I told them that I would need to give you two months' notice, and they've agreed. I won't start until the first Monday in October, so that should give you time to replace me."

"I doubt that we will be able to replace you," Linda replied. "Of course, we'll be able to hire someone else as our legal counsel, but it's unlikely that they will bring with them your level of dedication. You've done a very good job here—much better than I had expected. We'll all miss you."

"I'll miss everyone," Megan responded. "This has been a good experience, and I feel certain that I can put what I've learned here to good use in my new job. Being here has changed my perspective about the law and the legal system, and it's taught me to respect the needs of the people behind the legalities. I could never go back to viewing the legal profession in the same way that I did before I came here."

"When I interviewed you, I didn't think that you were at all suited for social work. I expected you to quit the first week, but you proved me wrong. You're not like anyone I've ever met, and I don't think I will ever meet anyone like you again." She laughed, and Megan suspected that there was a sense of relief in her statement.

"Anyway," Linda continued, "I'm glad you let me know. I'll begin looking for someone. Maybe Mike has another friend."

Megan rose to leave and then remembered something, "Oh, by the way, I've been called for jury duty. I need to take tomorrow afternoon off."

Linda swore and then laughed, "I guess you'll be spending your last two months here on a jury."

Megan shook her head, "Not a chance. I'm an attorney—instant disqualification. Neither side is going to want me sitting on a jury. I'll be there ten minutes before they send me packing."

"I hope so," Linda sighed, "I sure could use you here."

"I know so," Megan assured her.

Megan could not help being a little annoyed as she arrived at the courthouse for jury selection the following day. This was a ridiculous waste of her time. Yet, as she waited to be interrogated by the attorneys, she was reminded that she missed this aspect of her work, and she felt a sense of relief knowing that she was going to be practicing criminal law in the near future.

Anticipating every question, she mentally answered each query that the attorneys would pose. "How are you employed?" would be one of the first, and she would answer that she was an attorney. They would grimace and abruptly end the questioning.

She had selected jurors and knew the care that must be taken in the process. Recalling the Janet Dobson case, she thought of the difficulty she had encountered in selecting jurors who had not been prejudiced by the media attention given to the well-publicized shooting. She certainly would not have a bias in any case that might be going to trial in Buffalo. She had not watched the news since she had returned—at first because it was too depressing and more recently because she had been too busy. Her interest was now peaked, however, and she thought that she might follow this trial in the media since she would not be sitting on the jury.

Hours dragged by, and prospective jurors came and went. Finally, late in the afternoon her name was called. Taking a seat, she proceeded to answer the questions hurled at her by the defense attorney.

"What is your name?"

"Megan Cleary."

"How old are you?"

"I'm thirty years old."

"Are you married?"

"No."

"Are you a native of Buffalo?"

"Yes."

"Do you have a degree?"

"Yes, I…" she started to explain, but he cut her off.

"Yes, you have a degree?"

Megan nodded and again opened her mouth to tell him that she had a degree in criminal law, but he continued. She looked into his face—fat, bald and middle-aged, he was the kind of pompous, overly self-assured egotist who didn't believe that he was capable of making mistakes—just the sort of attorney she despised as a person but loved to go up against in court.

"Now Miss Cleary," he smiled at her patronizingly. "Have you ever heard the name Simon Winter?"

"No."

"Never? No one has ever mentioned that name to you?"

"No."

"How long have you lived in Buffalo, Miss Cleary."

"I was born here, and then I left for about ten years. I've been back for eight months."

"I see. Simon Winter is accused of rape and murder. Have you heard anything about the case?"

Megan gave a slight start that went unnoticed by the attorneys. The word "rape" conjured up terrifying images, and the idea of being called in on such a case was unnerving, but she answered truthfully, "No."

"Were you aware that this case was coming to trial? I understand that you may not have known his name, but did anyone mention to you that the man accused of raping and murdering a girl about a year ago was going to trial?"

"No."

"Did you see anything about it on the news?"

"No. I don't watch the news. I've been very busy."

He turned and said something to the prosecuting attorney who was standing close by. They both looked at their watches and glancing at the clock hanging on the wall of the small room, Megan saw that it was nearly five o'clock. The attorneys seemed to be in a hurry to be done with jury selections. Someone left the room and returned, and then the defense attorney turned to her. "Be here tomorrow promptly at eight-thirty. The trial starts at nine."

"Any others?" a clerk popped his head in the door to ask.

"Nope. That's it. She's Number Twelve."

"Wait," Megan was shocked. "You mean I've been selected!"

"That's right. You may go now." He turned his back to her, and both attorneys stuffed papers into their briefcases as they prepared to leave.

"But wait," Megan attempted to stop them. "You don't understand. I can't do this."

"It's your civic duty, Miss Cleary. If you fail to appear for jury duty tomorrow morning, the judge will issue an order to bring you in." He again gave her that patronizing grin. "We'll see you tomorrow."

That evening she discussed the situation with Jonathan. "I can't believe that they selected me. In fact, they almost didn't. I was the twelfth juror. The guy who's on trial should fire his attorney—I've never seen a worse jury selection. The only thing he seemed interested in was getting finished. He didn't even ask me how I was employed."

"Do you really believe it would have mattered?" Jonathan asked. "From what you've told me he seemed interested mainly in finding someone who hadn't heard anything about the case."

"He was—it must have been highly publicized. Still, other things are important too. There's another question he should have asked me."

"What?" Jonathan looked at the expression on her face and guessed the answer.

"It's a rape case, but he didn't ask me whether I had ever been raped. He should have asked me whether I had ever been raped or whether any members of my family or my friends had ever been raped, but he didn't. That question goes to the very heart of bias in this case, but he didn't even ask!

"I know that when he told me that the man on trial was an accused rapist I should have volunteered the information, but I just couldn't. I couldn't bring myself to confess to strangers something that I have spent months building the courage to tell you. My mind was racing because I was bracing myself to answer as honestly, but as briefly as possible. I was so busy preparing my answer for a question that never came that before I knew what was happening, the defense attorney told me to be at the courthouse tomorrow morning at eight-thirty for the opening of the trial."

"Don't you think you're putting yourself in a difficult position? You never went through a trial when you were raped, but by serving as a juror in this case, you will be hearing evidence that's bound to dredge up painful memories. Aren't you afraid that at some point in your own mind you will become the victim, and you will see everything through her eyes?"

"I thought about that very carefully after I left the courthouse this evening. I do have painful memories, and I'm sure that this experience will cause them to resurface. However, after I asked Jesus into my life, I made a real effort to make peace with myself about what had happened. I don't want the rest of my life to be consumed with hate. I've been a victim, but I'm also an attorney who understands the law, and that should give me an advantage. I will see things more clearly than many of the other jurors, and the evidence will mean more to me.

"I'm not going to hear the case with vengeance on my mind. I've never met the defendant; I've never even heard his name. I don't know whether he's guilty or innocent, and if he's innocent, I don't want to find him guilty. I've been the victim of cruelty, and I know how destructive unreasoning hatred can be. I would never want to unjustly inflict on anyone the kind of suffering I've experienced. I have prayed about it. In fact, I prayed for half an hour before I came over here, and I believe that this is the right thing for me to do. Perhaps the Lord knows that this experience will complete my healing process and help me put this nightmare behind me. At any rate, I'm certain that I can be totally objective. If I had any doubt about that, I would have myself disqualified immediately."

Jonathan put his arm around her. "I hope you're right."

"I'll be okay. If this is like most trials, it'll be over in a few days. By then it will be almost time for us to be married and start our life together."

"I know, and I want it to be a wonderful life. Just remember, it's not *your* rapist who's going on trial tomorrow."

That evening Megan called Linda at home and gave her the news. "I really never believed that I would be chosen," her tone sounded slightly embarrassed.

"I wouldn't worry about it," Linda sounded annoyed. "I thought something like this might happen when you told me that you had to report for jury duty. Anyway, there's nothing we can do about it."

"I'm not going to neglect my work during the trial," Megan assured her. "When I pick up Maria each afternoon, I'll take work back to my apartment. That way I'll keep up with everything. I'm sure the trial won't last long—I should be back full-time in a week or two."

"That's good. It sounds like you've got things under control," Linda responded. "I'll see you tomorrow."

Early the next morning Megan was up and dressed. Maria had to be given her breakfast before she could be taken to Safe Haven, and Holmes had to be taken for his walk. Megan wondered whether she would be able to stay on schedule and fulfill her other responsibilities, but by eight-thirty everything had been attended to, and she was walking up the steps of the courthouse.

She entered the room where the other jurors were assembling. To her surprise, several of the twelve were young professional-looking people not unlike her. A few middle-aged housewives and a couple of older women were milling about. It was a predominately female jury—out of the twelve only three were men. It was one of the most unique juries that Megan had ever seen, and she wondered whether it was by design or through carelessness that the attorneys had stacked the jury with middle-class women.

The jurors made their introductions, and Megan studied each of them with interest. Grace was the stereotypical housewife/soap opera addict who immediately explained that she was recording all of her favorite soaps so that she could watch them every evening when she went home. With two teens in high school, she found little to occupy her days, and she was very excited to be serving on a jury. "I hope they sequester us," she whispered to Megan, "so they'll have to put us in one of those big hotels and pay all our expenses. My husband will be so jealous."

Ralph was an independent building contractor who bore the worried expression of someone who has been taken away from extremely important duties. "They say that your job has to give you time off," he huffed. "But when you're in business for yourself, that's just money down the drain for every day you're gone."

Standing next to Ralph was Margaret, a sweet grandmotherly type with short silver hair and blue eyes that bugged slightly. Her two daughters were grown, and her grandchildren were the loves of her life. Megan could imagine her driving a car with a bumper sticker that read: "Happiness is being a Grandma."

Helen was a homeschooling mother of five who spent her days reading books rather than watching television. Actively involved in all aspects of her children's educations, she saw to it that they received music and dance lessons as well as proper scholastic training. A serious woman, she seemed to Megan to be both studious and intelligent.

Barbara and Anne were both data entry clerks who were delighted to have time off from their jobs for whatever reason.

Nancy was a hairdresser who greeted Megan with a warm smile and admitted that, as a fan of courtroom dramas, she was very excited about the prospect of sitting in on a real life trial.

Freddy looked very young. He was attending dental school and had been forced to take this time away from his classes. He seemed nice enough, in an irresponsible, flighty sort of way.

Harry was about Megan's age and considered himself the life of any gathering. Laughing loudly at his own jokes, he proceeded to try to entertain everyone. Though he did not say exactly what he did for a living—he was employed with a "major computer company"—he wanted all the other jurors to know that he was extremely busy and important, and he reminded them by constantly sending text messages and checking the voicemail on his cell phone.

Rita was a supervisor at a local bank and considered herself to be the ultimate independent woman. With her long thick black hair, bright blue eye shadow and gaudy gold jewelry, she was confident of her position as the undisputed beauty of the group.

Donna was a shy, mousy little woman who wrote a weekly column for the newspaper. Having never been attractive or popular, she prided herself on being brilliant and observant instead, and Megan imagined that her courtroom experiences would appear in a future article of the *Times*.

These eleven, along with Megan and two alternates, comprised the jury. Megan studied them with the strange fascination of someone seeing a familiar scene from a new perspective. As an attorney she had often wondered what jurors thought about as they waited to be called into court to hear the opening arguments. Now she knew—they thought about their own lives, work, and daily concerns.

At last they were called into the courtroom, and they filed into the jury box. It was a beautiful room in a stately old building that had heard many cases and seen many defendants during its years of service to the community. Year after year the guilty and the innocent passed through these doors, only occasionally receiving justice. Today another man would rest his fate in the hands of twelve strangers who, by a preponderance of the evidence, would attempt to determine what God and he alone knew.

Megan took her seat at the far end of the jury box and waited for the defendant to make his entrance. The heavy wooden doors swung open and, shielded on either side by his attorneys, Simon Winter entered. She could not see his face because of the wall of briefcase-bearing men surrounding him, but she could see that he was dressed conservatively in a dark blue suit. He took his place at the defense table, and again the attorney blocked her view of him. Megan watched Hank Dorson, the attorney who had selected her the day before, scratch notes on a sheet of paper. The defendant whispered something to him and Dorson stretched and leaned back in his chair, leaving Megan with a clear view of the defendant's profile.

As she stared intently at the clean-cut young man with his even features and clear blue eyes, the image of the cold gray face in the alley flashed before her eyes. That night the blond hair falling across his forehead had been drenched with blood from the bullet wound where she had shot him. She had stared into that face for just a moment before hearing the sirens and fleeing from the scene, but even in profile, she was almost certain that she recognized him. At that moment Simon Winter again whispered something to his attorney and turned to look at the jury.

Megan saw him clearly. It was he—there was no doubt. She had not known his name, she had known nothing about him, but that face had stayed with her in her nightmares. Simon Winter was the man who had raped her and left her for dead—the man she had shot and believed she had killed.

She was so shocked by the realization that the courtroom became a blur. When the judge entered, she tried to stand but found that her legs were almost too weak to support her. Pulling herself to her feet, she stood robotically until she heard the bailiff say, "You may be seated." She did not hear the prosecuting attorney or his impassioned argument; she did not see the defense attorney when he rose to make his opening statement. She saw nothing but Simon Winter, and she mentally relived all of the agony of her last months in New York City.

"How?" she asked herself. How was it possible that he could still be alive? She had been so certain that he was dead when she had fled the scene. She had been blackmailed for killing him...

Slowly a realization came over her that was darker than any she had already experienced. No one else had been in the alley that night or in the offices nearby. Only the two of them knew what had taken place. He had sent the blackmail notes.

Suddenly everything made sense—all of the questions that she had asked herself since this nightmare began were answered: why the police never came, why the murder was not reported in the media, how the blackmailer knew so much about her. He had orchestrated a cruel drama and tricked her into playing a part in it. She had been his victim—not once, but many times.

The thought crossed her mind that he had followed her to Buffalo, but she dismissed it immediately. She was not his victim now; she was on his jury. After almost eighteen months they had come face to face in court. Any minute now he would look up and recognize her. A look of horror would spread across his face, he would tell his attorney, and they would confer together trying to decide what to do. The attorney would ask for a recess, and then he would go to the judge to have her removed from the jury. They would declare a mistrial, and he would go to court again, but she would have caused him a few bad moments. She waited— it was her turn to see him squirm.

The defense attorney paced the floor in front of the jury like a caged animal as he extolled his client's virtues. Megan was aware of him only when he blocked her view. Simon watched Hank intently, making notes on what he was saying. His blue eyes followed the boorish lawyer until they stopped with Megan. Anticipating his first look of recognition, she sat perfectly still. Then a sunny smile accentuated by deep dimples and perfect teeth spread across his face, and without words he seemed to say to her, "I'm a nice guy who hasn't done anything wrong. I'm sure that by the end of the trial you'll understand that." He was trying to win her over. Megan felt a wave of shock followed by almost uncontrollable rage.

He didn't even know who she was! After brutalizing her, trying to kill her, and taking every cent she possessed, he had so successfully put her out of his mind that there was not even a glimmer of recognition. Before today she had not even known his name, but she had recognized him instantly. He had known everything about her: her name, her profession, where she worked and where she lived, but as soon as he had used her up and left her destitute, he had forgotten all about her. It was the supreme insult—after having done everything in his power to destroy her life, he had forgotten that she even existed. He had never lain awake at night fearing that she might find out that he was still alive and turn him over to the police. He had never been haunted by nightmares so frightening that he was forced to walk the floor at night to stay awake. This man who had done everything in his power to destroy her couldn't even recognize her. She meant less than nothing to him; he didn't even consider her a threat.

All of the anger that she believed she had conquered rose up inside her, and the hatred that she thought she had overcome was back again. At that moment she would have given almost anything to have been able to travel back in time to that evening in the alley and actually kill him. She could see herself with the pistol in her hand, shooting him over and over again. The fantasy was gratifying for a moment, but as Megan gave it more thought, she couldn't enjoy it.

Until the moment when she had believed him actually to be dead, nothing else had mattered. After she had shot him, however, she had been filled with remorse over having taken his life. Now as she saw him sitting there smugly, smiling at the jury, she could tell herself that her feelings were justified. If anyone deserved to be killed, he did. But the more she silently argued the point, the more something else inside her seemed to argue back. At last she screamed inside her head, "Everyone failed me! God failed me! If I had killed him, I would have been so much better off."

She had barely finished the thought when it was answered by another that came clearly to her mind, "If you had killed Simon Winter in New York, you would be in prison now, and your life would be ruined. You would never have come to Buffalo and found the life that I have for you." The statement surprised her, and she was certain that she had not inspired it, but it quickly brought her back to her surroundings.

"And in closing," Hank Dorson was practically yelling at the jurors, "I say that you *must* find Simon Winter not guilty of this crime."

"The crime," Megan thought, "the rape and murder of a young woman." She looked again at the defendant: rapist, blackmailer, murderer—a man without conscience hiding behind masculine good looks and boyish charm. Of all the heinous criminals who had ever sat in the defendant's seat, none had been more dangerously wicked than the one occupying it now. One thing she knew for certain, the man on trial today was capable of anything. She didn't have to occupy herself with thoughts of revenge; she was on his jury, and there was no doubt in her mind that he was guilty.

When they recessed for lunch, Megan tried to compose herself. The jurors had been instructed not to discuss the case among themselves, but as they walked out together she was surprised to hear Margaret whisper to Rita, "He seems like such a nice young man. Just the kind I always wanted my daughter to marry."

Rita giggled and whispered back, "And he's such a hunk! He's the kind of guy everyone's looking for."

Taken aback by their comments, Megan realized that she saw the trial from a very different perspective than her fellow jurors. Their vision was so simple—so uncluttered. "Uncluttered by what?" she asked herself. "The truth, or just bad memories and experiences?" To them Simon Winter was what he appeared to be—a nice, personable young man. Over the course of the trial that opinion would either be reinforced or reversed based on the testimony presented to them. She could never have that luxury—the knowledge of his past crimes against her clouded everything else.

In the afternoon the prosecuting attorney presented evidence about the dead victim and her family to give the jury a glimpse into the life that had been taken. The story of the young woman found brutally beaten and raped was gruesome enough to disturb the most placid juror, but Megan's mind was occupied by other matters. As she sat staring at the defendant, she wondered whether she had any place there after all.

The one question that Hank Dorson had asked her over and over was whether she knew anything about the defendant. When she had answered, "No," she had thought that she was answering truthfully. Now that she had recognized him, everything had changed. The law entitled Simon Winter to a fair trial by a jury of his peers—peers who had no former association with him. As an attorney, Megan was well aware of her obligation to uphold the law, but by staying on the jury, she violated its very essence.

In spite of her unwillingness for anyone to know that she had been raped, there were times when Megan had wished that the police had been able to find her attacker. She had wished that they had arrested him and put him on trial and that she had been able to take the witness stand and accuse him. That privilege had been denied her, but now he sat in the defendant's chair being tried for another crime against another young woman. Ironically, he was now at her mercy, and she would not have to tell anyone about the things he had done to her.

If someone had told her that one day she would find herself in this position, she would have been certain that when that day came it would be a moment of great personal victory. Yet, though everything in her cried out for justice, as an attorney she had to ask herself whether he might not be innocent of *this* crime. What if she voted for the guilty verdict and helped convict him of a crime he had not committed? He could never be punished for his crimes against her; was it right to punish him for a different crime, regardless of whether he had committed it?

She could have herself disqualified by coming forward and saying that she knew the defendant because he had raped her. It would be handled in the judge's chambers, and the other jurors would not know why she had been replaced by an alternate. If she did come forward, she was fairly certain that he would be acquitted. She could tell that the other jurors liked him. She had not yet heard the evidence, but she knew that his defense would explain away every detail of the prosecution's case. Having been in many courtrooms, she knew that testimony is contradictory, witnesses seldom tell the truth, evidence is weighted, and the jury's decision is little more than an exercise in determining how well they like the defendant. While it was possible that he was innocent of this act, it was much more likely that he was guilty. Megan suspected, however, that this jury would not convict him, and his freedom would mean that he would continue to rape and murder other women.

A horrible situation to be in, she thought to herself. At one time she would have known what to do—the old Megan Cleary would not have felt any qualms about taking justice into her own hands. Now she could not accept such an easy, clear-cut answer. As much as she wanted to make Simon Winter pay for what he had done to her, she could not allow her life to be ruled by hate; though she longed for revenge, she could not succumb. Other people had to be considered—her parents, Mother Harriet, Jonathan. Although they might never know what had happened, Megan realized that the outcome of this trial was going to affect her relationship with each of them.

She thought of her relationship with God. Simon Winter had tried to destroy her, but she had met Jesus, and He had rebuilt her life. She suspected that this was one final test. Her commitment and her faith were being challenged and how she responded to the challenge would affect the rest of her life. Her feelings versus her faith, her professional ethics versus the suffering she had endured—so many different forces working inside her. She wanted to do what was right, believing that if she did, God would give her the upper hand, but in this case she didn't know what the right thing was.

She thought of the two people who would understand and give her the advice she needed. When court recessed for the day, she lost no time in calling Jonathan and telling him that she needed to talk to him and Mother Harriet. "I have something that I need to discuss with the two of you. Could I come by and pick you up and drive you to her house?"

"Of course," Jonathan replied. "I'll be waiting for you."

Because Megan did not want to tell her story more than once, they hardly spoke on the drive to Mother Harriet's house. As soon as he saw her, Jonathan knew that something was seriously wrong, but he respected her request to wait until the three of them were together before she told him anything. Even Mother Harriet recognized the stress in Megan's voice when she greeted them at the door.

"I don't know whether I mentioned to you, Mother Harriet, that the day before yesterday I received a notice to appear for jury duty," she began. The old woman nodded her head.

"The trial started today," Jonathan added.

"Yes. It's a rape case. I was pretty sure that I wouldn't be selected for the jury, but I was. This morning when the defendant entered the courtroom..." She stopped abruptly and looked at both of them, "The man on trial is the man who raped me."

An expression of disbelief spread over both their faces as they sat up straight in their chairs. "Ain't he the one you shot? I thought ya said he was dead!" Mother Harriet looked confused.

"I thought he was dead. All this time I believed that I had killed him, but when I saw him today, I realized that I had been wrong."

"What about the blackmail notes?" Jonathan asked.

"He must have sent them himself. I realized today while I was sitting there that he had to be the one who blackmailed me."

At last Mother Harriet spoke, "Maybe it ain't the same man. Maybe it's just somebody that looks like him. Ya only saw him one time, just for a minnut, and it was kinda dark."

"No, he's definitely the same man. The alley entrance had a large security light right over the door. I saw him very clearly the night I shot him, and I recognized him immediately. Today, after the recess, he came down the hall behind me, and I heard his voice. My heart almost stopped. There's no way that I could confuse him with anyone else."

"Does he recognize you?" Jonathan asked.

"No. In a way, that's the most infuriating part. This morning when his attorney was making his opening statement, he looked directly at me and smiled. I could tell he had no idea who I was—after everything he's done to me."

"Well," said Mother Harriet, "You's on his jury now. Sounds to me like he's 'bout to get justice after all."

"No," Megan shook her head, "That's why I wanted to talk to the two of you. I want so much to see him punished, but I'm not sure that I'm doing the right thing by staying on the jury. When I look at him, I remember what he did to me; I don't see this case or this courtroom. I'm so sure that he's guilty that I'm ready to convict him right now. You know, I didn't hear one single thing that was said today."

"Then you need to open your ears and listen," Mother Harriet told her firmly. "You can't solve none of your problems by buryin' your head in the sand. You got to face up to this situation, and that means doin' your job as a juror."

"But I don't know that I can do my job as a juror. The law says that a juror should be impartial—that he or she should know nothing about the case. My past experiences with Simon Winter have prejudiced me against him."

"Did they ask you whether you knowed him before you got on there?"

"Yes. They asked me if I knew the name Simon Winter, and since I had never heard the name, I told the attorneys that I didn't. I thought I was being honest."

"Then why go back and try to undo it now? You did your best to tell the truth—now you need to go forward."

"But the law says that I should disqualify myself."

"Ya 'member when we first met, and I told ya that there's only one law, and that's God's law? How do ya know that He ain't put ya on this jury Hisself? Did it ever come to your mind that maybe you'd be doin' an injustice in not servin'? Of all the people in the courtroom, you's the only person there that knows what he's really like. The other folks—they's gonna hear what the attorneys wants 'em to hear, and that'll be it. They'll never know nothin' more than what's said right there in front of 'em. You's an attorney; has ya ever seen somebody that was guilty get off scot-free, or somebody that was innocent go to prison?"

Immediately Megan remembered Janet Dobson as someone guilty who had gone free. She couldn't think of anyone innocent being convicted until Sam Dyer's name came to mind. She remembered how he had proclaimed his innocence as he was dragged from the courtroom. "I've seen both," she finally answered.

The old woman nodded, "Ain't no justice in the justice system. Just a whole bunch of liars getting' up and sayin' things that ain't got nothin' to do with what happened. That's all a jury ever hears."

"It's true," Megan agreed. "A jury hears only a small part of what happened, and they try to reach a fair verdict based upon that. But the jury is supposed to start out impartial."

Mother Harriet waived her hand and cut her off. "Ain't nobody that's ever been impartial 'bout nothin'. People ain't that way; they gotta have opinions. Tell me, what do they think of him so far?"

"They like him," Megan answered. "I heard one of the old women say that he was just the kind of young man that she wanted her daughter to marry."

"That ain't impartial. She's done made up her mind he's innocent, and she ain't even heard the evidence. By the time they's through talkin' she'll be ready to set him free."

"Keep in mind," Jonathan turned to Megan, "the defense is probably going to call in several character witnesses to testify that he is a nice, responsible, non-violent guy who would never hurt anyone. You know things about his character that directly contradict that testimony. It's important that you stay on if only for that reason."

"I understand what you're saying," Megan told them. "But here's the problem: Simon Winter is not on trial for raping me. He's on trial for another rape and murder—one that he may or may not have committed. As an attorney, I know that he has to be tried only for that one crime."

"Then try him for that crime," Mother Harriet said. "When you go to that courtroom tomorrow, listen to what's bein' said. Look at all the evidence; pay attention to everythin'. When it's over, if ya think he ain't the one that killed that girl, then ya find him not guilty. But after you listened to all the facts, if ya think he did it, then say so. Don't run away; runnin' away don't never solve nothin'."

After hearing what Mother Harriet and Jonathan had to say, Megan knew that they were right. The next morning when she took her seat in the jury box, she determined that Simon Winter's future would not depend on what he had done to her but only on the case for which he was being tried.

The prosecution did a competent job of presenting its case, and Megan listened to each witness and every word intently. During each recess she made notes on the testimony she found most significant. Thus, by the time the district attorney's office had finished presenting its case, she had a clear outline of the information that had been presented.

The first witness called was one of the victim's co-workers. Cheryl McGuire took her place on the witness stand to testify as to why Sally Benson was still in her office at seven o'clock on the night of April 30.

"Sally was a very meticulous accountant," Cheryl testified. "A number of her clients had filed for extensions on their tax returns, and she was working overtime to catch up. She had worked late every evening that week."

"But the firm was closed?" prosecutor Dan Woodruff asked.

"Yes, the firm closes at five-thirty, and normally everyone is gone by six-thirty. Sally locked the place up and went on working."

"So all the doors were locked?"

"Yes."

"Where are the offices of the Davis Parker accounting firm located?"

"In a restored home located at 1515 Montana Boulevard. It's in a very good district; when that part of town went commercial, the property values went way up. All of the old mansions have been converted into offices."

"So there is no security there, such as one would have in an office complex?"

"No."

"Did Sally ever tell you that she was afraid when she worked late with no security?"

"No, there had never been any kind of trouble. We all worked late at times, and we never worried about anything like this happening."

The prosecution finished and Hank Dorson rose to cross-examine. "You and Sally Benson were friends, were you not?"

"Yes."

"So you saw each other socially, didn't you?"

"Yes."

"Did Sally have a busy social life?"

"I guess."

"Oh come on now, Miss McGuire. A pretty, single girl like Sally must have had a lot of friends."

"Yes, Sally was popular. A lot of people liked her."

"Did a lot of men like her?"

"I guess. She had a boyfriend, but she dated other people too from time to time."

"Did you and Sally ever go to bars together and pick up men?"

"Not really. Sometimes we went to bars together, but we didn't pick up any guys. Sally wasn't into that kind of thing."

"But you at least talked to men when you went to bars, didn't you? And when you went to parties, you and Sally flirted with the men there, didn't you? Did Sally tell some of the men she met where she worked and what she did for a living?"

"Sometimes."

"It's possible, isn't it, that Sally could have been killed by one of the men she had dated, or by a man she met in a bar or at a party?"

"Objection, your honor, calls for speculation on the part of the witness."

"Objection sustained," said the judge, and that ended Cheryl's testimony.

The police officer who had found Sally's body had been called to the scene when a passerby noticed that the employee entry door located at the back of the building was wide open. Joe Stanzik had arrived on the scene at seven-thirty to find Sally dead.

"Now, Officer Stanzik, describe for us what you saw when you entered the building."

"It's an old house with a long hallway and little offices on either side. When I got there, only one light was on, and that was the light inside Miss Benson's office. I was looking for the switch to the hall light when I almost stepped on the body; it was lying right there in the hall not far from the door."

"Describe the body for us."

"It was a young Caucasian female between twenty-five and thirty years of age. The body was almost nude, and the face was covered with blood and bruises. She had been beaten pretty severely and stabbed twelve times. When I touched the body, it was still warm. She'd been dead only a few minutes."

"Had the entry door been forcibly opened?"

"Whoever entered had used some kind of device to pick the lock. There were scrape marks around the lock; it had taken them a few minutes to get in."

"What other evidence did you find at the crime scene?"

"There was a lot of blood in the hall which we later typed back to the victim. There was no blood in the victim's office, indicating that the attack took place in the hall."

"So the evidence indicates that the victim left her office and walked into the dark hall where she was attacked and murdered."

"Yes, that's what our report shows."

"Was there any sign of a robbery having taken place?"

"No. That was one unusual aspect of the case. The victim's purse was on the desk in her office. It contained seventy-five dollars in cash and all of her credit cards. Nothing was missing from any of the offices. The perpetrator must have broken in specifically to rape and kill the victim."

"Officer Stanzik, why did you arrest the defendant, Simon Winter, for this crime?"

"There were a couple of things that made us suspect the defendant. First of all, his car was parked within two blocks of the crime—when we talked to the neighbors, one of them placed the car in front of her house at exactly the time when the attack would have taken place. We traced the license plate and learned that the car was registered to Simon Winter. When we talked to him the next day, he had some scratches on his face and neck that looked like he had been in a fight. We also learned that the morning after the attack he had taken his jacket to the drycleaners to have some bloodstains cleaned out of it."

"And you were able to trace those bloodstains back to Sally Benson?"

"No, By the time we got to the drycleaners, they had already cleaned the jacket. When we searched Mr. Winter's apartment for evidence, we took the jacket to our lab. They were able to tell that there had been bloodstains on it, but the cleaning fluids had gotten rid of any useful evidence." The prosecution turned the witness over to Hank Dorson, and following a brief cross-examination, the police officer left the stand.

Next, the coroner detailed the victim's injuries. Megan listened intently as he described the bruises and lacerations. "She must have walked out into the hall; probably she heard a noise. Judging from the marks on the body, he grabbed her from behind and threw her up against the wall before he started hitting her. She probably tried to run, but he knocked her down and continued to beat and stab her. One of the stab wounds was fatal."

Over lunch one day Megan heard Harry tell Donna, "There's no real evidence against the guy. A jacket with some blood stains that they can't prove were hers, and his car parked two blocks away—that's not enough to convict him."

"Yeah," Ralph added, "I mean, after all, two blocks is a long way. I might park within two blocks of a crime every day and never even know it."

"The main thing," said Helen, "is that there are no witnesses. Not one single person actually saw what happened. There are no finger prints, no hairs, no DNA—nothing to link him to the crime. The only person who really knows is dead."

"I'll be glad when we get to the defense," Rita said. "I'm so tired of hearing this prosecutor that I could scream. Every day it's the same old stuff told by different people."

Megan sat silently, taking in every word that was said and adding the comments to her outline.

On Tuesday the neighbor who had seen Simon's car parked in front of her home testified. "I was supposed to meet my husband at seven o'clock, and I was running late," she told the court. "I didn't leave until seven. As I was walking out the door, I saw this red convertible parked in front of my house. I ran past it, and when I did, I saw that it had a personalized license plate."

"What was written on the license plate?"

"It was the letters 'S-T-U-D'—Stud. I thought it was pretty ridiculous, but I remembered it, and the next day when the police came and asked if I had seen anything out of the ordinary the night before, I told them about it."

The clerk who had been on duty at the drycleaners testified that she recalled the defendant bringing in a suede jacket on the morning after the crime. "The whole front of the jacket was covered in blood, and he said he wanted us to get it all out. I was worried because the jacket was expensive, and I wasn't sure that it would clean up properly. We put it on a special ticket and sent it out to be cleaned by a special process. All the blood came out."

"Are you positive of the date?" the prosecutor asked her.

"Absolutely. It was the morning of May first. I wrote it on the ticket."

During the prosecution's last two days Dan Woodruff focused on the defendant's past. The jury heard that Simon Winter's father had committed suicide when Simon was thirteen because his wife had threatened to leave him. Simon's aunt testified that Peter Winter had worshipped his wife, although she was repeatedly unfaithful to him, and that when she told him she was leaving, he had gone into his bedroom and blown his brains out with his pistol.

"How did Simon handle that?" the prosecution asked.

"He was devastated," the dead man's sister replied. "Simon adored his father, and he blamed Madelyn for the suicide. One day I heard him telling some friends that he would kill her if he could. He told me that she was a whore who had killed his father."

"Did Simon's behavior change after his father's suicide?" Woodruff asked.

"Simon was always spoiled and undisciplined. Peter made plenty of money, and Madelyn spent plenty, but they still had enough to give Simon everything he wanted. After Peter's death, Simon's attitude became increasingly negative towards women and, especially, his mother. He began using obscenities as part of normal conversation, but it was the sexual, violent nature of his speech that bothered me. I'm no prude, and I know that kids today have their own way of expressing themselves, but I didn't think that Simon's behavior was normal. He was so full of rage. Finally, I told Madelyn that he couldn't visit me anymore; I was afraid of him. He was like a bomb waiting to explode."

"And he finally did explode, didn't he?"

"Yes, when he was fifteen. After Peter died Madelyn began having her lovers stay at the house overnight. Simon talked about it all the time;

he made jokes about what they did together. By the time George Carpenter came around he'd seen a lot."

George Carpenter was the last witness to take the stand for the prosecution. "Tell us," said Dan Woodruff, "when did you meet the defendant?"

"I met him just before his fifteenth birthday. Madelyn and I were dating, and one day I came over to the house, and she introduced us."

"What did Madelyn Winter tell you about her son?"

"She told me that she couldn't have guys sleep over any more because he had started acting crazy. She said that he had thrown somebody out and told her that if she knew what was good for her she would never bring another man there to spend the night again. So we stayed at my place, or I came over while the kid was in school."

"How did Simon behave around you?"

"Well, he had this big smile, and I knew from what his mother said that he was real popular with the other kids. But he called Madelyn dirty names right to her face, and he never would speak to me."

"What happened the day that he came home from school for Easter vacation?"

"It was early; the school gave the kids the afternoon off. He walked in and without knocking just opened the bedroom door and saw us together. Without saying a word, he turned and walked out. In a minute he came back with an iron fireplace poker in his hand. Before I had a chance to do anything, he started hitting us with it. We were both screaming, but he never said anything. I think that was the scariest thing about it—it was like we couldn't get through to him. We knew that he was planning to kill us. If I hadn't managed to get that poker away from him, he would have."

"What happened then?"

"After I got the poker, I ran him out of the room and locked the door. Then we called an ambulance; both of us had to be hospitalized. I filed charges against him, but his mother begged me to drop them; she said that she would be humiliated for this to come out in the news. Madelyn was afraid to have him live with her after that; she sent him off to military school the week after she got out of the hospital. She said that he was never setting foot in her house again, and I agreed with her. Personally, I thought he was nuts."

With this Hank Dorson stood and gave his final objection. The judge ordered the last remark stricken from the record, and the prosecution rested its case.

SIXTEEN

"This trial is awfully hard on you, isn't it?" Jonathan asked Megan on Saturday as they sat together with Maria playing on the floor close by.

"In a way," she responded. "Sometimes I come home at night, and I feel completely overwhelmed by everything I've heard. I've never had a courtroom experience that was even similar."

"Because the case brings back painful memories—I knew that would happen even before I knew who the defendant was."

"It has brought back painful memories," Megan agreed, "but it's also been good for me. There's something about sitting in that courtroom day after day facing Simon Winter that has forced me to come to grips with my own attack. After I was raped, I thought that nothing could be more shameful than having to talk about the experience. Later I felt that I couldn't talk because of the shooting and the blackmail. I realized in court this week that because of my own embarrassment I had allowed myself to be put in a position where I could be victimized repeatedly.

"I'm ashamed to admit this now, but when the police were looking for my rapist, there was a part of me that didn't want them to find him because I was embarrassed to go into court and testify. I just wanted to put the whole thing behind me and to never have to talk about it to anyone. Now I know that if I had taken a more aggressive approach with the police we might have been able to find him before he found me again. If I had gone into counseling in the beginning, as my mother begged me to, I wouldn't have suffered emotionally the way I did. Certainly, if I had called the police after the shooting, I would have learned that he had lived, and he wouldn't have been able to continue terrorizing me.

"Every time that I held back or remained silent, I gave him more power over me. If I hadn't come to Buffalo and met Mother Harriet, if I hadn't finally given my life to Jesus, I wouldn't have survived at all.

"One thing I've learned is that other people's opinions aren't important. I agonized as much over what people would think or say if the truth ever came out as I did over the memories of what he'd done to me. You and Mother Harriet have been very kind and supportive, and that's meant more to me than you'll ever know. But these last few days I've realized that even if everyone had been critical, I shouldn't have tried to hide the truth. People like Simon Winter are protected all their lives by the people they hurt. His aunt protected him; his mother protected him; her boyfriend protected him. They didn't care enough about him to try to stop his destructive behavior, and when he reached an age where he was beyond their control, they sent him away, but they never made him take responsibility for his actions. No one will ever know how many women have been his victims. Sally can never identify her attacker—she will never be able to take the witness stand and either accuse him or clear him of this offense. There may be many others who lived but protected him because of their own shame. I protected him for almost two years."

"You can't blame yourself for this," Jonathan said comfortingly. "You were doing what you thought was best at the time. That's all that any of us can ever do."

"Yes I was," Megan agreed. "But I know now that I was wrong. What is that scripture, 'You will know the truth and the truth will set you free?' The truth does set people free—free from guilt, and fear, and hatred. I remember when I sat down and told my whole story to Mother Harriet—she was the first person ever to hear it. I was worried that she would spread it around as gossip, but when I realized that she understood and supported me, I felt so relieved. All the secrets I had been keeping had turned into a tremendous burden, and when I told her, that burden lightened considerably. I went through the same thing when I told you."

"You know that you can always tell me anything. I'll always be here for you," Jonathan said with a reassuring smile.

"And I for you," she returned. "That's as it should be. Everyone needs someone they can trust completely, and in you I've found that person. Whatever happens in my life, you'll know about it and have a part in it—just as you've had in this case."

"What about the case?" he asked with interest. "Do you think he's guilty?"

"I'll know by the end of the trial," she returned. "Defense opens on Monday."

On Monday when Hank Dorson began interrogating witnesses in his overbearing manner, he paid no attention to the young blonde woman in the jury box listening intently to every word. He was an excellent attorney—even though Megan disliked him, she had to admit that. Much better prepared than the prosecuting attorney, he proceeded to counter the weak and mostly circumstantial evidence against his client with a series of witnesses who testified that Simon Winter was exactly the sort of nice, wholesome young man he gave the impression of being. As the days passed, she could see that he was accomplishing his goal—the jury was on his side.

The first witness called to testify for the defense was Simon's girlfriend Cynthia Harris, a bright, blonde twenty-year-old with dimples and blue eyes and a bubbly personality. An A student who had been the high school Homecoming Queen, she had the wholesome, fresh-scrubbed look of the girl next door.

"Cynthia," Hank Dorson began, "Tell us how you met the defendant."

"We met right after he moved here a little over a year ago—we're both students at the university. We had a psychology class together, and we started dating."

"What can you tell us about the defendant's character?"

"Cy is amazing! He's kind, caring, gentle—he has a great sense of humor. I've never met anyone who was so much fun to be with."

"We've heard testimony about Simon's violent behavior. Have you ever observed such behavior?"

"Oh, gosh no!"

"Has he ever threatened you or hit you? Have you ever seen him threaten anyone else?"

"No! Cy's not at all violent. He's so sweet; everybody likes him. I can't imagine him ever hurting anyone."

"Did Simon ever tell you about any problems between him and his mother?"

"Yes, after we had been going together a few months, I asked about his family. He told me that his father had died and he was having trouble with his mother. He never went into any detail, but he told me that he would give anything if they could be reconciled. I know he loves her, and it hurts him a lot that their relationship isn't very good."

When Cynthia Harris left the stand, Simon's psychology professor gave his testimony to the court.

"What is your relationship to the defendant?" Dorson asked.

"I'm a psychology professor at the university. Simon's been in two of my classes."

"What sort of a student is he?"

"He's an A student—his work is always at the very top of the class. I've seldom seen anyone more studious or dedicated. Simon doesn't just make good grades, though; he's really interested in the courses. His work surpasses undergraduate requirements."

"So, you would say that he's a good student?"

"He's an excellent student. He has a brilliant mind—he grasps the material more quickly than almost anyone I've taught."

"What do you know of his personal life?"

"Very little, but from what I've observed he seems to have very fixed habits. He's never missed a class—never even been late. He's always neatly dressed. He comes to class completely prepared; his assignments are always handed in well ahead of the deadline. I've seen him on campus with only one girl—Miss Harris. He's quiet and well mannered but in a friendly, personable way. Even his dorm room is perfect—I stopped by one evening to loan him a book he had asked for, and everything was spotless."

"Have you ever observed any abusive behavior from him or heard him use excessive obscene language?"

"No, all of the students seem to like him—he treats them all, from the oldest to the youngest, like friends. As for the language, he swears a little when he gets angry, but no more than normal. It's not a regular part of his conversation."

The criminology professor testified to the same effect. Simon Winter was an exceptionally bright, methodical student who was also personable, friendly, and well-liked by everyone. Hank Dorson was making his point well—Megan suspected that even the judge was beginning to sympathize with the defendant. Megan was surprised, however, when as his final witness Dorson called Simon Winter to the stand.

"Simon," Dorson said, "you are aware that you don't have to give testimony in this case. By law no one can force you to testify against yourself. Will you please tell the court why you have asked to be put on the stand?"

"Because, Sir, in testifying I'm not giving evidence against myself. I believe that the court has the right to know the truth, and I have nothing to hide."

"Thank you, Simon. Over the past two weeks this court has heard a good deal of conflicting testimony, starting with the stories about your relationship with your mother. Tell us about the incident that George Carpenter related."

"What he said was true," the young man's face grew serious, "except for the part about my threatening to kill my mother or trying to kill her that day. I would never have wanted to hurt her. But I was just a kid, and after my dad died, I was pretty mixed up. I missed him so much, and it seemed like my world was coming apart. I don't know what got into me that day, but I'm very ashamed of my behavior, and I've wished many times that I could go back and undo the damage I caused."

"Have you attempted to reconcile with your mother since then?"

"Yes, I've written and called her repeatedly. She's still angry, and I don't blame her. I know what I did was very wrong, and I can only hope that someday she'll forgive me."

"How long have you lived in Buffalo?"

"I was born here, and I lived here with my mother until I was fifteen. Then I was in upstate New York for a while. When I turned eighteen, I went to New York City where I attended the university until about a year ago."

"Why did you return to Buffalo?"

"One night in March of last year, I was walking down the street, and a mugger came up to me with a gun. He demanded that I give him my money, and when I resisted, he shot me. I guess he thought I was dead, because he ran off and left me. I regained consciousness and managed to get to a hospital. I was laid up for a few weeks, and when I was better I decided to come back here to recover completely."

"Do you remember the date of that shooting?"

"Yes. It was March 15 of last year. Somebody should've told me to beware the Ides of March."

At this point Dorson presented the judge with a copy of the statement that Winter had made to the police regarding the mugging. "That was exactly six weeks before the death of Sally Benson," he commented.

"What did you do after you arrived here?"

"I immediately enrolled in summer classes at the university. Then I got a room on campus so that I would be all set for the summer term."

"Did you meet anyone at that time?"

"Yes, my first day on campus I was invited to a party. I went and soon I was making friends."

"Why were you parked on Shipman Avenue on the night of April 30?"

"I was on my way to dinner at a friend's house, and I stopped to pick up some flowers for his mother, who was our hostess. I parked my car in front of the house because I thought it would be safer there on the side street than in front of the florist's shop."

"What time was that?"

"It was seven o'clock when I parked."

"What happened to you on your way to the florist's?"

"I was about a block from my car when a guy came up to me with a knife and demanded my wallet. I tried to take the knife away from him, and when I did, my hands were cut. Fortunately, all the cuts were superficial, but they bled a lot, and I got blood stains all over my jacket. The next day I took the jacket to the cleaners to see if they could get the blood out."

"Simon, did you ever meet or see Sally Benson, or even hear her name before the police questioned you?"

"No, Sir, I had never heard of her until the police came to my door."

"Were you ever inside the accounting firm of Davis Parker?"

"No, I didn't even know that there were accountants on that street. I'm still reacquainting myself with Buffalo, and I haven't been in that part of town very much."

"Mrs. Henson, the lady in front of whose house you parked your car, testified about your license plate with the word STUD on it. Would you explain that to the court?"

"Sure. It was a birthday gift from my fraternity brothers in New York City. I've always been quiet and kind of serious. I don't party much; I'm a one woman man. They thought it would be funny to give me a license plate with the word 'Stud' on it since I'm so totally not that kind of guy."

"So you don't consider yourself a stud?"

"Absolutely not. I've got eyes for only one girl, and that's Cynthia. We're going to be married right after we graduate, and then I want us to start a family. I want to be able to give my children the kind of close-knit family life that I didn't have growing up."

Simon Winter completed his testimony late in the afternoon, and the court recessed before the closing statements. Eleven of the twelve jurors went home that night to relax, but Megan returned to her apartment to work. Her outlines were now complete; all the facts were in. She had a detailed description of the crime. A girl had been found raped and stabbed in the old house that was home to the accounting firm where she worked. The building was dark except for the light in her office, and the lock had been picked. No robbery or vandalism had occurred. In every detail the attack paralleled what had happened to Megan, even down to Simon Winter's alibi.

Megan had promised herself that she would decide Simon Winter's guilt or innocence based solely on the evidence, and after examining the evidence, she knew that he was guilty—not guilty beyond a reasonable doubt, as she knew the law requires, but guilty beyond a shadow of a doubt. Over the years, she had heard many lay people say that a person must be proven guilty beyond a shadow of a doubt. She had always cringed at their ignorance and thought how impossible it would be to convict anyone of any crime if that were the criteria. Now, she realized that this was exactly what had happened in determining Simon Winter's guilt. He was guilty beyond a shadow of a doubt.

Her verdict was free from any vengeful motives; her conclusion was based on the evidence that had been presented against him in court. Yet, though she knew that he had murdered Sally Benson, she also knew that the other jurors were not convinced. At best, they were undecided; at worst, they had already made up their minds to set him free. If justice were to be served, it would be up to her to make certain that it was dispensed.

The following day the prosecution would make its closing remarks, but Megan's work would just be beginning. As the jury deliberated, she would be the deciding factor in their verdict. She was about to argue the most important case of her life.

The next morning as the jury entered the courtroom, Megan saw Rita looking at Simon. Glancing at the other jurors, she saw that several of them looked directly at him, a sign that told Megan they were inclined to vote for his acquittal.

Dan Woodruff rose to make his closing statements, and he summarized for the jury all that had been said in the courtroom. "Think of this young woman dying in pain and terror all alone at the hand of the defendant. Think of her parents, her sister, her friends. She could have been your daughter, or your sister, or your best friend. You cannot in good conscience let this man go free to do to other women what he did to Sally Benson. You must find him guilty of murder in the first degree."

Hank Dorson then rose to make his appeal and remind the jury of the lack of hard evidence against his client. "There is nothing to prove that Simon Winter is guilty of this crime," he told them. "The law says that you must be able to prove guilt beyond a reasonable doubt, and the prosecution has not done that. A brilliant young man with a promising future who is innocent of any wrong doing has been brought into court and put on trial because he had the misfortune to park his car in the wrong place at the wrong time. It is your duty to find him not guilty."

Even as the judge instructed the jury, Megan wondered whether her fellow jurors understood their true duty. At eleven o'clock Thursday morning they filed out of the courtroom to begin their deliberations. Simon Winter and both the defense and prosecuting attorneys nervously awaited the decision, but hour after hour dragged by without a verdict. Across the city Jonathan and Mother Harriet waited, but as evening came, there was still no word.

Evening turned into night, and the judge sequestered the jury. At eight o'clock the following morning they again began their deliberations, but Friday passed without a verdict. Saturday dawned, and the process continued. Finally, at four o'clock on Saturday afternoon they sent a message to the judge that they had reached a verdict.

Simon Winter was whispering to his attorney when the jury returned, but he immediately fell silent and rose to hear the verdict. Megan, as foreman, handed the verdict to the bailiff who carried it to the judge. After reading it silently, he turned to the jury. "To the charge of murder in the first degree, how do you find?"

"Guilty."

The blood drained from Simon Winter's face, and a look of utter disbelief contorted his handsome features. As Megan watched, he was handcuffed and led from the courtroom. Mentally she replayed the events of the past two and a half days. Of the twelve of them, only she had known he was guilty. Nine had been uncertain, and two had believed him innocent. Yet, in the end those two changed their votes to guilty, not because they had been convinced that he was guilty, but because they wanted to go home. "What a frightening commentary on the justice system," she thought.

Fall was in the air as she pushed the door open and stood on the courthouse steps. So much was happening in her life. She would once again have a position in a prestigious law firm, and she would once again be practicing criminal law. Now, however, her attitude about the law and criminals and victims was very different from what it had been when she was employed by Pratt, Forbes and Magoff. In a little more than a month she would have a husband and a child. The holidays were approaching, and before she knew it, she would be spending Christmas with her new family. She remembered what Mother Harriet had told her when they first met—that Christmas was a celebration of life in Christ. Now she understood what Mother Harriet had meant, for she had a new life and a new faith to celebrate. She had come to Christ asking for mercy, and He had given her that, but He had also given her justice for her own suffering and the suffering of all the other women who had been Simon Winter's victims.

Tonight she was joining Jonathan and Maria for dinner. Later, the three of them would go to her parents' house for the evening. Megan's right hand brushed against her engagement ring, and she thought with love of the man who had given it to her. As she hurried down the steps into the autumn twilight, she knew that she was free at last.

ABOUT THE AUTHORS

Joyce and Alexandra Swann are mother and daughter. Joyce homeschooled her ten children and is a well known author and speaker on the subject of homeschooling. For many years she was a popular columnist for *Practical Homeschooling* Magazine. Since her last child graduated in May of 2000, she and her husband and Alexandra have worked together in the family's mortgage business.

Alexandra is the author of *No Regrets: How Homeschooling Earned me a Master's Degree at Age Sixteen* and co-author of the creative writing course *Writing for Success*. Joyce and Alexandra's first novel, *The Fourth Kingdom*, was published in May of 2010.

The Swanns live in Anthony, New Mexico.

12387821R00213

Made in the USA
Charleston, SC
01 May 2012